MAEVE IN THE MORNING

AMANDA GALE

Will there really be a "Morning"?
Is there such a thing as "Day"?
Could I see it from the mountains
If I were as tall as they?

— EMILY DICKINSON

CONTENTS

CONTENT NOTE

This book addresses sexual assault.

CHAPTER ONE

SENIOR YEAR OF HIGH SCHOOL

*M*aeve took a final cursory glance at the last notecard and, exhaling, slipped it once again to the bottom of the stack. She tapped her foot a few times on the floor as she calmed her nerves. *Get with it, Sheering*, she scolded herself, lifting her chin and tossing back her thick mane of long dark hair. *You've got this.*

Across the stage, hidden behind the left-wing curtain, was her opponent. Kyle Langahan was standing with his arms crossed and his fingers pulling at his lower lip. In honor of the debate, he was wearing his navy blazer over his khaki uniform pants, blue shirt, and tasteful uniform tie. He was straight and serious, with not a modicum of humor. He didn't even seem to care that she was there; he was watching the principal as he spoke at the podium, waiting for his name to be called as if he already had it in the bag. His patience annoyed her. It was as if he couldn't even deign to be nervous. As if he knew the entire class was going to support him. As if this whole debate was just a waste of his time.

His smugness irritated her more than anything. You couldn't even have a conversation with him. Kyle was always right—at least, he was to Kyle. And no one seemed to question it. They took his arrogance as knowledge, his staunchness as superiority.

Well, not Maeve. Maeve had talked with him outside the principal's office before Mr. Heller interviewed them as candidates for senior class president. They'd been going to school together for four years, and she'd never really talked to him before; though they'd had many of the same honors classes, they always sat across the room from each other—his last name was L, hers was S. Their friend circles didn't overlap—come to think of it, she didn't even know who he generally hung out with. He talked to people, sure, but he had this attitude, so cold and impassive, like he didn't have time. Maeve guessed that's why his grades were so good: it was widely acknowledged he'd be valedictorian. Maeve herself would be second in the class. It was kind of a shame they'd never actually spoken.

Maeve had decided to give him a chance.

"Hey," she'd saluted him brightly as they met at the end of the hallway, having left their respective classes to walk to Mr. Heller's office. She'd smiled at him as they walked together, but he hadn't turned to look at her. "Are you ready?"

"Yes."

She'd waited for him to ask her the same question, but he hadn't.

"Congratulations on Princeton," she'd said. "I heard you got in by early admission."

"Thank you."

That was it. He gave her nothing.

Maeve tried again.

"I got in early admission to Vassar," she said, offering him a polite smile. "It's such a relief to know where you're going, right?"

"Yes. Congratulations."

They walked along in silence for a time.

"I guess you're going to be valedictorian," she said finally, "unless I catch up."

"You won't catch up."

She looked at him with raised eyebrows. *What the actual hell?* "How are you so sure about that?"

He shrugged. "I don't intend to let my grades slip."

They continued on down the hall.

"So what did you do last weekend?" she asked him, somehow knowing she'd regret it.

"I went with my parents to a protest at Brown & Little."

She looked at him again. "The chemical company right in Charlottesville?"

"Yes."

"I assume this is related to the PFAS leak."

"Of course. They've been ignoring regulations for years, but Virginia ClearStream lets them do it."

"They do? I hadn't heard anything about that."

"My parents are professors at the Virginia Science Institute. They're working on a paper on PFAS and its effects on our drinking water. They say it's all connected."

"And they dragged you along to the protest?"

"No," he said, a little testily. "I wanted to go. I actually care about the environment."

Maeve wasn't sure if he was suggesting she didn't and decided against one of her typical snarky comebacks, just in case. She waited some time before speaking again.

"Well, I also had an interesting weekend," she said, though he hadn't asked. "I went to a dinner in honor of Representative John Anderson. My dad's a state senator, as you may know."

"I know."

"Well, then you also know he was key in passing the Land and Water Protection Act."

"Yes, it was a decent start."

Maeve raised her eyebrows. "Excuse me?"

"I said it was a decent start."

"I heard you."

She let a few moments go by.

"My dad's cosponsored many similar laws, and he's called for strict sanctions on Brown & Little. We care about the environment, too."

Kyle snorted. "You have to make waves if you really want change. Politics is for sellouts and hacks."

"Tell me how you really feel." *Jackass,* she added in her head.

Kyle said nothing. He was walking along, his hand on his backpack strap as it hung over his shoulder.

"What did you do after the protest?" she asked.

"I bailed my parents out of jail."

Maeve burst out laughing. Finally, he looked at her. The seriousness of his expression told her he wasn't kidding.

"Oh." She cleared her throat. "What, you didn't get arrested, too, slacker?" she joked.

"My parents wouldn't let me in the building."

Maeve did not know what to say to this. She was regretting her decision to try to make conversation with him. He was really quite impossible to talk to.

"It's probably just as well," she said. "You don't want an arrest record before you even go to college."

"There are more important things in life than college," he said, surprising her with the firmness of his voice. "I wish they had arrested me."

"What good would that possibly do?"

"It would show them that I'm serious, that I won't let them get away with poisoning us."

"You can do that much more effectively if you're not incarcerated."

"It's all a distraction." They turned the corner; Mr. Heller's office was at the end of the hall. Maeve eyed it longingly: this conversation couldn't be over soon enough. "If you want to make a difference, you have to keep your eyes on the prize. You can't worry about yourself. You can't let emotion get in the way of your goal. No distractions. That's what my parents say."

"I just mean that there are ways to make change that don't involve potentially ruining your future."

"No offense, but how many protests have you been to?"

"'No offense' is the kind of thing people say when they're about to say something rude but don't want to look like an asshole."

"You didn't answer my question."

Maeve inhaled, her jaw working and her eyebrows turned downward. "I haven't been to any protests," she admitted. "But I've worked in my father's office and sat in on General Assembly sessions. I've been behind the scenes and watched him further the same goals you do, without pissing everybody off. I just think it's better to work within the system."

"Then you're incredibly naive."

Maeve stood still and glared at him, resisting the urge to kick him as he walked ahead of her into Mr. Heller's office.

Things hadn't gotten any better inside.

"Ladies first," Mr. Heller had said, smiling across his desk at her. He leaned back in his chair and swiveled in it casually. "What issue will you run on? How will Maeve Sheering improve the school?"

Maeve sat straighter and lifted her chin a little higher. "Well," she began, "I'd like to focus on wellness. I think we can be doing more to make sure students feel safe and healthy at school."

Mr. Heller nodded. "I see. And what do you propose for the improvement of health and wellness?"

"For starters, I'd like to institute a student mentor program between older and younger students. If a younger student needs some guidance, an older student can share their wisdom and support."

"Uh huh. Good. What else?"

"I think we can take girls' health more seriously here. For

example, I've talked to a lot of girls who feel that male athletes' health is prioritized. A lot of treatments in the trainer's office are catered specifically to male needs and aren't as effective for girls. Our needs should be more normalized."

Mr. Heller said nothing. The corner of his mouth twitched. "Oh?" he answered, folding his hands and swirling a little in his chair.

"And it isn't just athletes. We should have free tampons in all the girls' bathrooms. We shouldn't have to miss class to run to the nurse's office. We have..."

She trailed off, thrown momentarily by the change in Mr. Heller's face. It was something between a smirk and a grimace, and she watched it in profile as he turned from her, his face now beet red.

She cleared her throat and continued, making her voice steady. "We have girls getting late notes after nurse visits, and it can be embarrassing. Or sometimes teachers won't let them leave mid-class. It's time for us to be more evolved."

Mr. Heller suddenly laughed. "Ah," he said, rubbing his face in his hands. "Ah, okay."

"What's so funny?"

"It's not that it's funny, it's just—" He cleared his throat. "This isn't something we need to waste time on here, missy."

"But getting your period is a fact of life. It isn't something to be ashamed of. I think your discomfort is part of the point, which—"

"That's enough."

Maeve stopped talking and glared at him. Beside her, Kyle shifted in his seat but said nothing.

Mr. Heller leaned forward now and clasped his hands on the desk. "I advise you not to bring this up in the debate tomorrow. It's inappropriate, and you'll make the wrong impression."

"What impression would I make?"

Mr. Heller didn't answer, but Maeve knew what he meant. Fire burned within her, making her blood boil and race.

"It's only inappropriate to *you*," she said coolly, before she could stop herself, "because society is misogynistic."

"You saying I'm misogynistic?"

"I said society is."

"You're pushing the line, young lady."

"It just isn't a big deal." She'd reached a point she always did in these situations, when the tumbling of nervousness in her belly made way for all-consuming resentment—of patronization, of unfairness, of stupidity. "I'm talking about a normal bodily function, and you're telling me it's inappropriate."

"You'd better start showing some respect. Or you'll be removed from the running for class president."

Maeve's glare turned to ice, but she leaned back in her seat, momentarily silenced.

Mr. Heller turned his attention to Kyle. He now sat straight at his desk, giving him his full attention.

"Your turn, Kyle. What issues will you focus on as class president?"

"I'm very concerned about the pond behind the school," Kyle responded. "It's completely overtaken with algae. It's inhospitable for life. I'd like to form an environmental club. I'd like to test the phosphorus levels of that pond and, if we find them high, which we will, I'd like the environmental club to create a floating island with plants that will reduce those levels. It's probably the result of urban runoff. We should petition the Brown & Little factory in town to make them clean up their waste. We should also contact our state representatives to get them to change the laws that let them get away with it."

"A floating island, you say?" Mr. Heller was writing on a notepad. "Interesting. A noble enterprise."

Maeve discreetly rolled her eyes. A floating island? That was possible, but tampons weren't?

7

Mr. Heller put his pen down and smiled at Kyle. "Go on. How does that work, exactly?"

"It's essentially a floating wetland housing native plants that can reduce the phosphorous levels, preventing algae from thriving. The roots grow through a mat and into the water."

"That actually does sound cool," Maeve allowed, hating to admit it. "What's the benefit to the school? Just curious."

Kyle turned and stared at her.

"It helps the ecosystem," he said, slowly, as if she were incapable of understanding. "We all have to live here. Protecting our resources is the single best thing we can do for the school and the community. Conservation is the only important issue there is because our future depends on it."

"Well, I don't know that it's *the only* important issue," Maeve countered, deliberately quashing her irritation to make her voice casual. "My issue affects futures, too. You have no idea how girls' mental health is affected by things like this."

"I'm not saying it isn't. I'm just saying it won't be an issue at all if none of us are here because we've destroyed our Earth."

"Earth won't be destroyed if there's algae in the pond," said Maeve, beginning to feel her patience slip. "You want to feel like it's the end of the world, try waiting in the nurse's office with your period and hoping you don't bleed onto the chair."

"All right, all *right*," said Mr. Heller, waving his hands, a little desperately, in Maeve's opinion. "Just calm down. That's quite enough." He turned to Kyle. "My apologies for the interruption. Go ahead and finish."

Kyle cleared his throat. "I took it upon myself to draw up written plans," he said, digging into his backpack. "These files explain how to make and maintain the islands, as well as the levels we'd aim for. It would be a great assignment to add to the science curriculum. Students can continue to monitor phosphorus levels and test quality. We could even plant a butterfly garden."

"Well, it's plain that you've done your homework. I like your ideas very much."

Kyle nodded. Maeve looked to the side, frustrated.

After the interviews, Kyle and Maeve had exited into the hallway together before going separate ways toward their classes.

"You might have said something in there," she told him, slinging her backpack onto her back.

He looked at her. "What are you talking about?"

She didn't want to explain it to him; she was ready to just get to her class. "When Heller was being all Heller. Skeeving out just because I said the word 'period.'"

Kyle flushed but didn't look away. "I don't know what you think I should have said."

"You could have stood up for me. Told him it was a good idea. Objected when he called me 'young lady' and 'missy.'"

For a flicker of a moment, the corner of his mouth ticked upward. "I don't think you need a guy to stand up for you."

Maeve narrowed her eyes. *Look at him,* she thought, *with his curly brown hair and his tallness and his pretty green eyes.* He might have even been cute if it hadn't been for his personality. She shook her head. *Just look at him.*

"Of course I don't!" she told him. "It doesn't mean it doesn't help."

"It isn't my job to make your case for you."

"I'm not asking you to make my case for me." The fire was rising higher; he was completely missing her point. "But as a boy, you already have a leg up with Heller. You could call misogynists out on their shit, instead of leaving it all to girls. Civil justice sort of demands it."

"You weren't exactly supportive of me, either."

"You weren't being laughed at."

"Well, now you know," he said, hitching his backpack higher, "why you can't work within the system."

And with that, he'd walked away.

"Ladies and gentlemen, please welcome Maeve Sheering to the stage."

Maeve stood straight and inhaled to steady herself against the quick pounding of her heart beneath her ribcage. *Here we go*, she told herself. *No time to fixate on the past.* She took a step onto the stage, glancing once more at Kyle as she did so. He had turned his head to watch her take her place behind her podium. Their eyes met, locking for an unexpected moment of shared purpose and understanding. And just as quickly, it was gone, replaced by the sharpness of antagonism. Maeve raised her chin and stalked calmly to the center of the stage, where she shook Mr. Heller's hand and turned to the left to stand behind her podium. *Where is he?* she wondered, a little desperately, her eyes searching the crowd for one person in particular. Though she wanted to impress her classmates, his was the opinion she truly cared about.

"And now please welcome Kyle Langahan."

Maeve did not turn as Kyle emerged and took the podium beside her. A group of football players toward the front grew rowdy, knuckling each other and laughing, cheering Kyle on. Sitting among them, on the periphery of the group, was the one she was looking for.

Nate, she breathed, inhaling deeply, not even caring that her carefully constructed stone exterior was melting before the eyes of the entire senior class. *There you are.* The most attractive guy in the school, at least in her eyes—brown hair, average height, cute but in a quiet way—he'd occupied her dreams since junior year, when they'd worked on a Shakespeare presentation for their honors English class. He'd been nice to her, but shy, unyielding; they hadn't spoken since, but she'd thought of him every day. He wore the same easy, calm expression as always, and she smiled in spite of herself.

"Go Kyle!" one of the boys shouted, his hand at his mouth. The others cheered and clapped. Nate, still smiling, clapped, too, but said nothing.

Maeve braved a brief glance at Kyle. He was staring forward, serious as always, seemingly immune to the ruckus right before his eyes.

Maeve shook off her thoughtfulness and hardened herself once more. She looked out into the crowd. The entire senior class was here, and she had to convince them she was the right woman to get the job done. She gazed upon them and understood again what a tough job it would be. Some of them would ignore her; some would laugh. Still others would hate her, either for speaking her mind or for doing something they themselves could not. But she felt strongly that they needed her voice, whether they appreciated it or not. She couldn't change the world, but she could change her school. Maybe by putting herself out there, she could show other girls that they could put themselves out there, too. Maybe she could show the boys that her voice had power, and value.

"Biff!" someone shouted, and a murmur of laughter followed.

Maeve furrowed her brow and looked toward the front of the room, to the right, where the group of boys sat huddled together goofing off. What the hell was "biff"?

"Ahem," Mr. Heller said into the microphone, and the tittering in the room quieted.

"Thank you, seniors, for joining us for the class president debate."

"We were forced to!"

The room erupted in laughter. Everyone was now looking toward the boys in the right-hand corner. Mr. Heller stiffened and boomed into the microphone.

"That's enough!"

The room was silent.

Maeve glanced to her right at Kyle. He was standing straight and still, hands on the sides of his podium, staring stone-faced into the crowd.

She faced forward once more, then suddenly turned back to

11

her right. Kyle was now looking at her. Their eyes met. His face remained impassive. He turned again toward the class.

Mr. Heller waited a moment until he was sure he wouldn't be interrupted. Then he relaxed, took the microphone in his hand, and addressed the class.

"You're here today to hear from two of your talented classmates," he said. "Each candidate for senior class president will begin with a one-minute opening statement. Then we will allow questions from the audience. You will vote for senior class president at the end of the day."

The room hummed with mumbling and snickering. Mr. Heller tapped the microphone, and the noise died down once more.

"Mr. Langahan won the coin toss—" he began.

"Go Kyle!"

Mr. Heller ignored this outburst and continued.

"—and so he will give his opening statement first. I expect everyone to give the candidates their full attention."

Maeve's heart pounded as Mr. Heller stepped to the side of the stage, where a chair was waiting for him. Kyle had been watching him as he took his seat. At the principal's nod, Kyle turned to the crowd and began.

"Fellow seniors," he said, "welcome, and thank you. I'm here to speak with you today because I want to bring you on a journey. Let's be frank. We live in an affluent town in an affluent county. Most of us are members of privileged families, with many advantages. As such, we have many opportunities that others in our community do not. I'm talking opportunities not only to better ourselves but also to better the world for other people. And we should. We should make the world a better place. It's our responsibility to do our part to give back to the community."

"Kumbayah!"

Laughter once again from the crowd. Maeve was now seriously annoyed. In the audience, the group of boys were nudging each other and snickering; around them, kids were beginning to show they were over it, shaking their heads and rolling their eyes.

Maeve glanced at Kyle, who was standing straight and silent as before, his face stony and his jaw set.

After a moment, as the room quieted, he continued.

"As your class president, I will improve our school by helping us improve ourselves. For example, I want to start by doing something about the contaminated pond behind the campus. This is an easy project that can have huge ripple effects in the environment. I want our science classes to make floating wetlands—"

"Wetlands!"

"—that can counter the toxicity of the water and ensure more life can flourish there. It'll be not only valuable, but also fun."

"Wetlands!"

"Oh, grow up," murmured Maeve, rolling her eyes, before she could stop herself.

Kyle closed his eyes a moment, waiting for the laughter to subside.

"Ah, excuse me," said Mr. Heller, rising, his finger in the air. "That's enough. Enough!"

Maeve settled behind her podium, shaking her head. Her eyes were drawn to the boys to the side. They were all goofing off and snickering together—all except Nate, who was watching her with a smile on his face, his eyes twinkling slyly.

Maeve's heart tumbled in her chest, and her breath came a little more quickly. She smiled back at him, goofily, conscious of all the eyes on her but unable to prevent herself from falling under the spell.

The boy next to Nate shot Maeve a mischievous grin and nudged Nate with his elbow. Nate did not respond, but continued looking at her with that smile. Maeve blinked a few times, trying to gather her thoughts.

"Our school excels when it comes to making our own lives better," said Kyle, his voice firm as he spoke very close to the mic, demanding everyone's attention. "There's the gardening club, the spirit club, and of course the yearbook and prom committees. We should celebrate them, and we should continue to take part in them. But it isn't all about us. It's about looking at the world outside our own doorstep and recognizing that not everybody has it as easy as we do. If that's their burden to bear, then this is ours. Thank you."

Maeve clapped along with the audience. No denying it, his speech was very good. He really did care, she had to give him that.

The group of boys walloped and cheered; everyone else clapped politely. Kyle ignored it all, staring stonily forward. *Holy hell,* thought Maeve. *He wasn't kidding about no distractions.*

Mr. Heller rose and spoke into his microphone.

"And now we will hear from Miss Maeve Sheering."

"Biff!"

Maeve sighed with exasperation. At Mr. Heller's nod, she turned to the crowd.

She cleared her throat.

"Greetings, fellow seniors," she began, "and thank you for this opportunity to speak to you today. I think my opponent here"— she turned and gestured to Kyle, offering a conciliatory smile— "has some very good, unique ideas about how we can make a difference in this world." She faced the class once more and put her hands on the sides of her podium. "I, too, want to make a difference in the world, but I want to do it by starting at home. As your class president, I'd advocate for many changes, little changes that, by making your lives better, would provide a safer, more positive environment that can support us as we go out into the community." She paused. "I agree we need to look outside ourselves, but I think before we do that, we need to clean our own house, so to speak," she added, ad libbing.

She paused. The room was silent, everyone's attention rapt. To the right, the group of boys nudged and shouldered each other; Nate was watching her seriously, hands folded in his lap.

"Um," she began, blinking to clear her head. "I believe that in order for us to do our best for the community, we have to have confidence in ourselves and the guidance to achieve it. The first thing I'd do is institute a student mentor program. I don't know about you, but when I was a freshman, I felt lost and overwhelmed. I was lucky enough to have my sister, who was a senior, to help me figure out what to do. But not everyone has an older sibling to help. That's why I'm proposing establishing a program to provide student-led guidance for all incoming freshmen and for any other student who needs it."

Light clapping from sporadic hands throughout the room. Maeve took a breath and continued.

"I also firmly believe that in order for us to grow as a school, we all need to be represented equally. Many people don't realize this," she said, "but the last six senior class presidents have been boys. In fact, since the school went co-ed thirty years ago, there have been only two girl presidents."

She waited for a reaction from the room, but it was silent. She swallowed, then cleared her throat and spoke more forcefully.

"What this means in practical terms is that girls are underrepresented. As a result, this school largely is set up for boys, and there aren't a lot of people to advocate for our needs."

There was murmuring throughout the room, and a few giggles. Maeve took this as a sign that she had gained their interest, and kept going.

"There are many things we can do to level the playing field for our female students," she said. "The first is hiring a female athletic trainer so girls feel comfortable participating in our sports teams."

A boy in the group to the right let loose a high-pitched catcall, and a rumbling of laughter followed. Maeve leaned closer to her mic to make sure she was heard.

"I think girls' uniforms should include a pants option in addition these skirts. I'd also like to speak to our English teachers about opening up the canon to female writers. This year in AP English, we're reading six books by men and only one by a woman. We need to be more aware of women's voices so we can fight misogynistic tropes we witness every day."

She was losing them; she could see in the way they were whispering to each other or studying their fingernails, yawning. Maeve glanced over at Mr. Heller, who was watching her, and at Kyle, who was still staring out into the crowd. A hum of bored murmuring was beginning to spread throughout the room. She knew what would get their attention. Setting her jaw, she gripped the side of the podium and leaned into her mic once more.

"Also," she said, talking above the din, "we need to destigmatize the mere act of being female. We need free tampons in all the bathrooms."

This time, the reaction was extreme. The entire room seemed to explode with noise, the gasps and laughter and exclamations all jumbling together until, like an animal, it seemed to roar from below. No one was taking this seriously.

Maeve was irritated.

"You can pretend it's funny," she said, almost forgetting she was on stage and speaking into a microphone in front of her principal, "but I know each and every girl in here knows exactly what I'm talking about. How many times have you passed a frantic note to your friend in math class? How many times have you wrapped your jacket around your waist? The longer we laugh, the longer we don't have equal rights. The longer we—"

She'd noticed that her microphone had been turned off. She looked over at Mr. Heller, eyes blazing.

Mr. Heller was waving his arms as if he were bringing a plane in for landing. "Quiet!" he bellowed. The room gradually calmed.

He glared at her, his expression furious. Maeve met his gaze boldly, refusing to concede.

All this time, Kyle had been standing there expressionless,

assessing the chaos before him with total lack of passion, even with disgust.

Mr. Heller was telling the room the opening statements were done and that the candidates would now take questions. Instantly two hundred hands shot up into the air. He clarified that no one was to ask a question about what Maeve had just said. Almost every hand lowered once again.

The first question was about science labs and was directed to Kyle, who began to answer it in his usual self-possessed way. Maeve took the opportunity to gaze about the room, forlorn. It didn't matter what she said, or how sincerely she wanted to help; they were seniors, and uninterested in their causes, concerned only with getting through the year so they could reach graduation and transition into their own lives.

Kyle had finished answering his question. The next question was addressed to Maeve, whose heart sank as Jake, a boy from the group on the right, stood and smirked into the microphone as the boys around him stifled their hysterics.

"Um, yeah," he began, egged on by his friends. "You said how you're going to help girls." He turned as his friend punched him, doubled over with laughter, then turned to face Maeve once more. "But what are you going to do for the boys?"

Maeve's face froze over as she immediately understood his double meaning. Even from this distance she could tell their eyes were too low to be looking at her face; she instinctively pulled her cardigan more tightly around her round, ample chest, eliciting even louder laughter from the boys. She had developed early, and to her great chagrin had found that boys, and men, seemed to feel entitled to her body, to look at it, comment on it, and touch it, as if she were an object, as if she weren't even there. Years of snickers in the hallway came back to her, jokes whispered loudly enough for her to hear, the occasional grope she had come to see as normal. Grown men asked her on dates, asked to photograph her, asked to touch her. Sometimes they didn't even ask. Already, at eighteen, she was keenly aware of her role in their eyes, of her place in the world, of the need to protect herself from their gazes and their hands—and already, she was pissed off, on behalf of herself and every other girl she knew. Who the hell were they to subordinate her? Who the hell were they to dictate how she should act?

She watched icily as her classmates hooted and jeered at her, already over it, not even wanting this job anymore.

She leaned into the microphone and spoke.

"It doesn't surprise me in the least that you have to ask girls to do things for you."

"Ohhh!" yelled the boys, and the room rumbled as two hundred seniors roared with laughter or stared at her with wide eyes and open mouths. Maeve didn't bother to look at Mr. Heller; she knew she was done. She wouldn't recover from this, nor did she care. It wasn't in her nature to appease assholes. There was only so much bullshit she could take.

If Kyle wanted to deal with it, he was more than welcome.

She felt eyes on her. She snapped her head in Kyle's direction and realized he'd been watching her. She couldn't read his expression; his eyes were somehow softer. It didn't make any sense. She must have been imagining it.

What? she mouthed, self-conscious and defensive.

He straightened, and his mouth twitched awkwardly. He faced forward, his expression now hard.

Maeve shook her head with defeat and disgust, looking out into the jittery crowd. Her eyes were drawn to Nate, who was smiling at her, seemingly oblivious to the chaos around him. She inhaled and exhaled, returning his smile. He was different, she told herself—he gets it. Maeve blinked a few times, feeling delightfully dizzy. Maybe something good would come of this day after all.

～

"Hey, Maeve," said a female voice behind her. Maeve turned from her locker to find a trio of girls standing there watching her.

"Oh, hey, Stacy," she said, slipping one textbook into her locker and pulling another from the shelf. She stuck the book into her backpack. "What's up?"

"Interesting speech you gave today."

Maeve resisted the urge to roll her eyes, forcing a smile instead. "It didn't go exactly how I had planned."

"I don't know what you expected. There was no way people weren't going to go ballistic at the mention of tampons."

"Yeah, I guess I should have known better." Maeve turned to the inside of her locker door, combing her hair with her fingers as she studied herself in a magnetic mirror. She sighed. "I guess I have too much faith in humanity."

The girls laughed.

"Yeah, that's it," said the one on the right, named Ella. "You're the perennial optimist."

Even Maeve laughed. "You know me so well."

"Hey, are you going to the dance tonight?" asked Stacy.

Maeve snickered. "Yeah, no. Dances aren't my scene."

Lauren, the girl on the left, nudged Maeve with her arm, wearing a sly grin. "Nate's going to be there."

Maeve flushed despite her best efforts not to. "Why would I care about that?" she asked, with contrived nonchalance.

The three girls burst into giggles.

"Um, well," said Maeve, grimly; she had absorbed the shock of finding out that they knew, and she was already assessing how to move forward. She guessed she should have confided in them about her feelings anyway—she wasn't sure why she hadn't. Sometimes she felt guarded, like her priorities were somehow different from those of most of her classmates. The debate only proved it. But her friends had never given her a reason to mistrust them. It was probably fine.

"I guess it's okay if you know," she said, with contrived nonchalance, "since you're my friends."

"Oh my God, Maeve. Everyone knows."

Maeve pursed her lips, feeling like she might melt into a puddle and seep under her locker, and wishing she could. "Oh." She swallowed. "Okay. Does..."

"Does Nate know? Of course."

Maeve faced her locker, about to be sick. She fiddled with the pocket of her jacket, absentmindedly, pretending she had something to do there.

Maybe he likes you too, she dared tell herself. *He was smiling at you all during the debate.*

Don't expect it to work out, the other side of her said. *It never works out.*

"Anyway, you should go to the dance," said Stacy. "We're all going. Rumor has it John Beasley's bringing booze. It'll be fun."

Maeve rubbed her lips together and firmed up her face. She made herself smile and turned toward her friends. "Okay," she told them, slamming her locker shut. "I'll think about it."

"Yay!"

The three girls walked off toward their classes. Maeve stood for a moment, unable to suppress a rising feeling of hope. *Maybe I'll just go to that dance,* she thought. *Maybe I just will.*

"Hello?" Maeve called as she entered her house after school, having driven too fast so she could have more time to decide what to wear. The house was quiet; everything was still. Her father, she knew, was working; he was a Virginia state senator, and he was up for reelection this year. Every spare moment, when he wasn't at his law firm, was spent campaigning. She was about to call for her mother when she saw the note on the little table in the foyer.

"I went to lunch with Leanne and Constance. Help yourself to a

muffin. I hope you did well at the debate. Don't be disappointed if you lost."

Of course she'd lost. She'd had barely any chance in that boys' club, and any chance she'd had had been obliterated by the tampon fiasco. So much for change. But thanks as usual, Mom, for helpfully predicting her failure.

Maeve sighed and dumped her backpack by the door, shaking off her disappointment. She hadn't really expected to win. Hopefully her boldness would make other girls feel more comfortable being themselves.

She kicked off her shoes, then walked down the hallway, with its tastefully arranged end tables, lamps, and fine art, and into the immaculate kitchen. She grabbed an apple from a bowl on the countertop, biting into it as she bounded up the staircase and down the upstairs hallway, not to her room on the right but to her sister's room on the left, the larger room with the window that faced west. The late afternoon sun poured reams of gold onto the walls and across the floor; it made the already pretty room, with its white floral patterns and prints of roses and vintage women, look like the lair of a tasteful, intelligent princess.

Catherine, Maeve's older sister, was away at college. She hadn't given her permission to raid her closet, but she hadn't told her not to, and anyway, rules between sisters were only suggestions. Maeve did not generally covet her sister's clothes. First of all, her sister was tall and lanky, whereas Maeve herself was short; Maeve was bosomy and curvaceous, whereas Catherine had the more subtle curves of Audrey Hepburn or Lauren Bacall. More importantly, Catherine had a thing for vintage clothing, whereas Maeve preferred a more modern look. Therefore, Maeve did not go to Catherine's closet; rather, she made a beeline for her dresser drawer, where she knew Catherine kept her slips and nightgowns.

"And here we are," she said, pulling from the drawer a lacy red vintage camisole. She had seen Catherine wear this under sweaters, but Catherine, in her typical fashion, had been modest, buttoning the sweater to reveal only a teasing glimpse of red. Maeve had other ideas. If Nate was going to be at this dance, she had to dress to impress. She slipped out of her cardigan and pulled off her shirt, then shimmied into the camisole and stepped in front of the mirror on Catherine's closet door.

Damn, she thought, her eyes taking in the image of herself. As shapely as she was, she looked even shapelier in this camisole. It was heart-shaped, with lace all around. The deep cut in front brazenly revealed her cleavage, each side hugging her form and conforming to her body in glistening silk curves, accentuating the contrast between her waist and hips. There was no hiding in this camisole, that was for sure. On Catherine, it was demure and dainty; on Maeve, it was provocative and sexy, maybe a little sexier than Maeve liked to be. But damn, did she look good.

The sound of the front door opening and closing made her jump. She pushed the dresser drawer shut, then ran from the room and into her own bedroom, shutting the door quietly.

Once inside, she removed her skirt and stepped into dark jeans with tears in the knee and on the thigh. She straightened the camisole over her hips and twisted and turned in the mirror. There was no way Nate wasn't noticing her in this. Satisfied, she put her cardigan back on and buttoned it up. Then she went downstairs to meet her mother. Her mother would be surprised she was going to this dance. Maeve would have to tell her she was going to support a friend.

MAEVE PARKED the car in the high school parking lot and took a deep breath before swinging open the door and stepping outside. She usually didn't mind doing things alone, but tonight she was especially nervous. It was hard enough for her to muster the courage to go to a dance, much less the day she'd lost the election. It would be tough for her to face people. She'd called Stacy, Ella, and Lauren to see if she could go with them, but Stacy was arriving with some friends Maeve didn't know. Ella was going with her boyfriend. And she hadn't even gotten through to Lauren.

Since she was arriving by herself she had made it a point to be fashionably late—if nobody interesting was here, she could slip in and slip out without being noticed. As she stepped out of her car, she pulled off her cardigan, which had hidden her red camisole from her parents, and threw it into the passenger's seat. Then she slammed the door, her purse over her shoulder, and with an intake of breath walked with purpose up to the entrance of the school to find Nate.

The hallways looked darker at night, even though all the lights were on as usual. She heard the pounding of music emanating from the gym toward the center of the school. A straggling student lingered here or there, whispering frantically with a friend by the lockers about some crush or other, or hurrying out a side door to sneak a cigarette out of the teachers' line of vision. A few of them glanced in her direction, their eyes lingering a little longer than necessary.

"Holy crap, girl," said a female voice behind her, and then a hand was on her shoulder. Maeve turned her head to find Stacy, whose arm was across her back as she joined her outside the girls' bathroom. "You are smokin' hot."

"Thanks." Maeve caught a glimpse of herself in the glass of the trophy display and for a split second wondered if maybe she should have worn something less revealing. "How's the dance?" she asked, resisting the urge to inquire whether she'd seen Nate around.

"Kind of boring, but much more fun if you find John Beasley." Stacy devolved into hysterics, and Maeve realized her friend was pleasantly buzzed. "Grab a soda and look for him by the art room."

"How is he getting away with this? Aren't the teachers onto him?"

"They don't even know he's here."

Stacy was accosted by a group of girls in various states of excitement, and Maeve drifted off on her own toward the gym. The music grew louder, reverberating in her ears. Students were everywhere now, hanging around in couples and small groups, their faces bright with expectation or anxious with the desire to fit in, to seem like they had somewhere to go.

Maeve seemed to be drawing more attention than she had anticipated, but she wasn't sure if her own self-consciousness was making it seem more extreme than it was. She locked her gaze forward, ignoring their eyes, even as she squeezed through a group of students crowding the door. The inside of the gym was dark, with colored lights moving erratically around the room from a DJ station by the stage. It was hard to see in here, and everyone looked the same. Maeve frowned. She'd never find him.

A flock of students ran into the gym from the hallway, laughing raucously and shoving into her as she stood in the doorway. Maeve moved to the side, bumping into a folding table with a blue plastic tablecloth. Soda cans were lined up in uneven rows, big bowls of chips in front. Maeve swiped a can and popped it open, then downed a fizzy sip, not because she was thirsty but because she needed something to do with her hands.

After a couple of minutes of standing like this in the corner she decided to meander around to see what was what. She slinked around on the periphery of the crowd, staying in the shadows, her eyes darting here and there, recognizing faces for an instant before they went by in a blur.

"Skank," a girl muttered before exploding with laughter, followed by a group of three or four friends who pushed by Maeve toward the door.

Maeve's face fell, and her stomach roiled with anger—or something like it, something less biting and more grave. It was hurt, she realized, horrified to feel the swelling of tears in her eyes. She firmed her jaw and made her face stoic, forcing them back, reprimanding herself for letting other people tell her how to feel about herself. She pulled her long hair over her right shoulder and fiddled with it a little, something she did when she was nervous. It also gave her an excuse to cover her right breast—she was feeling conspicuous, wondering more and more if she should run to her car for her cardigan.

Someone was waving at her. Maeve looked to the right and smiled, her chest flooded with relief.

"Lauren," she said, walking toward her, confident once again now that she appeared to have someone to talk to. "Where were you? I tried to call you before."

"Yeah, sorry. I was out with my mom. Hey, tough break today. You look like you need to relax. Come with me to the art room for a sec. I want to show you my pottery."

Maeve followed Lauren out of the gym; her ears still pounded with the music. The two walked down the hall and around the bend to the art room, where a tall boy in a varsity jacket was standing there with his backpack, guarded by a couple of his friends who were stealthily on the lookout.

"Maeve just got here," said Lauren, grabbing Maeve's hand as it held her soda and pulling it toward the infamous John Beasley. Maeve lurched forward with the motion, ending up closer to John than she would have liked.

"Hey," John said, grinning, his eyes directly on her chest. He pulled a flask from his backpack and poured a stream of clear liquid into her can of soda. "Maeve Sheering. Who would've thought."

"Eyes up, Beasley," Maeve told him, watching the thin line of alcohol until it stopped, then pulling her hand back and giving the can a delicate shake. Maeve had dated John for a couple of months back in junior year. They were an odd couple, he the school's star basketball player and she on the math team, and they'd had nothing in common other than the fact that they liked making out in the back of his car after practice. It was just as well:

they never really had anything to talk about. Maeve wasn't sure, but she suspected their breakup was related to the fact that she wasn't ready to sleep with him, or with anyone—he'd hurt her with his rejection, but she was over it now. He wasn't all bad. He was otherwise nice to her, and she appreciated that they'd been able to remain civil.

John twisted the lid on the flask and slid it back into his backpack. "That's some outfit," he said, raising his eyebrows at her. "Makes me wish I hadn't broken up with you. Want to go out to my car, for old times' sake?"

"I'll pass," she said, and swigged her soda; she doubled over, cheeks puffed, resisting the urge to spit it out onto the floor. She swallowed with effort and shook all over. Everyone around her laughed.

"Jesus Christ, Beasley," she mumbled, wiping her lips with the back of her hand. "What the hell is that? Are you trying to kill me?"

"Nah. Just loosen you up a little."

"I hope you aren't driving home tonight."

"Yeah, my car's out back. I'm not drinking, though, just performing a public service. I voted for you, by the way."

He smiled at her, and she smiled back. She took another swig from her soda can, already feeling a lightening of her worries.

The group chatted for a minute or two before someone warned them a teacher was coming. They quickly dispersed, but it was a false alarm. Maeve didn't know where Lauren had gone. She looked up and down the hallway but didn't see anyone she knew. Numbed somewhat by the spike in her drink, she headed back for the gym, hoping to find Nate.

By now people had mostly split into groups; people were still dancing, but the crowd had spread out considerably. Everywhere she went, people were clustered together. They noticed her, but they were too much involved in their personal dramas to pay her much heed. Maeve tossed her soda into a nearby trash can. She didn't mind drinking, but she still had to drive home.

Maeve wandered around for some time, not really talking to anyone, merely observing and people watching, growing more and more disappointed when Nate was nowhere to be found. She made a pit stop in the girls' room and then, dejected, headed back to the gym with the intention of saying goodnight to Stacy. She'd might as well go home.

She found her friend in the center of the crowd, dancing her heart out. Stacy begged her to stay, though Maeve sensed it was half-hearted. Maeve hugged her and turned around to leave.

She started for the door and walked smack into Kyle.

"Oof," she said, straightening her hair, which had brushed into her face. She hadn't even seen him; he'd seemed to come out of nowhere. "Watch where you're going, Langahan."

"You bumped into me."

"Apology accepted."

"Likewise."

They stood for a moment, awkwardly. It was weird seeing him outside of school. His expression was serious, as always, but there was a thoughtfulness about his eyes. The soft curls of his hair were winsome, perhaps even charming. Without the protection of his uniform—he was wearing jeans and a tasteful oxford, neatly tucked in, and it loosened up his entire appearance—he looked almost human. If she hadn't personally witnessed his obnoxiousness, it's possible she would have found him attractive. For the shadow of a second, she wondered if maybe she had judged him too harshly—he was bristly, sure, but so was she. Then she remembered how he'd told her she was naive, how he'd dismissed the issue that was most important to her and how he'd blithely exploited his advantage over her, and she decided she'd been right the first time.

Still, she felt like she had to say something.

"So what are you doing here?"

He stared at her. "I'm here for the dance."

"I didn't know you were into dancing."

"Do you have to be into dancing to go to a school dance?"

"Point taken."

More moments passed.

"Hey, so um," he began, "I actually did want to talk to you."

"About what?"

"I wanted to congratulate you. On your campaign. You ran a good one."

Maeve blinked a few times, feeling the ice around her heart defrost a little. "That's nice of you, Langahan. Thanks." She attempted a smile. Maybe she had misjudged him after all. "As long as we're commiserating, you did a good job, too. You know your stuff, and you mean what you say. I guess if I had to lose to someone, it might as well have been you."

"Thanks." He shifted his weight. "I'm sorry you got heckled. That wasn't right."

"Thank you, Langahan." She warmed to him further, with caution. "I appreciate that."

The music was loud; it was hard to hear. Suddenly it switched to a slow song. The two of them looked around a bit, avoiding each other's gaze.

"Well, I should be going," she told him. "I was actually on my way out."

A shift occurred in his face, though it was already so impassive, it was hard to tell what. "Oh," he said. "Well, then go."

"Do you have a problem with my leaving?"

"Why would I have a problem with your leaving? I don't care if you leave."

"Well, okay then." Jesus. "See you Monday."

She turned to leave.

"Except that—"

She turned back to face him, waiting impatiently.

He straightened and took a breath.

28

"I just, um," he started. "I thought maybe we could dance. One dance, maybe."

Maeve's face contorted into a look of amused confusion. "... What?"

"Never mind. Just forget it. I was just trying to be nice."

"No, you already asked me. It's out there."

"Then what are we arguing about?"

Maeve watched him. "Why do you want to dance with me?"

"I didn't say I wanted to. I said I thought we could."

"What the hell is the difference?"

"The difference is that the former is a gesture of conciliation between competitive opponents. The latter suggests desire."

"So from this I surmise this is not about desire."

"Of course not."

Maeve laughed. "This has got to be the worst dance invitation ever."

"Look, if you don't want to, don't," he said, shrugging. "It was just an idea."

Maeve considered. The entire day had been such a bust, what difference did once dance make now.

"All right," she said, and stepped toward him. "Fine, why not. Dance with me, Langahan."

They were close enough to begin touching each other. Maeve was surprised by the physical reaction she had to his nearness. Up close, he smelled nice. Her face was just above his chest; if she were to lay her head down, she could nestle perfectly into his neck. His hands drifted to her waist, hers up to his shoulders. She had just begun to feel the light pressure of his fingers on her hips, enjoying an unexpected tingling sensation in her belly, when she spotted someone approaching, someone she'd been looking for all night.

"Nate!" she blurted, without thinking.

Kyle's hands fell, and he looked over his shoulder as the other boy grew nearer.

29

"Hey," said Maeve, delighted, and shocked, to find that Nate was coming over to talk to her. "Hey!"

Kyle had turned to face her.

"Nate McCallister? Seriously?"

But Maeve was not paying attention: she had already stepped back and favored Nate with a beaming smile. She didn't even notice Kyle widening the gap between them. She only knew that her dream had come true, that after all this time, he was finally noticing her.

"Hey, Maeve," Nate said, shyly, and Maeve's heart somersaulted.

Out of the corner of her eye, Kyle's movement drew her attention. She held her finger up to Nate and walked over to him, tugging at his arm to make him turn around.

"Hey, sorry to leave so abruptly," she told him. "He's actually the reason I'm here. I hope you understand."

He stared at her for a moment, then spoke in his usual off-putting way.

"Why Nate McCallister?"

Maeve raised her eyebrows. "Is it any of your business?"

"You know Nate McCallister is a complete asshole, right?"

"What are you talking about?"

"Wow. I can't believe you don't see it."

Maeve's blood was boiling. "And I can't believe you're even expressing an opinion."

"I'm just shocked you have such bad judgment. I mean, I'm seriously shocked. You of all people. Nate McCallister's one of these jocks who runs around with a sense of entitlement, never thinking of anyone but himself and his own asshole friends."

Maeve held her hands up, instantly defensive. "Whoa, whoa. And you know this how? And who do *you* think you're calling entitled?"

"I hope you're not calling me entitled."

"You just said I have bad judgment."

"You'd have to, to not see through McCallister."

Maeve felt all the old animosity boil up inside her. So now he knew better when it came to her love life, too? Who did he think he was?

"I don't even understand," she said. "They were all rooting for you at the debate. I thought you were friends."

Kyle scoffed. "You're kidding, right? Those guys wouldn't give me the time of day. They only rooted for me out of some warped sense of united masculinity. Sexism's your issue, right? How do you not see this?"

"What business is it of yours, anyway?" she asked him, in the back of her mind scolding herself for wasting precious time arguing with Kyle when she could be off doing whatever with Nate, but unable to stop the momentum of her anger. "Why do you care who I hang out with?"

"I don't care. And you're right, it's none of my business. If you want to hang out with him, hang out with him. Just don't say I didn't warn you."

Maeve shook her head and backed away. "You know what, never mind. I'm not sorry. Go make a 'gesture of conciliation' somewhere else."

Kyle waved brusquely and disappeared into the crowd. Maeve took a moment to fume in his direction, then turned around to face Nate, half expecting him to have given up and left.

He was still there, smiling at her. Maeve exhaled and joined him.

"Sorry about that," she said, tossing her hand in the general vicinity of the direction Kyle had gone in. "Just a little last minute political stuff. Very serious."

"He seemed pretty angry. Everything okay?"

"Yeah, sure. We were just arguing about what we should name our new floating island. You know, the one that's going in the pond. I suggested Florida, because Florida will be an island one day if we don't rein in global warming. He thought that was too

31

morbid and wanted to go with something that would evoke more positive images, like Martha's Vineyard."

Nate appeared to be trying to follow, without much success. His mouth was agape, and he was nodding along mindlessly.

Maeve cleared her throat and smiled. "Never mind. He's gone now, so it doesn't matter. Anyway, um." She pulled her hair over her shoulder and twiddled it in her fingers. "How are you?"

"Good." He blushed. "You have really pretty hair."

"Thanks." This could not be going any better. Hope lifted her heart higher with every passing moment. Suddenly, nothing else mattered, not the debate, not the vote, not Kyle's pompous criticisms. "Are you enjoying the dance?"

"Yeah, the dance is okay." Nate looked at his classmates dancing in the middle of the room and then back at her. "It would be a lot better if I were out there with you."

Maeve inhaled and exhaled, trying to stay cool. She nodded as he held out his hand for her, and followed him to the center of the crowd.

On the dance floor, he seemed aloof and distracted. Maeve kept trying to move closer to him, but he always managed to maneuver away.

"Are you uncomfortable dancing?" she asked, with sympathy. "It's fine if you are. I am, too."

"Yeah, a little, I guess." He glanced briefly at her, then looked around the room.

Maeve was watching him as she bopped to the music. "What is it?"

Nate leaned in toward her. "I am actually a little uncomfortable," he said. "I don't really like dancing. Do you want to do something else?"

Maeve was happy to do something else. Her heart fluttering, she took his hand. "Sure."

They left the dance floor and went out into the hallway, where they walked awkwardly together for a minute or two. His hand was very sweaty. Maeve hated to pull hers away, but she did, sticking it in her pocket instead.

"Hey, um," he said. "Do you want to go to the box with me?"

Maeve could not believe her luck and had to force herself not to scream and jump up and down. "The box," as it was called, was a place in the back of the school where the west wing of the building ran parallel to a fence dividing school property from a neighborhood yard. A dumpster blocked off the exit to the front of the school, creating a box-like formation where students often sneaked off to fool around or engage in other shenanigans.

"Oh," she said, as nonchalantly as possible, twiddling her hair. "Sure."

Nate didn't say anything, only glanced at her slyly and grinned. The two picked up their pace, exiting the school through a side door and walking along the west wing in the darkness until they approached the box. A few shadowy figures stood before them, needling each other and goofing off.

"Damn," she said sullenly. "Looks like other people got here first."

But rather than turn with her and go back the way they came from, Nate stepped to the side, narrowly missing being hit by dozens of objects the shadows were throwing at her. Instinctively, she ducked and covered her head, too bewildered to think. When the onslaught was over, the laughter began. Maeve opened her eyes and looked down at her feet. Tampons covered the ground.

She had just been pelted with tampons.

One had landed on her shoulder. She flicked it off, eliciting hysterics from whoever it was who had done this to her.

Maeve looked around for Nate, who had fallen behind a couple of steps. He picked up a few tampons from the ground and threw them in her direction.

"Here's for embarrassing me," he said, "staring at me like a pathetic puppy."

Mumbled laughter from the shadows. Maeve could not believe

this was happening. The letdown was almost too devastating to bear. Her face firmed as she commanded herself not to cry.

The shadows approached. Maeve's stomach dropped when she realized it was the group of football players who had harassed her at the debate that day.

"Hey, it's tampon girl," one of them shouted.

Maeve was frightened, but her hackles were up. "Good one," she said shakily, cocking her index finger at him in an effort to appear unfazed, looking around at the tampons at her feet. She began backing away, ready to end this nightmare and go home so she could curl up in her blankets and pretend this never happened. She shouldn't have even come in the first place. She pulled her hair over her shoulder and turned to leave.

"Hey, hey, hey, as long as you're here, you might as well stay," said one of them, and Maeve recognized the voice of Jake, the boy who had asked her that lewd question that day. *What are you going to do for the boys?* he had asked. Maeve had a bad feeling about this. Her breath came quickly with her heartbeat. She backed up stealthily as a couple of boys approached, then tried to bolt when they weren't expecting it; but they were too big and too quick, and they grabbed her arms and pulled her back.

"Let me go," she said firmly, through gritted teeth.

They laughed at her. "We aren't doing anything, relax."

"You can't keep me here against my will."

"Cry me a fucking river, tampon girl."

Maeve smelled alcohol all over the place. She cried out as one of the boys shoved her forward. She looked at Nate, who was hanging back, with an uncomfortable-looking grin on his face. He had entrapped her, exploiting her feelings for him by luring her into this, for the express purpose of humiliating her. How could he do this? How could anyone? And how could she have fallen for it? She closed her eyes, shaking, feeling nauseated.

"Hey, tampon girl," said Jake. "I hear you like sticking things in places."

To the background of laughs and catcalls, Maeve's face hardened into a stony frown.

"Hold her for me."

A couple of boys approached her, and she glanced to the side, assessing the exit. In response, one of them moved in that direction, blocking her path.

"I guess I was wrong," she spat. "You don't ask girls, you force them."

"Shut up. You talk too much."

Maeve tried to run again, but they had surrounded her. Two of them gripped her arms, their fingers digging painfully into her skin. She struggled to break free, but they only gripped her harder. A couple of boys poked and pinched her, their hands quick and numerous, too many for her to fend off at once. Someone grabbed her hair and pulled it back harshly, making her cry out, her neck bent back painfully.

One of the boys was unwrapping a tampon. "I say we stick it in her."

Jake rubbed his hands together. "Why should it have all the fun?"

The mood instantly changed: a new tension filled the air. Maeve's frantic heartbeat was making her dizzy; she felt she might actually pass out. Her breath was coming quickly, her skin prickling with alarm. She didn't want to be here; she wanted to go home. *Please, someone help me.* She struggled futilely to free herself. The boy holding her hair yanked it with a snort.

"Come on," she said, attempting reason as a last resort. She was now genuinely terrified. "What, so you're going to just assault me here behind the school?"

"Just pretend it's a tampon, bitch."

Maeve shook her head and shifted her jaw as the laughter grew vicious. Tears gathered in her eyes, and she scolded them back, desperate for them not to see her weakness, lest they exploit it.

"Please don't," she whimpered, her head hurting where her hair was being pulled, her neck strained. "Please just stop."

"Hey, guys," said Nate from behind them, raising his finger in the air. "Um, what are you doing?"

"Nothing," Jake snapped. "Shut up."

"Um, this wasn't supposed to happen. We were just supposed to throw these things at her."

Another boy chimed in. "Yeah, let's just let her go, okay?"

"Change of plans. Now everybody fuck off."

Someone from behind her lowered the strap of her camisole. She began to scream, but a hand clamped down over her mouth. She tried to bite it, but she was pushed against the wall of the school, and she was silent against the pain as her head crunched against cold brick. Jake stepped toward her, his snickering face dark in silhouette beneath the moonlight. Her view was blocked by the bulkiness of his form before her. He was all strength and muscle, and he stank of alcohol and rank masculine bluster.

All her bravado had left her; she was at their mercy, and she couldn't have felt more small. There was no hope, she was totally trapped. All the while, their laughter echoed cruelly in the background.

Jake had his fingers at the button of her jeans.

"Stop squirming," he grumbled, "and just—"

"Hey!" boomed a male voice from the far end of the box. "What's going on back here?"

The boys scattered, leaving Maeve by herself against the wall. She slumped down, her hair in her face.

Mr. Heller was stalking toward them; the boys were either fleeing or standing around awkwardly.

"I asked what's going on back here."

"Nothing, just hanging out," said Jake.

Mr. Heller took one look at Maeve and sighed. He went up to her and shoved her off the wall. "You shouldn't be back here," he said, ushering her out of the box. "Let these guys go back inside."

The boys had already dispersed. Maeve felt like she was floating above her own body. She let herself be pushed, unable to speak.

"And what's with this get-up you're wearing?" he went on, staring down at her with disapproval. "Go cover yourself up. You're just asking for trouble when you dress like this. For God's sake."

Maeve picked up her speed, her chin low and her shoulders hunched in a pitiful effort to make herself as small as possible.

Mr. Heller was hanging back. "What's all this on the ground? Oh, ha ha, very funny, guys. Someone has to come back here and clean all this up. Maeve, come back here and help."

But Maeve was already around the corner, biting her lips and breathing hard, her arms across her chest and her hair hanging over her eyes. She had to get out of here. The last thing she wanted to do was go back into the school, but she was afraid to walk alone outside the building in the dark. She kept her head down as she pushed her way inside, intending to make a beeline to the door down the hallway so she could take a shortcut to the parking lot.

The music was still playing; it was making her mind explode. She closed her eyes to block it all out and nearly knocked into Stacy as she passed the locker room doors.

"Oh my God, Maeve," she said, pulling her by the arm. Her face contorted as she looked at her. "What happened to you?"

Maeve's eyes were round with terror; she looked around at all the chaos, and a physical reaction overtook her. She couldn't identify why, but the thought of telling Stacy what had happened—of telling anyone—made her sick. She had to get out of here, now. Her skin was crawling, and bile rose in her throat. She tried to pull her arm from Stacy, but her friend wouldn't let her go.

"It doesn't matter," said Stacy. "You have to follow me."

"Let me go!"

"I'm serious, you have to see this."

Maeve frowned as her friend pulled her away. She glanced around her anxiously, praying she wouldn't see Jake or any of the other football players.

Stacy was leading her into the boys' locker room. For a moment, Maeve panicked, thinking her friend was about to betray her like Nate did. She cried out, shaking her head.

But Stacy had stopped anyway; she was pulling a folded piece of paper from a locker. She shoved it at Maeve, who took it mechanically.

"Open it."

Maeve made herself open the paper. She read the handwritten heading.

"Bitches I'd Fuck."

Number one on the list: Maeve Sheering.

"What did you have to do to get on that list?" asked Stacy, a bit viciously—was she laughing? "To be *first?*"

Maeve's head was spinning. She blinked a few times, trying to clear her vision. Her blood seemed to sink to her feet; her veins were empty and tingling. Her fingers began shaking as she stared at the list with disbelief.

Suddenly, a memory hit her.

Biff. Bitches I'd Fuck.

She must have dropped the paper, but she didn't remember doing it. Before she knew it, she was at the door to the locker room, vaguely registering Stacy's voice behind her. She glided down the hallway in a blur, knocking into people, stumbling away as fast as she could toward the door at the end of the corridor. The walls were closing in around her; she felt like she couldn't breathe. She burst through the door into the fresh air and ran to her car, stopping for a moment to throw up in the bushes. Somehow, she made it home, then up the stairs to her bedroom, where she locked the door and slumped to the floor, shaking in the darkness until morning.

CHAPTER TWO

TWENTY-THREE YEARS LATER

"Should we order an extra cream puff for Mom?"

"No."

"Don't you think it would be nice?"

"No."

"Aren't you worried she'll be sad we didn't think of her?"

"No."

"Maybe I'll get a cookie for Amy."

Maeve looked up from her compact. "Yes."

Maeve and her older sister Catherine were finishing up dinner at a café they liked in Charlottesville's historic Downtown Mall, an outdoor, brick-lined street with shops, restaurants, and other entertainments. Amy was Catherine's six-year-old daughter. Their mother Lois was watching Amy at Catherine's house while Catherine and Maeve met their father at the convention center, where Catherine's husband Wes, who was running for his second term in the US House of Representatives, was holding a town hall. Maeve had her purse in her lap and was straightening her chin-length dark bob as they prepared to leave. After powdering her face, she drew a tube of red lipstick from her bag and touched up her makeup. The server returned with their check as Maeve was popping her lips together, touch up complete.

"Excuse me, yes. We're going to add a dozen frosted cookies, please."

"Of course."

As the server took back the check and walked away, Catherine looked at her incredulously.

"A dozen?"

"My niece needs a dozen."

"But I have so much chocolate at home. I was experimenting with truffles for the Mayhews' shower, and Amy has been nipping at the leftovers."

"She always has chocolate. You make chocolate for a living. Let her have cookies. It'll be a nice treat."

"She can't have all that sugar. It'll make her feel sick."

"Relax, Mommie Dearest, she'll be fine."

Catherine sighed and slumped her shoulders in defeat: Maeve always won, especially against Catherine. Maeve suppressed a grin as she watched her elegant, lovely sister. Catherine was such a pushover. But Maeve could tell she was secretly delighted.

She decided to go easy on Catherine. "You're nervous," she said, with a knowing smile.

"Yes. How could you tell?"

Maeve laughed. "Just a sense. Though that napkin you're torturing might have something to do with it."

"Napkin?" Catherine regarded Maeve with wide, curious eyes.

Maeve gestured toward Catherine's fingers, which were picking a paper napkin to shreds. "You don't even know you're doing it, do you?"

Catherine glance downward and, catching glimpse of the little mess she'd left on the table, frowned ruefully. "Oh, dear. I'm sorry." She patted the shreds into a little ball and placed them neatly on her dish, no doubt out of consideration for the server. "I guess I'm more anxious than I'd thought. It's just so important that he do well. This is a lot more serious than when he was running for state Senate. Plus, back then, he'd had Dad to teach him the ropes."

"Yes, it was convenient that he was running for Dad's old seat." Maeve folded her napkin and placed it on the table, preparing to leave. She cast Catherine a sly look. "But Congress suits him. It's a bigger playing field." She thanked the server, who had returned with Amy's cookies, and handed her a credit card. "He's got it in the bag."

After Maeve paid the bill—it was her turn—the two sisters walked toward Maeve's tidy black car, Catherine in her modest navy blue 1930s suit, Maeve in her cocoa-colored pencil skirt, fitted white blouse, and stiletto heels. After all these years, Catherine was still drawn to vintage clothing—she rarely wore anything else. Maeve, on the other hand, was always on the cusp of fashion, quite naturally, preferring simple, classic clothing with a twist of sexy and a modern flair. The two were a study in contrasts as they walked down the street, though they had in common the quiet poise of the daughters of a politician. It was November, and the streets were bathed in gold: the trees were at the height of late-season foliage, and a canopy of colors danced and swayed in the breeze, seeming to sparkle with sunlight as leaves drifted toward their feet. Maeve enjoyed this time of year —except for Thanksgiving—because it was bright, brisk, and ulti- mately stark—just like her.

They drove to the convention center in cheerful conversation, then walked swiftly up the steps and into the auditorium. There were probably already about a hundred people gathered, some already seated, others standing about in small groups chatting. Standing by a seat about ten rows from the front was Maeve and Catherine's father, former Virginia state senator Fred Sheering. Tall and silver-haired, he was waving to them with a closed-lipped but friendly smile. Maeve nudged Catherine in the arm and began walking toward him, her heels clicking delicately on the polished floor.

"Hello, my daughters," he said as they approached, and kissed each of their cheeks in turn. "You're looking lovely today, as always."

"Thank you," said Catherine, smoothing down the front of her suit and fluffing the bottom of her shoulder-length honey-colored hair. "I like to look my best for Wes's events. I brought out a special suit today."

"As opposed to every other day," said Maeve, with a snide grin. "When's the last time you wore regular clothes?"

"These are regular clothes."

Maeve gave her sister's arm a few affectionate pats. "Sure they are."

"Do you not like it?" The shadow of a frown touched Catherine's lips. "I texted you before I bought it. You said the color was flattering."

"Of course it is. You look amazing." She softened her tone; she sometimes forgot Catherine could be sensitive to her snark. "Stop taking me so seriously. You know sarcasm is my love language."

Catherine was watching her, her eyes gentle. "You look like a queen today," she said. "I've always thought you look just like Hedy Lamarr."

Maeve playfully plumped up her dark bob. "I'm flattered."

"She's my favorite of the Depression-era actresses."

"Sounds about right."

"How was your dinner?" asked Fred. "You went to the new café, I assume?"

"It was excellent," said Catherine. "Smart menu, with a modern decor."

"Ah, that's good to hear. How's the wine list?"

"Extensive," said Maeve, "though I couldn't partake," she added ruefully. "Unfortunately, I was driving. Damn shame. These events are usually better after a couple of glasses."

They shook hands with some of Fred's connections who had made their way down the aisle. The room was filling up rapidly—Wes would have a good turnout.

"Aditi was going to try to be here," said Maeve, looking around as people took their seats, "but she just couldn't make it happen." Aditi was Aditi Patel, the freshman state senator who now held Senator Sheering's seat; before Aditi, the seat had been occupied by Wes, until he'd decided to run for Congress. Maeve worked as Senator Patel's communications director: though her passion for politics had never waned, she'd realized she preferred working behind the scenes.

"No, I suspect she couldn't. Not with her schedule."

"She's going to reintroduce the Right to Vote Act. She's going to ask you to write an op-ed."

"Of course. Good for her. You tell her she has my full support."

The three sat and chatted for a few minutes until the county commissioner approached the podium, to the polite applause of the crowd. After a minute or two of introduction, he held out his hand to the lefthand side of the stage, where Maeve's brother-in-law Wes had been waiting discreetly as he talked with the state representative and a couple of other local officials.

"So without further ado," the commissioner said, "I would like to introduce Congressman Wes Bickhart."

Wes strode to the center of the room with his characteristic coolness and ease, smiling brilliantly, his graying sandy hair impeccably neat, as always, and his expertly tailored suit falling perfectly on his straight form. At fifty-four, Wes appeared to be in his prime: he was entering the second half of his first term as congressman after a successful legal career, and he was still peppy, ambitious, and ever rising. Maeve smirked good-naturedly. With his almost blinding charisma and his ability to schmooze the socks off anyone, he'd always struck Maeve as just a little too full of bullshit. And though she was happy for her sister, who'd found love late and was almost obscenely smitten, she couldn't help but find her unsubtle worship of him to be a shade ridiculous—especially as they had overcome marital issues in which Catherine, in Maeve's opinion, was completely blameless. That said, as time had gone on, Maeve had realized that behind the bullshit was a good heart and a sincere desire to do the right thing. He enjoyed what he did, and he was efficient at it; he was dedicated to helping people, and he understood how to navigate the system to do it. Besides, he was good to her big sister: he lavished her with attention, and he frequently deferred to her advice regarding his political branding. Maeve had reluctantly decided to like him—though it didn't mean she didn't enjoy ribbing him every now and again.

"How is everyone tonight?" he asked as he pulled the microphone from the stand—Wes never stood behind a podium, preferring instead to pace up and down the platform, gesturing warmly to his constituents. "Thank you so much for joining me. No matter how many town halls I attend, it never fails to hit me how lucky I am to have the privilege of serving you."

Everyone in the audience clapped and welcomed him. Wes smiled and shook a few hands. When the din had quieted, he stood before them and said a few words about the last House session and the state of some issues in the national news. After these opening words, in which he shared his opinions and outlined his plans, the floor was opened to questions from the audience.

An older, gray-haired man stood. "Good evening, Congressman. My daughter is trying to go back to work after staying home for three years with my granddaughter, but the cost of childcare is so high, it's almost not worth it. She and my son-in-law can't make it on his salary alone. When is childcare going to be seen as a serious issue in Washington?"

The crowd clapped, and a couple of people stood. Wes listened carefully and waited for the applause to stop, then took a couple of steps forward, relaxing his stance.

"I agree with you," he said, nodding. "In many states, childcare costs more than college, and this keeps people out of the workforce, mostly women. We are the wealthiest country in the world. Why can't we ensure children—*all* children—get the best quality care, at a cost that isn't a burden to working families? Well, it's a funny thing, because I've been working with Congresswoman Heather Moon on this very issue. Our Fair Child Care Act would provide enough federal funding to ensure childcare is capped at five percent of a family's income."

From the center of the room came a man's voice: "You introduced it this week," the man said. "How are you going to pay for it?"

"Ah," said Wes, gesturing pointedly with his finger. "I am so glad you asked me that question." Wes dove into his answer, stepping casually across the stage, addressing concerns and ticking off points one by one until the questioners were nodding with understanding. At the conclusion of his response, the audience clapped again. Fred turned to Catherine.

"Pretty impressive, I'd say."

"Yes," said Catherine, swelling with pride. "Yes, I'd say so too."

Wes took a question from a young woman.

"I'm concerned about prescription drug prices," she said. "I have a medically fragile child and elderly parents. How will you address this?"

Once again, Wes deftly answered the question, laying out background and expounding on his beliefs, then explaining what he thought could be done, and what his own plans were to help solve the problem. As before, his answer was met with enthusiastic applause. Maeve had to admit he was nailing it.

The next question came from a man in a stone gray suit toward the front of the room.

"Yes, thank you, Congressman," the man said. "Sir, recently Congress failed to pass the Water Purity and Safety Act, which as you know, among other things more strictly regulates the levels of PFAS and other toxins that are allowed in drinking water."

Maeve's eyes shot in the direction of the voice. She knew that voice.

"You've cast yourself as an environmentalist," the man went on, "and in fact before you were a Virginia state senator, you made your name fighting the building of a toxic landfill on the outskirts of Charlottesville. However, you voted against the Water Purity and Safety Act."

"Holy mother of God," Maeve breathed.

"What is it?" whispered Catherine, leaning toward her.

"You are of course aware," said the man, "that the Water Purity and Safety Act would have required the EPA to assign a maximum contaminant level to PFAS, which would help eliminate carcinogens in our drinking water. Sir, as a public servant tasked with protecting the citizens of this community, why did you vote against the Water Purity and Safety Act?"

Maeve was watching the man, all sorts of emotions tumbling in her gut. The man was about her age, tall and well built, with curly brown hair cut short and an impassive, yet subtly demanding, manner of speaking. It was a manner she knew all too well, one she'd defended herself against too many times. It was definitely, most certainly him, the bane of her senior year existence.

"I can't believe it," Maeve whispered to her sister. "It's Kyle fucking Langahan."

"No way," said Catherine, too loudly, drawing looks from people nearby. She was now sitting up straight, unsubtly, with her chin in the air to afford herself a better view. Maeve elbowed her harshly; Catherine winced and reclined.

"I can't believe he's still at it," whispered Maeve, rubbing her sister's arm to amend for having nudged her. "After all these years, he still can't let this shit go."

"I suppose it's good that he's passionate," Catherine

responded, "though I wish he wasn't so accusatory toward Wes. Do you think this will hurt him, Maeve?"

The corner of Maeve's mouth ticked upward. "Wes can handle Langahan."

"...understand why this would concern you," Wes was saying. "It's a fair question. The problem with the Water Purity and Safety Act is that it contained a rider that cut funds for Women's Hope International. Now, I believe in regulating PFAS, but I'm not going to do it at the expense of women's healthcare, neither here on our own shores nor overseas in developing nations. We're talking about women who are most in need of the care the International provides. I don't think we need to pick and choose our causes. We can keep our water healthy and also uphold our responsibility to support under-served women. That's why I've been working with Representative Carrie Woods to write a similar bill that strengthens regulations, including on PFAS, and also protects water sources, allocates funding for infrastructure, and establishes protocols for emergencies. It strengthens enforcement and penalties for companies in violation. And best of all, it doesn't cut funds for women who need them most."

Wes's voice had grown louder for the last few words of his statement as the room erupted into cheers and applause. To her right, Fred was nodding and saying, "That's right." All the while, Kyle stood waiting, unfazed by the uproar around him. As the applause quieted, Kyle shifted his weight and began speaking again.

"The only real way to ensure we aren't sold out to special interests is to eliminate privately owned water companies and transition to public management." He paused. "Does your bill eliminate privately owned water companies, transitioning to public management? Sir?"

Wes's face turned sly. "Well, you must know that it doesn't, or you wouldn't have asked me that question."

Light chuckling from the room. Kyle remained unmoved.

"Sir?"

Wes relaxed, sticking his hand in his pocket, the other hand holding the mic, and made his voice conversational. "This is a very important question, and I appreciate your holding us accountable. I don't disagree with you. But we don't want to over-shoot here. Transitioning from private to public ownership would mean a lengthy legal battle, and we'd face incredible challenges as we restructured the entire system. Our first concern is getting the PFAS out of the drinking water. In order to do that, we need to impose strict safety standards for manufacturers disposing of wastewater. PFAS is a 'forever chemical,' so called because it's created with a bond that doesn't break down. This makes the matter that much more urgent."

"Yes, yes," said Kyle, with contained impatience, and Maeve found herself sucking in her breath at the familiarity of that tone. "I'm a scientist, Congressman, so I'm knowledgeable about chem-ical bonds. What I want to know is, why does your bill not address the problem at its source, and what are you going to do to remedy this weakness?"

"Representative Woods and I believe that the most important thing now is for us to stop the bleeding. Once we've ensured the contamination has stopped, we can look at solutions with wider implications."

"With all due respect, sir, this smells like a sellout. We've got companies like Brown & Little, right outside Charlottesville, who have likely been covering up their non-compliance for years. Brown & Little was ordered to clean up after the leak, but twenty-three years later people are reporting odors and chronic health problems. Who's lobbying against real regulation? Who in Congress is benefiting financially from this?"

"My friend," said Wes, quite seriously, taking a step forward to speak more warmly, "I want you to understand that I am doing everything in my power to ensure that we do what's right. We're on top of the residents' reports; swift action has been taken, and these complaints are being investigated by the relevant agencies as we speak. I know the importance of regulation—that's why I fought against Munson's landfill. Believe me, I won't let this go."

Kyle chuckled humorlessly. "You'll forgive me, but I've known too many politicians."

"I understand, and I don't blame you for your skepticism. I can't erase years of partisanship and inefficiency, nor can I deny that money in politics is a huge problem. What I can do is assure you that the regulation will come. Our water bill contains the strictest safety standards ever proposed, and it comes down hard on those not in compliance, so we can ensure this doesn't happen again. Sometimes, though, we have to do one thing at a time."

"Well," said Kyle. "I don't agree." He raised his hand briefly, as if in parting, and took his seat. "Thank you."

The tension lingered for a moment or two. Maeve was holding her breath. Out of the corner of her eye, she noticed Catherine's fingers fidgeting with the hem of her jacket. It didn't last long, however. Without missing a beat, Wes had resumed his congenial pacing, having taken it upon himself to choose a hand from the audience.

"Yes, you right there with the beautiful baby, what can I do for you today?"

Maeve exhaled, and the mood in the room relaxed. Catherine briefly turned to Maeve, and the sisters shared a look of understanding. Maeve raised an eyebrow at her and grinned—Wes was nothing if not sharp. As she turned back to the front of the room, where Wes was discussing healthcare, Maeve tried to consciously calm her heartbeat. She was still processing what she had just seen. Kyle Langahan, after all these years—still pushy, still condescending, still on a rampage about Brown & Little. And now, it appeared, he was once again intermingled with her life, facing off with her brother-in-law, calling into question a bill about which she herself had helped him brainstorm. And all this, over Wes's defense of Women's Hope International. It figured, Maeve thought, her lips now curved into a sneer. It just figured he'd throw women under the bus because his issue was more important.

It went like this for another hour or so, until the commissioner returned to the stage and, after a few parting words, thanked everyone for coming and asked for a round of applause for Wes. Most people in the room stood for a standing ovation. As she rose to her feet and clapped, Maeve glanced over at Kyle. He was squeezing out from the center of his row, excusing himself as he climbed over audience members.

As he fell into the aisle, his eyes met hers. He stopped dead short, and stared.

Maeve didn't even have time to look away. Other audience members were emptying into the aisle, and before she could blink, he had already moved on.

SHE DIDN'T EXPECT that he'd be waiting around in the lobby; still, as she made her way out of the auditorium with her father and sister, Maeve's eyes darted about anxiously, unsure whether she feared she would see him or that she wouldn't. Consciously, she had no desire to talk to him. At the sight of him, her anger, long suppressed, had begun bubbling at the surface; her blood seemed to tingle with their old antagonism, the instinctive preparation to fight. But, inexplicably, part of her was curious. An even smaller part of her itched for confrontation. Once in the lobby, she kept her eyes on her family. On the off chance he was still here, she didn't want to appear to be looking for him.

She and Catherine followed their father as he shook a few hands and chatted with important contacts. Eventually, they crossed paths with Wes: he had been talking with a group of constituents who had approached him to ask questions and take pictures and had finally made his way to the lobby.

"Hello, sweetheart," he said to Catherine, slipping his arm around her waist and kissing her tenderly. He rubbed her back and grinned at them. "Well, another one down! And a lively one, at that."

"Indeed," said Maeve as she accepted a kiss on the cheek. "Back to complimenting babies, are you, Congressman? The tougher the questions, the more of them you notice."

Wes cast her a sardonic grin. "Touché."

"You did a wonderful job," said Catherine, gazing at him adoringly. "You handled Kyle's questions with such grace, I don't see how anyone could doubt your sincerity."

"Kyle? Who's Kyle?"

"Kyle Langahan. The one who asked you about the water bill. He went to high school with Maeve."

"Ah." Wes's grin grew wider. "So he's a friend of yours, is he?" he asked Maeve teasingly. "I suppose I should have known."

"God, no," said Maeve, grimacing. "She said we went to school together, not that we were friends. In fact, we were the opposite. You might even say he was my nemesis."

"You disappoint me. I thought I was your nemesis."

"A girl's got to have more than one nemesis."

"Wes, I was interested in your comment about tax reform," said Fred. "I didn't know that bill was in the works. Come over tomorrow and we'll discuss it over scotch."

"Sure thing."

They shook a few more hands and watched as Wes took a few more pictures, then meandered through the crowd.

"Do you really think Wes had a good night, Maeve?" asked Catherine, leaning in toward her.

"I already said he did." The words came out more harshly than she had intended. Her habitually business-like expression softened. "Don't worry, dear. He did very well."

Catherine and Wes were held up by someone they knew. Maeve waved goodbye and headed for the door.

As she approached, she spotted Kyle. He was standing in the corner, separated from the mayhem, staring out the door as if he were waiting for someone.

She considered attempting to sneak out unobserved; she had come too far in her life to be bothered with bygones. It felt like escaping, however, and escaping wasn't her style.

She made her way toward him, a sassy sway in her step.

"Kyle Langahan."

He turned and looked at her. His face registered no emotion. It was as if twenty years hadn't passed, as if it wasn't a huge coincidence that they should run into each other after all this time.

"Hello, Maeve," he said, sounding as bored and put-upon as ever.

"What are you doing here?"

"I came to see the congressman."

"You gave him quite a run for his money."

"They need to work for their money."

Maeve studied him. He was looking out the door again, evidently having said his piece. Maeve used this opportunity to size him up. Time had been good to Kyle Langahan. His once boyish face was now sharp in profile, the lines of his jaw straight and square, his neck thick enough but not too thick, a nice balance of slim and strong. His hair was cut short, in a professional manner, but the loose curls gave him a subtle roguish air that was completely at odds with his demeanor. He was not clean-shaven, but he wore it well; it was a carefully curated five o'clock shadow, enough to be noticeable but not quite enough to be a beard. He gave the impression of a casual person who wore a suit out of necessity, but Maeve had been around enough men in suits to know when that impression is contrived. Kyle pulled it off perfectly. Maeve was simultaneously intrigued and annoyed by the ease with which he manufactured this look.

"You know, he's my brother-in-law," she told him.

A glimmer of surprise registered in his eyes; otherwise, his face remained stoic. He returned his gaze outside. "Really?"

"Yes. He's married to my sister Catherine. I'm surprised this is news to you. I thought you knew everything."

"I haven't been back that long," he said, still looking outside, ignoring Maeve's sarcasm. "I've been living up north."

"Where's 'up north'?"

"New York. Way upstate. My girlfriend and I lived there for years."

"Uh huh. And you came back here when?"

He looked at her, finally. "You sure ask a lot of questions."

"Well, you see, Langahan," she retorted, gesturing patiently with her hand, her compact purse hanging from the thin strap over her shoulder, "this is what's called a conversation. It involves parties asking questions and responding. It typically happens when—"

"Thanks, I got it." He hesitated, then seemed to relax, as much as Kyle Langahan could. He shifted his weight, and his expression became a shade less stiff. "I came back about six months ago," he said. He paused again. "How about you?" he ventured. "What have you been up to?"

"I've been here since high school, with the exception of college. I went to Vassar for undergrad, then got my master's right here at UVA."

"What did you go to school for?"

"Women's studies and political science."

For the first time, maybe ever, Maeve detected a grin in his face. "Ah. That makes sense."

Neither said anything for a moment or two. Maeve was getting ready to say goodnight. She didn't really know why she'd come over here in the first place and figured she'd quit while she was ahead.

He surprised her by reopening the conversation.

"So how close are you to your brother-in-law?"

"As close as I get to people, I guess. Why?"

"I mean do you agree with all his policies?"

"Usually, yes."

The shadow of a sneer crossed his lips. "I guess I should have figured."

"What the hell does that mean?"

"I mean you were all about the establishment, even back in high school. You've always had faith that the system would come through."

"Oh, spare me," said Maeve, rolling her eyes, and sighing. *I swear to God, nothing changes.* "'Establishment' just means experienced. It's what people with big ideas and no plans call the people who get shit done."

Unexpectedly, Kyle laughed. "That's what you think, huh? No plans? You know nothing about me, Maeve. You have no idea what I've been doing the last twenty years."

"And you don't know Wes." Maeve could add "made me defend Wes" to the ever-growing list of things she hated about Kyle. "Calling him 'establishment' is an easy way for you to dismiss all the good work he's done. Wes's voting record is stellar. Yes, he works within the system. That's because he's learned that you have to play the game."

"He's just a typical politician, compromising his morals to play nice with the other side."

"You are a piece of work, Langahan." Maeve's heart was pounding, as if it wanted to jump out of her chest and smack Kyle itself. Years of animosity were making her blood boil; she had so many things she wanted to say to him she felt incapable of choosing which to go with first. "What would you expect him to do? Do you think the opposing party simply vanishes into thin air upon one's inauguration? Need I remind you that you'd defund a necessary program for underserved women? You're the one compromising here. What would you tell those women? That their cancer screenings have to wait? That their birth control is disappearing overnight? You've been after Brown & Little since high school, and I know this cause is your baby, but Jesus, have a heart."

"Have a heart?" Kyle was staring at her incredulously. "Let me tell you something, Maeve. Brown & Little never fully cleaned up their mess, and they're still cutting corners to avoid adhering to safety regulations. My parents studied them for years. They're paying off Virginia ClearStream executives, mark my words. I'm telling you, the water company's been turning a blind eye to the violations—concealing quality testing, falsifying documents. It's been years, Maeve. Years. What kind of effect do you think that's had on our children?" There was genuine fear in his face, and Maeve straightened, surprised; a moment later, it was gone, and Maeve wondered if she had imagined it. "Don't tell me to have a heart. Anyone with a heart would care about this issue."

"I do care, and so does Wes. What about the bill he's working on with Carrie Woods? And aren't you aware that Aditi Patel is working on a corresponding bill in the Virginia General Assembly? They've been collaborating for weeks." Maeve was growing increasingly frustrated; it was one thing to disagree, but it was another to disagree with someone who was almost belligerent in their opposition. "But we can't let them take us hostage. I'm proud of Wes for voting against that bill. It took courage to refuse to sacrifice those women."

"It was progress, and he let it slip away."

"The bill failed because it was wrong. He wasn't the only one who voted against it."

"They're all the same. Nothing gets done."

"Langahan, I've worked in politics my whole adult life. Not everything has to be a conspiracy. Sometimes the system does work."

"The system moves too slowly. You of all people should know that."

Maeve had nothing to say to this. It felt like some sort of

twisted conciliation, but she was frazzled and couldn't be sure. In any case, he wasn't wrong; the system could, in fact, move infuriatingly slowly.

"What do you do?" he said then.

Maeve stared at him. "What do I do?"

"For work. You said you work in politics."

"Oh." The heat of indignation still flushed her skin, but she took a deep breath, and relaxed somewhat. "I work for Senator Patel. I'm her communications director. I volunteer for Wes when I can."

"So you don't actually write legislation."

"No." Maeve's hackles prepared to rise again, but she made them stand by. "My dream is to be a policy advisor, and I'm working up to it. But in the meantime, it's my job to write about it, so I know what I'm talking about."

"I wasn't suggesting you didn't." He cleared his throat. "So what does a communications director do?"

"I write or review press releases. I set up interviews and press conferences. Sometimes I help with speechwriting. I write marketing communications and work on branding. I write scripts and fact sheets to be released in the media, I oversee charity functions, I review public opinion research, I create messaging that reaches constituents."

Kyle's eyebrows rose briefly, and he studied her a moment, as if impressed, but averse to saying so. He cleared his throat again. "That sounds like a good job for you."

Maeve was cautiously appreciative of this acknowledgment, which she knew must not have come cheap. "Thank you. It is. I love my job." She cleared her throat. "What about you, Langahan? What do you do?"

"I'm a hydrologist with the Virginia Conservancy Society."

Maeve couldn't help but grin. "Shocking."

He was staring out the door again. "I've only been there a few months. I worked for years for the Lakes Preservation Institute in New York. That's where I met Melissa. But they've restructured since losing their funding, and I wasn't on board with some of the changes."

"How does Melissa like Virginia?"

"Melissa stayed up north."

"Oh," said Maeve, her heart almost touched by a vague tremor of sympathy. "I'm sorry."

"Don't be. It wasn't meant to be." He straightened. "Here's my daughter."

Maeve's jaw dropped as a little girl ran into the lobby and wrapped her arms around Kyle, who to Maeve's utter shock bent low and hugged her, then lifted her in the air and kissed her a dozen times. He was now a completely different person, warm and smiling and actually full of life. Gone was the humorless, pissed off Kyle; in its place was one who enjoyed things, who knew how to feel, and liked it.

"Hi, Daddy," said the girl, whom Maeve estimated to be about eight. Kyle had placed her back on the ground and was straightening her flaxen hair around her shoulder. "How was the meeting with the congressman?"

"It was good, I got him thinking," said Kyle. He thanked and waved off the babysitter and returned his attention to his daughter. "What did you do in school today?"

"Nothing of great consequence. Who's this lady?"

Whoa. Maeve blinked a few times, her brain struggling to catch up.

Kyle turned to Maeve briefly, and he started, as if he'd forgotten she was there. "Honey, this is Maeve Sheering. She and I went to school together. You know, a million years ago."

The little girl was looking up at Maeve with wide blue eyes. "You were the salutatorian."

Maeve's brow rose higher.

"Yes," said Kyle, and if Maeve hadn't known better she would have thought she detected his reserve falter a little. "Yes, honey, great memory."

"Hello," said Maeve, recovering, and sticking her hand out to the child with a warm, friendly smile. "How do you do? What's your name?"

"My name is Nicole Langahan. It's lovely to meet you, Ms. Sheering."

"You can call me Maeve. All my friends do."

The child smiled at her. To her own surprise, Maeve was instantly entranced. She was not one for children, having made a singular exception for her sister's daughter Amy. This little girl was precocious, though subtly so; she was dressed primly, in a skirt and button-down shirt, but it wasn't a uniform—it was how she wanted to look. In her hair was a pink glittery headband, and it kept tidy hair so blonde and shiny it looked like it came from a porcelain doll. Tiny brown freckles dotted the bridge of her nose. Maeve's eyes darted to Kyle. *Look at you, Langahan*, she told him in her mind, bewildered and impressed. *Just look at you.*

"My dad told me about you, once," said Nicole. Hanging on her shoulder was an old-fashioned leather purse; the little girl had her thumb looped through the strap like a tiny grown woman. "He said you ran against him for class president, but you lost."

"Yes." Maeve was more amused than she cared to admit. She firmed her jaw to suppress a grin. "Yes, your dad was just too good a candidate. I tried to beat him, but alas, I could not."

"I'm going to run for president one day. Not for class president. For president of America."

Maeve nodded her approval. "I have no doubt you will. You'll be the first female president."

"No." Nicole's face had suddenly hardened, and Maeve saw her father in that look. "By then, we'll have had several female presidents."

"You," said Maeve, cocking her finger at her, "are my kind of girl."

"Honey, we need to be going." Kyle was visibly uncomfortable. He turned to Maeve. "It's Tuesday. She has school tomorrow. The babysitter brought her over from a violin lesson."

"The violin, how lovely." Maeve looked at Nicole. "I'll have to introduce you to my sister Catherine. Catherine just adores the violin."

"Does she play?"

"No, she does not. But she knows every note of Brahms."

"I prefer Chopin, but Brahms has his merits."

"Indeed." Maeve could not have been enjoying herself more. She couldn't get enough of Nicole's subtle spunk. Making Kyle uncomfortable was the cherry on top. Who was this child, with her porcelain doll hair and freckles, her adult conversation and her desire to be president? She couldn't believe she was Kyle's daughter, but somehow it made perfect sense.

"Well," she said, "I'll let you head home and get ready for school tomorrow. It's almost my bedtime, too."

Nicole held out her hand. "It was nice to meet you. Maybe we'll meet again."

Maeve shook it. "Maybe we will."

Nicole headed for the door. Maeve watched her go.

"She's something else," she said.

Kyle sniffed in agreement, and smiled. "Yeah, she is."

"She's got quite a vocabulary on her."

"She reads a lot," said Kyle. "A real lot."

"And she's got smart parents." Maeve looked at him. "She must get her seriousness from you."

"She's not serious all the time. She likes to have fun."

"She must get that from her mother."

Kyle sighed silently. "You're enjoying this, aren't you."

"A little bit, yes."

Nicole poked her head back inside. "Daddy."

"Coming, honey." Kyle smiled at his daughter and shot Maeve an indecipherable look. "Well," he muttered, then nodded awkwardly and waved. "Good to see you, Maeve. Take care of yourself."

And with that, he chased after his daughter, and was gone.

～

THAT NIGHT MAEVE lay in bed thinking about time, how it changed so much, how it really changed nothing at all. Images of high school flitted across her brain, and she squeezed her eyes shut, simultaneously trying to summon them and to force them away. After the night of the dance, Maeve had made a conscious decision never to think of it again. If she didn't think of it, it couldn't affect her—it couldn't define her then, and it couldn't impact who she'd become. She'd gone back to school Monday with her head down, eyes directed solely at her tasks; she'd pushed her friends away, focusing instead on completing her senior year so she could get the hell out of there and forget it ever happened. Her friends, in any case, couldn't understand. They sought the attention of boys just like the ones who had attacked her; they'd called other girls "sluts" and surely would think her one, too.

Maeve had finished out the year brilliantly and accepted her diploma with a steadfast smile, already looking forward to the better years of her life. She'd sat behind Kyle as he'd given his valedictorian speech—she had hoped to overtake him, but despite her efforts, she had failed—and as she'd listened to his calls for charity and public service she'd been thinking about the future, of Vassar, of her career, of all the ways she'd do the things she'd only imagined in high school.

In college, she had been more free. It was a college that had suited her; it was forward thinking and aware. She wasn't laughed at for centering women's rights; no one batted an eye when she helped organize a drive to donate menstrual products to libraries and recreation centers. If she was serious during the day, she unleashed herself at night; she was a partier all through college, finding early that alcohol and casual sex provided release after a day of hard work, could make her forget herself, and the world— at least, for a time. She discovered that in losing control, she gained it; there was power in emotion, in honesty, in physicality. She understood that she could wield power rather than submit to it. She was able to connect with herself when losing her inhibitions. And in boys' dorm rooms, she had the power to make them lose theirs.

The moon was high above the window behind her bed, which faced directly east; silver light flooded through the curtains, illuminating the modern floral print bedspread, the curves of her form evident beneath. Maeve rose and cast the bedspread aside, a halo of moonlight around her. She looked about her bedroom. It was the finished attic of her 1920s-era cottage house, and with its gables and dormer windows, and slanted roof, it held plentiful nooks and crannies, places for hiding and for secrets. Built-in bookcases and recessed shelves were like secrets within secrets, unexpected hideaways in unexpected corners. The room was cozy, with cherry hardwood floors covered by the occasional woven rug and white-painted panels on the walls and ceilings. The northern side of the room was a recessed office, with lavender walls and a window seat with tufted pillows; the south side held a cottage-style bathroom, with the same white-painted panels and a large soaker tub. Maeve's bare feet lowered to the floor, and she stepped toward her office, where a recess in the wall held a flower vase, a photo of Maeve and Catherine, and a couple of bottles of wine. She uncorked a bottle and poured some into a thin-stemmed crystal glass, then sat in a wingback chair catty-cornered across from the bed. This room was precious, her respite; it was hers and hers alone. She never brought men up here; when she entertained male companions, she took them to a guest room on the second floor. Simple yet comfortable, sleek yet feminine, the room was exactly what she needed, exactly what she wanted to be. She'd bought this house partly because of this room: she enjoyed being as high up as possible, as far away from the problems of the day as she could be. She loved this house, at the end of a street in a quiet suburb of Charlottesville. Every day was a fight, whether obviously so or not—a fight for fairness, for justice, for happiness, for peace. It was high heels and lipstick and witticisms; it was personas and strong fronts and masks. Maeve loved retreating to this house every day. In this house, she was herself; she was free.

She sipped her wine and stared out the window above her bed. She'd need a glass or two to fall asleep that night; too much was running through her head. She sat in her chair and took a few breaths, enjoying the stillness, enjoying the solitude. In the morning, she'd put on her high heels and her sleek-fitting skirts; she'd fix her face and smooth her hair, and she'd reenter the world with her chin held high. Tonight, in her sweatpants and tank top, she pulled her knees up and nestled her feet into the chair, her mind swirling not with tomorrow but with yesterday.

CHAPTER THREE

*M*aeve spent the next couple of weeks preparing for a fundraising event at a local art gallery. She also wrote an impromptu speech for a protest that had cropped up at the last minute, in which local elected officials were joining constituents in front of the courthouse to make their voices heard about the importance of Wes and Representative Carrie Woods's water safety bill, which had been made more pressing by reports coming in from environmental agencies investigating local residents' complaints of foul-smelling water and health concerns. Brown & Little, tasked with cleaning up from their leak two decades ago, had been engaged in a massive cover-up involving years of violations, reporting of inaccurate data, and tampering with equipment to hide the extent of their non-compliance. Employees also had been instructed to mislead inspectors by providing false information and removing evidence of violations. Legal action was in the works, and the water bill was made that much more important. Today, elected officials were going to talk about their plans and make calls for those responsible to be held accountable.

Senator Patel was working on a corresponding bill in the

Virginia state Senate; it was, in Maeve's opinion, a wonderful example of state and federal officials working together to exchange information, coordinate efforts, and engage constituents in order to increase visibility and therefore, the bills' chances of success. Senator Patel, along with Wes and a handful of other public officials, would speak about the consequences of failing to pass these regulations. The protest came at an already stressful time—usually charity events were formulaic, but tight schedules and an uncooperative vendor had made this one a headache. However, Maeve was used to hiccups and was adept at multitasking. She also had incorporated time for a hiccup into her calendar: from experience, she knew something would interrupt her, though she hadn't yet known what.

Maeve was a hard, efficient worker with an eye for detail and a determination never to let things fall through the cracks. She would figure it out; she would make sure it all got done. One good thing, she knew, was that she had no qualms about lighting fire under people's asses, including her own. Obviously, more work meant more stress. But if she was going to have extra work, it might as well be for a good cause such as this.

The protest took place at a park only a couple of blocks from Senator Patel's office. That day, Maeve parked at work and arrived early along with the speakers; she stood to the side conferring with contacts, going over notes and speaking with reporters. As start time drew nearer, Maeve took a moment to look out at the growing crowd. After checking in with Senator Patel, she strolled toward Wes, who had just finished an interview with the local news.

She took her place beside him and nodded in a playfully cordial fashion.

"Congressman," she acknowledged.

"Ms. Sheering."

"I'm looking forward to hearing your speech today. I trust it will be poetic, as always."

"I'm no poet, Ms. Sheering, but I hope you won't ode it against me."

Maeve shook her head. "You're incorrigible. Don't you ever stop performing?"

"No, but I'm not averse to trying."

Maeve sighed. "I knew it had to be a small step from political bullshit to dad jokes."

Wes laughed. "I suppose it is."

Maeve settled in her spot and folded her arms across her chest, her eyes on the waiting protesters. She thought about why they were gathered and shook her head, turning serious.

"I'm sick about all this."

"Yes." Wes's voice had turned serious, as well. "It is truly sickening, in all senses of the word."

"There's already been a lot of pushback from ClearStream. It doesn't bode well," she said.

"For Congress, or for us?"

"Both, or neither."

They were silent for a time. Maeve glanced sideways at him. He was standing tall, his head up as he assessed the crowd before him.

She was reminded of something Kyle had said.

"Hey," she said, leaning in, and lowering her voice. "I need a favor."

He leaned in, as well. "Name it."

"Look into Virginia ClearStream. I've had word that they may be in on it."

"I'm two steps ahead of you. Grady's already handling it," he said, referring to his brother, his law partner before he'd moved on to Congress.

Maeve smiled. "I should have known."

"I'll keep you posted."

"Thanks."

She leaned in further, playfully nudging him with her hip. He did the same.

A few moments of silence passed as they scanned the large group before them.

"Not a bad turnout," he said.

"No." Maeve put her hands on her hips as she watched the crowd with him. "No, not at all."

"That, in fact, does bode well. Don't you think?"

Maeve met his gaze. He was doing that Wes thing, where he was smiling, but not—where he kept his face serious, but where knowing mischief flashed in his eyes. Maeve knew that look well: it meant tricks were up his sleeve. It meant it wasn't time to give up yet, that it was all about playing the game.

She reluctantly offered him a crooked, conspiratorial grin. He returned it, then winked—and then joined the cluster of colleagues called to the podium.

As she listened to the host's introductions, Maeve gazed about at the people who had gathered with signs and candles, and she nodded with satisfaction. This was an important issue, one which would have serious repercussions for Senator Patel's constituents, and she was impressed with the speed with which the protest had been planned. Maeve had been working closely with the leaders of the grassroots organization hosting this event, and she had been heartened. It was so easy nowadays to feel hopeless, like power was out of your hands. Maeve was a cynical person, and a wary one; she questioned people's motives and looked for the catch, and was never surprised when good things came with conditions and qualifications. Her time in politics had made her even more skeptical; she had seen too much of greed and self-interest. But it had also shown her the power of the good, that there were, in fact, politicians who cared, that the system, though imperfect, if supported, could make a difference. Maeve admired Senator Patel, a bright-eyed new senator who had been drawn to politics by her time as a doctor, when she'd witnessed firsthand how one's place in the socioeconomic hierarchy could be a matter of life or death. Then there was Wes, who had turned from corporate law to consumer protection and public interest law, having made the decision to fight for the everyday person so often squashed between feuding corporate powers. As much as she liked to tease him—though his charisma effortlessly attracted people's admiration and trust, Maeve was a little too much of a misanthrope to join them in their fawning—deep down, she knew that he cared, and though she wouldn't ever admit it, she respected his agility. Events like this, with so many people coming together with a shared purpose, suggested to Maeve that, while human nature could be vicious and selfish and cruel, there were plenty of people who wouldn't stand for it, who would force light to shine in the darkness.

The day was especially warm for November. She had chosen a figure-fitting black skirt and a cream blouse; she'd topped it off with a light jacket and tall red heels. Before the protest started, she discarded the jacket and stole a glimpse of herself in the window of the courthouse. The blouse was just sheer enough to offer a glimpse of the lacy slip beneath, and the skirt hugged her waist and accentuated her hips. She fluffed her dark bob a few times and strolled along the periphery of the crowd, noticing how diverse were the people in attendance. Senator Patel was the first to speak. Maeve turned toward the podium and watched her, pride swelling in her heart as her respected boss passionately recited her speech. Maeve may have written the words, but the sentiments came from Senator Patel's own heart. Maeve and her boss had formulated a quick understanding, and Maeve knew how to take the senator's ideas and mold them so they had the most powerful impact.

A man approached her, sidling stealthily as if he were used to sneaking through crowds. He was about her age, dressed in a kind of modern preppy style, in camel-colored slacks, navy sweater, and blazer. Maeve acknowledged his presence with a quick eyebrow raise, then leaned in toward him as he took his place beside her.

"Nice job," the man whispered, nudging her with his elbow. "She's on point."

Maeve nodded in gratitude, still watching her boss; she knew he was referring to the senator's speech, which he'd correctly assumed Maeve had written. "Thanks, Darney," she whispered back. "Not bad for such short notice."

"Not bad at all."

Maeve allowed herself to offer him a smile, and he smiled back. Rhys Darney was a *New York City Times* Southern correspondent Maeve had worked with many times before. He had integrity, and she trusted him. He winked at her and slipped away, and she stared after him for a moment, the shadow of a grin on her lips.

When the senator's speech was over, the audience erupted with applause. Maeve clapped, too, and looked proudly into the crowd to witness the emotion in the people's faces.

One face stood out. Maeve's heartbeat picked up its pace. She scrunched her eyes to focus. Sure enough, the face in her line of vision belonged to none other than Kyle Langahan.

Nicole stood beside him; Kyle's hand rested on her shoulder. Maeve noticed that Kyle hadn't clapped. Nicole, however, was clapping with enthusiasm.

Wes took the podium, and his crisp, animated voice resounded through the crowd. Maeve watched Kyle as Wes began his speech. Kyle's face remained impassive. He was utterly unmoved.

Maeve's jaw firmed with annoyance. She decided to forget Kyle, who was determined not to be pleased. Instead, she turned her attention to the podium, putting him out of her mind.

Maeve spent the rest of the protest meandering along the edge of the crowd, observing reactions and speaking with a few friends and colleagues. Toward the end, she returned to the front to consult with Senator Patel and to say a few final words to those with the press. She did not attempt to speak with Kyle again. They had nothing to say to each other, and she wasn't in the mood to revisit the past. Last time she saw him, she'd thought maybe they could at least let bygones be bygones, but it had quickly been made clear they repelled each other like poles on magnets. It was best if she pretended he wasn't even there.

She had just slinked her arms back into her jacket when she felt someone tugging at the jacket from behind. Thinking it some belligerent constituent or a presumptuous man looking to be slapped, she reeled around quickly, preparing for battle. She nearly jumped when there at first appeared to be no one there, then started when, upon glancing downward, she looked right into the wide eyes of Nicole Langahan.

"Oh," said Maeve, startled. "Hello, Nicole."

"Hello, Maeve."

"Did you enjoy the protest?"

"Yes, it was very interesting."

"Is this the first protest you've been to?"

"Of course not."

"Of course not." Maeve forced back an amused grin. "Your father must take you to these things all the time."

"This is the first one I've been to here. I used to go to them all the time when..."

Nicole's voice drifted off, and for a glimmer of a moment, the girl's trademark Langahan impassivity faltered. However, she recovered her lapse in seriousness with impressive ease.

"What did you think of the speeches?" asked Maeve; she really wanted to dig deeper into what Nicole had been on the verge of saying—she couldn't help a certain curiosity about her mother—but this of course would have been wildly presumptuous, not to mention cruel. She looked around suddenly. "And where is your father?"

"I thought the speeches were good, substantial and refreshingly lacking in platitudes," said Nicole. She removed her thumb from the strap of her leather purse and pointed behind her. "And my dad's over there, talking to someone he works with."

"Lacking in platitudes, huh." Maeve affected a serious expression and let her eyes dart over Nicole's shoulder, where Kyle and another man were deep in conversation. She looked back at Nicole. "So did you learn anything today?"

"I did," said Nicole. "I learned I probably shouldn't aim for president as my first goal."

"Indeed?"

"Yes. As I watched Congressman Bickhart, I realized it's better to start with local politics. He was a state senator first, and now he's a congressman. So he's gotten to know his constituents really well, you know?"

"I know." Maeve raised her eyebrows at the little girl's sharpness. "So what will you do? Will you start at the state level, or more locally?"

"Hmm." Nicole furrowed her brow. "I hadn't thought about it." She hesitated. "What do you think I should do?"

"Well, it depends on what your goals and interests are. Some professions are good precursors to politics. Or you could work for the town or county first, becoming treasurer or commissioner."

"What did Senator Patel do?"

"Senator Patel started on the school board. She moved on to Wes's state Senate seat from there."

"You mean Congressman Bickhart."

"My apologies. Yes, I do."

"I'm glad I got to see him, because my dad saw him last week."

"And did you like what he had to say?"

"Don't answer that."

Maeve looked up with surprise at the sound of Kyle's voice. He was standing right beside her; she hadn't even noticed him approach.

"Hi, Daddy," said Nicole, standing primly, head held high, content smile on her face. "I was talking to Maeve about politics."

"Honey, you really shouldn't wander off like that."

Nicole's face fell. "Sorry, Daddy."

"It's fine, just be careful."

"Don't worry, I don't bite," said Maeve, cocking an eyebrow at Kyle, with a tight-lipped, crooked grin. "Why can't she answer my question?"

"It's entrapment. You're setting her up. She has no idea Wes Bickhart is your brother-in-law."

"Congressman Bickhart is your brother-in-law?"

Maeve's eyes drifted downward to Nicole. Nicole was staring at her with her mouth agape.

"Yes," said Maeve. "He's my sister Catherine's husband."

"The sister who likes the violin?"

"The very one."

"Do you have more than one sister?"

"No, Catherine's it."

"Do you have a brother?"

"No."

"If you did, would he like the violin?"

Maeve stared at her. "Yes," she said. "Yes, he would."

"Would he prefer Chopin or Brahms?"

"Beethoven."

Nicole settled back and nodded, satisfied.

"Honey," said Kyle, smiling kindly, "no one could possibly know that."

"But we can imagine," said Nicole.

"Right," said Maeve, turning to him, brow raised in challenge. "We can imagine."

Kyle blinked, clearly holding his tongue. "Well," he said. "Nice to see you, Maeve. Honey," he said to Nicole, "we really should be going."

"Do you want to come to lunch with us?"

Nicole had said this to Maeve, who now returned her attention to the round eyes below her. Oddly, she would have loved to continue her conversation with Nicole—the little girl was fascinating, and Maeve was somewhat mesmerized by her—but she was repulsed by the thought of enduring more forced conversation with Kyle.

"Oh, thank you for the invitation," she told Nicole, "but I can't."

"Why not?"

Maeve's lips twisted with uncertainty, and her eyes darted involuntarily to Kyle. Judging by the discomfort contorting his face she was pretty sure he didn't want her there, either.

"Honey, I'm sure Maeve has things to do."

"Yes," said Maeve, "and you should spend some quality time with your dad."

"*Please*," said Nicole, taking Maeve's hand, and pulling. "We're going to the Happy Apple. They have a unicorn sundae, and Daddy says I can't get it unless I share it with someone." She cocked her head and raised her eyebrows, attempting an enticing look. "You can have the rainbow candy."

Maeve bit her lips and rubbed them together to prevent herself from smiling—she didn't want to appear condescending, and besides, she'd been smiling too much today. She sighed and turned to Kyle, who appeared to have reluctantly relented: his shoulders had slumped, and he was frowning, but his eyes were warm with affection.

"I suppose," said Maeve, "I could join you, as long as your dad says it's okay."

Kyle's nose wrinkled as he stifled a grimace. "Great." He shot Maeve what appeared to be a weak attempt at a smile. "Yes, please join us."

~

MAEVE PERUSED the menu of the chocolate-themed Happy Apple Café, brow raised and lips straight, as if intrigued. She didn't want Nicole to suspect she found the options utterly ghastly: peanut butter and hazelnut sandwich, chicken with a chocolate barbecue sauce, a burger with a pepper and chocolate rub. In short, it was just the kind of place a kid would love. Maeve was used to salads and meal replacement drinks—sometimes her meals consisted of nothing but coffee—and her stomach revolted as she imagined ingesting these heavy, greasy dishes.

A server came by to take their order, and Maeve was resigned to telling Nicole she wasn't hungry and sticking with her water. At the last minute, she noticed a crudité appetizer with a choice of three dips—blessedly, there were non-sugary options—and rattled off her order as she passed the server her menu.

"Oh, and also," said Maeve, pulling her menu back. "I'll take a dirty martini."

She held the menu forward with a smile and settled into her chair. Across the table, Kyle had raised his eyebrow at her.

"A martini?" he asked skeptically; he was sitting straight in his chair, hands folded on the table, and he looked as stiff as ever.

"Yes," Maeve challenged. "Do you have a problem with that?"

"It's eleven-thirty in the morning."

"I've been up since four. Relax, Prohibition ended in 1933."

Kyle sniffed. Maeve ignored him and turned to Nicole.

"Now," she said, propping her elbow on the table and looking at her seriously. She pointed at her. "You and I need to plan your campaign."

"Her what?"

"Her campaign." Maeve turned to Kyle, affecting what she hoped look like an innocent expression. "You didn't know your daughter is running for office?"

"She's eight."

"Well, Langahan, it's never too early to start."

"That's right, Langahan." Nicole looked at her father and stuck out her chin. "It never hurts to be prepared."

Kyle stared at his daughter, saying nothing. It was enough, and Nicole slinked back in her seat.

"Anyway," said Maeve, thanking the server as she set down her drink, "I think it's great that this young person is so into politics." She gestured toward Nicole, then raised her martini glass and sipped her drink, relishing the crisp coolness as it slid gently between her lips. "Kids should care about politics. They're going to need to fix the mess we've left them."

Kyle smirked. "This is a new position for you."

"What is?"

"Kids caring about politics."

"What do you mean?"

"In high school, you laughed it off. You teased me about going to a protest with my parents."

"I did no such thing." Maeve took another sip. "I admired that you cared. What I didn't like was your suggestion that my issue didn't matter."

"I never said it didn't matter. I said water purity was more important."

"You know," said Maeve, leaning back in her chair and crossing her arms, "if you haven't lived something, you should consider taking the word of people who have."

"Living something isn't essential to understanding it."

A corner of Maeve's lips drifted upward. "I love when a man explains women's experiences to me."

"There's no need for sarcasm."

"Tone policing, too. All my favorites."

Kyle opened his mouth to say something but appeared to think better of it, and remained silent.

"Daddy, what's tone policing?"

Maeve and Kyle turned to Nicole.

"It's nothing," said Kyle, patting his daughter's hand. "Let's change the subject."

He glowered at Maeve, who turned away. His point was taken, though. Best to check the antagonism in front of Nicole.

The server arrived with their meals, providing a blessed interruption to the tension. As they dug in, Maeve's spirits lifted. She downed the rest of her drink and swiftly ordered another, ignoring the steel gaze emanating from Kyle's direction.

Nicole wanted to be excused so she could look at the aquarium on the other side of the room. Kyle smiled and allowed it, telling her not to go too far.

"So," Maeve asked him, digging into her crudité. "Did you find anything of value in the speeches, or were they the mere mindless drivel of paid shills?"

"They were acceptable," said Kyle, with a hard look, "though I see Congressman Bickhart hasn't committed to retroactive penalties."

"That would never pass," Maeve replied, dipping a sliver of celery into her hummus. "You can't penalize for something that wasn't illegal at the time."

"I was under the impression that bribery's always been illegal."

"But they can say it was a 'consultation fee' or other such nonsense. All we can do is strengthen the language now."

"Let's just forget it, Maeve." Kyle took a sip of his water, seemingly to avoid looking at her. "Seriously. Let it go. You and I just have two very different philosophies."

"I don't think we do, though." Maeve knew, as she said these words, that she was escalating the conversation, but she did it anyway; she was competent in many things, but "letting it go" was not one of them. "We want the same things. Don't you see that?"

"I've always seen that. And I don't disrespect it." As he cut into his lunch, Maeve stared at him, eyes sharp: his comment seemed complimentary, in a weirdly indirect way. He must have misspoken. She brushed it off. "I just don't believe in settling."

"No one's settling here. If anything, I'm trying to ensure

something gets done. You have to be realistic. Sometimes—not all the time—*sometimes*, you have to take what you can get."

"Well, you're free to think what you want. Your brother-in-law worked for corporate firms for years."

Maeve stared at him. "What's that supposed to mean?"

"I have a hard time believing his intentions are pure here. But you have to keep the Thanksgiving table peaceful."

Maeve took a deep breath and clamped her jaw together; her blood was pulsing, and her face was on fire. She leaned in toward him and spoke quietly, forcing down the lid of her anger.

"You," she said, able to control the level of her voice, but not the words themselves, "have a hell of a lot of nerve. First of all, that was years ago. Wes left that type of law for a reason. You're ignoring all the work he's done since then, all the ways he's fought for the right people, all the ways he's made good on his promises. But more importantly, I am not a sellout, nor do I care about the Thanksgiving table. I'm an educated woman. I think for myself. I don't give a damn about what anyone thinks of me. I'll be the first to criticize Wes, when he deserves it, regarding this or anything else. You don't know me. You don't know anything about my relationship with Wes." He had touched a nerve now, whether he realized it or not. "I bow to no one, and if you knew anything about me, you'd see that."

Kyle was calmly spreading butter on a slice of bread, and the easiness of his motions enraged Maeve further. "Maeve, they're all guilty," he told her, then chewed a bite of bread and swallowed. "Every single one of them. I'm not picking on Wes in particular. We'll never have transparency until we get money out of politics."

"Of course not! But you're painting with way too broad a brush here. Not all politicians are ass—" Maeve's eyes darted to Nicole, who had returned and reclaimed her seat, then back to Kyle. "—Asking for favors."

Kyle snorted as he stabbed his lunch with his fork. "Says the daughter of a politician who works for a politician, whose sister is married to a politician. Not the most unbiased source."

"I hate to tell you this, Langahan, but politics is full of politicians. I, too, would love to live in a rainbow-filled utopia, but in the real world, public servants have to figure out how to pass laws in actual legislative bodies. It doesn't mean you have to sell out to do it."

"I see it differently, but to each their own, I guess."

"Well," said Maeve, utterly fed up, swallowing an especially large sip of martini, "if you're so convinced you know everything, then do something about it."

"I am. I'm going to primary him."

Maeve looked up from her glass, which she lowered to the table with a clink. "You're what?"

"I said I'm primarying him."

"You're primarying who?"

"Wes Bickhart."

Maeve stared at him. "I thought politics was for sellouts and hacks."

"It is. But I'm not a politician. I'm a concerned citizen exercising my rights."

Maeve settled back in her seat with her water and grinned. She was glad she'd had that second drink. "You really think he's that bad."

"I can do a better job."

"Wes is extremely popular. He won his race by almost twenty points."

"I wasn't running then."

Maeve watched Kyle for any sign that he was joking, but as always, Kyle was not joking.

"Well, godspeed to you, Langahan." She cast him a subtle, crooked grin. "You're going to need it, especially with that attitude."

"I think you'll be surprised by how many people agree with me."

"I think you're delusional."

"Hey."

Maeve turned in the direction of the sad little voice. She had almost forgotten Nicole was there.

Maeve smiled at the girl and leaned in to rub her shoulder. "I'm just kidding, lovey. Just a joke between old friends."

"I don't think you're friends." Nicole shook her head, frowning. "Friends aren't mean to each other."

Maeve and Kyle looked at each other. Neither said anything for a moment or two.

"Honey," said Kyle, tidying her hair around her ear, "it's just grownup talk. It isn't mean."

"Well," said Maeve, gesturing with her hand as if allowing him the opportunity to concede, "when you suggested I compromise my values, that was a little mean."

Kyle shot her an annoyed look.

Maeve turned to Nicole and smiled. "Nicole, you're very smart to perceive that your father and I disagree on some things, and we probably should have been more careful with our tone. But truthfully, you know, disagreement is healthy. In fact, it's necessary. Disagreeing is a great way to gain knowledge. If we all agreed, we'd never hear any different ideas, and if we never heard any different ideas, we'd never learn anything new. We'd never grow or make any progress. Right?"

Nicole watched her with wide blue eyes, and nodded. Maeve's eyes were drawn to Kyle. He was staring at her with an indecipherable expression. He didn't appear happy, but the animosity was gone.

She turned back to Nicole. "Anyway, not everyone has to agree all the time, and that's not always so terrible."

"The important thing," Kyle added, addressing his daughter, "is that you have to disagree respectfully."

"Most of the time."

Kyle's head snapped in Maeve's direction. "No, all of the time."

"No, not all of the time. If someone is threatening you or putting forth ideas that are abhorrent, you do not owe that person your respect."

"I can't think of any situation in which respect is not warranted."

"Then you've never been in the box with the football team."

"What?"

"Nothing."

Kyle was regarding her quizzically. Maeve ignored him. The server came with their check. Kyle reached for it, but Maeve was closer, and snatched it up first.

"No, let me," she said, reaching into her purse. "My treat today."

"No, I can't let you do that."

"Yes you can."

"Maeve, give me the bill."

"No."

"Please." Kyle was frowning, his hand extended, looking so perturbed Maeve chuckled.

"Really, it's on me." She pulled out her credit card and slipped it into the leather sleeve. "You two were nice enough to invite me. Thank you."

"You're welcome." Kyle watched her silently as she downed the remainder of her second cocktail and stuck the toothpick in her mouth, where her tongue slid down the olive until her lips sucked it dry. "Don't you have to go to work after this?" he asked her.

"No." Maeve's jaw worked the olive to a pulp, and she swallowed. She stirred the straw around in her water. "Aditi's taking the rest of the day off and told me to go home after the protest. Does it matter?"

"No. Anyway—" He sighed and turned to Nicole, placing his hands on the table and smiling. "—Shall we go?"

"Sure, Daddy." Nicole looked at Maeve with round eyes; her freckles looked especially pronounced in the midday sunlight. "Will you help me with my campaign later?"

"Later as in next week, or later as in twenty years from now?"

"How about," Kyle said, with transparently forced enthusiasm, "we see how things go for now?"

"Okay, Daddy." Nicole stood and stuck out her hand to Maeve. "It was lovely seeing you again."

Maeve took her hand and met her gaze. "It was lovely seeing you, too."

Kyle stood, too. "Aren't you leaving?"

"No, I think I'll sit for a minute."

"You're not okay to drive. I can give you a ride home."

"Very noble of you, but I'll wait it out or call a car."

"Ah." He hesitated. "Well, thank you for paying."

Maeve smiled and waved, and Kyle and Nicole waved back. She leaned back in her chair and closed her eyes, enjoying a moment of solitude before rising to once again face the outside world.

"Buy you a cocktail?"

Maeve opened her eyes and looked right into Rhys Darney's: he was leaning over the side of her chair, his hand on her shoulder, a large grin on his face.

"How can I say no," said Maeve, kicking back the chair Nicole had just vacated. "Have yourself a seat, my friend."

Rhys had called over the server and ordered two more dirty martinis.

"I thought you went for bourbon," she said.

"I do, but you go for martinis."

Maeve gestured with her hand in deference as Rhys took his seat. He pulled his chair close and spoke conspiratorially.

"Want to hear a secret?"

"Always."

"Hardwick's resigning."

Maeve gasped and stared at him with her mouth wide open. "No way!"

"Shh," Rhys scolded, lowering his hands to indicate she should lower her voice; however, his expression was playful. "Nobody knows yet, not even his wife. I just found out this morning from a leaked personal email."

"But why?" Bill Hardwick was a congressman in a neighboring district; he was of the other party and frequently butted heads with those in Maeve's circles.

"It's about to come out he had a child out of wedlock. She was a staffer. He paid the woman off for years, but she's not keeping quiet anymore. We're still gathering comments and fact-checking."

Maeve clicked her tongue. "So who will the governor appoint?"

"Your guess is as good as mine, but whatever the choice, it'll be contentious."

"Indeed." The server delivered their drinks, and Maeve clinked her glass with Rhys's. "So why are you telling me this? Shouldn't you wait until the rest of the info comes in?"

"You were sitting here all by yourself looking like you could use some juicy gossip."

Maeve grinned over the rim of her martini glass. "Rhys Darney, you always could read me like a book."

His face turned serious, and he leaned in further to kiss her. Maeve met his kiss, wholeheartedly, letting herself be swept away for a moment before pulling back, conscious of her surroundings. His face still close, the corner of his mouth ticked upward: he knew what was coming, as did she. Maeve had dated Rhys briefly a number of years ago; though their sexual chemistry was electric, they hadn't seemed fit for a relationship. They were both too wrapped up in work; they were too in love with their independence to be in love with each other. They'd parted with no hard feelings and still reunited for a casual tryst now and again, when their busy lives impeded their ability to form romantic attachments but the urges of human biology still demanded sating.

Maeve stared into the coffee-colored eyes of her friend. He was really quite good-looking. He was stylish and clean cut, his dark hair neat and professional and his body tight from religious exercise. She let her hand drift to his face, where her fingers fiddled seductively with his ear. His grin widened, and he kissed her again, then settled in for conversation, the two leaning intimately toward each other, speaking frankly about politics, their frustrations, their lives. She enjoyed the slow burn of the encounter, of anticipating the inevitable conclusion; stimulating conversation led to stimulating sex, and the view from where she sat was easy on the eyes. Anyway, it had been four months since she'd been with a man. There was no rush. She could wait an hour more.

An hour turned into two, and Maeve and Rhys moved to a bar a few doors down, where they indulged in a few more drinks, laughing raucously and playing footsie under the table. They ordered dinner and sat until nightfall, growing more and more passionate in their political treatises with every drink they finished. It was delightful to have someone to agree with, someone who understood her points of view and who saw the world so clearly, someone who could rail with her about the things she detested and hope with her about the things she believed in. By the end of the evening, they were both utterly intoxicated. Rhys suggested she join him at his place.

"Come on, I'm parked out back," he said, pulling his keys from his pocket. "I think it's my turn this time, eh?"

"You're drunk as fuck," Maeve laughed. "No way in hell am I letting you drive me anywhere."

"Let's call a car."

"Fine. Seriously, though." She slapped his arm. "Shame on you. You're better than that."

Rhys squinted into his phone to order a car to pick them up. They fell into the back seat together and made out the whole way there, then stumbled hazily into his condo, where they eagerly took advantage of each other, with no inhibitions, lending themselves to each other and gleefully taking what was given. Later, makeup smudged and hair disheveled, Maeve left him in bed and called herself a ride home; after grabbing as much sleep as she could, she showered and dressed, then got a ride to the office, where she'd left her car the night before. She stopped at a nearby café for a large coffee, then downed a few vitamins to stave off her hangover and got diligently back to work, tired but refreshed, and a little more able to face the messed-up world, at least for the time being.

CHAPTER FOUR

$\mathcal{O}$n Thanksgiving Maeve went to her parents' house, like she did every year. Also in attendance were Catherine, Wes, and Amy, as well as Wes's parents, Sarah and Charles, and his brother Grady and his family. Ever since Catherine and Wes had gotten married seven years before, the Sheerings and the Bickharts took turns: the Sheerings hosted Thanksgiving, and the Bickharts, Christmas. In Maeve's purse was a small white box that contained a present for Amy. It was a Mandarin duck charm on a gold chain, complete with a sapphire eye. It was strange, but Maeve knew Amy had to have it: the little girl inexplicably was obsessed with Mandarin ducks, and Maeve had seen the necklace quite by accident as she'd been walking past an antique shop on the way to work. She also tossed an overnight bag in the back of her car just in case. Though the thought of staying overnight at her parents' house was about as appealing as gouging out her own eyes, she wanted to be prepared in case she had too much to drink which, given she'd be forced to talk with her family for hours, she undoubtedly would. If it had been before Catherine got married, Maeve would have tried to hitch a ride. Maeve knew Catherine would still be happy to drive her. However, the older she got, the more distasteful it was to beg rides from her family. Also, though she hated to admit it, she was embarrassed to ask, fearful of appearing in any way vulnerable. In any case, she could always call a rideshare. She didn't like the thought of having to return the next day for her car, but needs must.

She chose for the occasion a low-cut red satin blouse and high-waisted alabaster slacks with a wide leg over a black stiletto heel. She made the mistake of leaving too early and arrived before Catherine, which meant she was by herself among her parents and the Bickharts. Maeve had no problem with the Bickharts, and she might have even gone so far as to say she liked them had it not been for the fact that being in her parents' house prompted a physical reaction in her that made socializing unbearable. Also, she questioned how they could tolerate so much of her parents' company and was deeply suspicious of anyone who came here willingly. When she was honest with herself, she had to admit that her father was not all that bad; though pompous at times, and attention seeking, and a little too prone to ass kissing, he probably wasn't any worse than anyone else's father. Her mother, however, was a passive aggressive nightmare, and her father, though well intentioned, had never protected either Maeve or Catherine, and even himself tended to subtle criticism that was just innocent enough to make her gaslight herself that she wasn't really hearing it.

The house was full of luscious savory scents, intermingled with the sweet scent of cranberry and the deep aroma of coffee. Maeve said hello to those present—her parents; Wes's parents, Sarah and Charles Bickhart; and Grady and Helen Bickhart, Wes's brother and sister-in-law, who were there with their eight-year-old daughter Olivia. Maeve poured herself some wine and asked her mother if she needed anything, though she knew she didn't: her mother had help for that. She then stood in the corner by the drink table and watched the gathering, making light conversation with whoever happened to walk past her and force her to lift her lips from her glass. The elegant, tasteful sitting room, with its cream-colored walls, crimson drapes, and antique furniture, led into the dining room, and Maeve watched with increasing dread as the preparations of her mother's assistants brought them closer and closer to the formal dinner. Her thoughts were interrupted when her mother and Sarah Bickhart approached. Maeve breathed deeply, steadying herself.

"Hello, dear mother," she said as Lois wrapped her arm around her daughter's back. Maeve took a long sip of wine to hide the rolling of her eyes. She then forced a smile on her face and met the women's gazes. "How are you? Great party."

"Thank you, dear. What are you doing over here all by yourself?"

"Just making sure no one steals the crystal."

Sarah laughed heartily at that. A petite woman with a neat silver bob of hair and strong feminine features, she wore a navy boat neck sweater with a slender-fitting gray skirt. She shook her head and patted Maeve's arm; her nails were painted a handsome crimson. "Lois, have I told you lately how I simply adore your daughters?"

"They are adorable." Lois smiled at Maeve, then looked her over and straightened a stray few strands of Maeve's hair. "You look very lovely today. Is this a new outfit?"

"Yes. Do you like it?"

"Mmm." Maeve's mother was staring at her chest. "It's a little revealing for Thanksgiving, don't you think?"

"I must not, or I wouldn't have worn it."

"Mmm." Lois tidied Maeve's shirt around her shoulder, then turned toward Sarah and sipped her wine. "Maybe just don't bend over too far."

Maeve inhaled sharply and worked her jaw, for Sarah's benefit suppressing a wisecrack.

Sarah laughed again, watching Lois with good-natured disbelief. She leaned in toward her with playful camaraderie, placing her hand on Lois's arm. "Lois, darling. It's the twenty-first century. Maeve's outfit is the epitome of glamor in modern-day America."

"Oh, I don't disagree." Lois's face was all sweetness, her sable-colored eyes crinkled in a smile and her rose-painted lips turned upward. "It's just that, you know. Maeve is already blessed with such generous curves..."

She trailed off, and Maeve peeked over her glass at her in challenge.

Lois conceded, tossing her hand up and laughing stiffly. "Oh, ladies, don't mind me. I suppose I am a little bit behind the times."

"Well," said Sarah, winking at Maeve, "I think you look fabulous. I say celebrate it if you've got it. Lord knows I wish I did."

Sarah clinked her glass, and Maeve downed the rest of her wine.

"Did you volunteer at the Food Rescue this morning?" she asked Sarah, with a smile, appreciative of the older woman's coming to her defense. "You always go bright and early on Thanksgiving."

"I did," Sarah returned cheerily. "We had a group of about six this year."

"Fantastic. It's a meaningful way to spend the holiday."

"Thank you, darling. I think so, too."

They chatted a few minutes longer, until Sarah was called away by Charles. Maeve caught sight of Catherine, Wes, and Amy in the foyer to the left. They were, as always, well-dressed and elegant, Amy in her fall-themed floral dress, patent leather shoes, and little rouge-colored pea coat; Catherine, her long legs and graceful figure tastefully filling out a cranberry vintage dress and gray jacket, her honeyed hair pushed back in a black velvet headband, as plush and shiny as Sleeping Beauty's; and Wes, tall and handsome, immaculately dressed in wool trousers, a cashmere sweater, collared shirt and tie peeking out from beneath, his graying sandy hair tidy and perfect. Maeve watched them as they hugged relatives and passed their dishes to an enthusiastic Sarah; Wes then helped Catherine slip from out of her coat, hanging it in the closet before, hand on her lower back, ushering her toward the festivities. Amy, polished and polite, walked beside her parents.

A tugging ache pulled at Maeve's stomach, for the briefest of moments, and then was gone.

She turned away, poured herself another drink and one for Catherine, and then slipped away from her mother toward her sister.

"Thank God you're here," she told her after the necessary double cheek kisses. "Mom is hassling me."

"Oh? What is she hassling you about, Maeve?"

"She thinks my boobs are too big."

"Well, that's rather silly. People aren't responsible for the size of their body parts."

"No, but I don't hide mine properly."

Catherine was a few inches taller than Maeve and was currently staring down into Maeve's cleavage. "Actually, I think they look beautiful. You always look beautiful, Maeve."

"Thanks." Maeve touched Catherine's chin with her finger and tucked it upward to direct her gaze higher. She handed Catherine a glass of Chardonnay and sipped her own, welcoming the soft haze of an oncoming buzz. She tweaked the collar of Catherine's lacy dress. "Is this the new dress you texted me about? The one you couldn't decide on?"

"Yes." Catherine looked down at herself. "Did I make the right decision?"

"It's fab." She directed her eyes downward toward her niece, then crouched beside her, balancing in her tall stiletto heels. "Amy," she said confidentially to the little girl. "I have a present for you."

Amy's wide brown eyes widened further. "You do? What is it?"

She straightened and crooked her finger to indicate Amy should follow her. She walked into the den on the right, relieved to have a momentary respite from the chaos of the living room. She opened her purse and retrieved the box. She passed it to Amy and watched as Amy opened it.

Amy gasped, her hand at her heart, and in that gesture Maeve could only see Catherine.

"Oh, Aunt Maeve, it's so beautiful." Amy pulled the necklace from the box and with childlike eagerness slipped it over her neck. She beamed up at Maeve, eyes sparkling.

"How does it look?"

Maeve, hand on hip, gave a chef's kiss with the other hand. "Perfection."

"Aunt Maeve, can I sleep at your house one night?"

Maeve's eyebrows rose. "I guess so."

Amy was twisting this way and that, looking like a little doll, a miniature version of her mother. "I sleep at Grandma Lois's house, sometimes," she said, "and also Grandma Sarah's. They go to bed early." She paused a moment. "Do we have to go to bed early?"

"Oh, God no," said Maeve. "I hate going to bed early. All the fun stuff happens at night."

Amy smiled happily; Maeve noticed she'd lost another tooth. "We should eat popcorn and watch a movie."

"Obviously."

Amy was holding the charm in her hand, studying it. "Where did you get this, Aunt Maeve?"

"There's a shop by my office that sells a lot of cool old stuff. It was in the window, and it made me think of you."

"I want to show it to Mommy and Daddy. Can we go back now?"

"Do we have to?"

Amy looked at her quizzically. "Don't you want to have Thanksgiving?"

"Eh." Maeve shrugged. "I've never been one for big holidays."

"Why not? I like holidays."

"All kids like holidays, as you should."

"My favorite holiday is my birthday."

"My favorite holiday is your birthday, too."

Maeve put her hand on the little girl's shoulder and, resigned, ushered her out of the room.

Everyone was standing around in the living room in boisterous conversation, each holding a glass and gesturing emphatically with their hands. Amy ran off to play with Olivia, her beloved dark-haired older cousin.

"He's not going to support it," Fred was saying to Wes. "I'm hearing from a number of sources. It's because of his ties to the industry, of course."

"Of course. I don't think we need him, though."

"Like hell you don't. Who else have you got?"

"Public opinion is on our side."

"What are you talking about?" asked Maeve, coming to a stop between them. "Am I to hope for some drama on Thanksgiving?"

Wes smiled. "Sorry to disappoint you. But your father and I are in agreement here. We're talking about the green energy bill. Your father seems to think Jackson won't support it."

"He won't support it," said Maeve. "You can count on that."

"See, that makes me nervous," Fred insisted. "Jackson's the yardstick. If Jackson's not on side, you've got trouble."

"Wes is right." Maeve took a long sip of wine, then rubbed her lips together and took a deep, relaxing breath. "You have public opinion. The media narrative is good, for once. I've been tracking it. I have data."

"Do you?" asked Wes, interested. "I'd love to see what you've got, if you don't mind."

"Certainly." Maeve was simultaneously put off and eager to help, and confused by her own ambivalence. But she couldn't focus on that now. She downed the rest of her wine as a distraction, then shot him a quick nod of acknowledgment. "Call me Monday."

"Will do. Much obliged."

"On a somewhat related note," she added, with deliberately exaggerated interest, "any word on Curt's support of the water bill?" Maeve's lips turned up at the corner—she wasn't being serious. Curt Tonelli was a US senator from Virginia who frequently voted against such measures. The other senator, Barbara Johnson, was certain to support it.

"No," said Wes, sipping his own drink. "But I think we know where he stands. It's going to be tight." He frowned, swirled his drink, and took another sip. "I'd sure love to see Curt come through."

The conversation turned to the following year's election. Wes had handily won his first term the previous year after winning his primary against a seasoned state representative. There were whisperings that the state rep would challenge him again, but nothing had been confirmed.

"I don't know what the hell Doug thinks he's doing," said Fred. "The last primary showed him to be painfully out of touch. Poor bastard."

"'Poor,' my ass," said Maeve, taking a long sip of a cocktail she'd fixed herself as they were chatting. "His point of view is horribly outdated. His debate performance was cringeworthy. The way he talked down to the moderators. And that line he had about how Puerto Rico has so many 'beautiful women'! Jesus."

Wes shook his head. "What a disaster," he said, nipping at his whiskey, standing casually with one hand in his pocket. "He had some good ideas back in his day, but good lord. He'd better get with the program, or he'll lose the seat he's got, and he'll deserve it."

Fred laughed and sighed. "Doug is definitely of a certain age."

"He doesn't get a pass because he's old," said Maeve, coldly. "Even old people can learn."

"I don't recall the debate being so terrible."

Fire instantly ignited in Maeve's belly. "Seriously? Come on, Dad. It was a question about the hurricane, and he's commenting on the victims' beauty. So insulting. That shit just doesn't fly anymore."

"Now, now," said Fred. "I don't disagree with you. But Doug's done some good things in his time. He was right there in the equal pay fight. And he cosponsored the domestic violence bill."

"It doesn't work like that. It doesn't excuse it. He can't call for equality in one breath and subordinate us in the next."

Fred watched her with raised eyebrows; Wes lifted his glass to her and took a drink of his whiskey.

"I'm just saying," said Maeve, staring into her cocktail; she was suddenly overwhelmed, without really knowing why, "that what really matters is how he treats people behind closed doors. We've come too far to tolerate implicit bias."

She arched her back and rear end suddenly as Olivia and Amy came running by, nearly knocking into her. The little girls were giggling and carrying on in their best Thanksgiving dresses, chasing each other in a brisk game of tag. They made a turn around the room before Wes, anticipating his daughter's return, scooped her up brusquely and held her in the air before sweeping her back down and tickling her until she was in red-faced hysterics. He then picked her up and held her on his arm, kissing her cheek as she lay her head on his chest, totally content.

"Attention, attention," Sarah called from the doorway, her eyes sparkling. "I've just been informed that dinner is ready to commence. Bickharts, Sheerings, let Thanksgiving begin."

Everyone cheered. Catherine joined Wes's side, and the two strolled toward the dining room, Amy still in Wes's arms. As they filed through the doorway, Maeve found herself next to Helen, Grady's quiet wife. Helen was dressed today quite simply, as always, in a knee-length black skirt and black cardigan sweater, a pale pink blouse beneath. Helen smiled at Maeve, and Maeve returned it; Helen was nice, and Catherine adored her, but Maeve usually found herself at a loss for what to say to her. Though she'd married into a political family, Helen did not take much interest in politics. Politics was Maeve's life, and she sometimes felt she had little in common with those who saw it as mere background noise.

"Happy Thanksgiving, Maeve," said Helen, her round eyes kind. "How have you been? I haven't seen you in a while."

"Thanks, I've been well. Yourself?"

"Great. We just got back from Wisconsin a few days ago."

"Catherine mentioned you were there visiting your family."

"Yes, my parents are there, and all my siblings. It was a nice trip, but I'm glad to be back. I miss them, though."

Maeve glanced at her sideways. Helen was a small woman who tended to wear her mousy hair in a low ponytail; she never wore makeup, and she preferred clothing as quiet as her demeanor. Most of the time, she seemed to blend into the background, at least to Maeve, who always stuck out. However, every so often, Maeve was inadvertently struck by Helen's subtle beauty: she was wide-eyed and rosy-cheeked, her appeal that of an Earth mother, or an angel. Maybe that's why Maeve had never connected with her. Maeve had no patience for angels.

"How nice," Maeve said, already bored with the conversation; she could not relate to missing her family, except for Catherine, and of course Amy.

"It was good for Olivia to see her cousins," Helen continued as the two squeezed into the dining room and walked around the table toward their seats. "She has so many cousins she never gets to see. She had fun, but she was happy to come home to Amy."

"Amy is her best friend," said Maeve, absentmindedly, as she scanned the place cards for her name.

"Yes." Helen reached out for her daughter, who had just appeared at her side. She tenderly stroked her daughter's hair, then looked up at Maeve with a smile. "I love seeing the little girls run around the room together, sharing secrets."

Maeve smiled politely at Olivia. "So many little girls." *No, only two*, she corrected herself. *Why do I think there are so many?* Out of nowhere, the image of Nicole Langahan popped into her head. *Huh*, thought Maeve. *Strange.*

Thinking of Nicole reminded Maeve of Kyle and of how he had said he was going to primary Wes. She would have to catch Wes later and have a chuckle over it.

They took their places. Maeve was between Catherine and Grady. Grady was a quieter, darker-haired version of Wes, with a humbler, more subtle wit. Less gregarious than his brother, and totally lacking the interest to be in the spotlight, he was less visible in social gatherings, speaking up only when compelled out of his shyness, or when asked. When Maeve wanted the sharpness of a hawk, when she had a question about the next maneuver—she went to Wes. When she wanted the sharpness of an owl, the even-handed answer of an observer—she went to Grady.

"Grady," she said to him now, figuring she'd make some light conversation, as the two settled into their chairs and passed around the wine, "what are your thoughts on the water bill? Does it stand a chance?"

"I think anything always has a chance," Grady replied, reaching for a crystal pitcher and filling her water glass, and then his own. She thanked him and smiled. "Wes certainly seems optimistic."

"Wes always seems optimistic. It's sort of his thing." Maeve's smile turned crooked. "I mean that as a compliment, mostly."

Grady grinned. "Fair enough."

"In all seriousness, though, Grady. You're an honest, thoughtful kind of person. Is there anything we can do? Is there anything we're missing?"

"Hmm," said Grady, considering with a furrowed brow. He began pouring her wine for her, and she thanked him; he glanced up at her for her to say "when," and she raised her eyebrow, which he correctly interpreted as a sign to fill it to the top. "If you're looking for technical help, there are of course plenty of cases to serve as precedent. I know Wes has been spending a lot of time on that."

"Anything we can do to build further momentum?"

Grady rubbed his lips together, concentrating. "It's not the kind of thing that would be helpful, but I was just thinking...This conversation reminded me."

Maeve waited patiently as he gathered his thoughts.

"It was more philosophical, really. Not anything with any practical import. But Thoreau writes about the pond, and how it was thought to be bottomless...Of course it wasn't, but it worked as a symbol of sorts, enchanting the people, who saw it as divine and wanted to protect it."

Maeve's brow rose. "Interesting."

"It served as a reminder of endless possibilities, of something greater than ourselves. The pond is bottomless, we are bottomless. Life is bottomless."

Maeve nodded, thinking. "I'm going to keep that in mind."

Grady chuckled. "I'm really just musing. It isn't anything you can use. As I said, you reminded me." He smiled kindly. "But it demonstrates how we're all connected, to nature and to each other. People need to believe in bottomlessness, to have faith. To feel the infinite." His eyebrows knit thoughtfully. "Does that make any sense?"

"It absolutely makes sense." Maeve regarded him earnestly, impressed. "Thank you, Grady."

"You're very welcome."

Dinner was blessedly cheerful, with some upbeat discussion of the election and some excitement about future vacations and family gatherings. Maeve's distance from her mother meant she did not have to answer any personal questions or fend off any criticisms, and she spent her time in peppy conversation with

Catherine and with Sarah, who was seated across the table. The mood was bright and good-natured, and they rose from the meal full and happy. Maeve braced herself when her mother made a point of finding her as they filtered from the dining room.

"Maeve," Lois said, gently holding her elbow as they made their way to the living room. "I met the nicest young man the other day."

"No."

"It was at Colleen's annual hospital fundraiser."

"No."

"Please listen, you don't even—"

"No."

Lois didn't sigh, but Maeve could feel a sigh in the air. Her mother let a few beats pass, a sure sign she was losing her patience.

"My dear," said Lois, facing her as they crossed the threshold. "I simply cannot understand what you have against meeting someone. You don't have to be embarrassed. Many women don't get married until later in life. Why, look at your own sister. There's still plenty of time for you to—"

"Mother."

Maeve had thought she would make it through the night without a breakdown, but her mother was quickly obliterating her defenses. The old familiar feeling began rising from her belly—it was like needles prickling her blood, deflating her lungs, draining her heart until she was nothing but smoke and shadows.

Her mother was staring at her, frowning. Maeve wondered at how you could hate someone so much while still loving them.

"I don't," said Maeve through clenched teeth, seemingly for the thousandth time, "want to meet anyone."

"But why?"

"I've explained to you why. I like my life, and my independence."

"But you're all alone."

"But I'm not. I have Catherine, and Amy, and Senator Patel. I have my job. And at the end of the day, I have myself."

"You don't have any friends. I never hear you talk about anyone, no one except work people."

Maeve's jaw stiffened as she resisted the urge to tell her mother to fuck off. It was...so much more complicated than she could ever understand. How to explain that "friends" was subjective and that she didn't want the same kind her mother thought she should? That trusting people did not come easily to her? That she was perfectly happy being her own best friend, that she got by with support from a few select people? That work was where she felt her strongest and that she'd built her identity around that persona, that if she let people look inside of her then the whole structure would collapse at her feet? That sex to her didn't require love or intimacy, that in fact it often spoiled it, that she liked the low-pressure nature of casual flings, that the biggest turn-on was saying goodbye before morning? That she was very often misunderstood, that it was hard for her to be herself with other people, that she would scare people with the depths of her darkness? That she didn't fully understand this darkness herself? That she didn't think she had to? That she didn't think she wanted to?

"Thanks for this fun chat, Mother," she said stiffly, the urgency of fleeing a tangible feeling in her skin. "Now leave me alone and bother someone else."

"Dear, I'm only trying to help."

"Stop helping. I don't need your help. I don't need anything."

"Well, just in case you change your mind," said Lois, gliding to the little end table by the door and pulling a business card from the letter holder, "you can find his information here."

Lois held out her hand, the card perched between her delicate fingers. Maeve looked her mother in the eye and took the card, then stuck it in her cleavage and enjoyed a split second of her mother's shocked expression before turning on her heel and striding toward the kitchen.

She pulled the card from between her breasts and tore it up without looking at it. She then tossed the pieces in the trash and went to find Wes and Catherine, stopping at the drink table for a refresh on her wine. *Maybe I should start taking it easy*, she wondered, but left the table with a full glass, blithely in search of her sister and brother-in-law.

She found them in the living room, where the lamps cast a golden glow over the cream-colored walls and antique furniture. With its warm hues and tasteful art and drapery, the room was formal and elegant, much like her parents. Much of the furniture had belonged to her mother's family, a stately old family from Massachusetts. Maeve's mother, Lois Darlington Sheering, had met Fred Sheering in Washington, DC because Lois's mother and Fred's father were both members of the House of Representatives. Fred had followed in his father's footsteps and pursued politics, preferring to remain in the Virginia State Senate; Lois had no interest in politics but, as the daughter of a congresswoman, was keenly attuned to the political world, the perfect match for a man of political ambition who was happy not to be outshone. Apparently the forward-thinking gene had skipped a generation of Darlington women: while Maeve's grandmother had been outspoken and unapologetically eccentric, Lois was status conscious and traditional, and she had, in Maeve's opinion, made her daughters' lives a living hell.

"Congressman," she said to Wes as she approached him; he was standing with Grady, who had been momentarily distracted by Olivia. "I have some inside information for you."

"You do, do you?"

"Yes."

"I'm all ears."

Maeve took a long sip of her wine and relaxed. "You're going to be primaried."

Wes raised his eyebrows with interest. "Is it decided, then? Doug is in?"

"Not by Doug. By Kyle Langahan."

"Kyle Langahan." Wes's eyes narrowed. "Now where have I heard that name before?"

"He grilled you at the town hall that time. You know. About the water bill."

The light of recognition reached his eyes. "Ah. Of course." Wes grinned and sipped his scotch. "So he's throwing his hat into the ring, eh? Good for him. I'm game for a little sport."

Maeve shook her head. "There are no games with Langahan. Take it from me. He is all business, and he's tenacious as fuck."

"Maeve, dear, watch your language."

This from Lois, who had passed by on her way to the kitchen. Maeve closed her eyes and took a deep breath, then drew a sip of wine from her glass and continued.

"I'm not saying you won't beat him," she told Wes. "What I am saying is, take him seriously. He could be a pain in your ass."

Wes considered. "And water is his issue, is it?"

"His only."

"Is that right." He gestured with his finger as if struck with an idea. "I wonder if I should engage him. Try to bring him around. I can't imagine we don't mostly agree. Maybe he'd work with us."

"Langahan doesn't work with anyone. He's the only one who can save the world."

"Got it," said Wes, his jaw working subtly as he swallowed a sip of scotch. "I know the type."

"Anyway, I thought you should know."

"I appreciate that, Maeve. Thank you." He grinned. "If I didn't know better, I'd think you were trying to help me."

Maeve shrugged. "It's my duty as Cat's sister. Sabotaging Langahan's the cherry on top."

"Do you have a history with him, then?"

"You could say that."

"Were you romantically involved?"

Maeve choked on her wine; she swallowed and cleared her

throat. "Me and Langahan? God, no. He beat me for class president. And also..."

She trailed off. Wes waited expectantly, his eyes wide.

"And also—?"

Maeve rubbed her lips together, enjoying the last vestiges of her wine. She shook her head. "Never mind. It doesn't matter."

"What doesn't matter?"

Catherine had sneaked up behind her and was now standing between Maeve and her husband. In her arms was a gold box wrapped in a rose-colored ribbon. Maeve knew what it was; the only question was, what was the occasion this time.

"Kyle Langahan doesn't matter," she said, momentarily ignoring the box; Catherine would surely get to it. "I was just warning Wes that he's primarying him."

"Oh?" Catherine watched her with a serious expression, thinking. "But...why?"

"Because he's Langahan."

"Do you think he can win?"

"Anything is possible," said Maeve. "But my gut says not to worry."

"I hope it doesn't get too ugly," said Catherine, frowning. "He seemed pretty angry at the town hall. I'm nervous."

"You're always nervous," said Maeve, rolling her eyes.

Catherine's eyes grew thoughtful. "Maybe he'll see how dedicated Wes is, and he'll do the right thing."

Maeve sipped her wine, then laughed. The sound was sharper than she'd expected it to be. "Preposterously wishful thinking, though I guess I shouldn't be surprised." She immediately caught herself. "I mean," she said tucking her hair behind her ear, then fiddling with her collar a little, "that that's politics."

"Oh. I guess you're right."

She looked at her sister, who was standing there prettily, wearing the same blank, uncomfortable look she always did when she'd absorbed a critical comment she didn't deserve.

A sick kind of feeling seeped into Maeve's gut. "I'm sorry," she managed to croak.

"It's okay."

The two sisters looked at each other, their eyes connected with silent understanding.

"We talked about this," said Wes, his voice stern. Maeve's eyes darted to his: his face was as stern as his voice.

"I remember," she said coldly. "And I said I was sorry."

But he wouldn't let it go. "You'll forgive me," he said quietly, but the words held latent reprimand, "but despite our agreement, we seem to continue to have this conversation."

"And you'll forgive *me*," Maeve uttered, seething, "for pointing out that we only continue to have this conversation because you insist on not minding your own business."

"Stop," said Catherine. "Please stop."

"It is my business," said Wes, ignoring her plea, "because she's my wife."

Maeve narrowed her eyes as she looked at him. It was times like this when she felt validated in all her past resentment. There he was, the picture of elegance, his clothes neat and pressed and his posture straight and firm, his hair like something out of classic movie, even the touch of gray at the temples almost iconic in its perfection. And he knew it—and he acted as if he knew it, as if his charm would draw people like magnets, as if it was a get out of jail free card.

"She is your wife, but she's also my sister," she said. "I've known her longer than you have. Back off. There are some things you don't understand."

"There's no reason to get mad at me, Maeve. I'm just calling it as I see it."

"Stop," said Catherine.

"Yes, you alone see things clearly," said Maeve, the sarcasm dripping from her voice. *I probably shouldn't have had that last glass.* "Cat's so lucky to have you to protect her."

"Stop! Stop, stop, *stop!*"

The entire room went quiet. Everyone was staring at Catherine. Catherine blushed furiously and tipped her head forward, letting her hair hide the fluttering of her eyelashes, a nervous tic she'd had for as long as Maeve could remember.

Maeve and Wes looked at each other, their faces grim.

Wes turned to Catherine, slinking his arm around her back.

"I'm sorry, sweetheart," he said, placing a soft kiss on her temple.

Maeve took a breath. "I'm sorry, too."

"Look, Maeve, I'm not trying to fight with you," Wes continued, offering Maeve a somber smile; Maeve noticed it didn't reach his eyes, and she knew he'd been rattled but was playing nice for Catherine. "I care about you, and our relationship."

"Understood."

"Can we let bygones be bygones?"

"Yes, bygones. Of course."

"In any case," he said to Catherine, "Maeve's right about politics. There's no need to worry, sweetheart. I can handle a little ugliness. I knew what I was getting into when I started this game."

He smiled at Maeve in earnest. Maeve smiled back at him, but it melted from her face as soon as he'd looked away.

"Sweetheart," he said, gently nudging Catherine's arm. "Why don't you show Maeve what you have for her."

"Oh." Catherine started, then held out the gold box to Maeve. "I made this for you."

"You shouldn't have." Maeve took the box and slipped off the ribbon; already the smell of chocolate wafted toward her nostrils. She lifted the lid. Inside was a chocolate crown.

Maeve stared at it. She suppressed a grin, shaking her head instead.

"It's a crown," said Catherine, unnecessarily, peeking into the box. "I made it because you looked like a queen that day."

Maeve turned the box this way and that, studying the detail. "What day was that?"

"The day of the town hall when we saw Kyle Langahan. Don't you remember? I said you reminded me of Hedy Lamarr and that you looked like a queen."

Maeve didn't remember, but how could she? Catherine was always saying nice things to her; it was impossible to keep track of them all. As she examined her sister's creation, she thought about the time it must have taken her: Catherine always made her own molds, carefully carving them in wax with her special little instruments. In her mind, Maeve could see her in the stark light of her basement workshop, her face bent over the block of wax, her doe-like eyes wide with concentration as she impressed the wax so delicately; she saw her pouring the freshly made chocolate, concocted with love, then attaching the colored chocolate stones, giving the finished product the appearance of a fairyland rainbow.

All for her.

"Jesus, Catherine," she said, her voice soft with admiration; despite Maeve's preference for stoicism, which she wore proudly like a mantle, Catherine never ceased to amaze her, crumbling her defenses and leaving her raw.

"Try it on! Try it on!"

The three adults turned. Olivia was behind them, jumping up and down. Amy stood calmly beside her, her hands folded in front of her, but her face wore a sly little grin.

"No, I—" Maeve started to say, then thought better of it and sighed. She reached into the box, which Catherine instinctively took for her; she slipped her fingers inside and slowly removed the crown, then held it over her head with a smile, turning for the girls to see.

The little girls clapped and laughed. Maeve stifled a chuckle, not wanting to go too far.

"You're a queen," said Catherine from behind her. Maeve turned to face her, removing the crown from her head.

"I am not a queen," she told her, laying it back in the box.

"You are."

"The Queen of Hearts, maybe. The one who yells 'off with her head.'"

"The Queen of Hearts has heart, silly. That's the entire point."

Maeve opened her mouth to reply, but Catherine had been distracted by Sarah. The party was breaking up, and the conversation was over.

As people mulled about around her, saying goodbye and kissing each other's cheeks, Maeve stood still and silent, staring at the box in her hands. Catherine liked to say she wasn't very perceptive, that her head was too in the clouds for reality. Incredulous of her own opinions, Catherine had gotten in the habit of consulting with Maeve on pretty much every decision, from what to wear to what to have for dinner, and Maeve had grown used to guiding her. When Catherine didn't feel confident in her ability to read social cues, Maeve had helped her read the signals. As the years had gone on, however, Maeve had begun to realize that actually, it was the reverse. Catherine may have had her head in the clouds, but when your head's in the clouds, you see things that others can't. In viewing the world from above, you may miss the details, but you see the whole picture—like a bird, like a star, like a goddess.

Maeve had had too much to drink and knew she couldn't drive home. She accepted a ride from Wes and Catherine, humbled and mortified by her need for their help but even more horrified by the thought of offending her angelic older sister.

FIVE YEARS AGO, about a year after Amy was born, Wes and Catherine had a fight. Catherine left to clear her head and was assaulted by a man who'd been stalking her. Wes, who had followed Catherine, was shot trying to save her. He and Catherine reconciled, and Wes miraculously recovered. But everything changed after that day—for Wes, for Catherine, and for Maeve.

The fight had been about a woman from Wes's past. Though he never actually had an affair, he'd remained beholden to her long after she'd left him, regardless of the ever-growing rift in his marriage. After that fateful day, he'd said goodbye to her forever; he'd had a life-altering experience, and he'd made big changes to prioritize what was important. He and Catherine had worked tirelessly to overcome this. They had hard conversations, and they attended months of counseling. To his credit, Wes owned full responsibility. His apology was thorough and sincere, he subordinated himself completely—and he spent every day since striving to make himself worthy of his sweet, deserving wife.

Maeve had always suspected his heart had been split. She'd told Catherine so, had warned her of what she'd seen; but Wes had been good at hiding it, and Catherine had missed the signs. It was only Maeve's own keen perception that had made her suspect in the first place: to everyone else, he was pristine and perfect, seemingly flawless, and overflowing with charm. When something hadn't seemed right to Catherine, he always had a convincing defense. And as he never actually cheated—the only betrayal locked deep within his heart, hidden from everyone, including the woman herself—there was no evidence of any real wrongdoing.

After that day, Maeve and Wes had had a chat. It was high time they cleared the air. Maeve had watched for too long as Wes had gaslighted her sister, making her believe she was imagining what was happening right before her eyes, and though it had been unwitting, it was selfish, stupid, and cruel. Maeve came to accept that Wes had tried, that he'd wanted more than anything to move on and had wrestled demons silently for years; in fact, he'd over-compensated, his desperation for normalcy and his guilt at his heart's betrayal inspiring him to lavish gifts and attention on his ever-loyal wife. He did not shirk from Maeve's accusations or attempt to defend himself, and in the years since, he'd proven to her that his dedication to Catherine was earnest and complete. She appreciated his honesty and his humility, the latter of which did not come easily to him. But though Maeve liked him, she hadn't fully trusted him, and she wanted to make sure that he never hurt her sister again.

Then Maeve learned how she'd hurt her sister, too.

It seemed that in their therapy, Catherine had revealed that her problem with Wes had only exacerbated a feeling that was already there, a feeling that was reinforced every day in her interactions with her family. It was a feeling of inferiority, of being minimized, of not living up to anybody's standards. When Maeve confronted Wes with what he had done to her sister—as Catherine's sister, Maeve felt she saw changes no one else could, the way Catherine didn't meet anyone's eyes, the way the life had gone out of her voice—Wes suggested the problem was bigger than Maeve had thought. At Wes's encouragement, when she was ready, Catherine had an honest talk with Maeve herself, informing her that she had felt hurt by her for years, that Maeve's critical comments had stressed her more than she'd let on, that she'd internalized these messages until they had become part of her consciousness. As she spoke, Maeve had been speechless; as she rolled back images in her mind she could not deny their truth. Sassy and cynical by nature, Maeve had taken advantage of Catherine, exhibiting emotional displacement with her in a way she couldn't with anyone else in her life. They say that after a long day of false smiles and restraint, we take out our frustrations on the people closest to us: Maeve had only Catherine, who not only was forgiving of her indiscretions but also was naturally kind, and naturally deferential. It only made sense that Maeve would project her frustrations onto her—and that Catherine, her accommodating big sister, would let her. She came to realize her sarcasm was a defense, one that walled out insecurity, one that had done such a good job it had been a barrier between her and the person she loved most.

It wasn't just that Maeve had been chastised for something she knew instinctively to be true, and it wasn't only that she couldn't stop imagining Catherine crying as she talked about her with her therapist. It was that Maeve had almost lost her, that when she'd received that call from the hospital she'd felt what life would be like without her sister. The sense of loss had broken her; the emptiness had consumed her. She'd realized in that moment something she'd never seen before: that her sister was her life, that without her, she had nothing. Work, as much as it was a part of her, would be meaningless without something to work for; work identified and sustained her, but Catherine breathed life into her. Catherine reminded her that things were beautiful, that despite the world's horrors, there was joy to be found in every day. Whether it was a richly colored fabric or a detailed square of chocolate, the lace hem of a 1930s suit or a compliment offered with a pure, earnest heart, Catherine noticed, and focused on it, and built her perception around it. Maeve wished desperately that she, too, could believe in this beauty, that it would keep her, too, afloat, that she could simply look around her for reminders of what it was all for. Whereas Catherine always saw the beautiful, Maeve seemed always to see the tragic—including, it turned out, when it came to Maeve herself.

In Maeve's view, Wes had almost left her niece fatherless and her sister a widow, all because he was selfish—and before that even happened, he'd torn Catherine's heart to shreds. But how could she even chastise him when she had hurt her sister, too? The thing was, she hadn't meant to hurt her; she didn't know why she did the things she did. Catherine was always so nice to her, had always seen the good in her even when she hadn't deserved it. Truth be told, Maeve was jealous of Catherine's goodness, her capacity for forgiveness and her almost innocent belief in people. She sometimes grew frustrated to see her taken advantage of— but hadn't she taken advantage of her herself? No, she hadn't meant to hurt her, but she supposed Wes hadn't meant to hurt her, either; and the realization was painful, that we hurt each other without realizing, even—especially—those we love the very most. Wes had been selfish, but she had been selfish, too: what made her any better? At least he had mended, had made it all right; at least he'd stood straight and faced his failings and flaws. This was more than could be said for Maeve, who barely understood why she was the way she was, who couldn't explain her feelings to herself, much less to anyone else. Sometimes she felt as if she only made things worse, as if the people around her would be better without her there.

The conclusion she had come to was that we all are selfish, we all bring pain to the ones we would protect—all of us, except for Catherine, and the knowledge Maeve would never be as good as Catherine ripped her apart almost as much as the guilt she felt for resenting the best person she knew.

MAEVE LAY in bed staring at the ceiling, tears leaving streaks on her face as they fell to her pillow. She did not know what the tears were for, but she resented them, too, reminders of her weakness. She wanted to talk to someone, but where to even begin? It was too much, it was too many years; one would have to get inside her brain, live her experiences, see the nuances of her heart. And besides, there was no one—no one who knew her, no one to trust —no one, of course, except Catherine, the very last person she could ask.

MORNINGS ARE A FRESH START: you can forget letting your guard down the night before.

The next day, Maeve felt better. She set her alarm for five o'clock in the morning, rose and had her coffee, then headed to work. In her tall heels and form-fitting skirt, her shiny bob bouncing and her lips as red as Thanksgiving cranberries, she once again had purpose, once again was important. She got to the office early and buckled down without hesitation, catching up on emails until her colleagues began trickling in. The gradually increasing bustle of the office was like lifeblood to her heart, and she could breathe again, could once again feel alive. The brusqueness and bite that were detriments to her relationships with her family were the very qualities that made her so good at her job, and she reveled in it, secure in the knowledge that she was helping real people. The world wasn't perfect, but it wasn't to be given up on, and neither was she.

CHAPTER FIVE

$\mathcal{T}$he holidays passed. Maeve spent them the way she always spent them, hovering in corners and skulking between Catherine and the drink table, enduring conversations with her parents and discussing politics with the Bickharts. Christmas was spent at the Bickharts' sprawling white manor house. Though she dreaded family get-togethers, Maeve had to admit she had a certain affection for that house, which was elegant and cozy under normal circumstances and positively exuded warmth at Christmas.

"And what are your New Year's resolutions, darling?" asked a buoyant Sarah who, looking all grace and glamor in her red knit dress, had approached Maeve and rested her hand on her arm.

Maeve sipped her wine. "I don't do resolutions. If I think something's important, I'll do it when I think of it."

"Fair enough. Though I've always liked the idea of making a commitment, of connecting an improvement with a lesson from the year."

"To each her own."

"Indeed."

Sarah brought her glass to Maeve's, and Maeve clinked it. The women stood for a moment sipping their wine and watching the family mingling in the spacious sunroom. It was after Charles Bickhart's famous Christmas dinner feast, and they'd gathered by the Christmas tree, a magnificent white spruce bedazzled with white lights and crystal globes. Strings of white lights hung across the molding, reflecting in the floor-to-ceiling windows that at this time of evening let in the soft purple glow of winter dusk. Wooden beams were visible in the vaulted ceiling. It was a room so inviting even Maeve could not resist its charms.

"What are your resolutions, Sarah?" she asked her sister's mother-in-law, feeling suddenly and inexplicably inspired by the holiday spirit.

Sarah took a deep breath as she thought. "I suppose they're the same as they are every year. Learn something every day, use my privilege to lift the less fortunate, use my voice to speak for the voiceless, and be a light for my family."

"That's cheating," said Maeve, taking a long sip. "The whole point of resolutions is that you're supposed to pick things you're not already doing."

Sarah turned to her, her brow lifted slightly with surprise.

"That's lovely of you, Maeve," she told her, her eyes sparkling in the light. "Thank you."

Maeve smiled, and Sarah was called away by Grady. Maeve had been drinking steadily and had passed the pleasant numbing stage where she was indifferent to the annoyances of her family and seemed to see small miracles in the people she liked most. She had wanted to tell Sarah she admired, even loved her, but it was probably just as well.

Early in the new year, Doug Tomlinson announced his intention to primary Wes for his House seat. Shortly after, Kyle Langahan formally announced his own candidacy.

"For too long, it's been business as usual in Washington," he said at a press conference; he was standing behind a podium, Nicole to his side and a few feet behind. "For too long, we have seen the ineffectiveness of the political machine. People are tired of establishment politicians who are bought and sold by special interests. I am not a politician; I'm a citizen, a scientist, and a father who cares deeply about his country and about his child's future. I will not be a big money candidate. I will not bow to corporate interests. It's time to shake things up in Washington. As your congressperson, I will fight wealth inequality, I will fight big money in politics, and most importantly, I will fight to protect our planet to ensure our children's future. I will reverse rollbacks to clean water bills and introduce new bills to fix pollution problems at their source: corporations."

"Of course there's nothing inherently wrong with what he's saying," said Maeve to Catherine as the two of them watched him on the evening news. Congress was in session, and Wes was spending most of his time in Washington; Maeve had stopped by on her way home from work to bring Amy a Mandarin duck coloring book. "I mean, I don't disagree with it. No one disagrees with it. And that's precisely my point. It isn't like Wes has to be told any of this. Just who does Langahan think he is?"

"I'm afraid I have to agree," said Catherine; ever the diplomat, she evidently could not bring herself to agree with Maeve's diatribe willingly. "Wes has shown to be dedicated to all those things."

"I guess the fact that he's not totally lacking in political experience makes him untrustworthy."

"I don't really understand it. Besides, he's only finishing his very first term."

"It's not to understand. Kyle said it, so it must be true."

Maeve followed the news as Kyle held protests outside the water company, outside Brown & Little, and outside the General Assembly building in Richmond. He always called for change, not just in policy but in leadership, which he believed was moving too slowly.

I get it, Maeve texted to Catherine, having just finished

watching his latest protest on her phone. *He's right that it's moving too slowly. But that isn't our fault. Aditi and Wes are working tirelessly to get this done. Kyle acts like we're sitting on our asses. It's infuriating.*

I agree, was the simple response. Catherine wouldn't lie, but she wouldn't go out of her way to complain, either.

By March, Wes was back home, and he was dedicating most of his time to campaigning. He had begun preparing for a debate with his opponents. The primary was in May, and this would be their first debate.

Wes had a solid team and a sharp strategy. The night before the debate, he and Maeve bounced ideas off each other; Maeve, along with a handful of others, had joined him in his office for a working take-out dinner.

"Just remember, Wes: Kyle's passionate, but he's got no experience," said Maeve, biting into her grilled vegetable wrap. She chewed, swallowed, and wiped her lips with a napkin. "Be sure to exploit that. Go for the jugular."

Wes grinned through a bite of club sandwich. "You sure this is just about politics?"

"I don't like what you're implying."

"I'm not implying it, I'm saying it straight out. It seems personal."

"Well, it's not. You're better for the job, whether I like it or not." She chugged her water, then placed the bottle on the table with a thud. "Just destroy him."

Before the debate, which took place at a local college, Maeve joined Catherine as she spoke with Wes in the green room. Maeve could tell by looking at him that he was ready to play his best game: he was sharper and crisper than usual, like a deceptively jovial cat ready to pounce. One thing Maeve had to say for Wes: he knew his stuff, and he knew how to show it. He had a way with words and the passion to choose them well. His law background helped; he was a good attorney, and he was nearly impossible to argue with. Maeve glanced across the room, where Kyle stood by himself, arms crossed, rocking on his heels, fingers picking at his lower lip. Dressed smartly in a gray suit, white shirt, and blue tie, he was staring at an invisible spot on the floor. He looked sober and stern—and nervous, Maeve realized with a start. Well, he should be. Tonight he would be forced to put his money where his mouth was; he was no longer a big fish in a little pond. This was a primary for a federal seat, and it was his to lose. Wes would be in his element; Kyle would be on the spot. He was finally going to be challenged in his belief that he knew everything. He would see it wasn't so simple, that dreaming it didn't make it so; he would see the gaps in his knowledge, that he wasn't the smartest guy in the room. Maeve suppressed a little smirk. She couldn't help looking forward a little to seeing him put in his place.

Sensing her eyes on him, Kyle glanced in her direction. He stiffened as she approached him.

"Well, well, Langahan."

"Hello, Maeve."

She crossed her arms and shifted her weight to one round hip. "I'll give you this. When you say you're going to do a thing, you do it."

"I don't like to stand in the sidelines."

"Where's Nicole?"

"She's in the audience with my parents."

"You trust her with those jailbirds?"

Kyle grimaced and shook his head. "Why are you such a wiseass?"

"Someone's got to be." She looked him up and down. "You're so serious. Loosen up a little. Have some humor."

"I do have humor," he said, a little testily. "I just don't find poison in our water humorous."

She decided to take pity and stop teasing him; clearly, he was in no mood for her snark. "Relax, I'm not here for a fight. I just wanted to wish you good luck."

Kyle inhaled and cleared his throat. "Thank you."

She softened somewhat. "Are you nervous?"

Maeve expected him to deny it, but instead, his lips turned down frankly.

"A little."

"Can I give you some advice?"

He stared at her. "Sure."

"Try to have some fun out there, you know? People already know you're smart. They want to know you're a person. If they can't relate to you, they won't vote for you."

"Whether they can relate to me has nothing to do with my ability to do a good job in office."

"Of course it doesn't. But these are people we're talking about. They don't always distinguish the difference. Look at Wes." She glanced over her shoulder, where Wes was talking with his campaign manager. "He knows how to schmooze. That's partly why he's so popular. It isn't just that he's a good congressperson. It's that he plays the part well."

"I don't 'play parts,'" said Kyle, with a sniff. "I hate bullshit. Bullshit is what people fall back on when they have nothing of substance to offer."

"That's a little harsh." She was already regretting coming over here. "Bullshit and substance are not mutually exclusive. A little bullshit is required for politics."

"That's what I'm here to change."

Maeve released a close-lipped sigh. "Look, I'm trying to help you, okay? This isn't high school class president anymore. You can't run on one issue alone. It isn't enough. They have to know you care about what they care about."

"I do care about what they care about. I'm trying to help them. I don't want people getting sick. Everyone cares about not getting sick. And if they don't, I'll make them see."

"Uh," said Maeve, scratching her head. "It isn't quite that easy. Your telling them something doesn't necessitate their buying it."

"Thanks for the help, but I've got this. I've been planning this for weeks. I know my strategy. I'm not about to go changing it now."

"Well, I'll tell you this, Langahan. You can listen to me or not. But Wes won for a reason. You can choose not to take heed, but I guarantee, it'll cost you."

Kyle shook his head. "I refuse to believe that in order to win I have to dumb myself down by becoming some kind of court jester. Everyone will see right through that. What they really want is sincerity, someone who's serious about getting the job done."

"No offense, Langahan, but that's a little simplistic."

"It's not simplistic; you're just cynical. You're not giving people enough credit. They don't want bullshit. They want logic and reason."

"And what if they don't agree with your logic and reason?"

"Then I'll explain it to them. They just need to understand the issues."

"Oh, well that's it, then. Thank goodness they have you to explain their feelings to them."

"What does that even mean?"

"Just what I said. You think your way is the logical way, and that people who don't agree with you just don't understand it. This is a uniquely male attitude, based on centuries of unchallenged privilege. It isn't your fault, really, when you think about it."

Kyle closed his eyes a second and took a deep breath. "Look, I don't have time for this. I have to get my thoughts together before I go out there. Are you done helping?"

"Yes." Maybe she had pushed it a little too far. She hadn't meant to, but he was so damn easy to tease. She really should cut him some slack. In a way, she felt sorry for him: she was a wiseass, not a monster. "All I'm saying is, be human. It isn't really about bullshit—it's just about showing some warmth. An argument could be made that your ability to relate to your constituents reflects your willingness to listen to them, to learn something new."

He looked at her a few moments. "Why are you trying to help me? Isn't it kind of like going behind enemy lines?"

"I have a naturally magnanimous personality."

The hint of a grin pulled at his lips. "Right."

They stood in silence for a moment.

"You know," he said then, "you shouldn't tolerate his bullshit. It distracts from the message, and from the point. We can't afford any distractions."

"First of all, don't tell me what I should or shouldn't do. In any case, Wes just understands human nature. He may know how to bullshit, but he's also sincere. I may tease him, but I've always known that. He just knows how to play the game."

"It's not a 'game,' Maeve." He air-quoted "game"; Maeve glanced briefly heavenward. "There's nothing funny about any of this."

"I know that." She should have known he would inevitably get back on his high horse. She didn't know why she'd bothered to come over here. It seemed that every time she tried to talk to him, she was reminded why she couldn't stand him. "It's a figure of speech. For God's sake."

"Well, I can do it without all that. You'll see. People don't need to be buttered up in order to do the right thing. I have more faith in humanity than that."

"Yes, you're a veritable beacon of light," said Maeve, rolling her eyes.

"You can joke, but you're only skeptical because you haven't tried it. The time for games is over. No dis—"

"No distractions." Maeve sighed internally. "I know."

"The point is that we'll never change politics without someone taking a stand. And I'm going to take it."

"You do that." Maeve had had enough. She cocked her finger at him. "Good luck, Langahan."

She turned and walked away, leaving him to watch her retreat.

She caught sight of Rhys Darney in the corner. His head was bent over his cell phone, and he was typing furiously. He laughed as he appeared to send a message, then caught her gaze and grinned.

He waved her over. She glided toward him, slinking beside him and leaning over him into his phone.

"What do you have there, Darney?" she asked. "I smell dirt."

"You have a knack for sniffing out dirt," he said, nudging her with his elbow. "I can't tell you yet, but it's huge. *Huge*. It'll knock your socks off."

"Yeah?" She nudged him back, leaning into him a second longer than necessary. "Just my socks?"

They turned their heads at an announcement that the debate was about to start.

Rhys turned to her, his eyes molten. He lowered his voice. "Gotta go. Catch me after."

Maeve smiled coyly and watched him scamper off.

Maeve and Catherine sat together. The two sisters chatted in their seats as they waited for the event to begin. Catherine's fingers were fidgeting with her scarf, a telltale sign of her nervousness. Catherine was always nervous at Wes's events. She wanted him to do well and couldn't bear the thought of seeing him chastised or embarrassed. As for Maeve, though never nervous like Catherine—she had been to enough of these events to know they were generally all the same, and Wes, adept at thinking on the spot, could handle himself—she often felt a little tingle of anticipation. Tonight, however, she was especially curious. The event encapsulated three very different sides: Wes, the sturdy, forward-looking incumbent; Doug, the old-school politician of the past; and Kyle, the grassroots non-politician upstart. It would be action-packed, as action-packed as things like this could be; it promised sparring and disagreements, the kind that forced candidates to say it straight.

Maeve lightly slapped Catherine's hands as they fussed with the strap of her purse.

"Stop that," she chastised her, though there was no malice in her voice. "He's going to be fine! Just like he always is."

"Do you really think so?" asked Catherine; Maeve could see her chest rising and falling as she attempted to calm herself by breathing. "I'm not so worried about Doug Tomlinson. It's Kyle Langahan who concerns me."

Maeve relaxed in her seat. "Langahan doesn't know what he's doing. He's sharp, yes, but he's a total wild card. He's got no branding, no data, no following, and no plans except for water. Langahan is not a threat. An annoyance, maybe, but that's all."

"I hope you're right, Maeve."

"I am right. I just talked to him. Trust me." Maeve cast a glance at her sister. She couldn't help but grin a little at Catherine's pure earnestness. "Wes is a pro. You know that. He's going to trounce him, Catherine. *Trounce* him."

Everyone clapped as moderator Eleanor Kang, county commissioner, introduced herself and sat; then the candidates entered as their names were called. Maeve was briefly reminded of another time she had heard Kyle's name called for a debate, but she pushed the memory away, suffering only a mild discomfort in her belly before it passed.

The three men stood behind their podiums, Doug to the left, Wes in the middle, and Kyle to the right. Eleanor went over the rules and then announced that Kyle had won the coin toss and therefore would answer the first question.

"Mr. Langahan," she said, "how important to you is diversity in government, and what would you do to encourage diversity in our representatives, both on a local and national level?"

"Diversity in government is very important," said Kyle, his hands on the sides of the podium. He shifted his weight and continued. "Now more than ever, we need to ensure that we're leveling the playing field for people whose voices have been

119

silenced. When people see themselves in their elected officials, they know their voices are being heard. That being said, it isn't enough to vote for someone simply for their demographic. We need people who are going to stand up to corporations, who are going to fight for tangible structural changes that will benefit everyone. For example, as your congressperson, I will dedicate my life to ensuring factories like Brown & Little can't contaminate our drinking water. This issue is particularly important because it so often leads to environmental discrimination, in which marginalized communities bear the brunt of the effects of climate change and lack of regulation. I believe we should encourage diversity in government, but we also need to elect the best candidates to promote important issues like conservation and water safety. When we fight for clean water, we fight discrimination by making sure the most vulnerable among us are protected. Thank you."

The audience clapped. Eleanor turned to Wes. "Congressman? Do you have a response?"

"Yes, I do. I agree with Mr. Langahan that people need to see themselves in their elected officials. But I'll tell you, I disagree that this isn't enough reason to vote for someone. When legislatures are diverse, they prioritize issues historically put on the back burner. Look at what happened in Nevada. For the first time in history, a state has a female-majority legislature. Almost immediately, bills that prioritized women's health, maternal mortality, and sexual harassment were brought to the table. These are issues that never would have been prioritized without a female majority—we know it, because they weren't. I'll be the first to admit majority-male legislatures have for too long cast these issues aside. The same can be said when legislatures are disproportionately white. We need more people of color in office, specifically because they're people of color—it's the only way to ensure the most privileged will fulfill their obligation to all of the people."

Applause erupted in the room. Eleanor waited until it had subsided.

"Congressman Bickhart, I don't know if you've noticed, but you yourself are a white man," she said, to the laughter of those in the room. "In fact, before Senator Patel, a woman had never occupied the General Assembly seat you recently vacated. Does this mean that you would have stepped aside if an equally qualified woman had been running for your seat?"

"Yes, it does," Wes responded, in a low, serious tone Maeve knew from experience was serious. "That's exactly what it means."

"Mr. Langahan," said Eleanor, over light applause, "do you have a response? Hypothetically speaking, would you step aside to ensure others had representation?"

"I think it's an irrelevant question," said Kyle, shifting his weight once more. "I've never run for office, and our House district has been represented by women in the past. But more than that, it's about who is most qualified to do the job. People should vote for who can get the job done."

"But the question is," Eleanor continued, "would you step aside for an equally qualified woman? Representative Tomlinson, your response?"

"I agree with Kyle," said Doug, emphatically. "I've got nothing against women holding office. I'll be the first to support them. But if I'm the most qualified candidate, I can't see stepping aside for the fact that they're female alone."

Kyle had grimaced at Doug's agreeing with him.

"As Ms. Kang stated," said Wes, with a sardonic, crooked grin, "that wasn't the question. When the Commissioner asks, 'Would you step aside for an equally qualified woman,' and your response is, 'We should elect the most qualified person,' you're doing one of two things: you're either suggesting there couldn't be an equally qualified woman, or you're deflecting to avoid admitting you wouldn't step aside. The question is not, 'Should we elect the more qualified person?' The question is, 'All things being equal, would you step aside for a woman who would do as good a job as you?' And I think any man who truly wants to close the gap would make space at the table for them, not profess to know better the issues that are important to them."

The audience applauded, and Eleanor moved on. Catherine raised her hands high as she clapped. Maeve smiled and joined the applause, proud of Wes's answer. He'd had a great start.

"Representative Tomlinson, next question," Eleanor said. "As you're aware, senators in Congress have recently unveiled a new universal childcare bill, which would cap childcare costs and institute a sliding scale. Early reports suggest you will not support this bill. Are these reports true, and if so, why will this bill not gain your support?"

"Now, don't get me wrong, it isn't that I don't believe in universal childcare. But we also have to be fiscally responsible. I want to put money directly in the hands of those who need it most, not those who are going to exploit the system to buy drugs or what have you."

There was a rumbling in the room as shocked audience members reeled at Doug's statement.

Wes held his finger in the air. "If I may respond."

"Of course, Congressman."

Wes shook his head. "I think we all know what Mr. Tomlinson said is ignorant, at best, and vicious at worst. Data shows that people who receive these benefits overwhelmingly use them for food, housing, and other necessities. Childcare and child tax credits have lifted millions of children out of poverty. Sounds to me that Mr. Tomlinson's afraid of opposition, and using scare tactics to make us afraid, too."

Eleanor turned to Kyle. "Mr. Langahan? Do you agree with Congressman Bickhart?"

"Yes," said Kyle, begrudgingly, but without hesitation. "Yes, Mr. Tomlinson is flat out wrong, for all the reasons the congressman said. I agree with Congressman Bickhart."

Light applause from the audience. Kyle shifted his weight, visibly unnerved.

"While the attention is on you, Mr. Langahan," said Eleanor, "you've made water safety your signature issue. Congressman Bickhart is getting ready to introduce a water safety bill in Congress, but you've insisted it doesn't go far enough. How would you tackle this important issue, if elected?"

"Thank you, Ms. Kang. As I've said, I believe we can't fully tackle this issue without going to the source. Increased regulation and oversight are necessary and good. But I have major concerns about water privatization. Publicly owned water companies are accountable to the public, not their bottom line. When they're motivated by profit, there are conflicts of interest—just look at what happened in Flint. That's how safety is compromised and public health is endangered. In short, privately owned companies prioritize their own interests over the good of the people. I will fight to ensure the good of the people is always the first priority."

Eleanor turned to Wes. "Congressman Bickhart? Response?

"I'll start by saying, I absolutely agree," said Wes. "And I admire Mr. Langahan's passion."

Kyle laughed humorlessly. "Let's do without the patronization."

Wes paused, eyebrows raised for an almost imperceptible moment. Maeve straightened: Kyle had managed to break Wes's composure, but the break was short-lived, and probably not noticeable to anyone but her and Catherine. A split second, and Wes had recovered; he grinned slyly and held up his hands in acknowledgment.

"Sincerest apologies. Not my intention at all."

Maeve and Catherine exchanged a quick, tense look.

Wes resumed his casual, easygoing affect. "Unfortunately, it's just not something we can get done. I want what Mr. Langahan wants. I really do. But we have to be realistic. I think this is something we can study and take action on—after further safeguards are in place. We're in a good place with the current bill, and I worry we're letting the perfect be the enemy of the good here. I don't disagree with a ban on privatization in theory, but the legal and constitutional concerns give me pause."

"You're a lawyer, Congressman," said Kyle, leaning in close to his mic. "Isn't it your job to figure these things out?"

"My job is to legislate so I can keep my promises to the people who put me in Congress. I'm just not going to sacrifice good, effective solutions because I can get only ninety-five percent of what I want. We'll get there. But we need a solution right now."

"Right now," sneered Kyle, "people are displaced because Brown & Little's poisoned them in their homes. They've done this to avoid investing in proper technologies and to gain competitive advantage. What are you doing for those people, right now? What are you doing to make sure Brown & Little is held accountable for their actions?"

"I am no stranger to holding criminals to the fire," said Wes, with a bit of fire, himself; he gestured with his pointer finger for emphasis. "One of the first cases I took as a public interest attorney was that of the Munson landfill. I flew to Texas to inspect the original Munson site, I investigated their violations of safety standards, and I had lengthy interviews with their victims. And though I largely credit the disintegration of Munson's Charlottesville deal to the hard work and passion of activists like yourself—activists who attended town halls, wrote letters, and drove great distances for protests—I will say that I worked tirelessly to solidify their efforts. And we were successful. My point, Mr. Langahan, is that I've done this before. And I am confident that with my guidance and support, we will do it this time, too."

The audience applauded. Eleanor leaned into the microphone. "Mr. Tomlinson? What are your comments on Mr. Langahan's suggestion for a ban on private ownership of water companies?"

Doug put his hands on the sides of the podium. "This is a case of government overreach, and it's going to hurt us. Water management is regulated at the state and local level—that's just the way that it is. If you want to pass regulations, you're not going to do it by antagonizing half of your constituents, or half of Congress. A lot of people would argue that privatization brings innovation and competition and that the government should not interfere with market forces. They may even be right."

"A lot of people believe women shouldn't have gotten the right to vote," inserted Kyle. "That doesn't mean we give in to it."

"Mr. Langahan, you've got gumption, that much is clear," laughed Doug. "But when you're in office, you have to see the big picture. You're out of your league here. You're a one trick pony."

A ripple of surprised exclamation rumbled through the audience. Maeve's mouth had opened at the harshness of Doug's comment; she almost felt sorry for Kyle, who had flushed and was now standing silent.

Wes spoke above the din. "Look, look, everyone," he said, holding up his hands, "I think the point here is that we all want the best. Now, we can do this while still acknowledging we're all on the same page. No matter where we stand on things or where we're coming from, we all have the same goal, which is to ensure something gets done to keep Americans safe."

The debate continued in this fashion. Questions were asked and answered, with the occasional blowup or spat. By the end of the debate, Maeve had learned one thing, and that was that each candidate was exactly who she thought he was before the debate began.

"Well, that was informative," she told Catherine, perched on the edge of her seat as she slipped into her jacket. "When backed into a corner, everyone digs in their heels."

"There was that one moment," said Catherine, rather brightly —she'd clearly relaxed once she'd seen the debate was going in Wes's favor, "when Kyle agreed with Wes. I thought that was big of him."

"Kind of sad," said Maeve, standing, "that acknowledging someone is an elitist asshole is considered 'big' these days."

"Still, though. It was the right answer."

"Yes." Maeve buttoned up her jacket, then stood looking around as Catherine gathered her things. Kyle had answered honorably; in general, he'd held his own. Credit where it was due. "I'll concede it was well done."

Across the room, Maeve caught sight of Nicole with a couple she assumed to be Kyle's parents. They were spilling out into the aisle, Nicole in front, her grandparents behind. Kyle's parents were gray-haired and inconspicuous. His mother wore olive-colored slacks, a cream sweater, and a buffalo plaid shawl, and her long hair was pulled back into a low ponytail. His father wore dark slacks, a sweater, and a sports jacket, and his white beard and receding hairline gave him the appearance of a sea captain. Nicole was wearing what appeared to be a tiny navy blue pantsuit.

Maeve was still watching when Nicole glanced over. Spotting Maeve, she waved, then looked up and back at her grandparents, indicating she'd seen someone she knew.

Catherine drifted off in search of Wes. Nicole met Maeve at the back of the room. She had her leather purse slung over her shoulder. She wore patent leather shoes with kitten heels.

"Don't you look sharp," said Maeve, looking her over, hand on hip. "Did you come here right from work?"

"I wore this to school," Nicole responded, without batting an eye. "I wanted everyone to know I was coming to my dad's debate tonight."

"That's fabulous." Maeve extended her hand to Nicole's grand-mother. "Hello. You must be Kyle's mother."

"Gillian Benson-Langahan," she replied, shaking it. "This is my husband Gus. And who are you?"

"Maeve Sheering," said Maeve. "I went to school with Kyle."

"I'm glad you were here to see this," said Gillian. "He was brilliant. He let Wes Bickhart know we won't put up with his crap."

"I'm not here for Kyle, though it was good to see him," said Maeve. "I'm here because Wes Bickhart is my brother-in-law."

Gillian's face hardened, but didn't flush. "I see."

"Nicole, what did you think of the debate?" asked Maeve, ignoring Gillian's comment about Wes. "You must be pretty proud of your dad."

"He did great," said Nicole, her face alight with excitement.

"He sure did, honey," said Kyle's father, patting her shoulders. He looked at Maeve. "You'll excuse us if we don't share your support for Wes Bickhart. We've been fighting Virginia Clear-Stream for years."

"So has Wes," said Maeve. She could definitely see where Kyle got his lack of humor. "He's been working on a groundbreaking new water bill, both in Congress and here at home. Maybe you didn't hear."

"I heard," Gus said; he sniffed, and in his testy tone Maeve heard Kyle's voice. "It's a spineless bill meant to dupe the public and placate donors."

"Really?" said Maeve, scrunching her face with feigned confusion. "I wasn't aware of any connections to donors. I'd love to hear any evidence you have."

"All you have to do is look at his history. He was a shill for corporations for years."

"I don't know that I'd go that far. And besides, he's been very vocal about his change of heart. That's why he moved down here to begin with."

Gus snorted. "How remarkable that he found his conscience right when he stepped into politics."

The corner of Maeve's mouth turned up snidely.

"Come on," said Gillian, tapping Gus's arm. "Let's go congratulate Kyle."

Nicole tugged on Maeve's jacket. "Will you come with us?"

Maeve followed them through the crowd and toward the green room, where the candidates were chugging water and shaking off the excitement of the evening. As the Langahans drifted toward Kyle, Maeve stepped subtly away toward Wes, Catherine, and the slew of Wes's team members and other local officials who had gathered to celebrate what everyone viewed as a clear victory.

"Way to go, Congressman," Maeve murmured to Wes, who was currently enjoying having his back rubbed by a beaming Catherine. "I must say, you knocked it out of the park, you nimble old dog."

"Thanks," said Wes, thoughtfully, screwing the cap back on his water. He gestured toward Kyle. "Say, how much do you know about him? Do you know what his plans are?"

He didn't add, "when he loses," but Maeve sensed it was implied. "I think his plans are to try to bring down Virginia Clear-Stream until he dies."

"I've been learning about him. His work is pretty impressive. He's only been back in Virginia a few months, but already he's got a great reputation as a knowledgeable, creative thinker."

"He's a smart guy."

"Mmm." Wes was looking at Kyle. He absentmindedly unscrewed the cap of his water bottle, took another sip, and screwed it back on. He had something on his mind, but whatever it was, he wasn't yet ready to say it.

Maeve glanced over her shoulder, where Kyle's parents were giving their son a final hug and holding their fists in the air in a gesture that appeared to be telling him to fight the good fight. They then escorted Nicole out the door, leaving Kyle to speak with his manager and a handful of other team members.

Maeve chatted with Wes and Catherine a little, and then the three of them walked out into the hallway and toward the front of the building. Maeve didn't know where Kyle had gone, and was glad for it. When they'd approached the entrance, she kissed her sister goodbye. Rhys was just outside the doors. She came upon him as he was clapping the photographer on the back and sending him on his way.

"Hey," he said, checking his watch. "I need to hunt down this lead. It shouldn't take me too long. Wait up for me?"

"But of course." She cast him a sly grin. "I can always wait a couple of hours for you, Darney."

"Great. I'll text to let you know I'm home."

"It's a plan." She smiled, nudged him, and turned to walk away. "See you later."

"Hey."

She turned back.

He was watching her with a look she hadn't seen him give her before. It was quiet and earnest, his eyes wide and his lips straight.

"Want to stay over?" he said.

She turned to him fully. "What? You mean, all night?"

He shrugged. "Yeah."

She thought about it. "I don't know," she said. "I mean, I have so much to do tomorrow."

"Okay, that's fine. You know, whatever."

She looked at him curiously. "You really want me to?"

He shrugged again and smiled. "Yeah."

She blinked a few times, then smiled cautiously. "Maybe," she said. "I'll think about it."

He smiled more widely. "Great."

Maeve watched as he bolted toward his car to chase his lead, her head muddled, her thoughts hazy. As he peeled out of the parking lot, Maeve noticed movement further up toward her car. The person parked next to her was putting something into his back seat. As she grew closer, she saw that it was Kyle Langahan.

"Stop following me," she told him as she unlocked her car from a few feet away. "It's beginning to look suspicious."

"I'm not following you. You must have parked here after me."

She peered into his car. "No Nicole?"

"She's staying with my parents tonight. Why?"

"No reason." She let a beat pass. "You've got yourself quite a daughter, Langahan. I like that kid a lot."

"I like her, too."

"She was really proud of you tonight."

"Yeah, well." He was standing straight, his jaw tight. Their two cars between them, it felt like they were a mile away from each other. "Kids are always proud of their dads."

"Not necessarily."

"I do it for her, you know." He glanced back at the building where he'd just laid his heart on the line, shown his passion, revealed his vulnerabilities. "All of it. I always believed in it, of course. But it didn't have the same meaning."

Maeve's eyes softened. "I'm sure."

"She's taught me so much about what matters. I have to put her first, no matter what else. I've got to make a difference, to make the world a better place—to make it a livable place. Her future depends on it." He studied her. "Does that make sense?"

"Of course." She was surprised by the gentleness in her own voice. "It absolutely makes sense." She bit her lip, cautiously grateful for his honesty, for his willingness to peel back the layers somewhat. She decided to meet him there, to return this little act of trust. "It makes you a good dad, if you ask me." But he was already a good dad. "An even better one."

He didn't smile, but acknowledgment of this compliment registered in his face. He turned serious; he shook his head, then looked down at the ground. "It's really a shame," he said, "what politics has become. It's all grandstanding and infighting. It's impossible to contribute anything of value in this environment." He looked up at her. "It's really discouraging. It's not even about the issues anymore, it's just about entertainment."

"So what you're saying," she suggested, a playful lilt in her voice, "is that I was right."

"No, that's not what I'm saying. I'm saying it's not what it used to be."

Maeve shook her head sadly. "How soon you forget the caning of Charles Sumner."

"That was before the Civil War. You just proved my point."

"No, I didn't. The point is that politics is politics, because people are people. It's the way it is, and it's the way it always will be."

He was watching her carefully, frowning. "We only spent five minutes talking about the water bill."

"It's an hour and a half debate, Langahan. They don't have time for everything."

"Don't they see how important this is? Doesn't anyone? While we're up there bickering about a hundred other issues, Brown & Little is getting away with actual murder."

"Those other issues are also important to people." Maeve had moved beyond frustration and into pity; for as confident as he was, he was beginning to see his ill-preparedness, and as someone who had seen it all along, Maeve was pained to witness his awakening. "Just because they don't matter to you doesn't mean they don't matter to others. That's what you have to understand."

"I'll tell you what I understand," he said coldly, "and that's that nothing is getting done under the status quo. And I refuse to accept that."

"Why don't you consider working with Wes?" Maeve had a feeling that's what Wes had been pondering earlier, and the more she thought about it, the more sense it made. Kyle would bring passion and knowledge, and Wes would bring the sharpness necessary to make something of it. "Or with—" She stopped. She was going to say, "Or you could work with Aditi," but working with Aditi would require him to work with her, too.

"You talk like the race is already over," he said. "It's only just begun. I have no reason to believe I can't win against Bickhart."

"I'm just saying, it can't hurt to have a backup. Even if you lose, you can still have influence."

"We can do better, Maeve. It's like I said in high school: you can't depend on the system. Have a little hope. Think outside the box. Limiting beliefs only mean more of the same."

"Really?" Maeve's brow had risen high, and her jaw had dropped; she had gone from sympathetic to livid in the space of half a second. "I should think outside the box? I got up in front of our senior class and all our teachers and talked about tampons. How is that 'limited'? You think I felt comfortable doing that? You think I didn't know how people would react? That's the point, Langahan. I understand people. I understand how shitty they are, and I put myself out there anyway. You just think it's so easy, like you'll just glide in here and the sea will part for your brilliance."

"Well, you can think what you want. But the fact is, they don't care. We need to vote them out. Just vote them all the hell out. Bring in non-politicians who aren't beholden to special interests. That is the only way we will ever make progress. Your brother-in-law is only in the way, and if you support him then you are, too."

"I am so done with you, Langahan. I've tried to be nice, but it's clear you know everything and that you have no patience for anyone else's opinion. So good luck with that, Langahan. Good luck with that, and when the race is over and you've been clobbered, maybe you'll see that I had a fucking point."

"I'm not going to be clobbered!" His face had turned red, and he was breathing rather heavily; Maeve had never seen him lose control of his emotions, and she was simultaneously alarmed and proud that she'd managed to break his façade. "I'm not going to lose. I'm not! You'll see, Maeve. You'll see. The people want a fighter. They want someone who tells them the truth. I'm not giving up, and I'm not giving in. I will never work with Wes Bick-hart or any other political sellouts. I'm going to win this thing. I am. I'm going to win, and then you'll see how anything can happen. Anything!"

But it wasn't to be. Kyle never did pick up momentum, lagging way behind Wes and Doug. His debate performances were predictable, his appearance stiff and unyielding; he was erratic but without humanity, coming across as neither likable nor qualified. Moreover, despite advice, he refused to expand his platform. As unlikely as his candidacy appeared in the beginning, as it progressed, he only continued faltering in the polls. Maeve was following the polls closely, and she wasn't at all surprised. It was always the same with Kyle: he knew it all, he had all the answers, and everyone else was in the way of true progress.

In May, Wes won the primary in a landslide. Maeve watched Kyle's concession speech, frowning and shaking her head. It was really too bad about Langahan, she thought. He was smart, he was passionate, he was good-looking, and he was on the right side of history; he could have really done something great. He might have had something to offer—and she might have had sympathy for him—if he weren't such an insolent, insufferable, self-satisfied prick.

ONE DAY IN JUNE, Wes called Maeve at work.

"How well do you know Kyle Langahan, anyway?" he asked her. "We never did finish that conversation."

"Not well," she told him, "and even that's too much."

"I want to get this water bill taken care of, and I want to do it right this time. Do you think he'd come on as a consultant?"

"My sense is no, but you could always ask."

"I was hoping you would."

Maeve nearly spit out her coffee. "That's the surest way for him to say no."

"Okay." Wes paused, thinking. "Well, I'm going to reach out to him. Thanks, Maeve."

"You're welcome. Good luck."

The next day, Wes called her back. Kyle had told him he'd sleep on it and had gotten back to him that morning. He would do it, he'd said, but he had conditions. He was not to be considered on staff, and he had the right to quit at any time if Wes proved himself to be a deceptive opportunist—his words, not Wes's. Wes had readily agreed to these conditions and had asked him to come in on Monday. Kyle would keep his job at the Virginia Conservancy Society; he would meet with Wes for a weekly Monday evening appointment, in which they'd discuss the science, brainstorm plans, and work on details. Wes asked, mostly ironically, if Maeve wanted to join them. Maeve laughed and told him she'd rather pluck out her own eyes with her mascara wand.

Maeve hung up the phone and leaned back in her chair, thinking. Kyle had told her he would never work with Wes or any other politician, and yet, here they were. She had to hand it to him, that Langahan. No matter how much he hated politicians, and no matter how much it had undoubtedly wounded him to lose, he cared more about that water than he did about his pride, more than he did about anything.

CHAPTER SIX

*I*n June, Maeve ran into Rhys at a bar party following one of Aditi's events. They hung out partying together for a while, then headed back to her house, where she treated him to a night of unrestrained bliss in the guest bedroom she reserved for encounters with men. She hadn't told him, or any man she took here, that it wasn't her actual bedroom; she'd just let them assume the door upstairs led to the attic. In any case, when stumbling into bed, no one ever seemed to care.

It was late as they lay still, and Maeve was getting ready to kick him out. Thankfully, leaving before morning was part of their understanding. Maeve had declined his offer to stay over the last time: she felt it was better to avoid things getting too complicated.

She had indulged in snuggling up close to him; his arm was around her back. He had that post-sex masculine smell, full of sweat and energy and power. She went so far as to kiss his neck, her nose tickling his jaw; he moaned once, and laughed, then turned to his side and propped his head in his hand.

"Here's a doozy for you," he said, the back of his finger

brushing the upper curve of her breast, from which the top of the blanket had fallen. "I think we should give it another shot."

"Give what another shot? Another round? Honestly, Darney, I'm tired."

"No, I mean us. Give us another shot. Our relationship."

Her face froze into an incredulous half-smile. She flipped slowly onto her back, running her fingers through her hair. "Oh, shit."

"'Oh, shit,' what?"

"Rhys, I am just not cut out for relationships. You know this. What we have is working fine, so why change it?"

"Because it's not working fine. Not for me."

She looked at him. "It isn't?"

"I mean, it's fantastic, don't get me wrong." He grinned slyly and bit his lower lip, his eyes roaming up and down her body's curves beneath the blanket; he stuck his hand under the blanket and pinched her, and she laughed, pushing his hand away. "But I'm turning forty this year, you know? I need to settle down."

"So you feel like you're too old to be single, and I happen to be in your line of vision? That's a hard no."

"It's not just that." For a moment, he looked hurt, but he shook it off, and his frown turned pensive. "It's just that...I don't know. Don't you ever get tired? Of casualness? Of the game?"

"So you want to renew our relationship because you're tired? I'm flattered, Darney, but you're not helping your case."

"That's not what I mean." He was serious now, his brow straight and his eyes intent. "I just mean, we keep doing this, you know? Hooking up like strangers, except we're not. And I like you."

"No, you don't."

"Yes, I do. I always have."

"You're in a sex haze. It happens."

"You can drop the act, Maeve. We've done this enough times

for me to know you're not really a hardass. At least, not deep down."

"Even you don't get that deep down inside me, Darney."

"Shut up." The words were harsh, but his voice was gentle; he nudged her leg with his own. His brow crinkled as he looked at her thoughtfully. "Have you been with anyone since we started doing this? You know, aside from me?"

"Yeah, a few," she said, briefly recalling a succession of occasional and anonymous one night stands that had floated from her memory as quickly as she'd scrambled from their apartments. As buttoned up and dependable as she was in her job, she was more impulsive in her sex life—a person had to let go somehow, somewhere. "Have you?"

"A few."

Maeve lay staring into nothingness, trying to find a reason to say no, something he would accept without a fight. Everything was so great; they had this no-pressure, equal opportunity thing going. It seemed unwise to mess with it.

"So?"

Maeve sighed. "I don't know. I mean, I like you, Darney. I do. But—"

"Look, I don't want to pressure you." Maeve looked at him. He had pulled his phone off the nightstand and was scrolling through a message; Maeve knew from past experience that it was a sign he was getting ready to leave. He punched in a quick reply, then turned to her. "Just maybe keep it in mind."

She nodded once as he hopped out of bed and into his clothes. Maeve watched him, his tight, fit body bending and stretching, the straight lines and curves of him, his quick, easy movements. When he was dressed, he leaned in and kissed her once, passionately, then once more on the cheek. Maeve took his hand and squeezed it, and he squeezed it back before pulling away.

"Thanks for the roll in the hay, gorgeous. You always rock my world."

Maeve listened as his footsteps pattered down the stairs and across the foyer, then as the front door opened and closed. She lay back for a while, thinking, then slipped from bed and made her way up to her actual bedroom. As she always did when she had a man over, she'd change the sheets in the guest room in the morning. Normally she'd change the man, too, and why shouldn't she? Relationships always seemed to devolve after you got to know each other too well; when it was casual, you never had enough time to annoy each other, never enough time to see all each other's flaws. You never got bored, never settled; you never saw anyone at their worst, never let them see you at yours. As she climbed the stairs toward her skyward bedroom she thought about what it would mean for her to commit to another try. What would she have to give up, she wondered; who would she have to become?

She pulled the covers back and settled into her plush, cozy bed, throw pillows around her, the lavender walls almost glowing in the moonlight that filtered through the curtains. *This is mine*, she thought, *and I don't want to share it*. And she wouldn't, she decided, at least not for now. Rhys hadn't seemed to require an immediate answer; he at least knew her as well as that. If there were anyone she'd be serious with, realistically, it was probably him. She tried to imagine it, a real commitment, knowing he was hers and she was his. What would it be like to have him with her always—to let him see her in the morning—to let him see her when she cried? To let him hold her every night, to let him comfort her—to see him in the morning, too?

As she lay staring up at the ceiling, she wondered why she hadn't let him stay, when she was enjoying snuggling into him, enjoying the warmth of his arms. She had gotten so used to defending her independence that she might have been keeping herself from some things she actually wanted. What did she want? What did he? Would she ever know? Did she have to?

No, she decided—*no, I don't have to right now*. She tucked herself tighter in the blankets, curling up in a tight little ball, then smiling in the comfort of her haven, she drifted off to sleep.

BY EARLY JULY, they were only four months away from the election, and Wes's campaign was in full swing. He faced a tough challenger, and he was working harder than he ever had before, as were Catherine, Sarah, Grady, and Maeve. Wes, whose signature issue when running for state senator had been stopping the building of a toxic landfill on county surplus land, had taken a special interest in water safety after the revelation of Brown & Little's coverups. Wes was on a mission. He took Kyle to a House hearing, where he presented him as an expert in water safety and PFAS. Kyle, while easily flustered on the debate stage, was in his element when advocating for his cause; he was bold, firm, and convincing, his expertise obvious to everyone in the room. He answered committee members' questions with deftness and skill, and he did not falter, the tenacity Maeve had always seen as pigheaded proving invaluable when put to firm purpose.

"That was impressive," said Catherine as the two watched on her phone over lunch. They were in a restaurant near Aditi's office, hunched together over the screen so as not to miss a word of the hearing. She looked at Maeve. "Don't you think?"

"It was very good," said Maeve, sipping on her wine.

"Kyle's very talented."

"Yeah, he's all right."

Catherine studied her, then looked back at the screen. "He's quite handsome. He looks good."

"He's not unattractive. He looks okay."

That Friday night, Maeve watched Amy so Wes and Catherine could go out to dinner. After Amy's begging, it was decided Maeve would watch her at her own house and that they would finally have their long-awaited sleepover. At the last minute,

Grady and Helen were invited to join them. This meant that Olivia would be at the sleepover, too.

After feeding the girls takeout in the kitchen, Maeve settled them on the couch in her sunroom, which with its moss-painted walls, built-in bookshelves, and stylishly upholstered furniture was one of the more comfortable rooms in the house. During the day, the tall windows let in copious amounts of light, which reflected off the glass coffee table and the bright colors of the throw pillows; at night, they offered a clear view of the stars, which twinkled from between tree branches and in the soft halo of the moon. Maeve gave the girls a chunky knit blanket to snuggle under, and popcorn in a big ceramic bowl. The girls sat munching their popcorn, waiting, and watching Maeve as she selected a movie to stream on the TV.

The girls chose an animated film about unicorns. Maeve took a chair and dimmed the lights.

"Aunt Maeve," said Amy, shoving popcorn into her mouth. "Why are you on your phone?"

"Just a sec," Maeve said absentmindedly; she was scheduling an appointment for Aditi. She hit "send" and put her phone back in the front pocket of her Vassar College sweatshirt. "What's that now?"

"Why were you on your phone?"

"I was on my phone for work." Her phone vibrated from inside her sweatshirt. She picked pulled it out, read the message, and put it back in. She smiled at the girls. "When you're a grownup, work doesn't wait."

"But you're missing the movie."

It buzzed again. She bit her lip, forcing herself to ignore it.

Suddenly, the girls burst into hysterics: something funny had happened on the screen. They laughed uncontrollably with their mouths wide open, half-chewed popcorn visible inside. In their laughter, they leaned this way and that, their eyes watering with tears.

Maeve smiled. Anyone with a heart would.

The girls settled back down, a few stray giggles escaping here and there.

Maeve's phone continued to vibrate for a while, but somehow now it was easier to let it go. Eventually, the vibrating stopped, and she concentrated on the movie, when she wasn't distracted by her thoughts.

"What does that mean?" asked Olivia, shyly.

Maeve looked at her. "What does what mean?"

"'Feasible,'" said Olivia. "That word they just said."

"Feasible means possible. It means that somebody can do it."

"Oh." Olivia thought about it. "So it was feasible for Dovetail to go with Adelaide on her quest," she reasoned, referring to the movie's characters.

"That's right."

"It's feasible for you to understand feasible," said Amy, and the girls erupted into laughter once more.

Maeve chuckled. "It's feasible for me to explain feasible."

"It's feasible for me to eat popcorn."

"It's feasible for me to laugh."

"It's feasible for me to ask for some water, please."

Maeve grinned. "It's feasible for me to get it for you."

Maeve rose and went into her kitchen, a bright, cozy room covered in white subway tiles with black and white patterns along the edges. While she was there, she preheated the oven. She had bought ready-to-bake cookie dough, the kind in the tube that pops. They had little heart designs in the middle, and Maeve thought the girls would like them. She pulled a cookie sheet from her cabinet and, retrieving the tube from the refrigerator, laid the cookies in even lines. Before walking off, she took her phone out of her sweatshirt and plugged it into a charger on the counter.

When she returned to the sunroom, the girls were leaning their heads on each other. They were growing tired. Maeve handed them their water, and they thanked her.

"I hope you're not too tired for cookies," she said as she sank into her chair, her feet under her bottom and her knees leaning on the arm. She stuck her hands inside the pockets of her sweatshirt and made herself comfortable. "They'll be waiting for us when we're done."

"Mmm," said the girls, shaking their heads. "We won't be too tired."

A couple of minutes went by. The ever-changing light from the television screen flashed its colors across the walls, the ceiling, the girls' faces. Maeve glanced toward the girls. They looked cute snuggled together, two cousins, two best friends. She looked back at the screen, watching as the unicorns danced in some sort of forest celebration.

"It's feasible," said Olivia, "for me to call you Aunt Maeve."

Maeve glanced back at the girls again. Neither was looking at her; their wide eyes were on the movie, their hands digging in the popcorn. For a few beats, a strange ache encircled Maeve's heart. Her eyes returned to the screen. The unicorns were flying toward the horizon.

"It's feasible," she said, and laughed with them at the movie.

THE FOLLOWING WEEK, Maeve was busy preparing for a special joint fundraiser for Aditi and Wes, who continued building a coalition for the passage of their respective water bills. One day, as she and Aditi pushed through a working lunch, Maeve was walking from Aditi's office toward the waiting room, a three hundred-page report in her arms, when the door opened, and in walked Kyle and Nicole Langahan.

"Mr. Langahan. Miss Langahan," she greeted them, nodding. "How delightful to see you."

Nicole waved. "Hi, Maeve."

"Hi, Nicole."

"I have an appointment with Senator Patel," said Kyle. "We're going to go over the economic impact assessment. I sent it to her last week."

"Yes, I know." Maeve leaned back against the desk, her bottom perched on the edge, resting her weight on one hip. She crossed her feet casually and hugged her papers against her chest. "It was fascinating. Good work, Langahan. We're using it in a comparative analysis of existing regulations. We think it'll help with public opinion."

Kyle watched her. "Yes, I know. Wes told me all about it. It's a good plan," he added, perhaps a little reluctantly.

"How is the Wes gig going?"

"It's going okay, I think." He was frowning, as if he found his own words baffling. "He seems to be all in."

"Of course he is. Didn't I tell you he was?"

"I'm not letting my guard down yet. These things have a way of falling apart at the last minute."

"How fortunate that he has you to hold him to a high standard of integrity."

Kyle glared at her with a look that said, *Really?*

"Mr. Langahan," said Aditi, walking briskly toward him, her arm extended. "The man of the hour. Thank you so much for coming in."

"My pleasure, Senator," said Kyle, nodding, and shaking her hand. He placed his hand on Nicole's shoulder. "This is my daughter Nicole."

"Hello, Senator Patel," said Nicole, reaching her hand up to shake.

"Hello, Nicole," said Aditi. She stood back and looked at her, her face playfully serious. "You look like a girl who means business."

What gave it away? Maeve thought ironically—was it the brief-case, or the notebook in her hand, or the suit, or her little leather purse? In fact, Nicole looked more serious than her father, who was dressed more casually today, in jeans and a sweater, and an army green jacket.

"Nicole likes to dress up to meet her representatives," explained Kyle, affectionately patting his daughter's shoulder. "She thinks it's important to be respectful."

"That is wonderful, Nicole." Aditi beamed brightly. She turned to Kyle and beckoned with her fingers. "Kyle, come on back to my office," she said, already marching back down the hall.

"Sure." Kyle looked at Maeve. "Can she wait here?"

"Of course."

"Thanks." He leaned down to whisper to Nicole. "You stay here with Maeve, honey." He smiled. "Okay?"

Nicole nodded, and Kyle walked off.

Maeve turned to Nicole. "How are you, Nicole?"

"I'm good, and yourself?"

"Fantastic."

Nicole was studying her. "I like your outfit."

"Thank you." Maeve looked down at herself. She was wearing a form-fitting teal pencil skirt, a tight turquoise plaid sweater vest, and soft white silk blouse. She had finished the look with tall beige patent leather heels. The look was curvy, flirty, and fabulous, with an undeniable stylishly professional edge. "I was feeling like some color today."

Nicole was digging in her purse. Her fingers emerged holding a little square of paper.

"Here," she said, holding it out to Maeve. "You can have this."

Maeve took it from her fingers and looked at it. It was a sticker with the picture of a mermaid swimming in the sea.

"Thank you," she said. "What is this for?"

"It matches your outfit."

Maeve nodded, regarding her seriously. "So it does." She pulled the sticker from the paper and stuck it to her sweater. "How's that?"

"Great."

Maeve was studying her. "I like your purse," she said. "I used to have one just like it."

"It was my mom's," said Nicole, looking at it. She patted it affectionately, then looked up at Maeve. "My mom still lives in New York. She really wants to see me, but she's doing very, *very* important work."

Maeve smiled at her. Nicole walked slowly around the room, taking it all in. "Is this Senator Patel's only office?"

"No, she has a few offices, and one in Richmond."

"Do you only work in this one?"

"I largely work from this office, though I've been known to travel on occasion."

Nicole looked at her curiously. "How did you decide to work in politics?"

"It was a natural path for me. My father, as you may know, was once a state senator, in the very seat Senator Patel has now. Politics is my lifeblood, my air. I always knew I'd do something in this field."

"Why haven't you run for office?"

"I prefer to run the show from behind the curtain."

"But you ran against my dad."

"The follies of youth."

Nicole watched her thoughtfully. "My dad likes to fight for clean water," she continued. "What do you like to fight for, Maeve?"

Maeve shrugged. "For everything, I guess. Women's rights. Civil rights. Compassion, respect, human dignity."

"What did you fight for when you ran against my dad?"

"I fought for equality for girls. I thought girls weren't treated fairly."

"Why?"

Maeve paused a beat. "Girls' needs weren't taken as seriously."

"When I'm president, everyone's needs will be taken seriously."

"You have my vote, Madam President."

Nicole brought her fingers to a photo on the wall of Aditi being sworn into the General Assembly.

"Senator Patel is pretty," she said.

Maeve smiled. "Yes, she is."

"When I'm president, I want to help girls, too."

"That's wonderful."

Nicole faced her. "Why were girls' needs not taken seriously in your school?"

Maeve thought carefully about how to respond. "Women's rights have been suppressed throughout history," she said. "And though we've made a lot of progress, unfortunately, people have gotten used to women being submissive."

"But the Nineteenth Amendment gave us the right to vote."

"That's true." Maeve couldn't help but smile at the little girl's innocence. "But why do you think they needed to make it an Amendment?"

Nicole hesitated. "Because if it wasn't the law, they wouldn't give it to us."

"Correct."

The little girl's face was serious. "But why aren't we equal today?"

"Well," said Maeve, shifting her weight, "opinions don't change overnight, especially opinions that give people more power."

Nicole was nodding and rubbing her lips together thoughtfully.

Maeve watched her astutely. She lowered her voice. "Is there something on your mind, Nicole?"

Nicole's expression sharpened. She met Maeve's eyes, boldly, but her feet shifted, as if she were nervous.

"Do you remember what my dad said?" she said. "At the café that time. I mean about always disagreeing respectfully."

"Yes." A little flutter of alarm occurred in Maeve's chest;

somehow she sensed she was entering an uncomfortable situation. "I remember."

"So yesterday in STEM class, I tried to join some boys who were building a robot. I like robots. My dad got me a kit once, and we even built one. Have you ever seen those kits? They're really fun."

"Yes." Maeve smiled in spite of herself. "That's very nice, that you built a robot with your dad."

"Well, I wanted to help the boys, because I have experience, you know? I even asked nicely. And they said no."

Maeve crossed her arms and looked at Nicole seriously. "They said no? Why did they do that?"

"They said girls aren't as good at science."

Maeve's face turned to stone. This went right to the core of her being. Her heart ached for Nicole, who was realizing something for the first time, something she herself had realized too early, along with every other woman she knew. She wanted to tell Nicole this was exactly what she had been talking about when she'd disagreed with Kyle that day—but Nicole wasn't her child, and it just wasn't her place.

"And what did you say?" she asked, consciously controlling herself.

"I did what my dad said. I was respectful. I asked again nicely. I even told them I'd built my own robot. I thought I'd use reason. You know?"

"Mmm." Maeve rubbed her lips together, waiting to see where this was going. "And then what happened?"

"They laughed."

Maeve turned her head to the side, out of Nicole's view. Nicole's words had prompted a visceral reaction in her. Images emerged from the back recesses of her mind—visions of hulking shadows, echoes of laughter. They were images she'd locked away, denying their very existence. It had been a while since they'd made it past her defenses; she'd worked hard at keeping them hidden. Her face contorted with disgust and fury; she rubbed her temple to hide it.

"How horrible," she muttered, taking a deep breath and meeting the girl's gaze once more. "What did you do next?"

"I walked away."

Maeve nodded, thinking carefully about what to say next. "Nicole," she began, and stopped; it was essential she find the balance here, to convey her sympathy without crossing the line into inappropriate. She herself would have told them off, and it probably would have involved a slew of profanities, but obviously she couldn't say that to Nicole. Besides, the boys involved were just kids, kids who clearly hadn't been taught very well. "I don't blame you for walking away." She smiled sadly. "It's hard to be rejected like that, just because you're a girl."

"Is that what you meant? When you said girls' needs aren't taken seriously?"

"That's part of it." She relaxed her stance, talking more intimately now. "You know, next time, you can tell the teacher what happened. They can make sure the boys include you."

"I didn't want to." Nicole shook her head in defiance. "I don't want to work with people who don't want to work with me. You know?"

Yes, Maeve knew. She knew all too well. "Well, you know what they say," she told her, trying to lighten the mood. "The best revenge is living well. You'll just have to build your own robot, and it'll be bigger and better than theirs, and then they'll see."

"Why do people think girls can't do things?"

"Nicole," said Maeve, not trusting herself to answer, "don't you want to talk about this with your dad?"

"Do you not know the answer?"

"Oh, I know the answer." Maeve stifled a grin. "It's just, I'm sure he'd be happy to help you."

"I know he would." Nicole flushed. "I...I wanted to talk about it with you."

Maeve nodded solemnly. "I understand."

"So why do they?"

"Well..." Maeve rubbed her lips together, thinking. "I think it's because..." She stopped herself. There was no good way to answer this question, and whatever she said was bound push the limit. "Hey, are you sure you don't want to wait until your dad is back?"

"No. I don't want to talk about this with him. *Please*."

"Okay." She took a deep breath. "I think it's because they know girls actually *are* good at those things, and that if they were allowed to do them, they might even be better."

"Why is that bad?"

"Well, it isn't. But men in charge might see it as bad, because then, they'd have less power."

"Why do they have so much power to begin with?"

"Because they made all the laws and built the entire system."

"Why are girls mean to other girls?"

Maeve was taken aback, then alarmed. "Was someone mean to you, Nicole? What did they say?"

"No, not to me." Nicole smiled, momentarily, in reassurance; it was a mature, perceptive, sensitive reaction, and Maeve's heart warmed. "There's another girl, though. Some girls are mean to her. But she seems nice."

"What do they do?"

"They just say mean things to her." Nicole thought about it. "She's really pretty. Like, *really, really* pretty. A lot of the boys like her." She furrowed her brow. "Do you think that's why?"

"Yes." Maeve was surprised by the force of anger roiling in her blood. *Skank*, said a shadow in her head. "Yes, I suspect it is."

"I get why *boys* do it, but why do *girls?* I just want to know why."

"Society teaches us to turn on each other," said Maeve, glancing toward the hallway where Kyle and Aditi had disappeared; it was the truth, and Nicole clearly was desperate for female guidance, but she was now genuinely worried about saying too much to someone else's daughter. "Unfortunately, girls are not immune to misogyny."

"What's misogyny?"

"You know what," said Maeve, patting Nicole on the shoulder, "I am *so* glad you talked to me about this, and I really, *really* want to answer all of your questions. It's kind of busy here in the office, though. How about for now, I show you what I do here all day, and we can continue this conversation another time?"

"Okay."

"You know you can come to me with anything. Right?"

Nicole nodded. "Right."

Maeve gentled her voice. "What did you do when they were teasing the other girl?"

"I told them to stop it."

Maeve smiled warmly. "What did they say?"

"They didn't say anything. They just rolled their eyes at me." Nicole met her gaze directly; fire shone in her eyes. "They stopped, though."

"Good girl." Maeve took a chance and pulled Nicole close, embracing her and rubbing her back. "I'm proud of you for doing that. More people should be like you."

Maeve offered to show Nicole around the office, and she introduced her to Aditi's staff. After, Nicole sat at a table in the waiting room while Maeve got back to work. Nicole opened her notebook and pulled some markers out of her purse. Maeve was surprised when she drew pictures not of debates or rallies but of rainbows and flowers. She found it unexpectedly heartwarming. She watched her for a minute before turning to her laptop. It couldn't have been easy for Nicole, new in town and not really fitting in. She'd have to talk to Kyle about it later.

After a time, Aditi and Kyle emerged. Aditi, with her typical haste and eagerness, approached briskly and squeezed Maeve's arm.

"Maeve," she said, "Kyle and I were just on the phone with George Collier. He says he can meet with us *tonight*."

"That's wonderful!" George Collier was a leader of a local grassroots advocacy group. He had a particular knack for getting important people to open up to him. He'd recently met with a handful of public health officials and representatives from water industry associations, who rumor had it had been surprisingly candid about the goings on at Virginia ClearStream. Aditi had been trying to get ahold of him for weeks.

"I'm going to have Tyler make a dinner reservation at French's. Kyle will join us to help collect info."

"Fantastic."

"Kyle, I'll update you ASAP with a time. Thanks a billion!"

Maeve walked Kyle and Nicole to the door.

"Good seeing you, Nicole. Langahan, it's been interesting, as always."

Kyle sighed, a little tiredly. "Maybe one day we can have a conversation without the snark."

"Don't push it."

Kyle and Nicole walked out. Maeve took a deep breath and got back to work.

"MAEVE?" Aditi's voice sang over the speaker in Maeve's car. "Maeve, I need you to do something for me."

"Sure, what is it?"

"I need you to go with Kyle to meet George at French's."

Maeve's stomach sank to the floor of the car. "Me? Go with Kyle?"

"Is that a problem?"

"No," Maeve said quickly, getting herself under control. "No, sorry, it's fine."

"I'm sorry to do this to you with such short notice. I have to go to Richmond for a last-minute Education Committee meeting. I would never ask you otherwise."

"I know, Aditi. I'm happy to help."

"Hey, at least it's French's!"

"Mmm." French's was one of the finest restaurants in town and was known for its atmosphere, elegance, and gourmet cuisine. "What time?"

"Kyle and George are meeting you there at seven. Maeve, thank you so much for doing this. You're the only one I trust to take my place. I really appreciate it."

"I'll do anything for you, Aditi. I'm glad you know you can ask."

"I'll send you my notes."

They hung up the phone. Maeve stared forward at the road.

"Shit," she sighed, and pulled onto her street.

AS SOMEONE who had been to many political and networking events, Maeve had a wide variety of outfits to choose from. For tonight at French's, she chose a little black dress with a sweetheart neckline, and long drop earrings accentuated by her short dark bob. She arrived promptly at seven and stepped out of the car for the valet, then swayed into the restaurant to subtle peeks and turned heads.

She had just given the host her name when she sensed eyes on her. She turned to find Kyle standing there staring at her.

"Langahan," she said, nodding in greeting. When he didn't say anything, she raised her eyebrows in annoyance. "What?"

He blinked. "Nothing." He began to step forward.

"You were expecting Aditi?"

"No, Aditi called me."

"She was disappointed not to make it. I'm sorry you're stuck with me instead."

"It's fine. I'll survive."

Maeve resisted the urge to roll her eyes. *Maybe you won't*, she was going to say, but the host waved them forward before she could respond.

They were led to a table for four and sat across from each other, waiting for George.

"You clean up nice, Langahan," Maeve conceded as they settled. She looked him over. He was wearing a charcoal gray suit, white shirt, and stylish blue striped tie. The loose curls of his hair had been gently swept back. He could be rather dashing, when he wanted to be. She reached for the cocktail menu. "I see you kept the whiskers. It suits you."

Kyle instinctively rubbed his lightly bearded cheeks between his fingers. "Thank you."

"I almost didn't recognize you the first time I saw you," she went on, perusing the menu. Immediately settling on a rosemary gin and tonic, she handed the menu to him. "You know, at the town hall."

Kyle grimaced, holding up his hand. "I don't drink."

She pulled it back. "Fair enough."

A server arrived, and she delivered her drink order. Kyle ordered an iced tea. They sat for a few moments in awkward silence.

"I almost didn't recognize you, either," said Kyle, his eyes on his menu. "You used to have long hair."

"Yes." The back of her head tingled as an image of her hair being pulled by a football player in "the box" instantly flashed in her mind. Of their own accord, her eyes turned hard. Why had she been letting these images free of their shackles? She'd been thinking too much about high school lately; it was probably his fault. Yet another strike against him. *Get yourself under control already*. She looked over her menu. "I cut it right after graduation."

"How come?"

She raised an eyebrow at him. "Does it matter?"

"No, it doesn't," he said, stiffly. "I'm just trying to make conversation."

The server returned with their drinks. Maeve took hers in her fingers and downed a large sip.

"What's keeping George," she muttered, checking the time on her phone.

Neither said anything. A text came through for Kyle. He answered it, put his phone back in his pocket, and sighed.

They each fiddled with their phones for a while. Maeve finished her drink and ordered another. Kyle stared at her as she did so.

"Is there a problem, Langahan?" she challenged.

"Can I ask you a question?"

"Depends on what it is."

"Why do you drink so much?"

Maeve glared at him. "Why is that any of your business?"

"It's not. I'm just asking. You don't have to answer."

"I'll make a deal with you, Langahan." She thanked the server who delivered her drink, then took it in her hands and sipped it. "I'll answer your question if you answer mine."

"What is it?"

"Is it a deal?"

He sneered. "Fine."

Maeve leaned back in her seat with her drink. "I live a busy life. I work hard. Everyone has a vice, and this is mine."

"It helps you to relax?"

"Yes, and to gather strength."

"But the logistics of it, the car situation..." He paused thoughtfully. "It doesn't become tedious?"

"I feel like this is moving into judgment territory, and I'm not a big fan of that."

"I'm not judging, Maeve, nor does my opinion mean anything. As I said, I'm just asking."

"And I gave you my answer. Are you ready for your question?"

"No, but go ahead."

"What happened to Nicole's mother?"

Kyle stiffened. "Nothing, really. It just didn't work out."

"Why not?"

He looked at her for a minute, took a breath, and relaxed. "Melissa's always been an activist. Even more so than I am. I admired her dedication. But she couldn't be around for Nicole because her work was always more important. Motherhood just isn't in her story right now."

Maeve's brow furrowed with thought. She didn't know what she'd been expecting him to say, but that wasn't it. "So what happened?"

"I told her I wanted a steadier life for Nicole, and she didn't object. We broke up, and I brought Nicole here so we could be closer to my parents' farm."

"So does she see Nicole regularly?"

"Not regularly, no. She's only seen her once since we moved here, and she's getting ready to spend a year in Antarctica."

Maeve's brow rose higher. "A year without her daughter? Wow. I can't imagine doing that."

"Yeah, well, that's why we're not together."

A text came through from Aditi: *George is running late. He'll be there in ten.*

Maeve responded: *Okay.*

She turned to Kyle, her face serious. "That must be hard for Nicole, to rarely see her mother."

"It is. Nicole's tough, you know? She tries to act strong, but she misses her mom."

Maeve watched him. "So you're a single dad. How do you do it?"

He shrugged. "You do what you've got to do for your kid. My parents' help has been invaluable."

"Does she see them a lot?"

"They pick her up from school sometimes, or watch her on the weekends. She'll stay the night every so often. I try to be around as much as possible, but sometimes things can't be helped."

"And you took on this work with Wes and Aditi, so now you're juggling that too."

He looked at her. "Yes."

Maeve couldn't help but be a little impressed. "Nicole is fabulous. You appear to be doing a decent job."

"Thank you." He chewed his lip a little and flushed. "It's funny," he said, suddenly and inexplicably awkward. He fiddled with his knife and fork. "She, uh." He scratched his head and chuckled. "She calls you Snow White. She thinks you look like her."

Maeve started, then laughed. "What?"

"Yeah, it's pretty weird."

"It must be my sweet, demure personality."

"I think it has more to do with your hair."

"Well." Maeve fluffed her dark bob, then sipped her drink. "Snow White is very beautiful. So I'll take it as a compliment."

"You should."

Maeve looked up at him, unsure of his meaning. There was no way he was calling her beautiful. She couldn't get a read on him—he was staring downward into his menu, intently, as if the secrets of the universe were written there. She let it go. She must have misunderstood him.

"This is the first time I've ever been compared to a Disney princess," she said, with a little laugh. "Usually I figure more as Cruella De Vil."

He laughed and shook his head. "You're so full of it."

She was taken aback. "What? How?"

"You put up this wall of sarcasm, as if you're some kind of people hater. But you don't hate anyone, including yourself."

"I never said I hated myself. Why would you think I hate myself?"

"I didn't say I thought that. You're the one who just compared yourself to Cruella De Vil."

"I said *other* people see me that way, not that I do."

"It's easier for you to believe that because you can block people out."

The blood rushed to her face. "What the hell are you talking about?"

He was watching her seriously. "The first night we met, I mean the first time I saw you after all those years, you told me you were as close to Wes as you get to people. That was an interesting choice of words. And you keep talking about how shitty people are."

"That's not hatred, Langahan. That's just realism."

"I don't believe it. I call bullshit. I think you're on defense."

"*I'm* on defense? You're the one who refuses to believe there's a single public official with pure intentions, that there's any hope of anything changing. You're the people hater here, not me."

"That's not hatred, Maeve. That's just realism."

"Throwing my own words back at me. Clever."

"Jesus, Maeve." He leaned forward, and his voice became low and harsh. "What is it with you, anyway? You tell me to relax, but you're the one who's so biting all the time. Why don't you take a break from the sarcasm? Just long enough to actually be real?"

"You have got to be kidding me." Maeve closed her eyes a moment, collecting herself. Well, that didn't take long. Where the fuck was George? She looked back at Kyle. "What do you know about me, anyway? Where do you get off? You have no idea who I am or where I'm coming from. You don't get to have any opinions."

"I can have whatever opinions I want to. That's the thing about opinions, is that you don't have to agree."

"We can disagree with opinions now? Funny, because when we're talking about politics, you don't seem to feel that way."

"Now you're moving the goalposts. We weren't talking about politics."

"But it's the same, don't you see? I mean, fine, I'll admit it—I hide behind sarcasm. Okay—? Who doesn't? Life is like politics, Langahan. A little bullshit is necessary."

"I just don't believe that's true."

"Then you aren't going far in politics. Politics is all about manipulating. I wish it weren't true, but it is. You have to know how to maneuver. You have to know how to feign interest."

"Let me tell you something, Maeve. When I was working at Lakes Conservation, we wanted the water company to implement smart meters. We knew it would encourage water-saving behavior and minimize water loss, to say nothing of how it would improve transparency. We made this happen, because we gathered evidence and forced them to change. We didn't do it by kissing anyone's ass. We did it by refusing to give in."

"You see? It works. I actually didn't care about a word you just said."

"I'll let that go because I know you're joking."

"How do you know that?"

"Because it's your defense mechanism."

Maeve was beginning to wonder if he actually had a point. She downed the rest of her drink to avoid having to think about it.

"I think it's safe to say that George isn't coming," said Kyle, as a server approached to take Maeve's next drink order. Normally she'd cut it off at two, but without George, it was no longer a business dinner, and she'd need another to get through a night out with Kyle. She didn't know what Kyle thought of her ordering another drink because she adamantly refused to look at him.

"At least we agree on something." She was beginning to have to think too hard for her words; she'd forgotten she'd skipped lunch. "Maybe we should order some food."

They looked over their menus in silence, which seemed to act as a buffer between them. By the time they delivered their orders, they'd calmed somewhat.

"How do you like working for Aditi?" he asked, his voice strained like he was forcing himself to make conversation.

"I adore Aditi." Maeve was feeling pleasant now, the third cocktail having begun to bestow the intended effect. "She's so smart and passionate, an inspiration. Just what we need right now. She's getting ready to introduce a bill to make it easier for sexual assault victims to come forward. It's long overdue, so it's good she's getting it done."

"Yes." Kyle paused a moment as the server replaced his iced tea. "I read you actually had a lot to do with the construction of that bill."

"I did."

"That's great. Good for you."

"Thank you."

"You deserve it."

Maeve was taken aback. "Thanks, Langahan." She grinned. "See, sometimes things do get done."

"I've noticed."

Maeve sipped on her drink. "This issue is important to me. It's always been." She didn't say anything for a few moments, deciding how much to reveal. She settled on half the truth. "But it became even more so after my sister was sexually assaulted five years ago."

He was noticeably rattled; his face turned warm and serious. "Wow, I'm so sorry." He stared at her. "Wait, I read about this. That's when Wes was shot. I just didn't realize at the time that it was your sister."

"Yes. She wasn't raped, thank God, but she could have been." The words were on the tip of her tongue; she blinked as images of the box, and of dark, lurking figures, made her heart beat faster and her stomach lurch. She took her drink in her fingers and gulped it. "Anyway, it's traumatic just the same. You see things differently after, you know? I should be in therapy."

"You should?"

"I mean, she's still in therapy." She opened her eyes wide to get her mind back straight; maybe she should lay off her cocktail for a bit. "But I probably should be, too." She laughed, as if it were a joke, but it wasn't convincing even to herself.

Kyle wasn't laughing. "I'm sorry that happened to your sister. I fully support that bill; any decent person should."

"Yeah, well this is why it's good when women are in office. These issues are prioritized in ways they aren't when men in are in power."

"If I'd won, I would have pushed for it. I'd do everything in my power to make sure women are heard."

"Where was this attitude in high school?" She leaned back in her seat, crossed her legs, and sipped her drink. "I could have used your voice when Mr. Heller was silencing me."

"Times change. I know better now. I was a stupid kid back then."

"Then you're a stupid kid now, to use your own words. You're still telling people their issues are less important."

He was silent for some time. "Point taken," he said finally, rearranging his napkin on his lap.

"What did you say?"

"I said point taken. You're right. I'm sorry."

She watched him for a moment, then inhaled and relaxed. "Much appreciated, Langahan." She sipped her drink. "Thank you."

The server returned with their dinners. Maeve had ordered salmon; Kyle had ordered ratatouille. Maeve took one bite of her meal, and her eyes drifted shut. It was her favorite, sweet and savory, with a miso ginger glaze. She savored it in her mouth a few moments, swallowed, and dug quickly in for seconds.

"You should try this," she told Kyle. "It's absolutely fucking fabulous."

"No, thank you," he said, spearing a vegetable with his fork. "I don't eat fish."

"Are you a vegetarian?"

"No, I'm not, though I don't eat that much meat. I just don't eat any fish."

"Why not?"

"Because I know what's in the water."

This made her pause a moment and eye her dinner suspiciously. She swallowed again and took another drink, putting it out of her mind.

"Have you been here before?" he asked.

"Yes, but not for five or six years. I was on a date, believe it or not. The date was godawful, but the filet mignon was marvelous."

"Why was the date bad?"

"Let me put it this way. We were discussing minimum wage reform, and he insisted Senator Wright was in favor of regional variations. When I disagreed with him, he directed me to read the senator's speech at UVA—and I'd written the damn speech. I should mention I was working for Senator Wright at the time."

Kyle sniffed wryly. "I take it you didn't see him again."

"That is correct. I only saw him the first time because a colleague had set us up. That was the last time I let anyone tell me what to do with my private life, and the last time I had a date."

He looked mildly surprised. "You haven't been with anyone in five or six years?"

"I said I didn't date, not that I hadn't been with anyone. I don't do relationships, but that doesn't mean I'm celibate."

"Oh." Kyle started, and his face turned crimson. "Sorry. I misunderstood."

"You don't have to be embarrassed. We're both adults."

"I'm not embarrassed."

"You're as red as a tomato."

"Well, now I am, because you keep talking about it."

He was trying to act normal by cutting into his food, but he was doing a lousy job. Maeve slowly grinned at his discomfort. She looked at him with interest.

"Are you bashful, Langahan? Who would've thought."

"For God's sake, Maeve." He laid his fork on his plate in a huff, looked to the side in an annoyed moment, then resumed eating his dinner. "I don't know why you have to push my buttons on purpose."

"Because you make it so easy! When you talk about pushing your buttons, what do you expect me to do?"

"I don't know, to act like an adult? To not make childish jokes?"

"Acknowledging the existence of sex *is* being an adult, Langahan. What's the matter, you don't like sex?"

Maeve thought he was going to explode. His face beet red, he looked downward at his plate, shoving food into his mouth and shaking his head, ignoring her.

"Am I making you uncomfortable?"

"No," he muttered thought a mouthful of food. "I'm just done, Maeve. I'm done."

"I just don't see what the big deal is. You have a daughter, so I know you've done it at least once. Why does this make you so squeamish?"

"I'm not."

"Well," said Maeve, sliding her fork into an asparagus spear, "if you don't want to talk about it, we don't have to talk about it. I'm just surprised you don't have an opinion, is all, since you have one about everything else. I expected more, to be honest."

"You want an opinion? Fine. Here's my opinion." He rested his wrist on the table and glared at her. "If I had to choose between having sex and *not* having sex," he ground out, "I suppose I would have sex." Fire shot out of his eyes. "Are you satisfied?"

Maeve grinned widely. "Not even remotely, though that was very well done."

"You go out of your way to ruffle my feathers."

"You could use your feathers ruffled." Done with her salmon, she leaned back in her seat with her cocktail. "I'm sorry. I'm just trying to lighten the mood."

"I don't think it's working."

"It's okay to have a soft spot, Langahan."

"This conversation is over."

A couple of minutes passed. Kyle finished eating; Maeve looked around the restaurant. It was a fancy, elegant place with a warm golden ambiance and intimate tables. It was a shame to be here with Langahan, though she didn't know who else she'd ever be here with. This wasn't Rhys's kind of place. She started when she thought about Rhys. She hadn't thought about him all night.

Thinking of Rhys made her think of the day she'd seen him after having lunch with Kyle and Nicole. She looked at Kyle curiously. She guessed now was as good a time as any to let him know Nicole had confided in her earlier that day.

"Hey, I have a question for you," she said. "That day in the café, when I had lunch with you and Nicole. You told Nicole we always have to disagree respectfully." She watched him. "I know you can't really believe that."

"Of course I do. I know you really can't not."

"But what if someone is disrespecting her first? What if she's defending someone else?"

"She's a child, Maeve." He brought his napkin to his lips, then folded it and placed it on the table. He looked at her. "I have to tell her to be respectful. What else should I do?"

"If you tell her to always be respectful, she'll think she should let guys walk all over her."

"You know that's not what I mean."

"It's a fine line." She downed the last of her drink, committed to not ordering another. She drank some water. "I'm not saying not to be nice, but I think it's a dangerous lesson. It can be confusing. It can make people walk away, when they should feel free to stand up for themselves." She placed her glass on the table, the words, *Speaking of which,* on her lips.

Then he said,

"Maybe it's harder to understand if you don't have kids."

Maeve looked at him. "I don't have to have kids to understand this. Besides, I have two nieces, nieces I dearly love."

"It's not the same."

"How do you know?"

"Because there is nothing like having a child, Maeve. Literally *nothing.*"

Maeve didn't like being devalued for being childless; it was something she dealt with far too often. "Are you saying I'm less qualified to have an opinion on matters of common decency, just because I don't have children? Don't be that guy. Maybe I can't relate to having a child, but I can relate to being a woman and a girl, and as a woman who has memories of men taking advantage of her, I feel confident in telling you that you need to teach that girl to stand up for herself, even when she isn't being 'nice.'"

"Men took advantage of you?"

"Men have taken advantage of every woman you know, Langahan. Wake up. Every single woman in your life has had experiences like mine."

"What do you mean? What happened?"

"I shouldn't have to reveal my personal history for you to believe me."

He seemed chastened; he paused a few moments, visibly calming. "You're right." His face turned serious again. "I'm not saying I don't believe you—that's putting words in my mouth. What I'm saying is that it's hard to judge a situation if you're not part of it. And I have to be very careful."

"Women always have to be careful, Langahan. That's the whole point."

"Let me teach her the rules. Then she can learn the exceptions."

Maeve was getting tired. What a waste of an evening. *Thanks, George.* "Forget it." He'd annoyed her now, as always, and she couldn't think properly. She'd tell him about Nicole another time. "It's fine. Agree to disagree."

They decided against dessert and asked for the check instead. Maeve could have used a cup of coffee but was ready to go home. She got up to visit the restroom, then flounced back to her seat. As she sat down, Kyle looked at her frankly.

"You obviously aren't driving home tonight. I'll drive you."

"No, I'm fine. I'll order a car."

"That's ridiculous. I'm right here."

"I don't need your help."

He stared at her, then rose. "Fine."

She followed him out the door, weaving around people as she ordered a car from her phone.

"Are you parked in valet parking?"

She lifted her face from her phone and looked at him. Usually, when she knew she'd be drinking, she parked somewhere discreet where she could leave her car overnight, or she just got a rideshare in the first place. However, she had thought this was going to be a business meeting, and she hadn't planned in advance.

"Yes, I am," she said. "Shit."

"Give me your ticket. I'll park your car on the street."

Reluctantly, she dug in her purse and handed him her ticket. He took it to the valet, then climbed in her car and parked. By the time he returned, her ride had arrived. They faced each other. She guessed she had to thank him.

"Well, this is embarrassing," she said. "I don't like to leave an argument in someone's debt."

"I don't care, Maeve. It makes no difference."

They both sighed.

"Fucking George," she said.

He snorted. "Fucking George. Yeah."

For a moment, she considered dismissing the car and letting him drive her home; it might smooth things over, but then again, it might make things worse. No, no; better to leave him here now, to chalk this up to a lousy evening and forget it, and to start over in the morning.

"Thanks for your help," she said. "Sincerely."

"You're welcome."

"I guess I'll see you soon."

"Right."

Awkwardly, she smiled, then walked by him toward the car. She looked back at him as she climbed in, and watched as the driver pulled away. He waited for her to leave, then meandered toward the valet to retrieve his own ride home.

MAEVE WAS AT WORK. She had a massive hangover. She didn't know why; she usually staved them off. This morning, though, she was living a nightmare: a freight train was running through her head, and all sound made her brain explode in pain. But worse than the pain of the hangover was the pain of feeling irresponsible. She had never had a hangover at work—never. Work was her life, her reason for being; it was the one thing that never failed to make her feel good about herself. Overindulging was one thing; overindulgence that affected her work was inexcusable.

She was sitting at her desk, squinting at her laptop and praying for some force to save her, when Aditi knocked at her open door.

Maeve waved her in, not wanting to speak.

"Are you okay?" Aditi asked as she strolled in and took a seat.

Maeve nodded, holding her head. "I don't feel so great today."

"Well, you should go home."

"No." There was no way she was giving in to this. She'd done this to herself, and she would suffer through it.

"Are you sure? You look awful."

"I'll be fine, Aditi. Thank you." She forced herself to look up and smile. "What's up?"

"I'm so pissed that George didn't show. He said he was held up at a meeting, but to not show up is so inconsiderate. I'm sorry you stood in for me for nothing."

"It was fine."

"Kyle didn't mind?"

Maeve grimaced at the thought of Kyle. That was the other thing giving her pain this morning, the way she had talked to Kyle last night. Not that he didn't deserve it, but she'd let her emotions get the best of her, and she hated that. She had the vague sense of owing him an apology, and she didn't like having that on her shoulders. In addition, though she hated to admit it, she'd begun to see a not unlikeable side to him—he'd gone out of his way to help her last night, without judgment, and he really was a good dad. That was bad enough. But the real problem was, when he was absolutely insufferable, she didn't concern herself with his opinion—now that he wasn't, it mattered more. She didn't like that she'd embarrassed herself in front of him, and she was furious with herself for caring. But most importantly, her behavior had been unprofessional and childish, and it reflected poorly on Aditi. Maeve knew better than that, and she was mortified.

"No, I don't think he did," she said, pretending to look at something on her laptop; she was unable to meet her boss's eyes.

Aditi was watching her. "Are you sure you're okay?"

Maeve breathed deeply. "I'm really fine, Aditi, but I appreciate your concern."

"Well, in that case, I want to talk something over with you."

Maeve looked at her, trying to hide her fear—did Aditi know Maeve had gotten trashed last night? Was it all more obvious than she'd thought? Oh God, please don't let this be an intervention, or even a scolding of some kind—Maeve didn't think she could take it. Feedback over her work was one thing, but a dressing down over a personal failure was more than she could bear.

Aditi looked at her seriously. "I know it isn't really in your wheelhouse and not really your job," she said, "but I'd like for you to take over work on this water bill with Kyle."

Maeve said nothing, staring at her. Relief the knowledge that her secret was secure fought with dread over the thought of seeing Kyle regularly. "That's fine," she said to Aditi, attempting a jovial tone, "though I thought he had a regular thing with Wes."

"Wes thinks he's gotten what he needs. Kyle's going to help us with the state bill now."

"Wouldn't Marcus be a better choice for this? I mean, he's your policy advisor."

"Marcus's time here is limited," said Aditi. "He's moving to Florida to be closer to family. I'm going to need another policy advisor." She waited in heavy silence as Maeve absorbed this information. "I know it's something you've wanted to do. I thought we'd ease you into it."

Maeve finally met Aditi's gaze, momentarily forgetting her embarrassment. She'd thought she was going to be scolded; instead, she was being offered a tentative promotion. She couldn't bring herself to smile, but her expression softened.

"I know you love your current role," said Aditi. "Think it over."

"I will. Thank you so much."

Aditi said nothing for a moment or two. "What's going on, Maeve?" she asked, not unkindly. "You don't seem yourself today. Are you sure you don't need a day off?"

Maeve stared at her, overcome by an anxious feeling she couldn't explain. She didn't want to work with Kyle, but that wasn't the issue. The issue was that somehow, the reason *why* wasn't totally clear. Somehow it seemed less to do with him, and more to do with her. It should be so simple. It made absolutely no sense. She rubbed her temples and closed her eyes; she had the sense that she was unraveling, but she didn't know why that was happening, either.

"You know," she said, pushing back from her desk, her voice surprisingly weak in her ears, "I'm not feeling myself." What on Earth was going on—was she on the verge of tears? "If you really don't mind, I think I might take you up on that day off."

"Of course." Aditi stood as Maeve rose from her desk. "Just go home and get well."

"I'm sorry, Aditi. I don't know what's the matter with me today."

Aditi rested her hand on Maeve's and looked at her confidentially.

"Maeve," she said. "You don't have to apologize for taking a sick day. You run this entire operation, and you're invaluable to me. You're also human, so be human." She raised her eyebrows. "Okay?"

"Okay. Thanks."

Maeve shut her laptop and shoved it in her bag, picked up her purse and her jacket, and went home.

"I PROBABLY SHOULDN'T," said Maeve, "but I will anyway."

It was early August, and Maeve was at Wes and Catherine's house. Her parents and Wes's parents were there, too, as were Grady and his family—in short, the whole gang. She had said these words to Catherine as she poured herself a second glass of wine. Maeve knew she would be there for a while and therefore, she could have another if she wanted. She just wouldn't have a third.

"It's a good thing Langahan's not here," she said, taking the first sip. She and Catherine meandered to a couple of chairs on the expansive stone patio. "He would give me the third degree."

"How are things going with Kyle?" asked Catherine, who was currently stroking Amy's hair. The patio looked out onto the perfectly green and manicured backyard. It was surrounded by woods, and the scene was idyllic. The weather was cool, and Maeve was trying to avoid everyone except her sister. As family events go, she supposed it could have been worse.

"Kyle is Kyle," said Maeve. Time had dulled her embarrassment; it had made it easier to return to objecting to him, which was good, because objecting to him was easier. "He's stubborn and impossible. He can't concede or compromise. He thinks he knows everything. We just can't seem to stop arguing."

"That's too bad." Catherine looked at her, her face turned downward in sympathy. "How often do you see him?"

"A couple of times a week."

"Maybe it will get better."

Maeve sipped her wine. "Ever the optimist, Cat."

Olivia joined them. She and Amy began playing a hand-clapping game, giggling and carrying on. Maeve smiled at them, then gazed out onto the lawn.

"Mommy," said Amy. "Ask Aunt Maeve about the thing."

"Oh, that's right." Catherine pulled Amy's hair back into a ponytail and tied it with a ribbon. "Maeve, I wanted to get your advice. I'm planning Amy's school field trip this year, and I can't decide where to go. It's between the botanical garden and Yates State Park. What do you think?"

"The state park, definitely," said Maeve. "Let the kids run free."

Maeve and Catherine watched Amy and Olivia playing. It was a charmingly sunny day, and the girls' hair shone like silk.

"The problem is that we're too different," Maeve said, her thoughts returning to Kyle. She sipped more of her wine. "We repel each other, like opposite poles of a magnet."

"No," said Catherine, distractedly; Amy and Olivia's clapping game had grown excited, and Catherine was trying to avoid being smacked. "It's the same poles that repel each other, not opposite. You repel each other because you're the same."

Maeve turned her head toward her. "No, it's opposites."

"It's the same."

"Are you sure?"

"I'm positive. No pun intended."

Maeve grinned snidely. "Well, that would make sense. You're positive, I'm negative."

"You're not negative, Maeve. You pretend you are."

Maeve looked at her again. "What did you say?"

"I said you pretend you're negative."

Maeve grew cross. "Kyle said almost the same thing."

"Maybe Kyle's right."

Maeve stood from her chair in preparation to walk away. Catherine tugged on the leg of her slacks.

"Don't go," she said. "I'm sorry."

Maeve looked at her sister's face, so pretty and pitiful in her remorse. She was always sorry, even when she hadn't done anything wrong. Maeve couldn't resist her. She sat back down.

A few moments passed in which neither said anything, both listening to the lively sounds of the party.

"If you're opposite poles," said Catherine finally, "that means you attract each other, not repel."

"Well, that's ridiculous."

"I don't think it's so ridiculous."

Maeve looked at her skeptically. "Are you kidding me?"

"No." Catherine looked at her innocently, as if what she'd said were perfectly normal. "Maybe you're attracted to each other. Maybe it's true."

"Who's on their second glass of wine, me or you?"

"You don't think so?"

"No. I definitely don't think so."

"He's very attractive, Maeve, and decent and also smart. Not to mention, you believe in the same things."

"We sure have different ways of getting there."

"But that's fun."

Maeve stared out into the yard, fixated on nothing in particular. What the hell was Catherine talking about? Lately Maeve had been thinking that Catherine seemed to know everything. But maybe Catherine was right to doubt her opinions after all.

"You're wrong," she told her. "You're not just wrong, you're delusional."

"Well, you would know."

Maeve watched as her sister now leaned forward so her daughter could braid her hair. Coming from anyone else, that line would sound sarcastic; however, Maeve knew Catherine well enough to know that Catherine was never sarcastic. If Catherine said Maeve would know better, then Maeve knew better. She settled in her seat, putting it out of her mind.

"We do work well together, though," she conceded. "There's no denying it. Funny how that happens."

"I think it makes sense."

"Of course you do." Maeve grinned, then sighed. "It's moot, anyway," she said, suddenly wishing to confide. "I may be sort of seeing someone. Don't tell anyone."

Catherine turned her head sharply, drawing cries of frustration from Amy. "What?"

"You know Rhys Darney, the journalist?"

"Of course."

"Yeah. I may be seeing him."

Catherine's jaw dropped. She smiled, then, and covered her mouth with disbelief.

"Do you…Do you have a boyfriend, Maeve?"

"No." Maeve wasn't ready for that quite yet; she hadn't even given Rhys an answer, though she'd seen him a handful of times the last few weeks. "I wouldn't call him that. We've been hooking up for years, but he wants to make it exclusive."

"What did you tell him?"

"I told him I'd think about it."

"Don't you want to?"

"I like being alone."

"You like him too, though, I assume."

"Rhys is my friend. He also scratches an itch. He serves a practical purpose, nothing more."

Catherine thought about this, for quite some time. Maeve watched the party, Wes and Sarah and Charles, her parents and Grady and Helen, all mingling like they were having the time of their lives.

Wes caught Catherine's eye; he winked and smiled. Catherine grinned goofily, always flustered under the spell of his affection.

Lois and Fred were talking with Sarah and Charles, laughing and telling jokes, playfully one-upping each other.

Grady and Helen were lying on a blanket in the lush grass, relaxing and chatting intimately.

It was an innocuous enough scene, but too familiar. She was lucky to have isolated Catherine. Usually Maeve skulked around by herself, weaving into conversations when necessary, like a sassy, high-heeled wallflower.

"I hate these family get-togethers," she said.

"I don't think you do."

Maeve sighed internally. "You're part of the group," she said. "That's why you love them."

"So are you, Maeve. You just don't think you are."

"As much I love you, Cat, you can't understand."

Catherine turned to her. "You're wrong." Her sister was glaring at her, her expression a mixture of confusion and hurt. "They're my parents, too. I know what it's like. I wish you knew how many years I felt alone, Maeve. I wish you knew."

Maeve didn't know what to say, and therefore said nothing. The wine was beginning to take effect; she was beginning to blitz out of her cynicism. Maybe she was part of it, and maybe she wasn't. Regardless, she still felt very alone.

"It's sad," she said, "when people feel like they don't belong."

"The world," said Catherine, "is too much with us."

Maeve sighed again, and Catherine reached out her hand. Maeve took it. They sat holding hands for a very long time.

"You should bring Rhys," said Catherine.

Maeve was silent a minute, then sighed once more. *Maybe I will*, she thought. *Maybe I will.*

Amy and Olivia ran off to play, and Maeve and Catherine withdrew their hands. They stood up to mingle with their family. Maeve attempted to enjoy herself. Sometimes she didn't know what, exactly, was stopping her.

CHAPTER SEVEN

oward the end of August Maeve had a lunch meeting downtown. After, she was walking briskly down the bustling street—it was a bright, sunny day, the kind of late August day that holds both the joy of summer and the early promise of fall—when she spotted Wes at a lemonade stand. It was his turn; he was in the process of paying. She slowed and smiled, then changed course to meet him.

"Good afternoon, Congressman," she greeted him as she swayed in his direction. Her voice was particularly upbeat: the cheerfulness of the golden sunshine and the sight of so many people enjoying it had made her feel content, optimistic. "Indulging in a little afternoon treat?"

She was surprised when, at the sound of her voice, not one but two men turned. The first, of course, was Wes—the second, just behind him, was Kyle.

"Oh." She straightened, startled. Recovering, she attempted a smile. "Hello, Langahan."

"Hi, Maeve."

"What a delightful surprise," said Wes, his smile as bright as the sunshine pooling through the trees and onto their skin. He gestured toward Kyle, who was already holding a tall cup of lemonade. "I invited Kyle for lunch because I can't make our usual nighttime meeting. The lemonade was calling to us." His smile warmed. "Care to join us?"

"I don't want to intrude."

"You're not intruding. Here, you take mine."

"Oh." She reached for the cup he handed to her. "Okay. Sure, thanks."

Wes turned back to order another lemonade. Maeve and Kyle faced each other. Like Wes, he was wearing suit slacks, tie, and dress shirt with the sleeves rolled up; each had eschewed his jacket, undoubtedly because of the heat. Once again she was struck by the way he managed to effortlessly encompass both formality and casualness. She supposed that suited him. Backlit by the sun, his loose curls and tall frame nearly in silhouette, he looked strong, but quietly so. That suited him too. She had never noticed that before.

She'd been so busy assessing him, searching for some hint as to how this encounter was going to go, that she hadn't realized he'd been doing the same to her. Suddenly she felt the weight of his gaze on her. She glanced down at herself. Today she was wearing a form-fitting herringbone skirt, in black and white, a white blouse, and thick black belt. She had finished the look with tall red heels and red lipstick. A strand of pearls was around her neck. She had the vague sense of being pleased she'd chosen this outfit today, but she brushed it off before it could materialize.

"How are you?" he asked.

"I'm fantastic," she told him, with a reflexive touch of challenge she hadn't fully intended. "Yourself?"

"Fantastic."

Maeve raised her eyebrows: this was about as much enthusiasm as she'd ever heard from him. "Well then. Why are you fantastic?"

"Why are you?"

She stared at him. "I just am."

"So am I."

There was no confrontation in his voice, or in his face; if anything, his eyes were gentler, as if he was being cheeky, as if he was playing with her. Her brow crinkled in confusion. A memory surfaced:

"Watch where you're going, Langahan."

"You bumped into me."

"Apology accepted."

"Likewise."

She didn't understand what was going on. It was their usual challenging, sarcastic banter, but it was somehow softened today. Glancing about at the happy scene around them, she realized it was hard to keep up fronts on a day like today. Maybe the cheer of the day had gotten to him, too.

Wes turned and stepped to the side, letting in the next person in line. He smiled widely. "Shall we?"

The three of them meandered toward a table to the side, and sat, each relaxing in their chair and soaking in the midday sun.

"So what brings you downtown?" Wes asked Maeve, his foot propped on his knee. He took a long sip of lemonade and placed it on the table, and grinned at her. "Or are you simply playing hooky on this beautiful day?"

"I don't play hooky," said Maeve, shaking her head. "It's one of the few games I don't in fact play."

"Work is your soulmate, eh? I guess I should have figured. I've always known that about you."

A couple of musicians began playing in front of a café. The music only added to the vibrance of the street. Maeve couldn't help but smile. She was glad she had made it outside today.

"You've got something in common with Kyle here, in that," Wes continued. He gestured toward Kyle with the hand holding the lemonade, then took another sip. He puckered his lips at the sweetness, then replaced the cup on the table. "Kyle never plays hooky, either."

"No reason to." Kyle took a sip of his own drink, then looked mindfully at the scene before him. "I can't concentrate when there's work to be done. Also, I enjoy it."

"Lucky for us," said Wes. "You're irreplaceable. I don't know where we'd be without you." He grinned. "I have to admit, I wasn't sure it would work out. In fact I wasn't even sure you'd join us. Maeve here was pretty sure you wouldn't. Isn't that right?"

"Indeed." Maeve had donned her sunglasses and was leaning back in her seat, each hand dropping over the end of an arm of her chair, her lemonade gripped loosely in manicured fingers. "I told Wes not to get his hopes up."

"Don't get too comfortable." Kyle was wearing his own sunglasses and met her comment with equal abruptness; however, the shadow of a smile touched his lips. "I still keep all my protest signs in my garage."

"I believe it." Wes sucked at his straw, pulling up the last of his lemonade. "In any case, we're very grateful." He chuckled. "We know how difficult it was for you to dirty your hands in politics."

"I guess even we civilians have to get our hands dirty in the trenches once in a while."

"And how does it feel?"

Kyle shrugged. "I've been dirtier."

Wes laughed heartily. Maeve listened to this banter in silence from behind her sunglasses. Wes was joking with Kyle, in his usual dry, ironic way, but Kyle appeared to be reciprocating. It was bordering on humor; it was almost as if he were comfortable with Wes, as if he and Wes were friends. She was unsure what to make of it.

"In all seriousness," said Wes. "You've given us a lot to think about. Thank you for trusting us. I know you were wary about the system."

"I was. I am," said Kyle, twirling his straw around the ice in his own cup. "But I see the big picture. It may be slow, but there's clearly genuine effort."

"Did I just hear you compliment the system?"

"I wouldn't go that far."

Wes's smile sobered. "Well, I'll take what I can get."

"Wes!"

They all turned. A man was approaching them, a smile on his face and his hand extended. Clearly recognizing him, Wes stood and greeted him brightly; the two shook hands and exchanged enthusiastic pleasantries.

"It's good to see you, Jerry!" Wes patted the other man on the back and gestured toward the table. "Let me introduce you. Jerry, this is my brilliant sister-in-law Maeve. She works for Aditi Patel. And this here's Kyle Langahan. He's the fellow who's been helping us with the water bill."

"Ah, yes!" Jerry leaned forward and shook their hands; Maeve and Kyle offered the usual polite salutations. "I've heard many good things about you both. Jerry Peterson. Wes and I go way back, but we haven't seen each other in ages."

"It's been too long, for sure. Say, how's Marcia? She had surgery recently, didn't she?"

As Jerry launched into a lengthy discussion of his wife's medical updates, Maeve and Kyle glanced at each other awkwardly.

"So," she began, making light conversation. "You're still meeting with Wes. I thought you were done."

"There were a few details he wanted me to help iron out."

Maeve nodded. She took a sip of her lemonade and stared into the crowd. "And did you?"

"I think so."

She nodded again. She didn't know what else to say. There was plenty to see here—the people, the flowers, the busy shops. She let silence hang in the air for a time, watching.

"I saw your op-ed," he said suddenly, surprising her. "About the sexual assault bill." She turned to him—he, too, was looking into the crowd, observing from behind his sunglasses. He faced her. "It was good."

"I didn't have an op-ed."

She couldn't see his eyes, but something about his mouth changed. Was that a smile? "I mean Aditi's."

"Oh." She looked at the street once more. "If you're guessing I had a hand in Aditi's op-ed, you'd be right."

"Well. As I said, it was good."

She was cautiously appreciative. "Thank you."

"I didn't know about the McNulty case you referenced. Do you think this bill would have led to a different outcome?"

Maeve was caught off guard by his interest, but she gladly explained the background of the case and how it had triggered events that led to the creation of the new bill. Kyle listened attentively, in silence, staring into the crowd, occasionally directing his gaze at her when she was making a particularly important point. He asked her clarifying questions, apologizing for his ignorance; he nodded in understanding and agreement. He did not insert opinion or commentary, and even when she had finished her explanation he remained largely silent. This reticence was a sign that he was thinking and absorbing; Maeve knew him well enough by now to understand this and was not put off by his lack of verbal response.

"It's interesting," she said when she was through, shifting in her seat and placing her now empty lemonade cup on the table. "A while back, I asked Grady for his thoughts on the water bill. He said something about Thoreau, about the bottomlessness of the pond. Of course the pond wasn't bottomless, but people thought it was. It helped them believe in the infinite. It became a kind of symbol." She shrugged. "I've been thinking a lot about that. I think it applies to any important issue. I'm a cynical person. But in the office, I believe in the infinite—I have to, or it would all be futile. Maybe the people knew the pond had a bottom all along.

They let themselves imagine, though, to believe in something. To keep making change."

Kyle was watching her carefully; his seriousness was evident despite his eyes not being visible. When she had finished, he leaned back in his chair and folded his hands, relaxing.

"I know that passage of *Walden*," he said. "I was heavily influenced by Thoreau."

"Really?" She thought about it. "I guess that's no surprise. I read it a million years ago, but I didn't remember a thing."

"I used to read it every few years. I haven't for a while, though. I should pick it up again." He indulged in a deep breath, taking in the rich summer air. "I was always drawn by Thoreau's idea of simplifying. I'm not really a minimalist. But I liked the idea of minimalism of the mind. A kind of mental minimalism, maybe."

"No distractions."

He turned his head to look at her. "Exactly."

"You keep your eyes on the prize, to use your own words. You don't stray from the path."

"In a sense, I guess."

"Let me ask you something, Langahan. Do you really think it's such a good principle to adhere to? Isn't it possible distractions make life interesting? Isn't it possible to do both?"

"Of course it is. And I'm not saying it's finite. I go off path all the time, because of Nicole."

"But Nicole *is* the path. That doesn't count." She looked at him again; his eyes were on the busy street. "You do it all for Nicole. You've said so yourself."

He didn't respond, but Maeve could see his jaw working. He moved in his chair; he was still facing the street, but he was leaning toward her now, and not away.

"Fair enough," he said finally. "Maybe we've got that in common, too."

Her head snapped back in his direction. "What do you mean?"

"I mean no distractions. You do the same thing."

"I most certainly do not."

"I think you do."

"It doesn't matter what you think." But Maeve couldn't help but wonder. Kyle avoided the distractions because his eyes were on the prize; maybe her eyes were on the prize because she was avoiding the distractions. The idea was jarring. It was like the two of them were simultaneously different and the same. It was like she and Catherine were both right.

"I guess it doesn't," said Kyle, his eyes following a group of cyclists whishing by. "In fairness, I probably get a lot of it from my parents."

"Is that so." Maeve's mouth turned crooked as she remembered Gus and Gillian's seriousness and bite. "That makes sense. Your parents are activists; mine's a politician. And look at us."

"Right." Kyle snickered good-naturedly. "Good point."

"I carry around a lot that comes from my parents." She thought of her mother's personal digs and criticisms, particularly about her body. She sighed. "I think it's pretty normal."

"Probably. I hope I can help Nicole be her own person."

"I think you're doing fine."

They watched the bustle of the street for a bit. A light breeze wafted by. Maeve closed her eyes, enjoying the way it sifted through her hair.

"On a somewhat related topic," said Kyle. "I have to tell you. Nicole absolutely adores you. She talks about you all the time. She was going on about you last night."

"Does she?" Maeve's face instantly brightened. She turned to him with a smile. "What does she say?"

"She loves your style and your high-powered job. She likes the way you talk," he added, and Maeve grinned at his expression, like he was amused, but trying to hide it. "Something about your humor appeals to her."

"Really," she said, shifting in her seat, delighted. "Fascinating."

She glanced at him, her lips turned up coyly. "Shall I take her under my wing? Teach her more of my snarky ways?"

"God help me."

With a closed-lipped grin, Maeve reached out and playfully tapped his arm with the back of her hand. He smiled and tapped her back, and they shared a brief, friendly look.

Wes, still in conversation with Jerry, caught glimpse of it and raised his eyebrows, suppressing a grin of his own.

"Well," said Maeve, her eyes on the street once more, "thank you for telling me. I really love Nicole. She's such a fabulous kid. You're doing a great job with her, and frankly, it speaks highly of you."

Kyle was silent for a moment. "Thank you," he said then, quietly. "I really appreciate that."

They chatted comfortably together for a while, on nothing in particular—on the pleasantness of the day, on weekend plans, on current events. They poked and jabbed at each other occasionally, as usual, but something about the loveliness of the day and the coziness of the setting allowed them to let their hair down, in a sense, and talk as real people. He was the same Kyle as always, and it wasn't that she saw him in a new light—it was that the same light looked softer, now, softer than she'd realized. She wondered if something had changed, if maybe he was feeling the serenity of the day, too—or if it had always been like this, and that she simply hadn't seen it. As the minutes passed, she found that she was enjoying herself. She was almost disappointed when she noted Wes and Jerry wrapping up their conversation.

The two men shook hands, and Jerry waved in parting. As he sauntered away, Wes resumed his seat.

"Apologies," he told them, pulling up his chair. "That went on longer than I'd expected, as these things always do."

"No worries," said Kyle.

"It's fine," said Maeve.

"What did I miss? Did the two of you solve all the world's problems?"

"We did indeed," said Maeve. "Expect a report in your inbox Monday."

"Fantastic. I'll look forward to some peace and quiet, even if it puts us out of business."

"I wouldn't worry about that." Maeve gathered her things, preparing to get back to work. "There will always be a need for bureaucrats and lawyers."

"No rest for the wicked."

The three stood and moved from the table. Wes and Maeve exchanged a brief hug, and Wes kissed her cheek. Maeve and Kyle faced each other, in one of those tense moments when one has just embraced someone and must decide in an instant whether to embrace the other, in equitability, or to hold ground, in deference to the less intimate nature of the relationship. It was a fleeting half-second, filled with a thousand thoughts; she jerked forward, almost imperceptibly, in hesitant decision. Evidently noticing, he started in her direction, and the two met clumsily until they were in each other's orbits but not quite touching, each bringing an arm around the other's back, and patting. As she pulled away she could still smell him, and her back still tingled where he'd touched her. Her cheek had brushed against his, quite accidentally, and the feel of his five o'clock shadow still bristled on her skin. Her heart was still recovering from a weird little flip. The entire incident took no more than three seconds, but it left Maeve unnerved; she felt awkward, something she hated, but she also felt confused, and that was even worse.

They stared at each other in silence, the words between them unsaid and unknown.

Wes's chipper voice broke the spell.

"Glad we ran into you, Maeve," he said, smiling kindly. "I'll see you soon."

"Yes." Maeve cleared her throat and collected herself. She was being ridiculous. She returned his smile. "Tell Catherine I'll call her."

She waved and walked away, her chest fluttering and her head full. On a whim, to take her mind off Kyle and ease herself back into reality, she popped into a stationery store to pick out something for Amy. A floral notebook in hand, she approached the register, but turned back—she should probably pick one for Olivia. Kyle infiltrated her mind again, though, when on her way back to the register it occurred to her she should also buy one for Nicole, and she almost went back for a third; it was presumptuous, though, and she refrained. *Too soon,* she told herself, and handed the two notebooks to the cashier.

As she returned to work she let her thoughts drift back to her conversation with Kyle. It had left her off kilter, but she wasn't ready to examine how, or why. Goddamn him, that Langahan. His uncanny ability to always make everything difficult and complicated really was so annoying. The thought calmed her somewhat: it was one more tally in the column against him. Ironically, the thing that had made him more likeable was the very thing that made him more intolerable. She laughed, almost relieved. For a minute there, she'd almost begun questioning her judgment, her perspective, her self.

As the summer began to draw to a close, Maeve grew used to Kyle. She saw him frequently now. Despite his inherent wariness of all politicians, even the best ones, like Aditi, he seemed to have mellowed somewhat by being in their constant presence, like exposure therapy. He now seemed to believe that if he couldn't beat them, he should join them, that like it or not, they were his best bet for getting what he cared about on the table, and that if he wanted to make progress, he needed a seat at that table. Since their chance meeting downtown with Wes, they'd been more cordial; one thin layer of defense had dissolved, it seemed, and they'd managed to preserve this slightly warmer connection.

One Friday, they were working together on an environmental impact report; Kyle was going to testify at a hearing in Richmond, and their work had taken longer than anticipated. Summer was fading into fall, and the days were growing steadily shorter. By early evening, the bright golden sunshine had made way for the more subdued, cool light of dusk. They were alone in the office, in a conference room, sitting among piles of papers, their laptops open in front of them.

"Where do you want to get into the info on the Danish groundwater reserves?" she asked him, finishing off the last of her coffee.

"I was going to tack that onto the discussion of monitoring. Where were those stats, by the way?"

"Hang on a second." Maeve leaned toward the end of the table and flipped through some paperwork. "Here it is. I'll send you the file, too."

Kyle took the papers and, reading, thought for a second. "The Devi study reiterates this. I should have thought of that before."

"Two steps ahead of you."

Maeve turned to her laptop and tapped out a few words, then punched the return button with a click. "It's in your inbox. Have at it."

Kyle was eyeing her studiously. After a moment or two, he directed his gaze to his own laptop, then read for a few minutes, nodding. He looked back up at her. "I don't suppose you also have the—"

"—the analysis of the corresponding Hemmings study? But of course."

She shuffled through some papers, then held out her hand, which now clutched about twenty pages held together with a paperclip. "I can send it to you, but this one has all my notes."

He scanned the report for a bit, then looked up at her, his

expression serious. "This is well done," he said, indicating the report with an upward nod of his chin. "Your notes are dead on."

Maeve looked up at him, surprised. "My notes? That was nothing."

"They aren't nothing. They're very perceptive, and they make good connections. You do good work."

Maeve was silent a moment. "Thanks, Langahan." A somber smile touched her lips. "I appreciate that."

"You really know your stuff. Thanks for your help."

"Thank *you* for your help. I'm good with details, but the structure's all you."

Kyle leaned back in his seat and folded his arms, thoughtful. "As an aside, I haven't heard anything new about Virginia Clear-Stream's role in the coverup. Have you?"

"Grady's been looking into it. I can get an update from Wes."

"It seems to be taking a long time."

"These things take time, Langahan. Grady's on it."

Kyle smiled. "Okay. I know he is."

They were silent for a minute as Maeve read a few emails and Kyle answered a text message. Kyle laughed silently, and Maeve looked up.

"Sorry," he said, clearing his throat and putting his phone back on the table. "That was Nicole. I mean it was Nicole on my mother's phone. The two of them are making cookies, and she sent me a funny picture."

"Let me see."

Kyle picked the phone from the table, pulled up the photo, and held it out for her to see.

"Aw." Maeve smiled. In the picture, taken from the higher standpoint of an adult, Nicole was smiling widely, showing her missing teeth, and holding two heart-shaped cookies in front of her eyes.

Maeve took Kyle's phone from his hand and looked at the

picture more closely. She handed it back. "That couldn't be more adorable."

Kyle took one last look at the picture before replacing the phone on the table.

"How's Nicole doing?" asked Maeve. "I haven't seen her in a while."

"She's doing okay." Kyle was sifting through the papers. He found what he was looking for and pulled it from the pile, then returned his attention to his laptop. "I worry about her sometimes," he mused as he scanned something on the screen. "She's doing well in school, but she has so much trouble talking to other kids. She clams up. It's like she has all this anxiety, you know?"

"That's understandable." Maeve paused for a moment as she finished reading. She looked up at him. "She just moved to a new place, with all new people. She'll adjust. Just give her time."

"I think not seeing Melissa has really had an effect on her."

Maeve's face softened. "I'm sure."

Kyle was staring absentmindedly at his laptop. He leaned back and folded his arms across his chest. "It's hard for me to explain to her why her mom isn't around to see her. It's not that her mom doesn't love her; she just doesn't have room in her life for her. But obviously you can't say that to a kid."

"No." Maeve tossed her papers aside and relaxed in her chair. "So what do you tell her?"

"I tell her Mommy wants to see her but is trying to create a better world for her future."

"Well. I suppose that's not untrue."

Kyle's brow rose and fell, and his mouth contorted briefly into a wry, cynical expression. "In its way, I guess it isn't." His face hardened. "Frankly, I think it's a generous way of putting it."

Maeve was watching him. "I don't blame you for being resentful. I'd also resent the person who abandoned my kid."

"Thanks."

Neither said anything for a while. Maeve attempted to read the report in front of her, but her mind kept drifting.

"So you have two nieces?" he asked. "I thought Wes had just the one daughter."

"Grady's daughter has decided that I'm her aunt. I like being an aunt, so I don't object."

"How old is she?"

"She's eight. A shy slip of a thing, but with a subtle sassy streak. I can feel it."

"I'm sure you'll coax it out of her."

"Damn straight."

He almost smiled. "Little kids are something else."

"They sure are." She had a thought. "You know, I watch my nieces fairly frequently. They're best friends, and really nice girls." She extended her hand in invitation. "Nicole would be welcome to join them. I'd love to have her."

Kyle offered a little nod of appreciation. "Thanks. I'm sure she'd like that." He watched her as she began typing an email. "Do you ever think about having kids?"

Maeve looked up from the screen. "That's not a question you should ever ask a woman."

"I don't mean any offense. I figured we knew each other well enough by now."

"It's a sensitive topic, Langahan. Childless women take crap from all directions. Most of us have reasons for being childless, and we don't necessarily want to discuss them."

"Okay. I'm sorry."

His expression benign and earnest, he appeared to mean no harm. She relaxed further.

"I've never had a desire to have my own kids," she ventured, allowing herself to risk opening up. "I like kids, though. I don't really think about it." She looked back to her laptop. "Do you think you'll have more?"

"I doubt it. Probably not, but who knows. Life happens. It did with Nicole."

"Ah. I hear you."

They lapsed into silence as they retreated into their laptops.

Maeve was finding it hard to concentrate; she had started thinking about what it must be like to be in a steady relationship, to plan to have children, to deliberately rearrange your lives to dedicate to somebody else. She couldn't relate to this; it felt like such a foreign concept. She hadn't even been in a really serious relationship; the closest she'd come had been Rhys, and as relationships went, it was pretty pitiful. Would she ever consider having children with Rhys? The question was almost laughable. She tried to envision it, she and Rhys working and sacrificing together, taking turns waking up in the middle of the night, canceling plans out when the baby was sick, missing deadlines because of school plays and PTA meetings. She somehow doubted that he was capable of this, that she was capable, that they were capable together. And even if they were capable, probably neither would be willing. There was just too high a price. It just wasn't in her priorities.

"Can I ask you something, Langahan?"

He looked up at her. "Sure."

Her eyes turned thoughtful. "Do you ever feel..."

His brow rose expectantly. "What?"

She waved her hand and turned back to her laptop. "Never mind. Forget it."

"No, what?"

"It's nothing."

"But now I'm curious."

She chewed her lip, suddenly embarrassed. "I was just going to ask if...if you ever feel isolated."

His eyebrows turned upward. "What do you mean?"

"I mean, do you ever feel like an outsider. Like you're on the fringes, like you don't belong."

Kyle took a few breaths and appeared to think about this. "I don't know. I guess we all feel isolated at some point."

"I mean as a matter of being."

He considered. "Maybe not as a matter of being." His expression crinkled thoughtfully. "Do you? As a matter of being?"

"Sometimes."

"Why?"

"Because..." She hesitated. *Because I isolate myself*, she wanted to say, but didn't. The thing was, she didn't do it on purpose, or for any particular reason; it was because she had neither the patience nor the room for people she didn't care about. Why endure another person when you could be by yourself instead? There were very few people in this world who were worth the trouble of socializing. Maeve was good at networking, at hobnobbing with coworkers and schmoozing politicians. It was easy to be Work Maeve because it didn't require sacrifices. Her personal life was different; people tended to ask her questions, to wonder why she wasn't married, why she drank so much, what was the matter. Despite her mother's assumptions, she wasn't unhappy—or was she? This arrangement had suited her for years. But Rhys's question had thrown off her equilibrium. Should she want to be with him? With anyone? How would she know if it was right? When she thought about Rhys, should she get a certain feeling? Though she liked Rhys, and though she enjoyed their spontaneous romps, she didn't feel the proverbial butterflies, and her heart didn't beat in the proverbial pitter patter. Rhys was smart, sexy, pleasantly mischievous—was there something wrong with her?

In her experience, getting close to people was much more trouble than it was worth. So few of them actually turned out to be good for her; statistically speaking, the work involved with testing a new person was unlikely to yield positive results. The numbers were exponentially lower when it came to getting close to men. They always...*wanted* something...be it flattery, or validation, or sex. They didn't appreciate her interests, or they patronized her, as if she couldn't discern the difference between sincerity and amusement. She didn't need that bullshit at this stage of her life. She wished she'd realized much earlier that she hadn't needed it at any stage at all.

Kyle was watching her, waiting, with uncharacteristic warmth in his eyes. *He's not such a bad guy*, she thought, *when it really comes down to it*. At least with Langahan, what you saw was what you got. He was honest, yes, and when he saw he was wrong, he could admit it—though granted, it was rare that he did, in fact, see it. But don't we all fail to see when we're wrong sometimes? Lord knows Maeve had been wrong on so much, to the point it had almost destroyed her relationship with her sister. Maybe Kyle was doing the best he could, just like she was. Maybe it helped that he was raising a child alone; it meant he didn't have time for bullshit, either.

Kyle was still looking at her, but now, she didn't know why; he seemed to be waiting for something entirely different than what he'd been waiting for before. His eyes had changed, but she couldn't pinpoint how.

Maeve blinked. What the hell had she been talking about?

"Maeve..." he began, but she cut him off.

"You know what, Langahan," she said, smiling. "It's really nothing. Forget it."

He stared at her, then shrugged. "Okay."

Maeve's phone rang. It was Rhys.

"Do you mind if I take this?" she asked Kyle.

"No, go ahead."

"Thanks." She picked up the phone. "Hey, Darney."

"Hey hey," said Rhys, his usual suave self, seemingly always ready for a good time. "A buddy of mine's playing at a jazz club at nine! What do you say—up for an adventure?"

"I'd love to, but I can't," she said, quietly; it was unprofessional for her to take a personal call like this in front of someone else, but it was only Langahan. "I'm babysitting Amy and Olivia tonight."

"Oh, man. Bummer." He paused. "I had a surprise for you."

"Oh, yeah?" The corner of her mouth turned up just slightly. She pulled up a game of solitaire on her laptop. "What's that?"

"Well, by definition, a surprise isn't meant to be explained, but since you can't go, I might as well tell you. I booked a room at the Piazza. I thought we could spend the night together."

In the depth of her stomach, a knot of anxiety instinctively tightened. "Oh. Well, it's just as well, then, because that's not part of the arrangement."

"What's not?"

"Mornings."

"I think when you stay up all night, it isn't technically morning."

She turned away from Kyle. "I'm reckless but not that reckless," she mumbled, pretending to wipe something off her lips.

"Where are you?"

"I'm still at work."

"Okay. Well, if plans change, let me know. Are they staying over?"

"No, they'll only be there a few hours."

"I'll swing by after?"

"What time?"

"I don't know. Does it matter?"

"I have Aditi's press conference tomorrow."

"That's never stopped you before."

"Are you done pressuring me, Darney? Because it's really not a good look."

"Hey, that's not fair, I've been pretty patient. I thought maybe I could entice you, but if not, it's cool, I'm not like that. We're good?"

"We're good, Darney. Text me when you leave."

"Will do. Later."

"Bye."

She sighed and hung up, replacing her phone on the table.

Kyle was scrolling on his laptop, but he didn't appear to be concentrating on it. His eyes were a little harder, and his face had turned a little red.

"Sorry," she told him. "I should have taken that outside."

"It's fine," he said. "Everything okay?"

"Oh yeah, everything's fine."

A quick rise of his eyebrows showed his acknowledgement. He then got back to work.

She was oddly compelled to put the situation to him; she spoke before she could stop herself. "I'm...I guess I'm sort of seeing someone. He wants to get together, but I can't."

"Mmm." He nodded, his eyes on his screen.

She scooted her chair closer to the table, feigning casualness. "It's a little weird because part of me is glad to have an excuse not to see him. I feel like that's not normal."

His eyes rose from his screen. "Probably not."

She rubbed her lips together and shrugged. "This is probably fairly common, though, right? Like when two people are moving their relationship forward. Those awkward stages, when you try to avoid someone. That's a thing, right?" Her voice had begun fading as she saw in his face that he didn't know what she was talking about. She attempted to shrug it off. "I'm sure everyone goes through it."

He blinked a couple of times, then returned his attention to his screen. "I don't know. Yeah. Sure."

She narrowed her eyes at him. "You don't sound convinced."

He sighed and looked at her, his eyes thoughtful, even a little confused. "I mean...I don't think it's normal. If you're hesitant early on..." He put his hands up and turned back to his work. "Whatever. It's not for me to say."

"I asked you, Langahan, so it is."

He leaned forward thoughtfully, his hands on his thighs. He

then ran his fingers through his hair. "You're asking the wrong guy, Maeve. I'm no good at this either."

"You were in a long-term relationship, though. You must be better at it than I am."

He leaned back in his seat, looking profoundly uncomfortable. He then rested his elbow on the table and scrolled through his laptop screen once more. "I guess I just feel like even when you're in it long-term, the person should still excite you when they walk into a room. I don't think you should be relieved to not have to see them. That to me doesn't seem all that healthy."

Maeve considered. "Well, it's not really that I don't want to see him. It's that he wants to take it further, wants to take a step up from casual. It's the fear that gets me, you know? The worry that I'll be trapped, that whatever we have now will be destroyed if we try to force it."

"So you'd rather sacrifice the possibility of tomorrow if it means no risk today? That seems kind of..."

"Cowardly?"

"I wasn't going to say that."

Neither said anything.

"Maybe it is a little cowardly," Maeve conceded, though he hadn't said it. She rubbed her lips together and scrolled mindlessly on her laptop, not seeing the screen. "I also have a secret bedroom," she told him, though she didn't know why, and regretted doing so even as she did it. She laughed, a little nervously. "Isn't that funny?"

His face twitched, and he blinked. "A secret bedroom," he repeated, as if bewildered.

"Yes. I take Rhys to my decoy bedroom, but my real bedroom is upstairs."

"Why?"

"I don't know."

He looked at her wordlessly, clearly holding his tongue.

"What is it?" she prompted.

He shrugged noncommittally.

A couple of minutes of silence passed. Maeve tried to read an email, but she kept glancing at him over her laptop. His brow was furrowed, his eyes on his own screen, but somehow she sensed he wasn't concentrating, either.

"I wouldn't mind, so much," she told him, "about tonight. It's the morning I always worry about."

"The morning?"

"Yes. The morning's when you're the biggest mess. It's a peaceful time for you to put your game face on and to get yourself together. I like having my mornings to myself."

"Yeah, but mornings are where life begins."

She stared at him, unsure what to make of this.

"Love," said Kyle, "is about trusting someone with your mornings."

The words were simple, but their profoundness touched Maeve. She watched him carefully, surprised.

"Well, well, Langahan," she said, leaning back in her seat, and grinning. "You have a soft spot after all."

"Everyone has a soft spot."

"I guess, but not everyone likes to show it."

His eyes rose from his laptop; his expression became wry. "No kidding."

Maeve flushed. She was taken aback: she didn't easily flush.

"In any case," he said then, clearing his throat, "it's moot if you can't see him anyway."

"Right. It's moot." She watched him as he sat there working, the sleeves of his oxford rolled up over his forearms, his sharp profile coyly peeking from beneath his five o'clock shadow, his short wavy hair a little looser at the end of the day. He was leaning casually, his elbow on the table and his fingers at his lips, his other hand scrolling whatever it was he was reading.

He looked at her suddenly. "What?"

She blinked. "Nothing."

They worked a little while longer, in silence. Eventually, Maeve checked the time, then closed her laptop.

"Well, I need to get out of here. I'm picking up Amy and Olivia at seven."

"Yeah, I need to get Nicole from my parents' house anyway."

Maeve looked at him. "Hey," she said. "Would Nicole want to come over and hang with the girls? We're going to eat grilled cheese and watch a movie, as per Amy's request."

"Not tonight. Melissa is coming in early tomorrow morning. She's leaving for Antarctica and wants to see Nicole first."

"Oh." Maeve's brow rose. "I assume Nicole knows she's leaving?"

"Yes. There have been tears. It isn't pretty."

"I'm so sorry." Maeve's heart felt cleaved in two. "The poor thing."

"Yeah, it sucks, pretty bad."

"I don't know how you do it."

"I hug her a lot, and I tell a lot of lies. I also spoil the crap out of her, which goes against everything I believe in."

"I don't blame you. I'd do the same thing." She hesitated. "Do you miss Melissa at all?"

"No. And even if I did, the pain she's causing Nicole would make me stop."

Maeve smiled ruefully. "Again, I can't blame you."

"Thanks."

They both were quiet for a moment or two.

"Anyway." He offered a mild smile. "Thanks for the invitation."

"Another time."

The mild smile faded; he was watching her carefully. "I have to ask you something. Don't be offended."

"Oh, God."

"Do you drink when you're watching the girls?"

Maeve sat up straight and glared at him. "*What?*"

"And do you ever drive with them after drinking?"

"Is this a joke?"

"I'm sorry, Maeve, but it would be irresponsible of me not to ask, if there's a chance you're ever going to watch my daughter."

Maeve was dumbstruck. "You've got a hell of a lot of nerve, Langahan."

"Well, you can go ahead and think that, but any parent would ask."

"I don't think I've ever been so insulted in my life, and that's saying something."

"You still haven't answered my question."

Rage oozed out of her skin, making her feel as if she were on fire. Eyes narrowed with fury, she put her hand over her heart. "*Of course* I don't drink with them. What the actual hell? What kind of a person do you think I am? I would never, *ever* do something so stupid. I take that shit seriously. I make sure I'm a good role model, and I'm prepared for all emergencies."

"Great." He put his hands up innocently, as if that were that. "That's all I wanted to know."

Maeve was stewing, sick with hurt. "I cannot believe you think so little of me as to ask me that question."

"It has nothing to do with what I think. As Nicole's father, it's my obligation to ask."

"I'm incredibly responsible. You see me arranging for rides—I don't even endanger myself, much less little girls I adore. That part of my life is my own business; I don't let it impact anybody else. I love those girls more than life itself. I'd jump in front of a fucking bus for them. I'd jump in front of a bullet."

"And I don't doubt that. I just needed to know for sure."

"Well, now you know." She stood. "I have to go."

"Come on, seriously? I think you're making too much of this. It's not an unreasonable question."

"It is." She threw on her jacket and shoved her laptop into her bag. "And I will tell you why, Langahan. It's because..." She stopped, gathering her thoughts. It was because of so much, none of which could be articulated. How to encapsulate it, how to make him see? This was the problem with people, they never seemed to understand.

"It's because," she told him, heading for the door, "I am not my drinking. I am not my being single. I am not my red camisole."

"What?"

She paused at the door, then turned to face him.

"People aren't perfect, and neither am I. But I swear to you, Langahan, I swear on my life, I love those girls more than anyone else on Earth. I would die before endangering them. I would die. I am not so selfish. I am not so weak. And anyone who questions that doesn't know me at all."

With that, she flounced from the room.

Five seconds later, she returned.

"I have to lock up. Get out."

He packed up his bag and stood, then faced her.

"If you're mad at me," he said, "you're just going to have to be mad." He slung his bag over his shoulder. "Have fun tonight."

He walked out the door.

Maeve locked up the office and went home.

THE NEXT DAY Aditi had a press conference and then a speaking engagement at the university. Maeve left her house well before sunrise knowing she wouldn't be home until evening. She and Rhys arranged to meet up after at a Mexican restaurant for tacos and margaritas—at least, for Maeve. Rhys was the designated driver: he was traveling the next day for a lead and couldn't afford risking having a hangover in the morning.

Maeve was into her second margarita. She'd downed the first one quickly, on purpose, so as to be more relaxed than usual when giving him the news.

"Fuck it," she told him, tossing her hand up. "Let's give us another try."

"Really?" Rhys's eyes widened with delight. "Hey, fantastic! Wow."

He reached across the table for her hand. She took it, and he leaned over and kissed her.

"What made you change your mind?" he asked.

"I don't know." She downed some more of her drink. "I just figured, why not."

"Why not, indeed."

Their server arrived with plates full of tacos. Maeve and Rhys dug in, the colorful pile of goodness nearly dispelling the vague gloom she'd been under since the day before. The margaritas helped, of course.

"We should take a vacation," said Rhys. "I really want to go away with you."

"Why?"

"Why? I mean, why not? Imagine it, Maeve—you and me at a nice resort, sitting by the pool, drinks in hand...Then retreating to our room for the night." He grinned. "That doesn't sound fantastic?"

Sure, it would be nice, or it would have been, before he'd gone and complicated things with his question about a relationship. Before, it would have been unfettered fun. Now, it was a further step toward something she wasn't sure she'd agreed to.

Maeve hid her ambivalence by filling her mouth with taco. "Mmm," she murmured, nodding.

They ate their tacos, talking about politics and the state of the world. Maeve's phone buzzed. It was a text from Catherine.

Hi Maeve. Do you want to go to a movie?

Maeve picked up her phone and responded. *Can't. I'm out with Rhys.*

You are? You should ask him to come to Dad's birthday party next weekend.

Maeve froze. *Um.*

Why not?

She thought about it. Why not, indeed? If she was going to try this, she might as well go all the way with it. It couldn't be worse than going to the party by herself; at least she'd have someone to talk to when Catherine was distracted by Wes and Amy.

"Hey," she said to Rhys, who was picking at a plate of nachos in the middle of the table. "Do you want to come to my dad's birthday party next weekend?"

He scrunched up his face. "I don't really do families."

Maeve glowered at him. "What the hell does that mean, you don't 'do' families?"

"I mean, I don't do families. No offense to you, gorgeous. Families are a headache, even my own."

Maeve narrowed her eyes at him and turned back to her phone.

I'll think about it, she texted her sister.

She could see Catherine responding, but it never came through—Maeve's battery died.

"Damn it," she muttered; she was usually good about keeping her phone charged, but she'd been out all day and had forgotten her backup battery. "Oh well." She put down her phone and ordered another margarita.

After another hour, Maeve was buzzed out of her annoyance. She and Rhys were in the middle of a hearty conversation about the upcoming election; everything seemed right with the world. Suddenly, Rhys's phone vibrated. He looked at it on the table, then picked it up in a flash.

"Holy fucking shit!"

"What, what?" asked Maeve, frantically. She leaned over the table, hoping to catch a glimpse of the screen. "What's going on? Is it bad?"

"No, no—it's amazingly good! Haddon wants to talk to me— he wants an interview. I can't fucking believe it!" Mike Haddon was the former aide to the White House Chief of Staff, who'd resigned suddenly and mysteriously. "I've been trying to talk to him all week, ever since the resignation."

"That's fabulous! Oh my God! He's like the holy grail of sources."

"I know, right? I'm like, in shock."

"When does he want to talk to you?"

Another text came in, and he did a double take. "Right now!"

"Seriously?"

"Yeah! Hey, I have to go." He looked at her. "Can you call a car?"

"Yeah, sure." She picked up her phone. "Shit," she said. "I forgot my phone's dead. Can I use yours?"

Rhys was already standing and shoving his arms into his jacket. "Would it be awful of me if I asked you to get the restaurant to do it? I have to get out of here, and Haddon is going to call me in—" His phone rang, and Rhys jumped. "Rhys Darney," he said as he answered it. "Yes, yes! Now's a perfect time. Thank you so much!" *Sorry*, he mouthed to her, and leaned down to kiss her cheek. He stalked out of the restaurant, the bells on the door tinkling as he left.

Maeve leaned back in her seat. *Great*. She finished her margarita and sat there a while to people watch, not quite ready to talk to another human just yet. After a time, the bell tinkled again. She looked over. It was Kyle Langahan.

Maeve averted her gaze. Moments later, she felt eyes on her. She looked up. He was staring at her.

"Hey," he mumbled, stepping toward the counter.

"Hey," she replied. "Fancy seeing you here."

"Yeah," he said, awkwardly, looking around. "I'm here to pick up some takeout."

She studied him through her buzz. "You look rough."

"Yeah, I know." His expression was grave, and he'd evidently been slacking in his usual careful attention to his appearance:

instead of a tucked-in shirt and slacks or more stylish jeans, he was wearing an old sweatshirt and jeans that looked like he'd had them since she knew him in high school. "Melissa just left. Nicole is heartbroken. She's back home with my mother."

"Oh, God," said Maeve, her shoulders slumping. "I forgot. I'm sorry."

"Yeah, well." He looked over her table. "Are you here by yourself?"

"No. I mean, yes. I was here with someone, but he had to leave."

He was watching her. "Do you need a ride home?"

"No, I'll call a car."

He narrowed his eyes. "What's the matter?"

"Nothing." She picked up her phone and put it back down. "I mean, my phone is dead, but it's fine. I'll ask the guy for help when I'm ready, or I'll walk."

"You'll *walk*? Are you kidding?"

"No, I'm not kidding. It's only a couple of miles."

"That's absurd. I'm right here. I'll drive you home."

"No, Langahan, no. You go back to Nicole."

"I'm not leaving you here by yourself, drunk off your ass, with no ride."

"I'm fine." She stared at him crossly. "And I'm not 'drunk off my ass.'"

Kyle looked angry. "He left you here drunk with a dead phone and no ride home?"

"Something came up. It couldn't be helped. And for what it's worth, I'm not fully drunk."

"That's a really shitty move, no matter what 'came up.'"

"I can take care of myself."

"That's not the point."

"I'm not a damsel in distress. Stop worrying. I'm fine."

He sighed and shook his head as a server slipped behind the

counter. Kyle spoke to him about his order. The server left to collect his food.

Kyle turned to her again.

"At least use my phone to call a car."

"Thank you, but I really don't need your help."

"Yes, you do. Don't reject my help on principle."

"I can take care of myself, not sure how many times I have to tell you that."

He inhaled and gritted his jaw, then turned back to the counter, paid for his order, took the bags in his hands, and walked out.

Maeve stood and visited the restroom. When she returned, a man was standing in the doorway. Maeve thought nothing of it until he approached her as she returned to her table and prepared to leave.

"Are you Maeve Sheering?"

Maeve halted. "Maybe."

The man indicated the street behind him with his thumb. "Car for you."

She eyed him warily. "I didn't call a car."

"Someone called it for you." He looked at his phone. "Kyle Langahan. Come on, I'm double parked."

Maeve started. She watched him, trying to assess. "I don't get into the car with strange men."

"Yeah, he said you'd refuse to get in the car. He said I should say to you, 'So you make it to morning.'"

Maeve just stood there staring at him, unsure what to do with these feelings. She was angry, and embarrassed, and grateful, three feelings she hated. Regardless, the car was here, and she desperately needed a ride. She walked outside, more soberly, and silently considered on the way back home.

～

MAEVE STOOD before her coffee maker and watched as it percolated. She had been thoughtful since last night, not sure what to make of what had happened. She had postponed coming to any conclusions, which likely would require a shift of her axis. As the sobering scent of coffee filled her kitchen, she stood there in her pajamas and bare feet, gathering strength. When the coffee had finished, she poured herself a cup; then she leaned against the counter and picked up her phone.

"Langahan," she said when he answered. "How's Nicole doing? I hope she's feeling more at peace this morning."

"She's inconsolable. It's awful. This is the most miserable day of my life."

Maeve frowned. "I don't know what to say. I'm really sorry."

"Me too."

"Is there anything I can do?"

"No. Thank you."

Silence. Maeve cleared her throat.

"I'm calling to thank you for the ride."

"You're welcome."

She hesitated a second. "Look, I also wanted to say, you didn't have to do it. I could have taken care of myself. You didn't have to feel sorry for me."

"I didn't do it because I felt sorry for you. I did it because you were drinking, your phone was dead, you were threatening to walk home, and I didn't want you to fucking die."

Maeve said nothing, for once in her life, utterly speechless.

"I have to go," he said. "Thank you for calling."

He hung up the phone.

"I STILL CAN'T BELIEVE he asked me that."

Maeve was standing with Catherine in the corner of her parents' living room. They'd just returned home from taking their father out to dinner; the Bickharts, of course, had joined them, as had a selection of other random friends and associates. The entire crew was now at the Sheerings' house for cake, coffee, and brandy. Maeve had been thoughtful all evening. She didn't like these thoughtful moods—they always seemed to lead to some kind of existential crisis—but the plus side was that it distracted her from making small talk with her parents and their pretentious friends.

"Have you talked to him since?"

"I've seen him a few times. He's been coming by Aditi's office to catch up on some work."

"Is it awkward?"

Maeve drew her lips from her glass and stared at Catherine. She raised an eyebrow.

"What the hell do you think?"

Catherine murmured acknowledgment and sipped her own wine.

"It's just a shame," Maeve went on, "because we have to work together now. You know? I mean, we're professionals, so we're figuring it out. But still. You can cut the tension with a goddamn knife."

They watched the party for a time. Grady was chatting up some of Fred's former colleagues. Lois and Sarah were entertaining a group of women around the drink table, laughing and carrying on. Amy and Olivia were playing cards together on the floor. Wes and Grady's father Charles pulled up a chair near the girls and began complimenting them on their game. Wes was on his way over to Maeve and Catherine, having finished a conversation with his father.

"I'm disappointed Rhys isn't here," said Catherine as Wes approached. "I would have liked to meet him."

"He felt it was inappropriate for him to socialize with my political family," Maeve told her, which wasn't completely untrue.

Wes kissed Catherine's cheek. "Who's that?" he asked Maeve, his brow raised with interest.

"Rhys," Catherine enunciated. She turned to Maeve with an unsubtle grin. "Maeve's new beau."

"He's not my beau."

"Rhys? As in, Rhys Darney? The journalist?"

"Yes."

Wes's brow rose higher. "Really!"

"It's not as serious all that."

"Rhys Darney's quite a journalist."

"Well, I'm quite a woman."

"I was telling Maeve," said Catherine, "that I would really like to meet him."

"His interview with Haddon was—" Wes cut himself off to perform a chef's kiss. He sipped his scotch. "Haddon's famously hard to get ahold of. I was impressed."

Maeve offered a half-hearted, rather irritated grin.

"It would be fun to talk to him," said Catherine, smiling at Wes as he sauntered off to speak with his brother. "You always say you don't have many people to talk to at these parties."

"It's fine. I have you."

"Don't you want him here?"

"Eh."

Catherine looked at her. "You don't want him here?"

Maeve sighed silently. "You know, Cat...I do. But..." She shrugged. "I don't know."

"Do you love him?"

Maeve cringed at the word. "No. We're so not there."

"Does he love you?"

"Doubtful."

Catherine turned back to the party and sipped her wine again. "I already knew you don't love him," she said, "because you love Kyle."

"God." Maeve rolled her eyes and took a drink. "You are a piece of work."

Catherine shrugged. "That's what I think."

"Why? We're always arguing. He makes me furious."

"You talk about him constantly. It's like you're trying to bring him up in conversation."

"Yes, because he makes me furious! He basically asked me if I get sloshed around the kids, Cat. He asked me if I *drive* with them."

"Can I be honest, Maeve? I don't think that's something to be mad over."

Maeve turned back to Catherine, her face dark with irritation. "You're serious."

"Yes, Maeve. I am." Catherine faced her, her earnest eyes wide with sympathy. "I know it hurts your feelings, but as a parent, I understand."

"You'd think he would know I was better than that. I mean, it's just so insulting!"

"But it isn't about you personally. His daughter is the most important thing in the world to him, more important than your feelings, more important than anyone's. He had to ask you that question. I would have, too."

Maeve's jaw worked as she tried to remain angry. She looked off to the side at Amy and Olivia, quietly playing, jostling each other, giggling.

"But you let me watch Amy," she argued. "I mean, you're fine with it."

"Because I'm your sister, Maeve, and I know you. Better than anyone else. Kyle doesn't. Not yet, anyway."

Try as she might, Maeve could not sustain the force of her anger. It fizzled from red-hot fury down to a mild simmer, not quite extinguished, but only licking at her feet rather than consuming her.

"I thought I was the one you came to for perspective," she said, "not the other way around."

"You *are* the one I go to for perspective, when it comes to everything but this."

Maeve watched her curiously. As usual, Catherine thought nothing of this bombshell she'd just dropped; she was straightening her skirt, fluffing her hair, checking the backs of her legs for runs in her stockings.

"I'm *not* in love with him," said Maeve, shuddering a little. "But it *was* nice to have a real conversation with him. And it was actually a good one. I was actually starting to…"

"Like him?"

"Yes, but not 'like him' like him."

They both laughed.

"I just don't know why he had to fuck it all up. Again."

"Maybe you're so upset because you let yourself be vulnerable and have feelings, and you felt like you were slapped down, the way you always fear you will be."

"It's nothing like that." Maeve glared at her sister, then inhaled and softened. "I just feel," she said, refusing defeat, "like he's always judging me."

"Why do you care?"

Maeve stared at her in silence. Catherine was drawn away by Wes, who wanted to introduce her to someone important. Maeve remained standing there by herself for quite some time, sipping her wine, deliberately recalling every obnoxious thing Kyle Langahan had ever said to her, every smirk, every stubborn rant, every reason she could think of that proved Catherine was wrong.

CHAPTER EIGHT

*W*es's water bill was held up in the Senate, which surprised no one. While it was not unexpected, they were disappointed by Senator Curt Tonelli's stance against it; they had held out a little hope he'd come around, given the bill's closeness to the hearts of those in Virginia. However, they had been planning for this, and they worked even harder to get Aditi's state bill finished. They also had to seek co-sponsors and, to Kyle's chagrin, draft amendments to address detractors' concerns. Kyle seemed to grit his teeth and do it, resigned to the tedious and, at times, heartbreaking negotiations of government, but he did it without complaint. In any case, Kyle and Maeve were forced once again to put aside their differences. Thankfully, they were professionals, as Maeve had said, and compartmentalizing went smoothly, if not easily.

Toward the end of summer, everyone gathered for the Labor Day parade. It was a warm, sunny, cheerful day, with a perfectly pleasant breeze. The mood was festive, with marching bands pumping and signs waving. Maeve was walking with Aditi, Wes, and other elected officials and their families. Kyle and Nicole were there. Kyle was dressed casually today, in jeans and a blue and white-checkered shirt. Nicole was wearing a white pantsuit and waving a little American flag. Maeve did her best to balance not looking at him but not obviously avoiding him. The two stayed away anyway, as Kyle chatted with a local commissioner.

Maeve walked with Aditi for a time, then with Catherine and Amy, until Catherine was drawn toward someone she knew. Amy stayed with Maeve. The two waved their flags and threw candy for the children. Maeve admired the way the sun kissed Amy's caramel-colored hair, making it look like warm honey. She straightened it affectionately, then patted her niece on the shoulder and looked out contentedly at the procession.

She found herself not far from Kyle and Nicole, who were now walking by themselves only a few feet away. As they drifted toward Maeve and Amy, the two girls caught each other's eyes. Amy waved at Nicole, and Nicole, with a little smile, waved shyly back.

"Amy," said Maeve, leaning down to speak with her niece, "that's Kyle Langahan's daughter Nicole. She's pretty new here. I'll bet she'd like to talk to you."

Amy eagerly approached Nicole, who blinked a few times, her eyes growing hopeful. When Amy, in her typical way, began chatting with her quite naturally, Nicole relaxed, immediately warming, clearly grateful to have a new friend. The two girls fell into quick conversation as they compared the contents of their candy bags and hid some choice pieces for later in Nicole's leather purse.

Maeve and Kyle were left walking side by side. There was nothing left to do but acknowledge his presence.

"I admire you for coming," she said as they walked. She herself was wearing a mermaid-shaped denim skirt and pink short-sleeved blouse. She had eschewed her usual high heels for tennis shoes; even she couldn't walk three miles in heels. "I know how painful it is for you to hang out with politicians, especially on your day off."

Kyle emitted a sound that was something like a reluctantly

submissive grumble. He paused for a moment, then chuckled, a little cynically. "Yeah, well. You know. Got to play the game, and all."

Maeve smirked. "Playing the game, are we? Now, who do I know who suggested that was a thing?"

"It was you. You won."

"Can I get that in writing?"

They walked on a few minutes in silence. With the luscious sunshine, the happy crowd, and the chirpy band music, Maeve could almost pretend he wasn't there.

Finally he stuck his hands in his pockets and turned to her. "Any news on the legal action against Brown & Little? How's it going?"

"It's definitely going," Maeve said, her gaze straight ahead. "Wes can probably give you more details."

"And there's no chance Brown & Little can be held accountable for the original leak."

"No." Kyle had been frustrated to learn that, because of the statute of limitations, the chemical company would get away with the original leak that had occurred decades before. However, they would face stiff consequences for the recent violations and cover-ups. "I know it's so disappointing. But unfortunately you're going to need to let that go."

"Just making sure."

There was something odd about his voice, something Maeve couldn't pinpoint. She glanced at him. He looked as normal, his expression serious and thoughtful.

"Everyone is optimistic about the bill, though," she told him, as consolation. "Wes says response to the amendments is very good, as it should be, as they're totally reasonable. We're getting it done." She looked at him again, and smiled. "You should be proud."

"I am proud." He met her gaze. Their eyes locked; he returned her smile. "You should be, too."

She wasn't sure what it was that she was seeing in his expression—it was deeper somehow, more meaningful. Her smile faded, even as her eyes softened; some kind of understanding, it seemed, had passed between them, some kind of connection made in shared work, in having a shared purpose. Maeve regarded his face in the bright midday sun: he looked more approachable out here, more human, his eyes squinted in the sunlight and first shimmers of perspiration on his brow. She moved her gaze, somewhat reluctantly, to the parade before her; but before doing so she couldn't help but note the broadness of his shoulders, the muscular angles of his forearms and the easy sway of his hips. He really wasn't all that bad, that Langahan. He'd shown himself to be human after all, even if he'd been slow about it. There was wariness between them, certainly, maybe even tension—but discussing the success of their bill had reminded her that they worked well together, despite this—or perhaps, even because of it.

Maeve frowned and faced forward. This was Langahan she was talking about. What was happening to her, exactly? It was all just so confusing.

"My parents are going away overnight," he said, a bit randomly, in Maeve's opinion. "I guess I'm on my own with Nicole. I mean, if something were to happen."

"I'm sure you'll be fine. Where are they going?"

"They've got a wedding tomorrow. They'll be home tomorrow evening." He paused. "What about you? What are your plans for the week? Anything interesting going on?"

Maeve looked at him curiously. He was walking casually, his face unemotional as he watched the procession before him, but there was still that something unusual in his tone.

"Not much," she said, looking forward again. She smiled and waved to a little boy who ran into the parade before his mother hastily retrieved him. "I have a few meetings, as always, but mostly I'll be in the office."

"So nothing really important, then."

"Well, it's all important," she said, a little testily. "Just nothing out of the ordinary."

"Right, that's what I meant."

She looked at him again, her eyes narrowed. "Why do you ask?"

"No reason."

They continued walking. Amy and Nicole were now a short distance ahead. Maeve was delighted for Nicole: Amy would make her a good friend.

"So," said Kyle, "nothing going on tomorrow, then, huh? Just a boring Tuesday."

"What is with you, Langahan? Why this interrogation into my schedule?"

"I'm just making conversation."

Maeve was going to counter with a sarcastic retort but suddenly thought better of it. It was clear he had a reason for asking her these questions—she just wasn't sure what it was. She was aware of a vague twittering in her stomach. Could he be trying to—no, he couldn't, and even if he was, so what? It wasn't like she wanted to; it wasn't like she cared. It didn't matter why he was asking; it was probably as he said, he was making conversation. It was awkward, yes, but so was Langahan.

"The only thing I have going on is babysitting," she said instead. "Wes and Catherine and their entire family have an event an hour away. They're bringing Amy to Aditi's around two, and she's going to hang with me until I take her back to my place for dinner."

"Oh! Oh, you're watching Amy?" Kyle turned to her with interest, and almost something like—relief? His eyes were wide, and if she hadn't known better she would have interpreted his expression as smiling. What was he up to? It made no sense. "Cool, cool, that sounds like fun."

"You're so weird, Langahan."

A tap on the shoulder made her turn. Finding no one but Kyle, who was staring thoughtfully forward, she turned in the other direction, where Rhys Darney had sidled next to her and was now looking at her with a playful smile.

"Hey, you," she said, accepting a quick kiss. "I didn't know you'd be here today."

"Anne sent me. Kind of a breather, I guess, after the excitement of the last few weeks."

"An easy story, but I'm sure you could use the break."

"Not a wasted day, though. I'll catch Aditi and Wes for some words about the water bill."

In front of them, Amy and Nicole were now arm in arm and waving to the crowd like a couple of princesses. Maeve nudged Kyle.

"You see that?"

"Yeah."

"I'm so glad they're getting along."

Rhys leaned in toward her. "Who's that with Amy?"

"That's Kyle's daughter Nicole." She gestured toward Kyle. "Rhys, have you met Kyle?"

"Haven't had the pleasure." Rhys reached in front of her to extend his hand toward Kyle. "Hey, Kyle. Rhys Darney."

"Hey," said Kyle, shaking it. "How's it going."

"Wait, Kyle Langahan, right?" Rhys stuck out his finger at him. "I can't believe I've never met you! I need to talk to you about the hearing. I'm talking to Aditi later, can I ask you a few questions?"

"Yeah, sure."

"Hey," Rhys said then to Maeve, leaning in toward her again. "Stay at my place tonight?"

"Sorry, Darney, I can't. I have to work tomorrow, early."

"You always have to work early. I have to work early, too. Come on, we'll grab coffee and leave for work together."

Maeve sensed Kyle listening in, or maybe she just worried he was. She lowered her voice.

"You know how I feel about this."

"Well, you know how I feel about you."

"This isn't going to work if you can't respect my feelings."

"You're not the only one here."

Maeve sighed and said nothing, watching Amy and Nicole as they walked. They were now handing out candy, enjoying being the bearers of gifts.

"I'm sorry I can't help you," said Maeve. "I have to do it in my own time."

"Yeah but at what point are we just going to say, We're doing this?"

Maeve gritted her teeth a little, aggravated under this pressure. "We're definitely not doing this here, Darney. So can it."

His impatience was a tangible presence beside her; it made her feel cold, and worse, small. It was the feeling she hated most, and he knew it, and she knew that he did.

"Maybe if you back off," she said, "one day, I'll come to you."

"And maybe you won't."

"In that case, we'd have our answer."

Rhys whistled. "Ouch. Okay."

Maeve softened and looked at him. "Look, can we do this another time? Come over later. We can still hang out."

"I can't. I'm meeting a source."

"Then tomorrow evening, after Amy leaves. I'll text you when she's gone."

He grumbled in acknowledgment, kissed her, and disappeared into the crowd.

Maeve faced forward and continued walking with Kyle.

"Sorry about that," she muttered, tucking her hair behind her ear.

"No need."

"That was pretty annoying."

"It's none of my business."

"This is our second try. I'm beginning to remember why it didn't work out the first time."

"I'm sorry."

They walked on. Before her, Aditi and Wes were talking together. Catherine was chatting with a friend just beside them.

"Is he the one who left you that time?" he asked her. "In the restaurant?"

"He really did have a work emergency," Maeve responded, immediately jumping to his defense; when it came to work, she understood. "An opportunity came up that he couldn't ignore. I can't blame him for that."

"I don't know." Kyle hesitated. "I think it was selfish and irresponsible."

"You're free to think what you'd like. He isn't a selfish person."

"Whether he is or he isn't, it was a dick move. Like something those guys from high school would do."

Maeve scoffed. "He's nothing like those assholes."

"Catcalling and pressuring are on the same continuum."

"I'm aware." Maeve tried to keep the annoyance out of her voice, and failed. "The thing is, though, that I know him, and you don't."

"I just think you deserve better."

Maeve paused at this, unsure of his meaning. "Let me be the judge of that."

"Well, as I said. It's none of my business."

Maeve stared forward, a little peeved. She was a grown woman, not a teenager. He had no right to an opinion. He should keep his judgments to himself.

They once again found themselves drifting, with Maeve mingling with people she knew and Kyle standing off to the side, his arm now around Nicole.

Amy was walking with Catherine. Maeve snuck up behind her and put her hand on her shoulder.

"How do you like your new friend?"

"Do you mean Nicole? She's super, super nice."

"She wants to be president. Isn't that neat?"

"She told me that. But she doesn't want to be president anymore—not yet, anyway. She's going to start local, she said, and work her way up."

"Smart girl." She walked with her niece a moment, taking in the scene. "Do you think you might want to hang out with her sometime?"

"Sure," Amy said eagerly. "I told her I'd help her make signs for her campaign."

Maeve grinned, shaking her head with amusement. How did she get so lucky to know so many amazing little girls?

When the parade was over Maeve said her goodbyes. Eventually she found herself face-to-face with Kyle Langahan, who had walked over with Wes as Maeve chatted with Catherine.

"Well, I should be going," said Maeve, stuffing her water bottle into her bag. "I have things to do."

"Thanks for helping Nicole today."

Maeve looked up at him. "You're welcome. Nicole's a sweet kid."

"Amy made friends with my daughter," Kyle explained to Wes and Catherine. "She went out of her way to reach out to her. My daughter's had a hard time adjusting to being here. I appreciate Amy's kindness."

"Oh, that's so nice," said Catherine, her face instantly brightening. "I'm so happy."

"You're a nice family," Kyle went on. "I'm glad I've gotten to know you a little better."

"Well, that's very generous of you," said Wes, smiling warmly, clearly moved. "The feeling is definitely mutual."

"I'm sorry if my criticism went too far. I enjoy working with you and being on your team."

Wes clapped him on the back. "Water under the bridge, my friend. No hard feelings at all."

Maeve watched all this in stunned silence. She blinked a few times, unsure she'd really heard what she was hearing.

As Wes and Catherine gathered Amy, Kyle and Maeve faced each other.

"All right," she said, looking around, inexplicably unable to meet his gaze. "I guess I'll see you next week for our regular meeting."

"Sure, sure, see you next week. Or before then."

Maeve met his eyes. "Is there something I'm forgetting?" she asked, incredulous, and reaching for her phone to check her calendar.

"No, I'm just saying, maybe I'll see you around. I mean we run in the same circles, now, sort of. So, maybe I'll see you."

Maeve stared at him blankly. "I mean, I guess."

A few moments passed, a tense silence amidst the joyful cacophony of the crowd.

"I really should be going," said Maeve.

"Right." Kyle watched her. "Hey, I'm sorry if I overstepped about Rhys," he said, lightly punching her arm in an awkward attempt to be casual. "You're right, you'd know better than I would."

"I'm sorry, Langahan, but did you just tell me I'm right? For the second time in one day?"

"Weird, right? It must be the heat."

"Must be."

"Well." He smiled at her, a genuine smile, not the typical Langahan grimace. It warmed his entire appearance. "Catch you later."

He waved and backed away, but lingered a moment before turning and, his arm around Nicole, disappearing into the crowd.

Maeve watched him go, that odd feeling making her forehead crumple with thought. Putting it out of her mind, she hitched her bag over her shoulder, kissed her sister and Amy goodbye, and went home.

~

THE NEXT DAY, Maeve was sitting at her desk waiting for Catherine to drop off Amy when Aditi poked her head into her office.

"I'm running late with my newsletter material," she said. "I should have it for you tomorrow."

"No problem." Maeve glanced at her phone to check the time, then looked at Aditi and smiled. "Take your time."

"Thanks, Maeve. Hey, can you also set up a time for me to talk to Brian from the Richmond office?"

"Sure thing."

Maeve checked her phone again, and sighed.

"Everything okay?" asked Aditi.

"Of course. Why?"

"You look anxious, like you're expecting a phone call."

"I'm not."

Aditi studied Maeve. "You look especially nice today."

"Oh," said Maeve, looking down at herself. "Thank you."

"Is there something special going on today? What did I miss?"

"Nothing. You missed nothing." Maeve sat primly, and smiled innocently, as if she hadn't spent an extra ten minutes in front of her closet that morning taking special care to choose an outfit in which she'd look her best. She had settled on a shapely black skirt and white blouse with a draped neckline. A pendant sparkled from just above her cleavage. She'd chosen her brightest red lipstick, and her tallest black heels. "I felt like looking my best today, that's all."

"Ah. I thought maybe you were meeting someone."

From the waiting room, they heard the sound of the bell on the door tinkling, then voices.

"I'm not meeting anyone," said Maeve, her hands on her desk in preparation to stand. "I thought maybe I was, but as it turns out, I'm not. That'll be Catherine and Amy," she said, looking at her phone once more, and rising—it was fifteen minutes after two.

"Go ahead and knock off a little early," said Aditi. "Take Amy out for ice cream."

"Okay." Maeve looked over her desk, forlorn. She normally wouldn't consent to leaving work early, but somehow today she wasn't in the mood to be here. "Thanks, Aditi. I think I will."

"Aunt Maeve," said Amy excitedly as she entered Maeve's office, Catherine trailing behind. Aditi and Catherine exchanged greetings, and Aditi excused herself; Amy met Maeve behind her desk and kissed Maeve on both cheeks, European style.

"This is new," said Maeve, accepting the kisses and kissing her in return. "Where did you learn to do that?"

"Nicole showed me. She said her mom showed it to her. Her mom has been all over the world."

"Thanks again for taking her," said Catherine, distractedly; she was digging in her large canvas bag and pulling out Amy's coloring books and special pens. "We should be back by around eight."

"That's fine."

"I have to go, I'm sorry. I'm late, I'm always late."

"It's fine."

Catherine bent her tall frame to speak to her daughter. "You be good for Aunt Maeve," she said, with kindness, tucking Amy's hair behind her ear. "I'll be back in time to tuck you in for bed."

"Okay, Mommy."

"I love you very much."

"I love you very much, too."

They kissed each other's cheek, and Catherine waved and scurried out. Maeve turned to Amy.

"Senator Patel told me to take you for ice cream," said Maeve. "Let's get out of here."

"Really? Thank you, Aunt Maeve!"

"Don't thank me. Thank Senator Patel."

They were in the car when Maeve got the call.

"Hi, Aditi," she answered, her voice unusually chipper; it was a beautiful day, her niece was in the back seat, and hell, she might even treat herself to some ice cream, too.

"Maeve." Aditi's voice was rushed, anxious. "Kyle's over at Brown & Little staging a protest."

"*What?*" Maeve started in her seat; she pulled the car to the shoulder so she could think.

"He didn't tell you he was going to do this?"

"Of course not! He knows I would have stopped him."

"Honestly, Maeve, I'm very upset. This makes us look awful, like we aren't doing enough, and it endangers all our efforts in trying to get this done."

"I know." Maeve ached for Aditi, who had worked so hard for such a good purpose and was now probably feeling betrayed. "I'm furious. I'm just beside myself, truly."

"His statements to the press lament the slowness and insufficiency of lawmaking, the fact that Brown & Little gets off the hook because of statutes of limitation and expressing frustration with the compromises we're making to get the law passed."

"Jesus. Goddammit, Langahan."

"We're on the verge of passing this bill, both here and in Congress. Why can't he see that?"

"Because he's Kyle." Someone else was calling in. She didn't recognize the number. She asked Aditi to hold on and answered it. "Maeve Sheering speaking."

"Hello, Maeve?"

Maeve's face instantly turned serious. The voice was high and hesitant, not scared, but meek: it was that of a little girl.

"Nicole?" said Maeve, alarmed. "Nicole, are you okay?"

"Yes, I'm okay. Can you come pick me up?"

"Yes." The word came out unthinkingly, without hesitation. "Where are you? What's wrong?"

"I'm at school."

"Why do you need to leave?"

"Because school is over for today."

Maeve glanced at the dashboard clock. It was after three o'clock. Fucking Langahan. He wouldn't even be back from the protest with enough time to pick up his daughter from school.

"Yes, I'll pick you up," she told Nicole. "Let me just call and tell your dad."

"You can't call him. He's in jail."

Fear turned to fury. "*Motherfucker.*"

Amy gasped in the back seat. "Aunt Maeve!"

Maeve glanced back at her, red in the face. "Sorry." She turned forward and inhaled deeply, collecting herself. "Nicole," she said, "why is he in jail?"

"For protesting at Brown & Little."

Maeve's head was spinning. Protest was legal, so what the hell had Kyle done to get arrested? Why would he do this right when things were looking positive? How could he put Aditi and Wes in this position? How could he leave his daughter without a ride home?

These were not questions with which to burden Nicole. Maeve cleared her throat and put on her game face. "What is the name of your school, Nicole?"

"Shady Valley Elementary. Mrs. Bleaker wants to talk to you."

Maeve waited in heated impatience as Nicole passed the phone to whom she assumed was the receptionist.

"Ms. Sheering?"

"Yes." Aditi was texting her—she needed to get off the phone.

"Thanks so much for picking up Nicole. We have her all ready to go."

"It's no problem." She hoped she'd managed to keep most of her annoyance out of her voice. She guessed this was why Kyle was so interested in her schedule yesterday. "Wait a minute," she said suddenly. "How do you have my number?"

"Oh, Mr. Langahan gave us all your information this morning when he dropped Nicole off at school. He thought it would be better if Nicole called you herself, but he told us you would come if you were needed."

By now Maeve was furious. It was really nice of Kyle to just assume she'd be around to help him. Of course she would be there for Nicole. But the idea that he left her with this huge responsibility without even consulting with her first—a responsibility that required her to essentially be an accomplice in something that was a threat to her own work—rankled her in ways she wasn't even yet able to fully comprehend.

"Great, that's just great," she told Mrs. Bleaker. Aditi had hung up and was calling her back. "Mrs. Bleaker, can you hold for just a moment?"

She clicked over to Aditi, who started speaking instantly.

"They've all been arrested, Maeve. *Arrested.* Maeve, this looks so bad."

"I'll handle it, Aditi. I promise. Let me call you back."

Anger was seeping out of her pores, making her skin feel like it was consumed by fire. She clicked back to Mrs. Bleaker.

"Shady Valley's on Oak Street, right? I'll be there in ten minutes."

NICOLE WAS surprised but pleased to see Amy. When they arrived, she was sitting in the office with her backpack on her back and her purse over her shoulder, slumped over, staring somberly into space, waiting. Upon seeing Maeve and Amy, she instantly brightened, going to Amy first and looking at her with a relieved-looking smile as Amy immediately launched into a description of the games they should play when they got back to Aunt Maeve's house. Nicole then turned to Maeve, hesitant but glad.

"Thank you for picking me up," she said, leaning forward for a hug.

"Of course."

"Are we going back to your house?"

"Yes, I suppose so."

Amy tugged at her jacket. "What about ice cream?"

Nicole perked up. "Ice cream?"

Maeve stared at them. Their eyes were wide, their faces hopeful.

"Oh. Right." She cleared her throat, distracted and unable to keep up. *Get it together, Sheering.* "Yes, we can get ice cream. Let's go." She turned to Mrs. Bleaker. "Thank you."

"Sure."

Her hands on their backs, Maeve shuffled them toward the door.

Once in the car, she made sure the girls were buckled in and then turned to Nicole in the back seat.

"Nicole, dear," she said sweetly, "why don't you tell me the story from start to finish."

Nicole shrugged. "Daddy told me this morning he was going to be arrested at Brown & Little. He told me not to worry, he'd been preparing for this for weeks and that nobody would hurt him. He said sometimes we have to stand up for what we believe in if we want to make change. Did you know my grandma and grandpa got arrested, too?"

"Yes." Maeve couldn't discern whether Nicole believed what she was saying or not; the little girl, like her father, was inscrutable when faced with a challenge. She turned to Nicole again. "I'm just surprised, is all, because usually, you can protest without getting arrested."

"My dad was trespassing. That means he entered the premises without permission and against posted restrictions. Also they refused to disperse, which means they were ordered to leave, but they didn't."

"Ah." Maeve stifled a wry grin. "Yes, that makes sense. You're very smart, Nicole."

"Do you think he'll be out of jail soon?"

Maeve could hear the anxiety in her voice, and her eyes were glassy, like she was trying not to cry. Damn Langahan. Always having to make a point, didn't matter that he had put his little girl through hell.

She took a deep breath. *Shit.* "Of course he will be." In all likelihood they'd book him and let him post his own bail. He'd be home before dinner. She reached back and patted Nicole's knee. "Don't fret."

"What flavor of ice cream are you getting?"

This from Amy. Maeve's eyes darted to her niece. She couldn't help but warm at the excitement in her voice.

Nicole's impassive face relaxed somewhat. She furrowed her brow, thinking. "Mint chocolate chip, I think. Or maybe strawberry."

Maeve smiled. She then faced front, turned on the car and, with a deep breath, pulled out of the parking lot.

"My dad told me that you would take care of me," said Nicole.

Maeve glanced in the rearview mirror. Nicole was looking out the window, smiling at the scenery.

"Did he," she answered, under her breath, her hard eyes now back on the road.

ICE CREAM CONES IN HAND, Maeve, Amy, and Nicole sat in the sunshine on the ledge of a fountain in the Downtown Mall. Maeve licked her black raspberry and sat listening as the girls joked and played together. If nothing else, their laughter was a distraction from her anger, which was so multi-layered and complicated she struggled to begin working it through.

She'd considered texting Kyle to let him know Nicole was safe and that they had gone for ice cream, but she'd decided against it.

He hadn't offered the courtesy of transparency, and neither would she. Fuck it. Fuck him. He'd get in touch when he needed her.

As the hour passed, her anger burned even hotter. Where the hell was he? Wasn't he worried about what was going on? She considered that maybe he'd actually been detained, that maybe the protest had gotten out of hand, but no—Aditi would have let her know. And besides, even if he had, fuck him then too. She'd already stepped up despite no warning and no consideration; he could use an hour or two in jail. Let him rot.

They finished their ice cream and walked around a bit, poking into a few stores and smelling flowers. Maeve let the girls make bracelets at a bead shop. At least this debacle had given her a chance to indulge a little in some unexpected pleasantries.

She was surprised when, exiting the bead shop, they saw Kyle walking toward them, hands in his pockets, a slowness in his gait that if she hadn't known better she might have interpreted as contriteness. Nicole flew to him upon first sight. Amy and Maeve hung back, letting them have their reunion.

"Daddy!" Nicole exclaimed, a wide smile on her face as he bent low and engulfed her in a tight hug. "You made it out of jail!"

"Of course I did, honey. I told you I'd be fine."

"Look what I made." She held out her wrist to show him her bracelet. "Amy made one too."

"Wow, that's really pretty. Did you thank Ms. Sheering?" He looked at Maeve then, for the first time. His eyes were pensive, as if trying to read her.

"Yes, she thanked me," said Maeve. "She always expresses gratitude to people helping her." *Unlike some people*, she added with her eyes, and with a subtle but unmistakable bite in her voice.

Kyle picked up on it, as intended. "Yes," he said, flushing a little. "Nicole is a very good girl."

Amy asked Maeve for some pennies to throw into the fountain. Armed with a fistful of coins, she and Nicole scampered a few feet away, leaving Maeve and Kyle to talk amongst themselves.

"How did you know where we were?"

"Nicole's watch has location services."

Maeve nodded. She looked about, rubbing her lips together and gathering her wits.

Finally, she met his eyes and crossed her arms. "So you got yourself into a little bind today, Langahan."

"I wasn't in a bind. I did it on purpose."

"You left your daughter in school without a ride home."

"She had a ride home. You picked her up."

"And what if I couldn't? What if I had last minute plans?"

"I knew you would drop everything to help her."

Maeve stared at him, steaming. "You were feeling me out yesterday. You knew about this, and you wanted to make sure I could cover your ass."

"I was trying to make sure the person I trust the most was available to take care of my daughter."

Maeve hated this shit, the manipulation and the lies. It was deceit, it was game-playing; it went against everything she stood for, everything she felt comfortable with. But even as she stood there so angry she couldn't even see, she recognized a spark of something curious, a tremor of something—was it pride? Relief? Something totally different? She didn't fixate on it; she pushed the feeling away.

"It's just so irresponsible," she told him. "I'm really surprised you'd do this."

He shrugged. "It wasn't ideal. But it had to be done before the bill went back to the Senate."

She watched him, frowning. "What you said yesterday," she said. "About working with all of us. I guess your professions of camaraderie were all just deception and bullshit."

"No, they were legit."

Another tremor had replaced the one before, something

darker and lonelier, something deep in her gut that ate at her soul. This, too, she pushed aside; it was all too much. She needed to think.

"Goddamn it, Langahan."

They stood there in silence. She rubbed her face in her hands.

"Thank you," he said, and this time, she was sure—he was contrite, and embarrassed. He knew he had pushed a little too far. "I do appreciate that I knew she would be safe."

She was watching him, her face hard. "You criticized Rhys for abandoning me for a work thing, and here you are, going behind my back."

"Yeah, but I didn't have a choice."

"One might say he didn't either."

"But I didn't abandon you."

"No, you only abandoned your daughter."

Kyle stared at her, his jaw tightening. He seemed to sigh, his shoulders slumping slightly.

"I'm sorry for not being honest," he said. "Can you forgive me?"

Maeve shook her head at him, in frustration. "It's not just that. You owe Aditi an apology, and Wes, too. It just looks so bad, on every level. It looks like you don't trust your own team, and if you don't, why should anyone else?"

"It's brought attention to our cause."

"You know what it is, Langahan?" she said, her hand on her hip. "It's that you think you have all the answers. You're not really a team player. You made us all think you were with us, but really, you were biding your time until you could do it your way."

"That isn't fair," he told her, his face hard. "I joined your team willingly. I swallowed my pride after a humiliating defeat, and I've done everything that's been asked of me. I've been working my ass off to help you."

"To help *us*?" cried Maeve, with a sardonic laugh. "This is your pet project, Langahan, and we let you put it front and center. You talk about swallowing your pride, but we're the ones who invited in an opponent to try to work together to get this shit done. You were helping us? Okay, yes. But don't pretend for a minute that we weren't helping you. No way could you be doing this on your own."

"I absolutely could have done it on my own!" Kyle threw up his hands, meeting her in her anger. "I've been doing it on my own for twenty years. And in case you've forgotten, I ran a pretty damn good campaign. I didn't have to tell Wes I'd work with him, but he convinced me we could get this done."

"And we *are* getting it done. You gave up too easily."

"I don't see it as giving up. I see it as lighting the match to start the fire."

"And you're willing to burn it all down in the process."

Kyle frowned. "Look, Maeve," he said. "I know the bill's going to pass. And I'm proud of the work everyone's done. But it doesn't change the fact that we're not getting everything we need to do it right. I was very careful in how I worded my statement. I didn't complain about Wes and Aditi, or about anyone. My point was that the system is slow and unfair, but not that it's anyone's fault; Wes and Aditi mean well, and they do the best they can, but they're working in a system that's stacked against us. I was trying to make a point about the system, Maeve—I wasn't trying to minimize anyone's work."

"Well, that's what it looks like, regardless. No matter what your intentions, you made it sound like you don't have any faith in anyone. You made it sound like what we're doing isn't enough, and that it's our fault. You make it look like we're fighting, like we aren't even on the same side—and worst of all, you did it right when we're trying to secure more support that can clinch its success."

Kyle's expression changed, and he blanched. "Okay, I guess I can see that."

Maeve shook her head, her jaw tight. "Unfuckingbelievable."

"Daddy!"

Maeve and Kyle turned toward Nicole, who was calling to him from the fountain.

"Can Amy come over and play today?"

"Honey, not today," he told her, his face instantly sympathetic. "Grandma and Grandpa are on their way home, and I told them we'd see them for dinner. Maybe another day."

They faced each other once more.

"I need to get her home," he said. "Thank you for picking her up."

"I was happy to pick her up. Not that you left me a choice."

"Thank you anyway."

She shook her head at him. "I'm really disappointed."

"And I'm genuinely sorry." He actually did seem sorry, but Maeve was frustrated—it was too little too late, and besides, while he might have been sorry, he did not appear remorseful. "I hope you understand that I did what I had to do." He glanced at Nicole, then back and Maeve. "For my daughter."

Maeve shook her head again, gathered Amy, hugged Nicole goodbye, and walked toward her car.

WHEN CATHERINE and Wes came for Amy that evening, Maeve was in a rotten, sour mood. The little girl was sitting in the sunroom working on a craft project. Upon hearing the doorbell, Maeve left her there and walked toward the door, her heart thumping. She had texted Catherine to let her know what was going on—she felt her sister had a right to be updated—but while she knew there had been nothing she could do, she still felt guilty for exposing Amy to this drama.

Catherine looked somber but elegant in her vintage black jacket and skirt. Wes looked dapper as always in his well-tailored suit.

Maeve kissed her sister's cheek and accepted a kiss on the cheek from Wes, then stood back and crossed her arms.

"How was your night? Worth the drive, I hope."

"It was lovely," said Catherine. "We had a nice time."

"We did," said Wes. "These things are part of the territory, but it's always nice when they turn out to be pleasant and entertaining." His face turned serious. "What happened with Kyle?"

Maeve inhaled and exhaled, resisting the urge to let loose a string of profanities. "He bailed himself out and met us downtown, and he and Nicole went home." She shrugged. "That was pretty much it."

"Where's Amy?"

"She's in the other room with her crafts. She's totally fine, Wes. It wasn't really that big a deal."

"I'm sure." Wes patted her shoulder and smiled reassuringly. "You did what you had to do. Don't sweat it."

"She enjoyed some unexpected time with her new friend. I think she sort of saw it as an adventure."

"What's life without a little adventure?" His chipper smile dimmed. "I'm more concerned about Kyle's brazenness and secrecy. It makes him look rather like a loose cannon. And it minimizes everything we've been working toward."

"I know, I know. I told him the same thing."

"Well," he said, and sighed resolutely, "I guess we'll have it out with him tomorrow." He patted her shoulder again. "I'm going to go see Amy."

Maeve smiled somberly and watched him walk away. She then turned to her sister.

"Hey," she said, affecting casualness, but poorly. She nodded toward the kitchen behind her. "Can I talk to you for a sec?"

"Sure," said Catherine, and followed her sister down the hall.

Once completely out of earshot, Maeve looked at her sister frankly.

"I'm really angry with Kyle," she told her, "and I don't know what to do about it."

Catherine stared at her blankly. "Okay," she said, then waited for Maeve to continue.

"I'm telling you this because you're better at containing your emotions than I am. How do you handle it when you're angry? Do you even get angry?"

Catherine blinked a few times, then scrunched up her face, then laughed. "Oh," she said, nodding with tentative understanding. "Oh, I see. You're teasing me again. That's very funny, I guess."

"Oh my God, Catherine, I'm not joking. I seriously need your help."

Catherine's face grew more serious. "Oh." She watched her for a second. "But I don't understand. I'm not good at containing my emotions. I break down all the time. Well, lately I've been better. But I used to break down all the time."

"I just don't know what to do."

Catherine was studying her. "What are you angry about, Maeve?"

"He jeopardized our cause and all our hard work. He made Aditi look like a fool. And also, I'm disappointed in him for having so many false pretenses. All that talk yesterday about being on our team. He made us think he wanted to patch things up, or whatever, that he had actually made a personal connection."

"Is that it?" asked Catherine, her eyebrows raised with genuine interest. "Are you angry because he didn't take you into his confidence?"

"No." Maeve was growing frustrated; why couldn't Catherine ever get what she was saying? "It's not about *me*, Catherine. It's about *Aditi*. It's about *dignity*. It's about, why can't he just be on the up and up? Why would you make someone think you care about their feelings and then go behind their back with something so important?"

Catherine bit her bottom lip and thought about this. "You know," she said, "I think he meant everything he said. I think he was feeling guilty, maybe, because he likes us all now and knew that he was getting ready to do something behind all our backs."

Maeve shook her head. "I'm just hurt on Aditi's behalf. I feel like he has more of a personal relationship with her than that."

"Yes," said Catherine, shifting her weight. "He does have a personal relationship. With Aditi."

Maeve didn't like her tone. She turned away from her sister and pulled a tumbler from the cabinet, then withdrew a couple of bottles to fix herself a cocktail.

"For the record," said Catherine, "I think this is even more personal, because of trust."

Maeve took a long sip of her cocktail. "What does that mean?"

"You're angry because you thought your relationship with Kyle was more personal. But I think it's even more personal, because he trusted you with his daughter."

"What the hell are you talking about? This has nothing to do with me."

Catherine was watching her; she nodded toward Maeve's glass. "Did he ask you if you had been drinking?"

Maeve swallowed and wiped her lips with the back of her hand. "No."

"Well, there you go."

Maeve clenched her jaw. She was beginning to feel sick, but she ignored the queasy tumbling and downed another gulp of her drink. "I really wish you'd stop acting like there was something going on with us, Catherine. It's getting really frustrating."

"But it's so obvious, even I can see it. I just think maybe you'd want to know that I think he likes you too."

"Stop it. Just stop."

"I'm just trying to help you, Maeve."

"Well, don't help me. You put these thoughts in my head, and they make me uncomfortable. I wouldn't ever have even thought of Kyle that way if you hadn't started pestering me. I don't even know why I asked your advice in the first place." Maeve's voice had grown involuntarily louder; her chest was now heaving, and her face was burning. She glared at her sister with fire in her eyes. "I'm the one who's supposed to be giving *you* advice, not the other way around. I don't need your help, Cat, or anyone's. So stop helping me, and leave me alone."

Catherine said nothing.

Out of the corner of her eye, Maeve saw Wes step into the doorway.

"What's going on?"

"Nothing," said Maeve, turning to him, away from Catherine's pained face. "It's none of your business."

He stepped into the room. "It sounds like you two were having some kind of disagreement."

"And?" she challenged, before she could help it; she usually tried to keep the peace, but tonight she was in no mood. "People disagree with each other, as you are well aware."

"I wanted to make sure it didn't get out of hand."

"Can't you ever let anything go without inserting your opinion?"

"Now let's calm down," said Wes, lowering his hands to demonstrate what calming down looked like, and Maeve had never wanted to punch someone as much as she wanted to punch Wes in that moment. "Let's just talk this over."

"I am so tired," said Maeve, through gritted teeth, her voice nearly a whisper, "of men telling me to calm down."

"Wes, it's fine," said Catherine, her hand on his arm; she was smiling, but she had never been good at pretending, and Maeve could see the hurt in her eyes. "Really."

Wes cast her a sympathetic look and turned to Maeve. "I'm sorry, Maeve, I don't mean to offend. But I know how these things end, and if I can help, I'd like to do so."

"I hope you can breathe up there on your high horse," Maeve blurted, and stormed from the room to say goodnight to Amy.

MAEVE HAD INTENDED to go up to her room with a bottle of wine and work her way into a hazy slumber. But somehow, the thought of drinking made her feel sick. She sat in her bed with a book, but she couldn't concentrate. She tried to sleep, but her mind was in a whirlwind. Finally she gave up. She threw the covers back, slipped quickly into jeans and her Vassar sweatshirt, and walked out her front door, keys in hand. She was going for a drive, a long one, with the music blasting, to clear her aching mind.

As she fell into the front seat, something behind her caught her eye. She turned to the back seat, where she saw Nicole's frumpy leather purse.

The fire in her calmed a little. Nicole would feel lost without that purse.

She imagined the little girl searching for it, crying for the one thing that connected her to her mother.

"Damn it," Maeve muttered, but there was softness in her voice. She had never been to Kyle's, but she had his address from work. She punched it into her GPS app: she would be there in about twenty minutes. Briefly she considered going back inside first and changing, putting on some makeup and doing something with her hair, but she didn't. Who cares. *Fuck it*, she decided, and drove off down the street toward Kyle's.

Twenty minutes later she pulled into a tidy-looking townhouse community and followed the road past dozens of identical two-story homes, most with minivans or sport utility vehicles in the driveways and playground equipment in the back. Toward the end of the road, she found the Langahan home. She pulled into a spare spot and stared at it. It was as nondescript as the others. It had a kids' picnic table beside the bushes. Kyle's sedan sat in the driveway.

Maeve grabbed Nicole's purse from the back seat and walked up the steps to the front door. She rang the doorbell without thinking, not giving herself time to worry about facing Kyle.

After a minute, Kyle opened the door. He was wearing jeans and a gray t-shirt that looked like it had been washed a thousand times. It looked comfortable and soft, and it hung neatly over his well-built frame. It said, "End Toxic Dumping. Water You Waiting For?"

He stared at her with confusion for a moment, his expression blank. Eventually, he blinked and attempted a mild smile.

"Maeve," he said. "What are you doing here?"

Maeve held out Nicole's purse. "She left this in my car. I knew she would need it."

Kyle looked at it, then slowly reached out to take it. His eyes returned to Maeve's. "Thank you," he said quietly, with an indecipherable look. "She's actually not here."

Maeve's shoulders slumped. "She's not?"

"She's spending the night at my parents'. She went over there after dinner."

"Then I guess I didn't need to run over here."

"It's okay. I can give you this." He gestured for her to follow him; she closed the door and did. She glanced around at his living room while he led her to the dining room table. There were built-in bookshelves overflowing with books. There were lots of houseplants. There were picture frames everywhere, most of them filled with Nicole's shining smile. It was warmly lit and relatively tidy, with a telltale stack of papers or pairs of shoes askance. It was comfortable, unpretentious, lived in.

"Here," he told her, handing her a sheet of paper with a child's illustration on it. "Nicole made this for you."

Maeve looked at it. It was undeniably a portrait of Maeve. She was wearing Snow White's outfit. On the top of the paper, she'd written "Thank you" in rainbow letters.

Maeve felt all fuzzy and sparkly inside; her heart momentarily warmed. "How sweet."

She stared at it a moment, then looked back at Kyle.

"Well," she said, "I guess I'll go." She turned to leave.

"Fine. I'll see you next week."

"Oh, no, no," she said, wheeling back around. "You're going to have to talk to Aditi about that."

"Why?"

"Why? How about because you went behind her back and sabotaged her signature bill? Because you basically told the press her work wasn't good enough? Aditi was pretty upset. You're going to have to face her before everything just goes right back to normal."

"I was trying to help," he said, his voice tense with frustration, though he looked tired. "Bringing attention to the issue will inspire more support."

"You know, Langahan," she said, her hands at the sides of her face, and pulling her hair back—she was done, she was just so done, "it's one thing to go behind everyone's backs, and it's another not to own it. Even if reasonable people could disagree on method, you still have to involve your team. How do you think it feels to think you're really making headway with someone, to begin to care about them, and then find out they don't even take you into their confidence? Can you blame Aditi for being upset? I mean, think of Aditi's feelings."

"I am really sorry about that. And I'll talk to her. I just knew what was right, and that it had to be done regardless of the inevitable pushback. You do things one way, and I do them another: why can't we do both, and make up for each other's gaps?"

"So your attitude is that it's better to beg forgiveness than ask permission. Got it. Does this same rule apply to Nicole?"

He scrunched his face. "Nicole? What do you mean?"

"You pinned your daughter's welfare on a hope and a prayer today. She was nervous, and scared. How do you justify that?"

"Nicole was fine, Maeve. She had a great time with you and Amy, and she bounced off to my parents' as if nothing had happened."

Maeve shook her head and started for the door. "You're a good dad, Langahan. But you operate with tunnel vision. You help her get over her mom, but what about after? What about her fears, her needs, her questions? She's not a little adult, despite dressing like one. She isn't mature enough to understand all this. It might be why she's turning to strangers to get her questions answered."

"Wait, what?" Kyle followed her toward the door with wide, quick steps. His voice was urgent now, his ramparts clearly shaken. "Who is she going to with questions? And what questions?"

Maeve had her hand on the doorknob. She paused, aggravated with herself for saying too much. She never had gotten around to talking to Kyle about Nicole's questions. Now it would look like she'd been hiding it. She closed her eyes a moment, fortified her voice, and turned to him. "It wasn't a big deal," she said, with deliberate calm. "She had some questions for me, that one day, when you brought her to the office. Questions about being left out because she's a girl."

Kyle was staring at her. His face softened, turning a little bemused. "Oh. I guess...I guess that's fine." His brow crinkled. "I mean, she can come to me with that stuff, but I get why she wouldn't." His eyes grew serious. "Was she left out of something? Is she okay?"

"Yes, she's okay." Maeve shifted her weight. "Some boys didn't let her build a robot with them because apparently girls aren't as good at science. She was also upset that a girl was being teased because she's pretty."

Kyle said nothing for a moment or two. "What did she do?"

"She walked away from the boys," Maeve told him, with undisguised anger in her voice, "no doubt because you told her to be respectful. But she stood up for the girl who was being teased." Inexplicably, tears sprang to her eyes. She frowned and firmed her jaw, ordering them to recede. "Your daughter's a strong, moral person."

"I know that." He was silent, thinking. "What else did she ask?"

"She wanted to know why boys think girls aren't as good at things like science and why girls are mean to each other too."

His eyebrows turned down. "And what did you tell her?"

Maeve braced herself. "I told her the truth, which is that girls' competence is a threat to male power, that men built the system by themselves and for themselves, that girls are taught to turn on each other and are not immune to misogyny."

Kyle's jaw dropped. "Are you kidding me?" He had his hands up at his sides, raised in a *What the hell?* gesture; his voice had grown louder. "That's a little much, don't you think? She's just a little kid!"

"A little kid with big questions! Nothing I said was wrong, or do you think it was wrong? Are you denying any of it? Would you deny any of it to her?"

"I'm not saying it's wrong, Maeve, just that I really should have been present for that, so I could know what was said and see her response. She's been going around with this ever since! I'm sure she's got a hundred more questions. It probably confused her more than anything else."

"You think she hasn't already seen it? You think she hasn't figured it out? She was asking those questions because she's a good observer. I didn't tell her anything she didn't already on some level know. I've been telling you this for weeks—for *years*. It's the same shit we talked about back in high school, back when Heller turned off my mic."

"You're not seriously bringing up high school. This is about right now, about you taking it upon yourself to project onto my daughter. I just don't think you had any business discussing such adult issues with her, especially in such heavy terms, and especially back then, before we'd become this close."

"All right, Langahan." Maeve threw her hands up in exasperation. "I'll concede. It was a lot, and it was heavy. But she was asking. I told her flat out she should talk to you about it; I cut off the conversation when things were getting a little too deep. But she was practically begging me to answer her questions. What was I supposed to do? Say nothing? Turn her away? I wasn't 'projecting,' I was meeting her in her own experiences. Not answering with the truth would only make it seem like more of a secret, and it would make her more upset."

"Why didn't you tell me about it? You don't think I had a right to know this? Talk about secrecy and confidence!"

"Okay." Maeve's heart was pounding, and she could feel the redness in her face—too many emotions, too many layers, and she was having to think too quickly. "Maybe you're right about that. But she specifically said she wanted to talk to me about it. Talk to *me*. She clearly needed a woman's opinion on this, and I gave her what she needed. At the time it seemed best to keep it between us. And then I was going to tell you at dinner that night, but you pissed me off, and I never got around to it."

"And yet here you are, talking to me about going behind people's backs."

Maeve set her jaw and glared at him. She'd been pushed well beyond her limits; she couldn't remember the last time she'd been this worked up. "I'm so over it, Langahan—over it," she ground out. "Why, why, *why* does it always have to be a fight. *Why* do you have to push my buttons. And why, *why* do you have to look so *fucking* good doing it."

Kyle's eyes opened wide, and Maeve's hand flew to her mouth. She stood straighter, and her face flushed. Had she really said that part out loud? When he merely stared at her in silence, she began to wonder if she'd imagined it. But any doubt she had was obliterated by one look at his face. His eyes were round as quarters, his jaw tight. Time stood still for a minute, for a year. She couldn't breathe, couldn't blink. She stared at him with horror.

"I..." she began, her stomach dropping, but she couldn't finish her thought: she sucked in her breath as he crossed the space between them, catching a fleeting glimpse of his piercing expression before he was kissing her, his hands clutching her face. She tilted her head and parted her lips, and let him do it. The force of her own reaction startled her. She watched the scene as if she were floating above it; there were two Maeves now, the rational Maeve who hated Kyle Langahan, who had always hated him—for good reason!—and the traitor Maeve, the one who was in control of the body and who was acting as if she'd been positively longing for him—desperate, even! frantic!—as if he didn't infuriate her— enrage her! inflame her!

Your fingers are in his hair, she marveled; *your thigh is lifted around his hip. You are inside his arms. You are inside his mouth.* What was she doing? What was even happening?

"Where's your bedroom," gasped body Maeve, and observer Maeve dropped her jaw with shock. *He's pulling you toward the stairs. You're stumbling down the hallway. You're in his bedroom! You're on his bed! Kyle Langahan's bed!*

"Mmm," she breathed, momentarily forgetting herself. He was lying on top of her, his sighs rumbling in her throat. Her hands were on his face; his five o'clock shadow was bristling on her skin. She brushed it with her fingertips, the roughness spurring her further. If she was being honest, it had always struck her as sexy, the way it showed off his angular cheeks and jaw...

What the hell are you talking about? observer Maeve objected. *Don't do it. Don't you fucking do it!*—but she was sighing as his fingers stroked her beneath her ear, was letting her eyes flutter shut and her breath catch, was parting her legs for him, arching toward him in invitation. She was squeezing him from behind, smiling at the groans he emitted in response.

He pulled his shirt off, his arms lifting, releasing the scent of him into her nostrils and offering her full view of his neat waist and broad chest, of the way his arms were rounded with muscle. Her eyes widened, and her stomach dropped. *Jesus.* She brazenly ran her hands over his biceps, grinning.

Don't do it! observer Maeve warned her again, even as she entangled her arms in the sleeves of her sweatshirt, let him help free her elbows and hands and toss it to the floor. *Don't you give too much ground here. Sheering! Get ahold of yourself.*

She cleared her throat. "Langahan," she murmured, swallowing, in an attempt to mask need with sarcasm, and aware of it. She firmed her voice. "You're actually hotter than I thought."

But his words were smothered by the swallowing of her lips. "I've always known you were hot."

She exhaled shakily: he was palming her breast in his hand, having pushed it down over her bra, breathing hard. His thumbs brushed her nipples. She watched on, stunned, as his head lowered toward her chest. *Okay...*she compromised with herself, her chin lifted into the air as his tongue took over for his fingers. *I'll let him do this. Just this!* But the silkiness of his tongue on her skin was sending warm ripples over her belly and thighs, and her fingers were tugging with his at the waistband of her jeans.

Oh, my God, they're around your knees. They're in his hands. They're on the floor.

This was getting ridiculous. She was taking back some control.

She pushed upward and flipped him onto his back, then straddled him, unbuttoning his jeans and unzipping his fly.

"I'll take the top, if you don't mind," she informed him, lifting her hips as he kicked off his pants.

"What's wrong with the bottom?"

"Why does it matter?"

"Do you not like it?"

"What if I didn't?"

"God, you look amazing."

She blinked and swallowed. "What?"

"I said you look amazing. Kiss me."

"Are you telling me what to do?"

"Please."

He tried to sit up. She pushed him back down.

She reached behind her back and unsnapped her bra, then tossed it to the floor.

"God, you look so fucking *amazing*."

His fingers had slipped beneath her red lace panties; they were brushing and circling *just right*. Between thumps of her heart, she registered surprise: she hadn't had this done to her before, not at this point, when they were still racing toward the finish. There was no reason for him to do this; it benefited only her. She had the sense of this being somehow important, but she couldn't think. She lowered her head to hide the bliss-heavy contortions of her face. *My God.*

What are you doing with your eyes? Why is your mouth open? Stop moving like that. Stop making that sound.

"You know," he said, pulling down his boxers, "if you don't try something, you won't know if you like it."

She clucked her annoyance, drawn momentarily from her haze. "Are you suggesting I make uneducated decisions?"

"Why would..." He squirmed and sighed as he throbbed inside her fingers. *You are holding him in your hand! You are positively gripping him!* "Why...would I do that. Why do you...always...You always think the worst of me."

These last words had trailed off into a kind of choked whisper. From underneath half-closed eyelids she caught view of his face. He was watching her with an earnest, breathy smile. He was enjoying this too much. She got herself under control.

"My opinions are informed, Langahan." He was pulling her panties down over her hips. *Don't even think about letting him do that!* She lifted each knee to slip them off herself, and leaned back into his fingers. A moan gathered in her throat, but she held it back. "Are you really going to do this right here, right now?"

"I'm just saying...that maybe...that maybe there's an experience...that you'd enjoy, if..."

She was cupping him from beneath. She let him suffer for a moment, enjoying the sight of his chiseled face in agony.

"...if you weren't so defensive. There's no point in...in being stubborn if...if it doesn't..."

"Are you going to get a condom, Langahan, or would you prefer to lie there arguing with me all night?"

Abruptly, he turned and reached into his nightstand for a condom. Their fingers intertwined as she helped him unroll it.

"Leave it to a man," she said, lifting her leg to make room for him, "to tell me my not acceding to his opinion is just 'being stubborn.'" She maneuvered in position, heart hammering. *Oh, my God. You're going to do this.* "Ever the know-it-all, Langahan, even in the goddamn bed."

"Fine! It's fine." He rubbed her hips as she adjusted herself on top of him. *God damn it, are you helping him! Are you actually fucking helping him!* His eyes drifted shut, then opened; he made them focus, clearly with effort. "You're arguing with me, but whatever."

"I'm pretty sure you started it."

"Fine, I'm sorry. I'll stop."

"Good." She brought her hand to his cheek, in an unexpected moment of softness. "Now, are we doing this, or what?"

He arched his hips upward, and she pushed down hard. They cried out simultaneously, then fell into motion with instant understanding, looking at each other and grinning through hazy eyes.

"Maeve," he breathed, his chest rising and falling under her hands. "You look...so good from down here."

A warm overturning of her insides. *Don't let him get to you.* "Are you saying I was right?" she demanded, but the words were rushed and quick. She shifted to take him in deeper; he sensed her intention, and shifted in return. She pressed into his hips; he was at the center of her existence. *Holy hell. You're in it now. Just don't let him know. Don't say anything. Turn your face away.*

He wouldn't stop watching her. What was he looking at? "You were right, you were right! You're always fucking right."

She released a quick laugh, which surprised her by morphing into a loud, shaky sigh. "You're kidding with me."

"No." His lips parted as she pressed down harder, picking up speed. "I...I'm serious. I...don't kid, as you know."

Maeve laughed wildly at this. Was this sarcasm? Right now? She spread her hands over his chest, squeezing his pecs. "Oh, Langahan. Always such a card."

"Maeve." His fingers were trailing over her shoulder as they moved together; she winced, not unpleasantly. "Can I please sit up. I really want to kiss you."

She turned her head to glance at his fingers. She couldn't get over how nice this felt. Her shoulder! What the hell? In all her experience sleeping with men she'd never been talked to like this, touched like this; they'd never deferred to her, asked to kiss her, shown actual endearment, except of course to get her into bed. But they were already in bed, so what exactly was he up to?

Don't give in. Just get this over with. This is physical. That's all this is.

At her hesitation, he took a chance, and rose. They were pressed together now, chest to chest. He wrapped his arms around her until she was enclosed in him, supported. All the while, their hips rolled in tandem, naturally, as if they'd done this a hundred times. Maeve exhaled as his fingers slinked over her throat and into her hair, his lips descending on hers in an open-mouthed kiss. She brushed his five o'clock shadow with her fingertips, clutching his jaw as it worked with hers.

"Kyle," she breathed, but she didn't know why. His lips were now trailing over her throat; his hand was gently gripping her hair, the other splaying across her back, driving them closer together. There was urgency in his movements, but also something else...

She couldn't identify it...She'd never seen it and didn't know what it was.

She moved her knees a little, and he shifted in return; she leaned back, to angle him, and he moved forward, meeting her where she was. Through the oncoming oblivion she was—what was she? grateful?—for his obvious attention, for his knowing what to do. Stranger still, he seemed eager to do it. He was mimicking her movements, letting her lead. He was beneath her, he was asking permission; he was arguing, but giving in every time. Where was the fight? The disagreement? She was trying so hard to take control, but you can't really take something that's given voluntarily.

They were holding each other's faces now; she hadn't even realized that had happened. His eyes were closed, he was panting; he was at her mercy, and he seemed to be enjoying it. Maeve was fixated on the bliss in his expression. There was a thrill in seeing him like this, in knowing him in this new way. She felt her animosity melting, right along with her defenses; the same fire electrifying her senses was turning it all to cinders.

You've got to stop this. From a distance, observer Maeve echoed through. *It isn't too late.*

She rode harder, perhaps foolishly, in half-hearted punishment; he groaned hoarsely in response.

"Maeve, you're amazing. Oh God."

You're losing it. Don't lose it.

She slinked her arms around his back and squeezed him, to shut him up; she rested her cheek on his so she was looking behind him, denying them the intimacy of a kiss. But it meant she could feel his breath and his heartbeat; now their movements were more in sync, and the bristliness of his jaw was enlivening all the nerves in her skin.

His voice was beginning to shake. "You're amazing. You feel so amazing."

"Stop saying 'amazing'!" she cried—but she was bearing down

into the concentrated fire, already anticipating the clenching release to come.

He obeyed, but sighed in raspy bursts now, and more often. Between her own breathless exclamations she relished the sound of it, understanding vaguely that it was not because he was suffering but because he wasn't.

Caring.

The word rose without warning into her consciousness from beneath silky oblivion. That was it—that was what she'd felt in his movements. It was unknown to her, but there was something wonderful in it, something safe—and through the oncoming mindlessness she knew that she was no longer running from it, but chasing it.

She leaned her head on his, her defenses dissolving.

You're hopeless. I give up.

"Well, go then!"

"What?"

"Nothing!" She pressed her hands to his temples, her eyes intent on his. "Just kiss me again."

She had now given in completely, the last defenses wafting upward and out into the universe. There was nothing now but him, in the darkness and in the present—no high school, no debates, no determined attempts to resist. Rather than push back, she held fast, undulating with him seamlessly in a steady, inevitable ascent. She was whispering his name, she was kissing him behind his ear; she was letting him guide her movements, unrestrained in her response until the climactic, furious end. After her quickening had subsided she watched him finish. The relief was beautiful in his face. His fingertips were taut on her back, and she leaned into him, the skin between them slick with sweat.

They slowed together, hearts racing, and fell backward together onto the bed. They looked at each other with wonder, and smiled through sex-drowsed eyes.

He was gazing at her from below, glowingly, with a look of pure contentment. He stroked her cheek with his finger, his expression more tender than she ever imagined it could be.

"You're so pretty," he told her, his voice gentle with reverence. "I've always thought so."

Maeve's face turned grave, and she pushed herself off him.

"You are such an asshole."

The ecstasy left his face, and he propped himself up on his elbows. "What?"

"I can't believe this happened. I can't believe you let this happen."

"Why? What? What's going on?"

She was shaking her head, searching the floor for her clothes. "And I wanted it! I can't believe it. After everything. After everything you did."

"What? What did I do?"

She was shaking. "The assault." She'd found a few of her things and was picking them up in the darkness. "The assault was all your fault."

"*What?*"

She was already stepping back into her underwear, then pushing herself into her bra. "The night of the dance, after the election."

"The election? You mean the primary?"

"No! Not the primary. There was no dance after the primary!"

"Then what, what election? What are you talking about?"

"The *dance*." She stopped a moment to glare at him, then pulled her jeans up over her legs and hips. "The night of the dance, when you asked me to dance with you. You remember that night. You remember Nate McCallister."

"Oh. Yes." He watched her in confusion as she zipped and buttoned her jeans. "But what did I do? What happened? What's this about an assault?"

Maeve stuck her head through the neck of her sweatshirt. "I

was sexually assaulted that night. In the box, behind the school. Nate lured me there, to tease me. It got out of hand. They almost raped me."

"Who did?"

"The football team."

He looked like someone had punched him; his face contorted with pain. "Oh, my God. Oh, my God, Maeve. I'm so sorry. What can I do?" He was sitting up in bed now, reaching out to her; he made to get out, but she pushed him back down.

"Don't get up. I'm leaving. Don't even try to stop me."

"But what did I *do*? Seriously, Maeve, I really just don't know. Please tell me what I did. Can I fix it? Can I apologize? Whatever it is, I can—"

"So you can get me into bed again? Don't go to the trouble."

"What? Maeve, I'm sorry. If I offended you, I want to make it right. I should probably know what I did, but you're going to have to help me."

She was fully dressed now, and she stared at him, pitiful in his bed, his hair mussed, his lips turned downward with a frown.

"You stopped me," she told him, through firm, gritted teeth; she was trembling violently, and she was dizzy, as if she were having an out of body experience. "You stopped me just as I was leaving, and that's the only reason it happened."

"You mean when I asked you to dance?" He was utterly confused, and his confusion made her even angrier. "I asked you to dance to be nice. To extend an olive branch. And also, I was attracted to you. I never would have hurt you. I'm not like those guys, I swear."

"Don't you dare 'not all men' me."

He was out of the bed now, having wrapped a blanket around his waist. She pushed him away, but he came closer; she was crying, and he tried to wipe her tears.

"Don't touch me!" she yelled, in a panic, smacking his hand away. "I don't want your pity."

"Maeve, Jesus, I'm sorry! I don't pity you, I just want to help you."

"They surrounded me. They pushed me against the wall."

"Fucking monsters." She stopped a moment to rub her running nose on her sleeve, and he took the opportunity to wipe a tear from her cheek. "I can't believe this. I feel terrible. If I had known they were doing it I would have done everything I could to stop it."

"They pulled my hair. They had their hands on me, all at the same time. They *laughed* at me. They fucking *laughed*."

"I'm so sorry." He tried to hug her, but she pulled away; she was out the doorway, and he followed her down the stairs.

"I never told anyone," she said, still shaking, and racing toward the door, "and you made me tell you, and I hate you for that. And I hate you for letting this happen, and I hate you for being right about Nate Mc-fucking-Callister."

He was calling her name, but she ignored him, and she fled outside into the night.

MAEVE WAS DRIVING in the opposite direction of her house. She hadn't even thought about it; she was drawn in that direction by a force that was larger than she was. It was after eleven o'clock, rather late for Catherine—but Maeve could at least drive by the house and see if there were any signs of life.

He called her three times; she didn't have to look to know it was him. Every time the phone rang, she cried out with panic. *Stop it, just stop it,* she begged him in her mind. *Just stop it, and leave me alone.*

She pulled up to the house and was relieved to find the lights still on downstairs. It was a nicely sized Tudor-style house, like something out of a fairy tale. It had dormers and decorative framework, eight-paned windows and a steep sloping roof.

Charmingly asymmetrical, it was surrounded by a meticulously cared for lawn and garden.

It was a gorgeous house, probably the most beautiful Maeve had ever seen. And yet she had always been put off by its overbearing perfection, as if it were personally calling her out on her flaws. It had been Wes's house, of course, before he married Catherine. Like Wes, it was impressive and pristine, and it knew it, and it didn't mind if you knew it, too.

She parked in the driveway and closed her eyes. He was texting her now: her phone was vibrating from the passenger's seat. She picked it up warily.

Maeve, please call me.

Maeve, I'm sorry.

Please, Maeve, please. Let's talk about this.

Maeve ignored him. She climbed out of the car and stalked up to Catherine's front door. Fearful of waking Amy, she knocked a couple of times rather than ringing the doorbell. She stood waiting for a couple of minutes, wondering if she should have texted her sister; then the door opened, and she was face-to-face with her brother-in-law Wes.

Maeve's already restless heart dropped with dread. Wes was the last person she wanted to see just then. Her relationship with him was erratic enough on a normal day; the fact that she had argued with him, and about Catherine, mere hours earlier only exacerbated her anxiety at having to deal with him at her moment of crisis.

"Hey, Wes," Maeve mumbled, distractedly; she was looking into the house to see if her sister was coming. "I need to talk to Catherine."

"Catherine's asleep," Wes told her. "She fell asleep tucking in Amy."

"Oh." Maeve's face fell. What was she supposed to do now? She supposed she'd go home and sulk with a bottle of wine. "All right."

She turned to leave, but Wes called her back.

"Is there something I can help you with?"

Maeve turned back around and looked at him. He was still wearing his suit slacks, but the tie was gone, and the sleeves of his white shirt were rolled up toward his elbows. He was a tall silhouette in in the dim light from the table lamp in the foyer.

She watched him for a minute. Her phone buzzed again from inside her purse, and she closed her eyes a moment, bracing against the rushing of her heart.

"No," she said finally. "This is really something I need my sister for."

"Why don't you try me?"

Maeve was getting irritated. Did he always have to swoop in and save everyone? "This is rather personal, Wes. But thank you."

"Well, if you're sure, I won't press you. But I might be able to help."

His expression was calm and thoughtful, with just the hint of a smile. Maeve firmed her jaw.

He seemed to sense her faltering. "Come on," he said, gently, and gestured with his head into the house for her to join him.

Maeve sighed ruefully and nodded in return. She stepped inside the foyer and followed him to the left toward his study.

Wes's study was lined with classic wood panels and built-in bookshelves; a heavy wooden desk sat at the head of the room. A large fireplace, by which one could prop one's feet up while sitting on the loveseat, was the focal point—unless you counted the large bay window that looked out on the lawn. The room had the warm, cozy feel of a professor's personal library. Maeve flopped onto the loveseat and stared into the cold fireplace, wishing she had a stiff drink.

Wes sat across from her in an antique wingback chair. He waited a moment for her to say something, but she only sat there rubbing her face in her hands.

"What seems to be the problem?" he said.

Maeve rubbed her lips together, trying not to lose it. She couldn't tell Wes she'd slept with Kyle. He would subtly criticize her choices; he would think it was unprofessional, as it was. Her heart was racing, making it difficult for her to think. Everything was hazy, thrown up into the air; if she didn't release it, the pieces would destroy her as they fell.

"I slept with Langahan," she gasped, and the words' being out there brought fresh horror. She leaned forward and dangled her head between her legs to stop the dizziness.

Wes didn't say anything. When she raised her head to brave a glance at him, he was staring at her with raised eyebrows.

"Is that right," he ventured finally.

His voice was tinged with humor that made Maeve seethe. "Yes," she said, now leaning her elbows on her knees and glaring at him sharply. "Do you have a problem with that?"

"*I* don't have a problem with it," he told her, shrugging with his hands raised, to illustrate. "It's none of *my* business. It appears *you* have a problem with it, though."

"You seem to think this is funny."

"I don't think it's funny. I do think it's a long time coming."

Maeve blinked, taken aback. Then she sighed and closed her eyes, hanging her head.

Wes said nothing for a moment, then spoke in a soft, quiet voice.

"You do know it was a long time coming. Right?"

Her phone continued buzzing. Exasperated, she withdrew it from her purse.

I'm sorry I hurt you.

What can I do? I really like you, Maeve.

I'm literally begging.

Maeve shook her head and held her face in her hands. What was the point.

"I guess it was."

Wes's voice was somber. "I understand your hesitation," he

said. "I've never been one to mix business and pleasure, either. But Kyle isn't technically employed by Aditi. I really don't think it's all that inappropriate."

"It isn't just that."

Wes was silent, and Maeve was grateful for his giving her the time she needed. She had to decide if she was really going to do this. She forced herself to meet his gaze. There was no judgment or condescension in his face, only patience and calm. She'd never fully trusted him—but Catherine did, and if he made Catherine happy, maybe Maeve should trust him, too. Catherine was an eternal idealist, and too often gave people the benefit of the doubt; but Maeve knew Catherine well enough to know that her contentedness with her life was full and sincere. Wes loved Catherine, and had done the work to prove it; he'd acknowledged his demons, and faced them, and it took a brave man to do it. Maybe, after all, he could help her with her own demons; maybe he'd understand.

She decided to trust him, to take a chance and be honest for once.

"I have spent years," she began, barely recognizing her shaking voice, "blaming Kyle for something that happened to me back in high school. It wasn't his fault. But I associate him with it anyway."

"What happened?"

She took a deep breath. "I was assaulted at school one night, following a senior class dance."

Wes's face softened. "I'm so sorry."

"I was lured there by a boy I liked. The whole football team was there waiting. They held my arms and pulled my hair. I was pushed against the wall and groped. The only reason it didn't go further was that the principal saw us and scared them away. He blamed me, though, for what I was wearing."

"What a terrifying experience. I'm furious that they did this to you."

Maeve teared up at the contained anger in his voice. He hadn't moved, but his face had turned hard. His body had tensed, and she could see his chest heaving.

"Thanks, Wes," she whispered, wiping away a tear. "I am, too."

"And nothing was done about this? There were no consequences, no repercussions, no one was held accountable?"

"I didn't tell anyone." She pulled a tissue from her purse and blew her nose, then sat back and took a deep breath. It was such a relief to talk about it, an unburdening she hadn't known she'd needed. "A couple of the boys tried to stop it at the time, but it was half-hearted. I could tell they were afraid."

She expected that next he would ask her why she hadn't reported it, and was already preparing herself to be defensive. But the question didn't come. From the look on his face she knew he didn't need to ask it, that he understood her secrecy and the hurtfulness of placing blame on her. She had never appreciated him as much as she did in that moment, when she knew he had listened to the conversations around him, when she realized he was not going to make her explain anything, only listen to her, and validate. She smiled at him, tears swimming in her eyes. He smiled back, and shifted in his seat.

"So what does Kyle have to do with all this? I can't imagine Kyle on the football team." His eyes widened. "He wasn't the boy who lured you there, was he?"

"No, no," Maeve assured him, sniffling and wiping her nose. "No, it was nothing like that. He..." As she went to say it, she was hesitant. She had held on so long to this bitterness, it had almost come to define her. Once the words were out there, they would be out of her control; they would drift into the air and take another shape, and she'd be forced to shift her entire axis.

Wes watched her with patient expectation. She had already started; there really was no turning back. She had opened the window, and it was wafting out with the breeze; she had to get to the other side of this, and something in his eyes told her it would be okay.

"I was on my way out," she began. "I was leaving. I bumped into him, and he asked me to dance. If he hadn't been there at that moment, if I had already gone, Nate wouldn't have found me, and this never would have happened." She paused. "I guess that's pretty unreasonable."

A smile touched his lips, but his eyes were rueful.

"You know," he told her, his brow furrowed thoughtfully, "we don't always respond to trauma in what other people would call a 'reasonable' fashion. What is 'reasonable'? How should someone respond to such a thing? Is there a right way to recover from that?"

Maeve inhaled, the knot in her chest loosening somewhat.

"I'm no psychologist," he went on, "but it seems to me only natural that you'd make this association."

Maeve smiled gratefully. It was what she needed to hear. She guessed he was able to relate, in some way, having recovered from his own trauma years before.

He reached out his hand, and she took it; he squeezed it, patted it affectionately, and retracted his arm.

"So," he said then, his voice lighter; he leaned back in his seat and propped his foot up on his knee. "I take it you're wondering what to do next."

"Yes." She didn't really want to think about it; what she wanted more than anything was to go to sleep and wake up in the morning and forget this ever happened, but she was here now, and she might as well deal with it. In any case, talking it over was less painful than she had thought it would be. "This is not something I expected to happen, and I'm at a total loss. I'm not used to making impulsive decisions. I'm thrown off my equilibrium."

"Is that all?"

Maeve blinked. "All?"

"My apologies. I certainly don't mean to suggest you need any more. I was just expecting you to say something about Rhys."

"What about Rhys?"

Wes stared at her, and she blinked again. Rhys. Right. She'd almost forgotten she was supposed to be in a relationship with Rhys. In fact she'd told him she would see him that very night. She narrowed her eyes: he hadn't even texted her to find out where she was.

Well then. She guessed she had her answer.

"Rhys doesn't figure into this."

For once, Maeve was glad Wes was so perceptive. She could see in his face he understood what she meant, and it saved her the trouble of saying it.

He watched her a moment, then spoke gently. "I think," he said, "that you should talk to Kyle."

"About what?"

"About what you told me."

"I tried. It didn't go well."

Wes's brow lowered. "Kyle wasn't understanding?"

"No, I wasn't."

Wes's mouth twitched with ill-suppressed humor.

Maeve sighed and leaned back in her seat. "I guess at some point I need to deal with the fact that what happened that night wasn't really his fault."

"I think talking to him about it might be a step in that process."

"Yes, but..." But what? But she'd have to let go of her anger, the thing that had sustained her and kept her memories at bay. She'd have to acknowledge that if it wasn't the fault of one person, it was the fault of people in general, that maybe it was possible she'd pushed off this knowledge successfully enough to move on with her life but not successfully enough to avoid bringing it into all her relationships ever since. She'd have to reevaluate her entire existence, everything she'd told herself about who she was and why, everything she knew about the world, everything she knew about Kyle.

"Also," she noted, raising her finger in half-hearted protest, "he's really just an asshole."

"Kyle's not an asshole."

"He is. He's an asshole. You don't know him like I do."

"What on Earth are you talking about?" Wes raised his eyebrows at her. "I've been working with him as long as you have —longer, even. I've taken him with me to Washington. Hell, he primaried me, for crying out loud."

"He's just so *stubborn*. You can't tell him *anything*. He's blunt, he's peevish, he's—"

She noticed Wes's expression, and stopped. He was nodding along with her, his face one of lightly amused interest.

She frowned at him. "What?"

He held his hands up innocently. "I didn't say anything."

"Your eyes say it all. You think this is funny. You think I just described myself."

"Hey, those are your words, not mine."

She shook her head; this was getting too confusing. "I think it's possible having him back in my life has made me think about things again, things I've made a point of forgetting. I was *so good* at keeping it all separate, and he mushed it all together. I think it's possible that's why I've pushed him away."

"I think that's possible, too."

"It could be a defense mechanism."

"A defense mechanism? You? I don't believe it."

She put her fingers to her temples and closed her eyes. "I need a drink."

"I can get you a drink."

"I have to drive home."

He didn't say anything. She sighed.

"If you're not ready," he said finally, "you're not ready."

"Ready for what?"

"Ready to move past this with Kyle. Hell, you don't have to do it at all. I'm not trying to push you, Maeve. What's most important is that you take care of yourself. If you don't want to see him again, you shouldn't."

"Right."

He noticed the hesitation in her voice. "What's the matter?"

She was eyeing him carefully. Goddamn him, that Wes.

"I know what you're doing," she told him. "You're using reverse psychology."

"What do you mean?"

"You're trying to make me imagine not seeing him again, in order to make me want to see him."

"Maeve." Wes leaned forward now, his face very serious. "That is absolutely not what I'm doing. I would never profess to know how this feels to you or to know more than you about how to handle it. I would never suggest you do something you're not comfortable with." His eyebrows rose in a conciliatory manner. "Do you believe me?"

"Yes." She smiled soberly. "Yes, I believe you."

"Don't get me wrong, I want you to be happy. If you think you can be happy with Kyle, I'd love to see you get together. But if you don't, or if you don't want to, I won't try to change your mind."

"I know. Sorry."

He leaned back once more. "And you don't owe me an explanation. You don't have to tell me what you want, if you don't want to."

Maeve watched him as he drummed his fingers on the side of his chair, looking steady but casual, in his usual way.

"Of course," she said, affecting her own best casual tone, "there's no guarantee he'd want to be with me, anyway. Not that I'm saying I would want to be with him," she added quickly.

"Of course not." He looked at her seriously, but there was a grin in his eyes. "But I think he would."

Maeve didn't know what this meant, but Wes was sharp. No

doubt he'd picked up on Kyle's signals. No doubt he'd picked up on hers.

Her phone hadn't buzzed in a while. She wondered at the fact that she wished it would buzz again.

"I mean," she said, a little shakily, "I guess I would consider it."

"I thought maybe you would." He smiled kindly, and shrugged. "Just a hunch."

Maeve smirked. "Here I thought I was hiding it so well. I hid it so well, I even hid it from myself."

"You can't put anything by me, Maeve." He grinned and held out his hands, as if it was a given; it was the old familiar confident Wes, the one who'd always struck her as full of it—though now she saw there was a shade of humor to his confidence, a self-deprecation that suddenly felt comforting and charming. "For what it's worth," he added, "I think you'd make a fine couple, personally."

Maeve's mind was all awhirl. "I almost didn't tell you what happened," she told him. "Things have always been a little weird between us. Honestly, I thought you'd be mad."

"Why would I be mad?"

"I thought maybe you'd think it was unprofessional. I thought maybe you were upset with me for what I said to Catherine."

"Well, you'll have to take that up with Catherine." His eyes turned serious. "Have you ever told her? About what happened that night in high school?"

"No." Maeve's heart began leaping; she knew she'd have to tell her. "I put it behind me and tried never to think of it again."

"I would consider telling her. She's your sister, and she'll help you. Besides, she's been through it herself."

"I've been through what?"

Wes's face lifted toward the door, and Maeve turned at the sound of her sister's voice. Catherine was standing in the doorway, a tall angel in her flowing ivory silk robe. Her honey-colored hair was tumbling over her shoulders, the hallway's soft light making the curves of her figure a silhouette through her nightgown.

"Hello, sweetheart," said Wes, his face suddenly glowing like the light that illuminated his wife. "I thought you were asleep."

"I was," said Catherine, gliding into the room, pulling her robe tight around her body, "but Amy kicked me, and I woke up."

"It's just as well." Wes reached out his hand for her as she approached his chair and sat on the arm; as she perched there, he rubbed her lower back. "Now you don't have to sleep in a twin bed, and I don't have to miss you."

Ugh, thought Maeve, turning her face as she rolled her eyes.

"Maeve, what are you doing here?"

Maeve turned back to face Catherine, her hand now rubbing her throat. "I had something to talk to you about," she said, "but your brilliant husband has been talking with me instead."

"Oh?" Catherine looked between them curiously. "Has Wes been able to help you?"

"A little."

"Maeve just needs time to work some things out," Wes told Catherine. "As always, she'll be okay. But I'm sure a chat with her sister wouldn't hurt."

"What did you think Maeve should tell me?"

"I think she'll have to tell you that herself, if she wants to."

Wes stood, and Catherine lifted her chin up as he leaned down to kiss her. Wes then faced Maeve on his way up to bed.

"Good luck, Maeve, with whatever you decide. And whatever you decide, it'll be the right decision."

"Thanks." Maeve was surprised by the catch in her throat. She swallowed and bit her lip. "And also," she said, firming her voice, "thank you for this chat."

Wes smiled, patted her shoulder, and winked at her. "You're welcome," he said, and strode out the door.

Maeve watched him go, then stared at the emptiness he left in his wake. She didn't have it in her, right then, to tell him everything it had meant to her, or to own to him her part in their argument earlier that day; she was overwhelmed, she was frightened, she had to clear her head. She didn't yet know how to reconcile this with her usual cool cynicism; it would require a reassessment of everything she knew. She would tell him, though, eventually—and she smiled as she realized their relationship would never be the same.

Turning back toward her sister, Maeve wondered at the warmth of goodwill that surrounded her heart and radiated through her soul. Catherine had slid into the chair and was watching her with interest; she crossed her legs and looked at her, a kindly goddess ready, as always, to work her power for someone else.

"What did you want to talk to me about, Maeve?"

Maeve inhaled deeply as a rush of emotion swelled her chest. Catherine...it always came back to Catherine. Catherine had been there since she was born and had no idea what a towering presence she had been in her life every day since. Maeve had to smile at the innocence in Catherine's face. Catherine had an infallible capacity for forgiveness, which was fortunate, as she also had a sister with an infallible need to be forgiven. How often had Maeve wished she'd had Catherine's sunny outlook, her faith in people and in the universe, her unselfish goodness and goodwill?

"I wanted to talk to you," Maeve began, "about..." She stopped; she couldn't say it. Instead, she turned the tables. "I was just curious," she said then, instinctively looking to twirl the long hair she hadn't had in over twenty years, "how you managed to... how you moved on, after that night."

Catherine looked at her curiously; the delicate patch between her eyebrows had crinkled. "Do you mean after Wes was shot?"

"No." Maeve hadn't noticed until that moment that "that night" always meant Wes's being shot, never Catherine's surviving sexual assault. "I mean, the other part."

Catherine's eyelashes fluttered, that nervous tic she'd had ever since she was a girl. "Oh." Her wide eyes had sharpened, and her fingers picked nervously at the hem of her robe. "Why do you want to know about that, Maeve?"

"Well," Maeve began, shifting in her seat; bile gathered in her stomach, stars behind her eyes, but she pushed forward—this was the moment, like it or not, "I'm asking because I...because I slept with Kyle tonight, and—"

"You slept with Kyle?"

Maeve had never seen Catherine's face look like this. Her eyes were wide, her mouth open. Her cheekbones were elongated with her shock.

"Yes, but that's not the p—"

"Oh my gosh, you slept with Kyle!" Catherine clapped her hands and bounced in her seat. "I knew it! Finally! I'm so happy!" She was positively giddy.

"Wait, wait." Maeve held out her hand in protest. She closed her eyes and sighed, getting herself together. "You're missing a big part of this."

"Okay, I'm sorry." Catherine made a visible effort to calm down, folding her hands in her lap and affecting a serious expression that under normal circumstances would have made Maeve laugh. "What were you going to say, Maeve?"

"I was going to say," Maeve continued, unnerved, "that as complicated as this is, it's further complicated by the fact that..."

Catherine was not as good as Wes at masking her feelings. She appeared to be waiting patiently, but Maeve could tell she was fixating on her joy in what she'd just heard.

Maeve sighed. "It's complicated by the fact that...that I was sexually assaulted in high school."

Catherine's face, which had been frozen into an expression of impatient excitement, now loosened, dropped, and hardened into stone.

"You were what?" she murmured, her eyes to the side as her mind attempted to absorb this information.

Maeve related the story, from the beginning, when she'd gone to Catherine's room for her vintage red camisole, to the very end, when she'd thrown up in the bushes and sat in her dark room, shaking until morning. Catherine sat transfixed, staring as Maeve spoke, her only movement the blinking of her eyes and the occasional rise and fall of her chest. With every word, Maeve felt marginally lighter, twenty years' worth of shame and secrecy peeling from her heart like ice crackling off a tree branch in the sun. But as she spoke, she saw that it didn't disappear; it now lay between them, and they had to sort through it before it would be gone.

When she finished, Catherine rose and sat next to her on the loveseat. Maeve smiled awkwardly and turned to face her, her foot tucked under her opposite thigh.

Catherine looked at her frankly. "I wish you had told me this when it happened, but I understand why you didn't. I'm so sorry this happened to you."

Maeve rubbed her lips together, trying not to cry. She hated being the subject of sympathy, and she hated crying. Both made her feel weak, and small, and vulnerable—like a victim—like a child. She bit her bottom lip, forcing herself into normalcy.

"Well," she said, her chin in the air, her elbow on the back of the loveseat as her fingers combed casually through her dark bob, "you were off in college by then, studying the 1930s or vintage clothing or whatever it was that you were doing."

"I was an art major."

"I know."

Catherine was watching her, her eyes thoughtful. "You're trying to act strong now, so you don't have to feel weak."

"I suppose you studied psychology, too."

"Please stop doing that."

The familiar sickness filled Maeve's belly. "I'm sorry." She frowned. "I don't know why I keep doing it."

"It's a habit. Habits are hard to break."

"You really shouldn't put up with me."

"I don't 'put up with' you. I love you."

Maeve knew she did, and loved her in return for it, but she didn't say so. Instead, she casually picked up her phone and glanced at the screen.

She had two texts.

Maeve I don't want to bother you or intrude. Just know that I'm sorry and that I'm here if you want to talk. I don't regret what happened tonight, but I understand if you do. I'll do whatever it takes to make you feel better about all this, and if that means leaving you alone then that is what I'll do.

And then, two minutes later:

I care about you. More than I've probably let on.

Maeve looked at Catherine. Why was it always so hard? Everything was always such a riddle; people never showed you how they felt. There were layers and layers to human emotions, deeply rooted fears and insecurities that made people act in bizarre and mysterious ways. True motivations were buried far below the surface, and feelings that should manifest as flowers rose as poison ivy instead.

She returned her phone to her purse. "I don't know how you make it look so easy," she told her sister.

"Make what look easy?"

"Everything. Relationships. Love. Life."

"Please stop making fun of me."

"I'm not!"

Catherine sat back, assessing. "You told me I don't get angry, but I do. Do you know what makes me angry, Maeve?"

"What?"

"It isn't easy for me. Any of it. I've always had anxiety. I've never felt good enough for all this. I spent my whole life questioning myself. I stayed home and worked on my chocolate, avoiding friends and missing experiences because it was too hard for me to cope. Opening myself up wasn't easy; I had to change everything I knew. I had to jump into new experiences after years of relying on myself. When I was by myself, I had my routines, and I was good at them. Then I got married and moved into this house, and I had to do new things and meet new people, and all the while I worried, 'What if I'm a big disappointment? What if he sees I'm not the woman he thought?' It's only in the years since that night that I've been able to try to move past it. Even now, I have to make myself believe it, that I'm here and I'm happy and I deserve what I have. It isn't easy for me, Maeve, not at all. It's a constant, conscious battle. I've suffered every day for it, and it makes me angry that you can't see that."

"Oh." Maeve blinked. Catherine had never talked so much about her feelings; usually her quandaries were petty things, like what color roses she should buy for her end tables. "I had no idea."

Catherine was fiddling with her robe hem again. "I thought I wore it pretty plainly."

The two sisters looked at each other across space, in silence.

Maeve narrowed her eyes.

"You never told me."

"You never asked."

Maeve's eyes drifted, seeing nothing as she pondered this statement. It was true, she had never asked. But why should she have asked? Catherine may be perpetually late, and she may take four hours to decide which color to wear to dinner, and she may be frustratingly, almost inappropriately compliant; however, to Maeve, Catherine had been a pillar—maybe not of confidence, but of strength, of being who she was, unapologetically.

"I always thought you were above me," Maeve said, "like I could never live up to your goodness."

"That's funny. I always felt like I was beneath you, like I could never live up to your success."

They studied each other, one soft and fair, the other brazen and sharp.

"I'm sorry I never knew this about you," said Maeve. "And I'm also sorry for what I said to you today."

"It's okay," said Catherine. "You're only human."

Maeve sighed and rubbed her face in her hands. She needed to go home. She was exhausted.

"A question," Catherine blurted suddenly.

Maeve's eyes returned to her sister. "A question about what?"

"No, it's a poem title. 'A Question.' It's a poem by Robert Frost. He won a Pulitzer Prize in 1931."

"Yes, I'm familiar with Robert Frost," said Maeve. "What about his poem?"

Catherine sat straighter, her expression quite serious.

Her hands folded solemnly in her lap, she recited:

"A voice said, Look me in the stars
And tell me truly, men of earth,
If all the soul-and-body scars
Were not too much to pay for birth."

Maeve had just begun to be lulled by the soothing rhythm of Catherine's sing-song voice when Catherine stopped. Maeve raised her eyebrows and gestured with her hand.

"Well, go on. Finish."

"I did finish. That's the whole poem."

"Oh." Maeve's brow crinkled with confusion. "It's rather short. And, what's the point?"

"The point," said Catherine, "is that to be human is to be hurt. But, it's the price we pay for life."

Maeve stared at her in silence.

The morning's when you're the biggest mess.

Mornings are where life begins...Love is about trusting someone with your mornings.

Catherine settled back into her pillows. "That poem is actually from a collection published in 1942, and of course the forties are not my decade. But I've always loved it just the same."

Maeve smiled but did not respond, her eyes brimming with tears.

Catherine's eyes rounded. "What's the matter?"

Maeve sniffled and shook her head to clear it. "Nothing," she said, retrieving a tissue from her purse. She blew her nose and tossed her hand up to indicate that it really was nothing. "I was just thinking about something."

Catherine watched her as she blew her nose again and rubbed her eyes with her fingers.

"I really am sorry," she said. "About what happened to you."

Maeve closed her purse and adjusted her feet beneath her bottom. "Yeah, me too."

"It hurts me to think of you in pain with no one to talk to."

"Mmm." Maeve looked at her sister frankly. "I wanted to tell you later. You know, after that night. I thought it might help you to know you weren't alone. But I..."

She held her hands up helplessly. Catherine waited for her to continue, but Maeve's voice was stuck in her throat.

She put her hand on Maeve's knee.

"You had to be ready. It's okay."

Maeve sniffled again. "Do you have any idea how many times you've said 'It's okay' to me? Probably close to a million."

"Well, it is okay." The mood relaxed. Maeve took out her mirror and checked her reflection, needlessly; Catherine watched her as she fiddled with her things. "As I said, we're human."

Maeve put her purse away and took a deep, calming breath. She really could use that drink. What time was it, anyway? She really should head home.

"So what are you going to do about Kyle?"

Maeve faced her sister. "I don't know."

"I should rephrase that. What do you *want* to do about Kyle?"

Maeve didn't answer. She turned toward the fireplace.

"How did it happen, if you don't mind my asking?"

Maeve faced Catherine once more. She pursed her lips. "Well," she said, shifting in her seat, "I went over there to drop off Nicole's purse. We were standing there arguing, and before I knew it, he kissed me."

Catherine's eyebrows rose dramatically. "He just kissed you? Just like that?"

"Yes, just like that. Although," she said, brushing some imaginary dust off her pants, "I might have let slip that I thought he was attractive."

Catherine's brow now creased. "Wait, that's very different."

"It was all completely consensual, of course," Maeve went on, examining her fingernails. "When he led me to his bedroom, I allowed him to do it. I mean, I asked him to," she added, twirling her hand up as if it were nothing, "but really he initiated."

"But you asked him to."

"It was implied."

"Oh." Catherine watched her sister as she fluffed up her hair. "It's okay if you initiated it, Maeve."

"I know that." Maeve's voice was sharp, but her expression was warm. "I'm just saying, for the record, that it was his idea, not mine."

"Okay."

Maeve looked absently about the room, then faced her sister squarely. "I'm joking."

"I know."

Maeve hesitated. "Can I tell you a secret?"

"Please."

Maeve closed her eyes and sighed. "I think I've actually wanted this for a while."

Catherine remained silent.

Maeve opened her eyes and looked at her. "Well?"

Catherine started. "Oh," she said. "I'm sorry. I was waiting for you to tell me the secret."

270

Maeve laughed and shook her head. She turned to face forward on the loveseat, leaning way back. "That evening," she said, "in Aditi's office. Right before we got into that big fight."

"What about it?"

Maeve closed her eyes. "I think that's when I knew. When I knew I didn't hate him. When I let myself acknowledge what I'd noticed in him all along. We were getting along so well, and he looked so relaxed and casual...I just...I just wanted..." She shut her eyes tight, and sighed. "I think that's why it hurt so much when he asked me about my drinking."

"I told you that, and you said I was 'a piece of work.'"

"I didn't say it quite like that."

"Those were your exact words."

"It's water under the bridge."

Neither spoke for a moment or two.

"He was..." She flinched, unused to bearing herself like this, but she was on a roll. "He was very caring." She paused. "No one's ever really been caring."

"No one? Not even Rhys?"

Maeve frowned and thought back to her frantic tumbles with Rhys. Rhys wasn't shy with his praise, but it was usually after the fact, when there was nothing to lose, when he had his game face back on. It seemed purely physical for him, a sprint to the end—which was not news, as it was purely physical for her, too. That was the deal—that was the point.

"I guess it's not really their fault," she said, "as I'd never let anyone in like that." Her eyes sharpened with consideration. "Or I never engaged with anyone I thought would do it."

Another few moments passed in silence.

"Rhys," said Catherine finally. "What are you going to do about Rhys?"

"I haven't even figured out what I'm going to do about Kyle."

"I'm sure Rhys is very nice. But I already know I like Kyle more."

"Same. Which is why Rhys is probably the safer choice."

Catherine was taken aback. "Isn't the person you like best the safest choice?"

"No."

Catherine sat back to ponder. Maeve didn't say any more.

In the silence, Maeve checked her phone. Nothing.

"Well," she said finally, "I guess I'm going to go home."

"Okay." Catherine hesitated. "Are you going to be all right, Maeve?"

"Yes, I'll be all right, of course I'll be all right." She put her phone back in her purse and stood. "Thank you for talking to me about it, and please also thank Wes."

"You're welcome. And I will." Catherine stood to meet her sister, and she leaned in for an awkward hug. "I love you."

"I love you, too."

Catherine walked her to the door. Maeve hiked her purse up on her shoulder, waved, and turned with a smile to head toward her car. As she strode down the walkway as if nothing had happened, her face darkened and fell, but she wouldn't let her sister see it.

CHAPTER NINE

Hi, Maeve. I'm going to assume you still don't want to talk to me, and I'm going to leave you alone. That being said, I don't want you to mistake my silence for apathy. Whenever, if ever, you're ready to talk, I'm here. This will be the last message from me for a while. I hope you have a great day today.

Maeve received this text just as she was stepping out of her car to go to work. It was precisely eight o'clock in the morning. It was as if he had been watching the clock waiting for the earliest appropriate time to contact her.

She stared at the screen for a moment or two, looking at his name. She jumped when another text came through.

Actually, sorry. I meant to tell you that I'm going to call Aditi this morning to apologize. I'd love to continue working with her, and with you, but I don't want to make you uncomfortable. I guess we'll cross that bridge when we come to it.

Maeve closed her eyes and sighed, leaning her head against the headrest while she took a moment to breathe. She exhaled brusquely as her phone buzzed a third time.

Last one, I promise. I want to leave you alone, but I also don't want to put the onus on you. I'll try to call you in a week or so to see how you're doing, if I haven't seen you at Aditi's before that. If you don't want to hear from me, let me know or ignore my call. Okay, well... Have a great day, Maeve.

Maeve waited anxiously for a couple of minutes, but that appeared to really be the last one. She sighed again, helplessly. She'd spent a sleepless night simultaneously reliving what happened with Kyle and scolding herself for the pleasure it gave her. Images of him had washed over and around her, drowning all reason, pulling her into a current of thought she had no more strength to fight. She'd imagined him naked and gasping, his hand on her cheek, or suited up and serious, with a wariness she now understood. She'd imagined his passion in facing Congress and his tenderness with Nicole, his trusting her with his daughter and their little townhouse, lived in and quaint. After finally falling asleep, she'd woken that morning with a pit in her stomach, a veritable fireball of anxiety that singed her insides and quickened her breath. He was in her head, every second, as if he were standing before her in the flesh. It didn't help that his stunt was all over the news. Worst of all was her inability to parse her own feelings, to determine the fear at the bottom of this vortex. She was so used to being in control and competent. She now felt out of control, and bumbling, and lost in a land where she didn't know the language. She was afraid of it, and didn't like it.

She saw his face beneath her, breathless in ecstasy and relief. She felt his fingers stroking her shoulder, remembered the gentleness in his voice when he'd asked to kiss her. She shivered and shifted where she sat, then with an angry curse threw her head back against the seat.

"What am I going to do," she muttered, her elbows on the steering wheel, her fingers rubbing her temples.

Inside, she dropped her purse on her desk and, holding her breath, called Aditi, who was in another office across town. Aditi did not respond. Maeve put her phone down and dove into her work, the perfect antidote to emotional strife.

After about a half hour, Aditi called her back.

"I just got off the phone with Kyle," she told her. "He apologized for his secrecy and practically begged me to let him keep working with us."

The sound of his name was like an electric shock to her blood. "But did he really apologize?" she asked Aditi, determined to remain objective. "Is he genuinely sorry, or is it an 'I'm sorry you were upset' kind of thing?"

"Honestly, Maeve, I don't know. And if I'm really being honest, I don't care. Kyle has been invaluable to us, and I want him on our team. Regardless of our differences, I know he's on our side. For what it's worth, I think he's genuinely sorry. He was very sincere. He's going to help us get this done, and I trust he won't do anything he thinks will jeopardize our chances."

"How can you say you trust him after he kept this from us? How can you be certain he won't keep something from us again?"

"Because I talked to him, and I think he understood. And then there's Curt Tonelli."

Maeve straightened in her seat. "What about Curt Tonelli?"

"You mean you haven't heard? He's going to support Wes's bill. He said he was already leaning toward it, given the amendments, but that Kyle's protest showed him how important it is to his constituents."

Maeve was silent. "When did this happen?" she asked finally.

"About fifteen minutes ago."

Maeve leaned back in her seat. *Well, well, Langahan.* She pursed her lips against a wry grin. It looked like they were both right: they had different approaches toward a common cause, and each needed the other. They really did fill in each other's gaps.

"I asked him to call you," said Aditi, "but I'm not certain he will. He seemed to hem and haw. He said he's busy today but will get to it when he can. It was unlike him to question me. Is everything okay with you two?"

"Yes, yes," said Maeve, quickly. "Everything is fine."

"All right, well, I have a meeting in five. Let me know if he calls you. And Maeve."

"Yes?"

"Thank you for having my back."

For the next couple of hours, Maeve attempted to lose herself in her work, but she was restless; a tremor of expectation was in her blood, faint but constant. Around ten o'clock, her phone buzzed. She nearly knocked over her coffee to answer it.

Anticipation made her gut contract in on itself. When she saw it was Rhys, she didn't know if the drop in her stomach signified disappointment or relief.

"Hey," he said. "You never texted."

"You didn't, either."

A beat passed in silence.

"What the hell's going on, Maeve? Really. I mean, what the hell is going on?"

Maeve leaned back in her chair and sighed internally. For not a single moment had she considered telling Rhys about what had happened with Kyle; it wasn't even a question that she would not. These two parts of her life seemed to be in completely different universes, unrelated and irrelevant to each other. It was not impossible for her to imagine that Rhys felt the same way, and she supposed this was part of the problem.

"You know, Rhys, something about this just doesn't feel right."

Rhys said nothing for a moment or two.

Finally, he said, "And by 'this,' you mean..."

"I mean us. We don't feel right. It was fine when it was casual, when there were no strings attached. But I don't think I'm made for this, and I don't think you are, either. I was hesitant, but I gave it a shot. It didn't work out. I'm sorry."

Rhys was silent, and Maeve exhaled slowly. She hadn't realized how strongly she felt about this until she said the words out loud; she hadn't known she couldn't breathe until she could. At least now she could put things right again. At least now she could move on.

"Well," Rhys said after some time, "I mean, if that's how you feel, that's how you feel. I guess I have to respect it."

"Thanks. We had a really good thing before, you know? I think it would have been best to stick with it."

"Right." A few beats passed. "Look, can I say something? At the risk of pressuring you?"

"I guess."

"I think we go great together. Neither of us really 'does' relationships, so we'd have the same expectations. We work in the same field, and we have the same ideas. We like to have fun."

"Yes, but—"

"I've always had a thing for you, Maeve. I think you're brilliant and sexy, and I like being around you." Maeve imagined him shrugging. "And we get along so well."

"Rhys," she began, "I'm not saying all that isn't true. But we shouldn't have to work so hard."

"Then let's not work so hard. Let's just do whatever we want, right? Fuck the rules."

Maeve considered. She did like Rhys, after all. And as much as she liked what they had before, part of her was asking herself, *Do I really want to do this forever?* Not the being alone part—that part, she enjoyed. It was the wondering, the running, the never knowing what would come next. Even as the thoughts floated up to the forefront of her mind, they surprised her; she had never asked herself these questions before.

"Look," she said gently. "It isn't that I don't like you. It's that I'm not cut out for—"

She stopped, because she realized what she was saying was a lie. Why was she tired of the running; why did she suddenly want to know what came next? Was it only a coincidence, she wondered, that her crisis was coming now?

"Not cut out for what?"

277

Maeve had frozen, her mouth half open with the unsaid words. She went to speak, but no sound came out; she was finally allowing herself to see something she'd refused to see before. She was asking herself these questions because Kyle had made her ask them—but she couldn't have Kyle, couldn't face that humiliation. It was bad enough to have ripped herself apart, exposed the innermost workings of her conscience, the demons that pulled the strings. It was bad enough to be vulnerable. No, no—better to let that be, to make it easy on herself, and on him. She asked herself, as Catherine had asked her, why she cared so much about what Kyle thought of her. If she were to allow him into her life, she would care about it too much, would run herself aground with it, would die of it. Rhys, on the other hand, wouldn't judge her; Rhys wouldn't even care. Kyle would care too much, would have expectations. With Rhys, there wouldn't be any expectations. She could disappoint Kyle, she could disappoint Nicole; she could never disappoint Rhys, because Rhys shared her vices and flaws. Rhys was a wild card, but he was safer, just the same. Kyle, with his earnestness, his transparency, and his darling doll of a daughter, had made her ask the questions, and they couldn't be unasked. Kyle was out of the question, but Rhys was the next best thing.

"Okay," she told him shakily, unnerved, and suddenly unwilling to make any big decisions. "As long as we can make our own rules."

"Awesome! Yes."

Closing her eyes and exhaling deeply, she shook off the conversation and dove back into her work. The fact was, she figured, she didn't have anything to lose. Rhys had made clear they could follow their own path; nothing in her life had to change, except a return to a sense of stability, the catalyst toward building a new normal. Yes, she thought—yes, a new normal would be good. She could still say goodbye before morning, could still keep her bedroom off limits. Maybe in time they'd grow closer; maybe one day she'd relent. Until then, she had something to hope for, something she hadn't known had been important. Unfortunately she couldn't forget the visions she'd created; it was funny how she'd only just recognized them, and now she was putting them away. No, she couldn't exactly forget them, but she could morph them into something that worked. It was still practical, still flexible, still *her*. And if it wasn't working, she could call it off for good.

Maeve felt better about the situation, feeling she'd come to some sort of compromise. She was a different person than she was before; she had to do something different. So when Rhys called her that night and invited her to dinner, she went.

"THIS WEEKEND, big party. New club just outside town. I know a guy who knows a guy. It's invitation only."

Maeve and Rhys were at an Indian restaurant, huge plates of fragrant food in front of them. Rhys was on his second cocktail. Maeve was not drinking: she had to be at work early the next morning, she was driving, and anyway, somehow she wasn't in the mood.

"So what do you say?" Rhys was stuffing his mouth with naan, then draining his cocktail and gesturing for another. He leaned his elbows on the table and, digging with his fork into his Tandoori chicken, smiled handsomely at her. "Great music, great friends, and free drinks for guests."

"I'll think about it." Maeve was picking at her own food; she found herself not very hungry. She'd thought going out tonight would distract her from her troubles, but instead, it put them front and center, forcing her to ask herself what the fuck she was doing here.

Rhys was looking at her inquiringly. "What's wrong? You lost your spunk."

"I don't know. Okay, I'll go."

Rhys's face lit up, his smile widening and his eyes sparkling. "That's my girl."

She forced herself to eat a bite as she watched Rhys pull his phone from his pocket and text someone. He stayed on his phone for several minutes. Maeve sighed and ran her fingers through her hair, picking up her water glass and putting it back down.

"You want to put that thing down for a minute?"

He looked up at her. "What?"

"Your phone. You've been ignoring me for at least five full minutes."

He appeared taken aback, but he put his phone away. "Sorry." He picked his fork back up and stuck it in a shrimp on her plate. "I didn't think that was a thing with you. It never was before."

"Maybe it is now."

"Okay." He appeared to roll his eyes, but Maeve couldn't be certain; he'd lowered his head so he was staring into his plate.

They ate in silence for a time, until Maeve felt guilty. Rhys didn't know she'd slept with Kyle. He hadn't been in her head all night. She shouldn't be unfair to him. It wasn't his fault the rules had changed.

"So tell me about the interview with the former governor," she said, vaguely remembering him mentioning an interview for an assignment. "That was today, right?"

"Good memory. Yeah, we met today. You would not *believe* the drama."

"Tell me."

Rhys launched into a dramatic story about a newly discovered scandal, and Maeve listened with genuine interest. Before long, she had forgotten about the new awkwardness, had forgotten about everything: it was like the old days, before it became complicated, when they'd meet over a meal and some drinks, and would talk passionately about politics all night. If Rhys was one thing, it was a good storyteller; he had an eye for detail and a knack for suspense, which was probably what made him such a talented reporter. Maeve found herself on the edge of her seat, breathlessly awaiting the next segment of his story. He answered her questions with seriousness and attention, fleshing out scenarios and deftly tying them to his ultimate point about what exactly they should take from all this.

"It was really something," he concluded, downing the last remnants of his drink, "to hear his side of the story."

"I'm sure." He was on his phone again; she didn't know what he was doing, but she was feeling better, and she wasn't in the mood to make a big deal of it. "You'd better keep me posted about the article."

"Oh, I will."

She watched him as he put his phone back on the table and resumed eating his meal.

He looked up at her. "Oh, sorry. About my phone."

"What? Oh, whatever, it's fine."

"I'm waiting for Ted to touch base on tomorrow's meeting."

"It's fine."

He looked relaxed and in a good mood, as he always did. She admired his lithe, narrow frame as he leaned casually on his elbow, his shirt sleeves rolled up over his forearms. A lock of his dark hair had fallen over his brow in a playful, jaunty manner.

"Rhys," she said suddenly. "I need to tell you something important."

"Yeah?" he asked through a mouthful, his eyebrows raised. "What is it?"

Her heart was pattering. "I was sexually assaulted."

"No, shit." He dropped his fork. "When? Where? Who?"

"It was in high school, by the football team. They attacked me during a dance, behind the school, where no one could see."

"Were you..."

"Raped? No. The principal intervened."

"Jesus." He picked up his fork and shoved a bite of food into his mouth. "That's terrible."

He didn't say anything more. Maeve watched him eat.

"Is that all?" she said.

He looked up at her. "What do you mean?"

"I mean is that all you have to say to me."

"What, about what you told me? I mean, it's terrible."

"You don't seem all that concerned."

"I am, I mean, I am!" He reached over and held her hand for a minute, then retracted it and resumed eating. "I don't really know what to say."

"You could ask me about it. You could say you're sorry."

"Does that even need to be said?"

"Apparently, it does."

"What are you getting at?" His face scrunched into a look of almost malicious confusion, as if she were hysterical and it was getting on his nerves. "Obviously I'm sorry. Do you really think I'm not?"

"I don't know what you think, because you're not saying anything."

He sighed and continued eating for a second, deep in thought. "Look, I really am sorry. Of course I am." He looked at her then with sympathy in his eyes, having evidently reconsidered his approach. "It's just, you know. It was a really long time ago. I thought you were going to say you were assaulted last week."

"Does it matter?"

"Well, no. Well, yeah. I mean, what girl wasn't assaulted in high school, right?"

Maeve stared at him in silence. Several minutes passed.

"This place looks good since the renovations," he said finally. "Not sure I'm a fan of the new tile in the bathroom, though."

The corners of Maeve's mouth lifted upward in a grim imitation of a smile.

The server brought their check, and she let him pick up the tab. He slipped his card into the holder and checked his texts as they waited.

"I think I'm busy this weekend," she said. "I can't go to the party."

"Bummer."

The words, "Rhys, I slept with Kyle" were forming in the back of her throat; her lips parted with the impulse to release them, but she held them back. It was not guilt that lured them outward, nor guilt that kept them inside. She was tempted by the unequivocal closure these words would bring. But the closure would nullify the need to say them. Maeve sighed internally at the irony of it all. She could tell him what she did, but it would only hurt him, and it would impart to the relationship a weight she didn't want. It would damage a friend unnecessarily, and would make things more complicated, and really, who needed that?

FOR THE REST of the week, Maeve tried to put Kyle out of her mind. She had to, or she couldn't concentrate. She could handle being a screw up at home; what she couldn't handle was the degradation of screwing up at work. Fortunately, with the news about the bill's new support—now that Senator Tonelli was on board, they'd garnered enough votes to ensure its passage—Kyle really did not have a role in the office anymore. If at some point they were forced to work together again, it was best that they kept their relationship strictly professional. Maeve could not afford to be vulnerable, or it would impact not only her job, but Aditi's. Kyle was a distraction, a liability—at least, that was what she told herself.

Maeve could forget him during the day, when she had important things to do. She was helping Aditi, and therefore fellow citizens. It was essential she focus, for the benefit of others, and leave the mess of her life at home.

But at night, in her bedroom, the armor she'd donned disintegrated, and she lay in bed remembering, deliberately drawing up his face in her mind's eye.

You really know your stuff. Thanks for your help.

It was amazing, really, how they'd gotten here, with as volatile a history as they had. Maeve had to strain to remember the reasons she hated him, and when she did, they seemed quaint and obsolete, the product of years of reinforcing her own narrative and of the misunderstandings between newly reacquainted strangers.

Now that she knew him as she did, the things that had bothered her before were the very things she appreciated in him—and while six months ago she might have bristled at his staunchness, what shimmered through the fog now was his willingness to listen. And besides, she knew something about staunchness, herself.

I care about you. More than I've probably let on.

The pulling in her chest made her breathless, the warmth emanating from her heart bringing life to her blood and tears to her eyes. There was no use denying it any further; she knew why this confession mattered. How was it possible that she'd wriggled into his heart, with her fierce humor and snideness, her guardedness and self-preservation? They seemed such an odd couple, he with his daughter, she with the secret upstairs bedroom where she hid from men and from mornings. But she loved his daughter, and he knew about her bedroom, and unlike a lot of men she knew, he could be trusted with her secrets.

Love is about trusting someone with your mornings.

She didn't know if she could do it, but suddenly, she was willing, desperate, to try. What was the worst that could happen? She retreated back to her life? She'd pick back up the armor, more assured of her life than ever; she'd have been open-minded, and learned something, and shown the courage she prided herself on. Somehow, the risk seemed worth it, seemed not like a risk at all. She felt terror of the vulnerability, but in her heart of hearts, she knew vulnerability would make her stronger.

Maeve was full of hope, but afraid; her heart fluttered joyfully, but her stomach roiled with anxiety. And it wasn't anxiety of rejection, and it wasn't anxiety of fear. It was because it made sense, because she wanted it, because it felt more right than anything in her life and because she was preparing to step through a vast transformative portal, into a life unknown.

SATURDAY NIGHT MAEVE babysat Amy and Olivia so the Bickharts could attend a dinner party. The girls wanted to sleep over, and Maeve was happy to let them. She did not talk to Rhys about the party. He didn't reach out about it, and neither did she.

On her way home from work, she stopped at the store and bought ingredients for the girls to make their own pizzas. She bought ice cream, too, and pancake mix for the morning. She pulled into her driveway and took the groceries inside, then changed into jeans and an oversized sweater. She returned down-stairs just as her doorbell rang. The girls ran inside and into Maeve's sunroom, ready to snuggle under blankets to watch a movie, as promised. Maeve laughed and waved off their parents, then joined them in the sunroom, where they watched a little television before dinner.

"This is so fun," said Olivia, pulling the blanket up to her chin. "I love sleeping over here."

"Yeah, me too," answered Amy, also pulling up the blanket, in imitation of the older cousin she adored. "It's so fun."

"And I love having you here," said Maeve, sincerely, looking forward to a night of innocence and glee. "I had a long week. I could use a night with the girls."

"Why was it a long week?"

"It was just a lot of adulting. Adulting can be tedious."

"What does 'tedious' mean?"

"It means tiring, difficult, annoying."

"What was annoying about it?"

Maeve shrugged; she wanted to keep it lighthearted. "You know, work stuff."

"Oh." Amy scrunched up her face. She didn't want to hear about work stuff. "But the parade was fun, wasn't it?"

"Yes." Maeve watched the television, keeping her voice bright. "It was a very nice day."

"Aunt Maeve," said Amy, "do you remember that girl Nicole?"

Maeve smiled to herself. Kids always asked if you remembered stuff. "Yes."

"Why did you think she wanted to talk to me?"

"Well, she's new in town, and I don't know how many friends she's made yet. She's a very nice girl, but I think she's a little bit shy sometimes. I thought it might help her if she had a friend in you."

"Mmm." Amy nodded sagely. "Nicole really is nice."

"Who's Nicole?" asked Olivia.

"Nicole is a girl I met. She's *really* nice and *really* fun." Amy's eyes opened wide. "Aunt Maeve, can we invite her?"

Maeve's heart skipped a beat. She looked at her niece. "Invite Nicole where?"

"Here, tonight. For the sleepover. Please, oh, please?"

Maeve frowned, giving her pulse a chance to slow. "I don't know, Amy. It's a kind thought, but it's a little late."

"Oh, please, Aunt Maeve? Please? Wouldn't it be a good deed?"

"Yes," said Maeve, though she was shaking her head. "I just don't think it's a good idea for tonight."

"But why?"

"Because it's not the kind of thing you spring on someone last minute. What if she's busy? What if her dad can't drive her?"

"You said they just moved here. They probably don't have any plans."

"But still."

Amy was frowning. "Aunt Maeve," she said solemnly, "you said it would be kind to include her. We're having so much fun. Don't you think Nicole would, too?"

Maeve's lips turned downward, and her heart overturned with distress. Of course she had her own reasons for distancing herself from the Langahans. But try as she might, she could not resist the chance to help one of her girls—nor could she justify preventing Amy from performing this gesture of kindness.

"I mean…" she began, hesitantly, "I'm sure she would appreciate being invited."

"Yay!" Amy clapped her hands. "Thank you, Aunt Maeve! Thank you!"

Maeve smiled nervously. She stood and smoothed down her clothes.

"I'll just… I'll text Nicole's dad from the kitchen."

She walked out of the room, leaving Amy and Olivia to their movie.

In the kitchen, she paced back and forth, breathing in and out, gathering her courage. *Don't make it more than it is*, she told herself. *You don't have to mention it. Just invite his daughter over.*

She stopped abruptly in the middle of the room, then pulled out her phone and typed in a rush.

Hey Kyle, she said. *Amy and Olivia are here, and they're sleeping over. Amy insisted I invite Nicole. Can she come?*

She paused a moment, then gave him a way out.

I understand if it's too last minute.

She stared at her screen with expectation. Her heart leapt when the three dots indicated he was typing his response.

There was no response for at least a couple of minutes. The three dots stopped. Maeve just knew he was anxious about leaving his daughter in her care. He would come up with an excuse, to let her down easy. She felt dizzy and deflated, unbearably ashamed.

Sure, that would be great, he texted back suddenly. *Nicole would love to. Thanks for inviting her.*

Maeve jumped and exhaled, overwhelmed with relief. She closed her eyes and smiled, and did a tiny little dance. He trusted her with his greatest treasure. All was not lost; there was still, then, hope.

Great, she typed back. *Bring her over here whenever. We're making pizza.*

Thanks, he responded. *She'll pack some things, and we'll leave in five.*

~

"COME ON IN," Maeve said to Nicole, who was staring into her house, her eyes darting here and there as her hand clutched her purse. Maeve smiled at the girl, her hand on her shoulder. "We're all so happy you could make it."

"Thank you for having me." Nicole seemed nervous. Maeve's face softened. The little girl tried so hard to be big, but really she was frightened behind her formality and grace.

"Nicole!" cried Amy from behind her, and Maeve stepped aside to let Nicole through. "Nicole, this is my cousin Olivia. Do you like pizza? We're going to make pizza. We have coloring, too, and games. And blankets! Do you like blankets?"

Nicole dropped her bag and followed Maeve's nieces through the house. Maeve laughed, and Kyle laughed, too. Maeve turned to Kyle in the doorway: she hadn't even looked at him since opening the door.

"Hey," she said casually, not knowing what to do with her hands; she rubbed them awkwardly on her sweater, then shoved them in her pockets, then smoothed her hair with one while leaning with the other on the door. "Hey, how are you?"

"Doing okay." His eyes locked on hers, and the intensity of his gaze set her insides on fire. "How are you?"

She held tightly to the door, lest she die on the spot.

"Doing okay."

They said nothing for what seemed like forever.

"I'm glad Nicole could—"

"Thanks for inviting—"

They both laughed again, without looking at each other. Maeve could feel his presence like the heat from off a flame; if she met his gaze again, she would melt in it, would fall apart before his very eyes. Too much was weighing on this simple conversation; there were too many consequences, too many potential mistakes. She was desperate for this to end; she was overwhelmed, nervous, and unready. She hadn't prepared what she was going to say to him; she hadn't even prepared what she was going to say to herself. She couldn't say the words she should have; it was all or nothing, and right now it couldn't be all.

"Well," she croaked, and cleared her throat, "I'll call you in the morning when the girls are up and fed."

"Great." He smiled at her, but the smile seemed sad. Maeve felt sorry for him; she could tell he'd been hoping to talk. *Thank you for respecting my boundaries*, she yearned to tell him, but she could not bring herself to go even this far.

"Okay," she said, and waved at him brusquely. "Thanks."

"Thank you."

He waved in return, smiled genuinely now, and walked away from her to return home alone.

"WHO WANTS PIZZA?" Maeve chirped, too loudly, and three little girls hopped up and ran to the kitchen.

After Kyle left, Maeve had washed her face in the bathroom, then stared at herself for a good few minutes to get herself under control before facing the girls as a pillar of adult strength. She had to take care of Nicole tonight; she had to get this right. She couldn't let her emotions get in the way of her job. She couldn't disappoint the greatest treasure he had.

Maeve laid out four individual pizza crusts, and put sauce, cheese, and toppings on the table. She sat at the head while the girls filled in the other seats. She watched with delight as they spread sauce and sprinkled cheese, then stared at the toppings very seriously, making serious big girl decisions.

"I love pepperoni on mine."

"I've never had mushrooms on pizza. Are they good?"

"I usually like red peppers, but I'll try the green."

The chatter cleared her head and warmed her heart. She poured them all some lemonade and made a pizza of her own, mindlessly spreading sauce in a slow even circle, her mind drifting despite her attempts to stay present at the table.

"So, Nicole, how was school today?" she asked.

"It was good," said Nicole. She was daintily sprinkling cheese on her pizza, sitting hunched in her chair, curled into herself. At Maeve's question, she relaxed a little, looking up and scanning the table for more toppings. She reached out for a dish of olives and began dropping them carefully onto her pizza.

"What did you do?" asked Amy helpfully as she arranged her pepperoni in a symmetrical circle.

"Um." Nicole thought about it, remembering. "We learned about the ocean."

"Oh, really?" Maeve leaned back in her seat with her coffee as the girls finished. "That's cool. What did you learn?"

"We learned about trenches. The Mariana Trench is the deepest part of the ocean."

"I'll bet it's dark down there." Maeve sipped her coffee and crossed her legs, relaxing. "And cold. Brr."

"Oh, you couldn't go there," said Nicole, shaking her head and turning to Maeve with a solemn expression. "Only three people have ever been there. Two scientists went a long time ago, and also, James Cameron."

Maeve looked up at her over her coffee cup. "Who?"

"James Cameron. He's a movie director."

"Yes." Maeve attempted to hide her skepticism. "James Cameron...went to the bottom of the Mariana Trench?"

"Yes. For the movie *Titanic*."

"Hmm." Maeve would have to look that up later. She popped a slice of pepper into her mouth. "Do you like to go to the ocean?"

"Sort of, but I like the lake more. When I lived with my mom, we went to the lake, and I swam."

"Did your mom swim too?" asked Olivia.

"No, she didn't swim. She liked to do tests on the water."

"Did you have to swim all by yourself?"

"My dad swam with me."

Maeve watched her with somber eyes. It was subtle, but it was there, the girl's fixation on her mother. Maeve noticed she'd mentioned Kyle only as an afterthought, as if his presence was a given, as if it didn't need to be said. Despite Kyle's attention, it was Melissa who featured in Nicole's story. Melissa was the star, the one Nicole was proud of—but it was Kyle who supported her, selflessly, behind the scenes.

Maeve didn't blame Nicole for not realizing this now. But she knew as Nicole grew older, she would remember her father as the true, genuine star.

"That's nice, that your dad swam with you," she said, draining the last of her coffee. "I guess he found the water clean enough," she couldn't help but adding, a bit snidely.

"He said it was problematic but that you also have to live."

A cozy halo of warmth encircled Maeve's heart. She blinked a few times, suppressing a smile.

"What's your favorite food?" Amy was asking.

Maeve brushed off her thoughtfulness and stood to put the pizzas in the oven. From behind her, Nicole answered shyly.

"Indian food," she responded, without hesitation.

"Ooh," said Maeve, licking sauce off her finger. "Indian is one of my favorites. Do you have a favorite dish?"

Nicole thought about this, for rather a long time. "No," she said. "I like it all."

Maeve returned to the table and began putting toppings away. "I'm a sucker for biryani," she said. "Do you like that dish, too?"

"Yes," said Nicole, nodding, too vehemently. "Yes, I love it!"

Maeve's brow furrowed; she had the feeling Nicole was lying, but she couldn't figure out why she'd be untruthful about so innocuous a question.

"My friend loves chicken Tandoori," Maeve went on, tightening the lid on the sauce jar, "but it's never been my favorite."

"Mine, neither," Nicole agreed loyally, clearly affecting false casualness. "I never liked that, either."

Maeve closed the refrigerator door and returned to the table for the cheese. She picked the bag from the table and zipped the bag closed. "I also like samosas. I make a mean tamarind chutney."

"My mom loves samosas," said Nicole then, with sudden enthusiasm. "Indian is her favorite, too."

Ah. So that was it. Maeve's eyes rose to look at Nicole; she was picking at the zipper of her purse. She looked so small sitting at the table, her little legs kicking in the air above the floor.

"My favorite Indian place is only a few minutes away," she told her, placing a pack of juice boxes on the table. "I'll take you there sometime, if you want."

Nicole looked up at her. "Okay." Her eyes were bright, and her face wore a warm smile.

Maeve squeezed Nicole's shoulders on the way back to the counter. She poured herself more coffee as the three girls chatted, three sweet voices brightening Maeve's already bright kitchen.

∼

DURING THEIR LAST SLEEPOVER, Amy and Olivia had shared the full bed in Maeve's other guest room, but now there was a third girl, too many for one bed. Maeve brought spare blankets and pillows up into her spacious bedroom, and they arranged them on the floor to form one big cozy bed. She herself would sleep in a guest bed. She'd considered putting them in the sunroom, but then they'd be two floors below her.

She had them brush their teeth and change into their pajamas. Then she tucked them in for the night.

"This is awesome!" said Amy, plopping herself onto the pile of fluffy comforters. "So comfy cozy. Thanks, Aunt Maeve."

"Yeah, thanks, Aunt Maeve," said Olivia beside her.

Nicole was snuggling deep into the blankets, looking around in the dark.

"Are you okay, Nicole?" Maeve asked her, kneeling on the floor at her side.

"Yes." Nicole lay back thoughtfully. "This is my first sleepover in Virginia."

"Is it?" Maeve had figured as much, but she didn't say so. "Did you—" She was going ask if she'd had many sleepovers in New York, but changed her mind; she didn't want to remind Nicole of the time when she lived with her mother. "Did you want to call your dad to say goodnight?"

Nicole nodded, and Maeve pulled up Kyle's contact information. She handed the phone to Nicole, who spoke solemnly to her father, promising to listen and to have a lot of fun. Maeve could hear his muffled voice but could not hear what he said. The sound wreaked havoc on her insides; her heart ached with something like both delight and agony.

Nicole handed the phone back to Maeve, and Maeve, on an impulse, lightly pushed a lock of hair from the little girl's forehead.

"Everything good with your dad?" she asked.

"Mmmhmm." Nicole blinked a few times, clearly tired.

"Do you need anything?"

"No, thank you."

"Okay then." Maeve patted her knee and rose to go. "I'll leave the light on in the hall for you girls."

"Thank you, Aunt Maeve."

"Thank you, Aunt Maeve."

"Thank you, Aunt Maeve."

Maeve turned abruptly; the girls were settling in for sleep. Amy and Olivia were chatting quietly. But Nicole was watching her, her hands gripping the blanket as it rested below her chin.

"You're welcome," Maeve whispered, and turned back toward the stairs.

THE NEXT MORNING Maeve woke to the sound of giggles from the floor above. She turned toward her window, where bright golden sunlight was pushing from behind the curtains. She rose, walked to the window, and pushed the curtains aside. It was a perfect, clear day, a beautiful manifestation of late summer cheer. The trees were still lush and green, and the air was still thick with the fragrance of gardenias and lilacs. Soon, the air would be crisp and brisk, the scent of dying foliage wafting in wide swirls with the falling of the leaves. Then, they would witness the retiring of nature, the hiding of the earth before the frigidity of winter. But for now, there was still promise, still adventures to be had before the cold forced retreat.

She yawned once, covering her mouth with her hand, then put her hands on the windowsill, deep in thought. Despite her dedication to rising early for her job, she was not, in fact, a morning person. She much preferred the late hours of the night, when she cast off the cares of the day, when she herself could hide. In the morning, she had to start all over again, put on a different face. At night, the face could fall, and there was power in watching the world around her sleeping, while she herself was alive. There was power in the morning, too, she supposed; she could choose to wear any face she wanted. And if it was a new face, well, what of it? She could try it and see how it went. She could stay where she was and be content, but no one ever gained anything by standing still.

She picked up her phone and texted Kyle.

Do you like pancakes?

She stood for a minute and waited, then jumped at his reply.

I love pancakes.

She pushed back a grin. *What's not to love about pancakes? Seriously.*

She took a deep breath.

I'm making pancakes for breakfast. She paused. *You can have some if you want.*

A few moments passed. *I'd love to.* Then, *Thanks for asking.*

Now that it was out there, a tremor of panic seized her. She dialed it back.

Don't get too excited. They're from a mix, not homemade.

I'm sure they'll be delicious.

I may fuck it all up. I'm warning you in advance so you can't give me shit about it later.

Are we still talking about pancakes?

Maeve hesitated. *Yes.*

A few agonizing seconds went by. Maeve watched the three little dots, awaiting his reply.

Whatever we're talking about, I'm game. What time?

MAEVE PREPARED breakfast in a kind of manic haste, unable to concentrate on the girls' conversation over the rushing of her own blood in her ears. Her hands shook as she measured and stirred; her vision was blurry as she dropped quarter cups of batter on the griddle. She rapped her fingers on the countertop as she waited for the pancakes to cook, straining her neck to look out the window every time her ears registered even the faintest noise.

It was when she was least expecting it that the doorbell rang, making her jump. The girls were carrying on as normal, the sound of their laughter mingling with the clanking of forks and knives. Maeve wiped her hands on a dishtowel and marched into the hallway toward the door. Taking a deep, calming breath, she ran her hands downward in the air in front of her, forcing herself to achieve a composed expression before swinging the door open.

She was face-to-face with Kyle. She took a moment to look him over. He was dressed neatly in tan slacks and a blue oxford shirt, tucked in. Around his waist was a canvas belt, and he wore complementing canvas shoes. His five o'clock shadow was carefully trimmed, and his thick wavy hair was swept mildly backward, giving him a tidy, well-kept appearance.

"Got a little business casual going there, Langahan," Maeve noted with a brief rise of her eyebrows, and a coy pursed-lipped grin. "Can't you ever just relax?"

"Look who's talking," he responded, nodding in the direction of her own carefully dressed figure. "Not exactly sleepover attire."

Maeve looked down at her russet three-quarter slacks and rose-colored, ruffle-sleeved blouse. "Oh, this?" she said, with an upward flick of her hand. "This is just something I threw on."

She stepped aside to give him room to come in, then shut the door behind them. He stood silently, waiting to be directed. He was straight and tall, respectable and neat. He was watching her, his eyes intent, waiting for her to begin.

Maeve couldn't handle his puppy-dog eyes or his Sunday best apparel. Now that she'd acknowledged her affection for him, she was swallowed by it, and it scared her. She wasn't used to being looked at like that. She didn't know what to do.

"Pancakes," she uttered, numbly, pointing toward the kitchen. "The pancakes are this way."

She turned and headed into the kitchen, letting him follow. The sounds of laughter grew louder.

"Look who's here," she announced cheerily, patting Nicole's shoulder as she made her way to the cabinet for another plate.

"Daddy!"

"Hey, honey." Kyle embraced his daughter, who had jumped up from her chair to greet him. "Looks like you're having a good time."

"The best." Nicole doubled over with laugher. "Amy was making bubbles in her chocolate milk, and then, woodles!"

"Woodles?"

All three girls were in hysterics. It was clearly some kind of inside joke. Maeve shook with silent laughter.

"Look, Daddy," said Nicole, holding up an antique teacup with a delicate floral pattern.

"Ah." Kyle nodded at it admiringly. "Very fancy."

"The girls wanted a pancake tea party," Maeve explained. "These were my grandmother's."

"They're beautiful." Kyle's face was solemn, his demeanor pensive. He looked at her, and her heart turned over. "Aren't they a little fragile for a kids' party?"

Maeve shrugged. "I never use them. They needed to be used."

They watched the boisterous scene at the table, they themselves silent.

Maeve turned to Kyle. "Do you want coffee?"

He returned her gaze and smiled. "Absolutely."

She pulled down a mug, and he stepped beside her to reach for the coffee pot. The air between them seemed charged with energy, and her blood tingled at his nearness. For a moment, standing beside each other, they seemed connected by a secret understanding.

She pushed a carton of cream in his direction. "I know you take cream."

"I do. Thanks."

His fingers on the carton were straight, strong-knuckled, and masculine. Maeve stared at them, remembering their firmness as they'd gripped her body and their tenderness as they'd held her face.

He'd long since put the carton back on the counter. He was looking at her again, with those wide inscrutable eyes.

He opened his mouth to speak. Maeve headed him off at the pass.

"Here's a plate," she said hastily, taking one in her hand.

She placed the plate in front of a chair and invited Kyle to sit.

"Can I help you do something?" he asked her.

"There's nothing to do. Everything's on the table."

Maeve and Kyle were absorbed into the girls' laughter. Maeve laughed along with them, finding comfort in their gleeful innocence. But the unsaid words between her and Kyle were like a ghost in the room, lurking behind every teacup, slinking their way into every movement. She was flustered by this masculine presence in her kitchen, among all these feminine faces; he was an intrusion, an anathema, but not an unwelcome one.

"Mr. Langahan," said Amy, sipping daintily from her teacup; she put the cup back on the table and raised her chin, as if a great lady, "I just returned from a visit with the queen."

"Did you." Kyle raised his eyebrows. "And what did she say?"

"She said she is having a grand dinner party tomorrow, and she wants to know if Nicole can come."

"Hmm." Kyle appeared to be considering this carefully. "Nicole doesn't have any plans tomorrow, but I'm not sure how I feel about her going all the way to the palace all by herself."

"Don't worry. The queen is hosting the party at my house."

"Well, in that case, I don't see why not."

"I," said Olivia, holding her cup in a regal manner, "am going to wear my *very* best dress."

"Me, too." Nicole held her cup high, too, and the two sipped their iced tea.

Maeve glanced over at Kyle. His eyes met hers, warm with a subtle smile.

After a time, the girls finished eating, and they retreated upstairs to build a fort in Maeve's room. Their absence was conspicuous, the silence heavy in the air. Kyle helped Maeve clear the table. They worked wordlessly for a minute before Maeve turned to face him.

"We should talk about what happened," she said.

He slowly rested the plates he was holding on the counter. He turned to face her, too. They were standing several feet apart, far enough to be safe but close enough to sense each other's warmth. Maeve was shaking inside, but she put her chin up. Her hand on her hip, she assumed an assertive, sassy stance, defying the crushing fear of her own vulnerability.

"Okay," he began, leaning his hip against the counter and crossing his arms; it was an attempt at casualness, but his voice was tentative and quiet. "Maybe you should go first."

Maeve eyed him narrowly. "Why? Do I owe you an explanation?"

"No, of course not."

"If we're going to do this, it has to be on equal terms."

"I know." He paused. "Are we...are we going to do this?"

"I don't know."

Neither said anything. Several tense moments passed. Maeve rubbed her lips together, thinking. She had just rustled up the courage to thank him for his text messages when he took it upon himself to begin.

"I understand why you blame me," he said.

Maeve blinked a couple of times, caught off guard. She shifted her weight and relaxed a little. "I don't really blame you," she said. "I just...associate you. Associated," she corrected herself. "Associated...you."

"Fair enough."

A few more moments of silence.

"If I really blamed you," she went on, "I wouldn't have been able to work with you at all."

"Makes sense."

"Much less go to bed with you."

This made him flush. Maeve, in turn, smiled, but checked herself, pushing it back into a flirtatious little grin.

"You always get so embarrassed," she said, "whenever I mention sex."

"I'm not embarrassed."

"You are!" Maeve laughed abruptly, and the sound broke through the room, dispelling some of the awkwardness. "You're bright red. I'm looking right at you."

He worked his jaw, as if agitated, but Maeve could see he was trying not to smile. "You have to understand," he offered, and the look on his face was so pitiful, the last of her nervousness dissipated. "I've been attracted to you since high school. When you talk about sex, I feel exposed, like you're able to read my mind."

"Are you saying you thought about having sex with me, Langahan?"

He flushed further. "Yes," he conceded, and laughed. "Yes, I did. I'm sorry."

"You don't have to apologize to me. I never even knew. I commend you for your restraint."

"Restraint shouldn't have to be commended."

They looked at each other, then looked away.

"All teasing aside," said Maeve, "I give you credit for arguing with me anyway. It shows your principles."

He shrugged. "I'm more stubborn than I am romantic."

"So am I."

They both smiled.

"I guess there were some signs," she said. "I didn't see them, or wouldn't. I suspect I didn't give you much opportunity to say anything, or much encouragement."

"No." He chuckled once, silently. "But I get it. I'm sure I didn't give you much reason to encourage."

"No." Her mouth worked as she stifled a grin. "In fairness, though. I wouldn't have said anything either, in your shoes." She hesitated. "I mean, I didn't either, once I..."

She trailed off. The process toward her own realizations and self-awareness was still sensitive to her, and she was unable to complete the sentence out loud. He smiled in evident understanding, clearly pleased at the thought of her harboring secret feelings for him, too.

"I considered telling you," he said. "I might have, but—"

"Let me guess. No distractions."

"Right." He blushed. "It sounds a little ridiculous, now that I'm saying it out loud."

"Maybe more cautious than ridiculous." She shot him a sly look. "You held out a long time."

"Honestly, I was afraid. I didn't think you were interested. And also, you said you didn't do relationships."

"I said a lot of things. I think I even believed them." She hesitated. "It seems a little ridiculous, now that I'm saying it out loud."

"Maybe more cautious than ridiculous."

Maeve turned serious. "I felt stupid. I mean about Nate. I fell for his lines, and I shouldn't have, and it made me resent you for seeing it when I didn't."

"You were eighteen. You were in high school. And even if you weren't, it wouldn't have been your fault."

"I know." She rubbed her lips together. "But just the same."

He shifted his weight. "Well," he said, "I was too hard on you that night, anyway. I was hurt because I thought I had a chance. I'm sorry."

"It's fine. Forget it."

She hesitated, then said,

"I have to admit I'm nervous. I'm never nervous. Usually I have all the power."

"It shouldn't be about power."

"Your not caring about power is what gives you power. I don't know how to do this."

He looked at her. His eyes were kind, and she found comfort there. "You don't have to know how to do this. You just do it."

"But what if I fuck it up?"

"You'll definitely fuck it up. So will I. That's the point."

"What's the point?"

"That you fuck it up and stick around anyway."

Maeve thought about this. It was scary, but appealing. She didn't know if she could bear showing the worst parts of herself, and having to face him again the next day. There was a certain... humiliation about it, about being with someone who knew all your flaws, who'd been hurt by them, and showing up at the table with your head still held high.

"I guess if I fuck it up, and you fuck it up, we're even."

"That's right."

"In other words, you know too much about me, and I know too much about you."

He grinned. "Sort of."

Maeve nodded thoughtfully. "Interesting."

He took a step toward her. She straightened and shuffled nervously. He now stood only a couple of feet away from her, and he spoke to her more intimately.

"I respect you, Maeve," he told her. "And I want to continue to work with you. I'd love for us to see where this is going, but I don't want to make you uncomfortable."

"I'm not," she assured him quickly, fearful he would change his mind. "I mean, I am, but it's not because of you."

His expression lightened marginally, with cautious optimism. "Thanks for inviting me over. I wasn't going to bother you again, but I'm glad we got to talk."

"I invited you over because I wanted to talk. I took a chance." Suddenly, from nothing, her heart lurched, and tears sprang to her eyes. Alarmed, she opened her eyes wide, ordering them away. Once they had retreated, she escaped by changing the subject. "As an aside, commendations are in order. I'm sure you heard Tonelli's on board. I have to confess your protest worked."

"Oh," he said, seeming to brush it off. "Yeah, that was great."

"Congratulations. You got it done."

"*We* got it done. I staged the protest, but the framework was already there. He wouldn't have relented had it not been for the negotiating."

A smile touched her eyes. She couldn't believe how easy this was.

"So," she said, playfully slapping his arm, "are we, you know... going to do this?"

"I don't know, are we?" He hesitated. "I mean, I'd like to."

"I'd like to, too."

He said nothing, and his face remained impassive, but Maeve had gotten to know him well enough to know when the impassivity was a front. His expression was serious, but his eyes were bright, and Maeve took the opportunity to approach him. He opened his arms for her, and she went to him, resting her head on his chest, sighing at the instant comfort of his arms around her waist. It was a feeling of safety she'd never known existed; it was awe-inspiring and beautiful, and she reveled in the humility of letting another person make her feel whole.

"You smell delicious," she told him. "Just so you know."

"So do you."

He kissed the top of her head, and she lifted her face toward his. They met in an easy, seamless kiss, anticipating each other's movements with instinctive understanding. Maeve sighed into him, and his hands pressed her tighter. She opened her mouth wider, taking him in, and ran her hand up his chest and over his

303

neck, letting it settle around his angular jaw. Her heart pattered. She could definitely get used to this.

A *thump* sounded from above them, and muffled laughter right after. Maeve and Kyle looked upward, then kissed once briefly and relaxed in each other's arms.

"I wonder what's going on up there," he murmured.

"It doesn't matter. Just let it stay up there."

"You're not worried about them breaking something?"

"It's just stuff." She considered. "They can't get into anything. I moved my wine before they got here."

His brow furrowed. "Your wine is in your room?"

"Well, some of it, usually. But it's locked away down here today."

He was watching her thoughtfully. "I want to thank you for being so good to Nicole."

She frowned. "But you're worried about me drinking too much around her."

His chest rose and fell as he sighed silently. "Yes."

Her face softened. She rested her hand on his cheek. "I understand that. And you don't have to worry."

His jaw worked. "Okay."

"I'll keep it under control. For Nicole. I promise."

He kissed her forehead and rubbed her back; resting his forehead on hers, he closed his eyes and nodded. "Okay."

"Mmm." Her eyes drifted shut as she enjoyed the warmth left by the soft movements of his hands. She shivered a little, and smiled. "So can we kick them out of here, or what?"

He chuckled. "I'm about ready to say yes."

"I can tell." She nudged him playfully, then nestled in closer. He grinned and hugged her tighter, a little groan escaping him.

She looked up at him, her hair hanging over the back of her neck. "So," she said, slinking her knee between his legs, "was it as good as you imagined it would be?"

"Better." He grinned wickedly; his eyes turned molten and

dark, then softened. "To be honest with you, I can't stop thinking about that night. I wanted to tell you how great it was, but I didn't want to creep you out if you were trying to forget me."

"I wasn't trying to forget you." She rested her head on his chest, and he locked his hands around her lower back. "I couldn't, anyway, even if I was."

His voice was barely more than a whisper. "Did you think about it, too?"

"More than I let myself admit." She hesitated. "I'm sorry I yelled at you." She realized she should probably specify which time. "You know. While we were having sex."

"It's okay."

"You were right, I was being defensive."

"I know. It's okay."

"I acknowledge it's not really considered normal. I'll try not to do it again."

"It's okay." His mouth twitched with a suppressed grin of his own. "I kind of liked it."

Her grin widened. "Noted."

Three pairs of footsteps pounded down the stairs. Maeve and Kyle separated quickly. When the girls entered the room, they found them washing dishes.

"Aunt Maeve. Daddy," Nicole gasped breathlessly. "You have to come upstairs and see the fort we built."

"It's so big!" said Olivia. "We're going to invite the queen."

"Okay. We'll be right up."

The girls ran from the room. Maeve's eyes moved to Kyle.

"Looks like you're about to see my secret bedroom," she told him, "something no other man can say he's done."

"I'm honored."

She put her hand on his back and guided him from the kitchen, as if they'd always done this, as if he'd been coming here for years.

"You should be," she said, and they hurried upstairs toward the girls.

～

"This coconut shrimp is *bangin'*," said Rhys, enthusiastically, his expression one of pure bliss. He pushed his plate in her direction. "Here, Maeve. Try this."

She stabbed a shrimp with her fork, then popped it in her mouth and chewed.

"Holy shit," she murmured, and swallowed. "You're not kidding."

"The mango salad is just as good."

She helped herself to a forkful.

"That's amazing."

"Right?"

They'd met here about an hour ago, and were taking their time, enjoying their usual politically charged conversation. Rhys had recently written an exposé that was gaining him a lot of applause, and they'd spent the last hour discussing the implications. Maeve had been able to forget for a while that she'd invited him there to break up with him—that is, to do whatever it was to end things, as "breaking up" seemed too serious a term to apply to whatever it was they had.

"Listen," she said finally, figuring she'd put it off long enough. "Rhys, we have to talk."

"No kidding." He swallowed the last of his shrimp and took a drag of his beer, then rested it on the table and looked at her frankly. "I have some news, and it's huge."

"What is it?"

"Well," he said, and inhaled, preparing himself, "I'm moving to New York City."

Her eyes bulged. "You're *what*?"

"I said, I'm moving to New York City!"

"Oh my God!" She shook her head as she stared at him. "When did this happen? And why?"

"I've been awarded a Wright-Burrows fellowship."

"Through NYU!"

"Right. Decent stipend, international travel, lots of cool opportunities and connections."

"Oh my *God!*" She reached out and took his hand, squeezing hard. "Rhys, that's fabulous! Wow, you so deserve this."

"Thanks, love." He smiled at her affectionately, wrapping his fingers in hers. "That means a lot, coming from you."

"I'm so happy for you. Really. You're going to be *marvelous* at this."

He nodded in gratitude. His eyes turned serious.

"Of course," he said, withdrawing his hand and picking up his fork; he stuck it into a bowl of rice, then brought the fork to his lips, "it has some heavy implications for you and me."

"Yes." She cleared her throat. "Actually, Rhys, that's why I asked you here tonight."

He looked up from his plate, his brow lifted curiously. "Oh?"

She sighed. "I was going to say I thought it was time we ended it."

He watched her for a moment, then smiled sadly. He returned his attention to his bowl, digging in.

"Right," he said, popping a forkful into his mouth. He swallowed and dabbed his lips with a napkin. "I have to be honest, that's why I took the fellowship."

"What do you mean?"

"I mean I knew it wasn't working. There was nothing keeping me here."

"Would you have stayed even if it was working?"

His hand froze as it went in for more rice. He stared at her for a moment, blinking once or twice.

"No," he finally conceded. "No, probably not."

AMANDA GALE

It was Maeve's turn for a rueful smile. "I guess that's kind of the point."

"Yeah." He chuckled, scraping the side of his bowl. "I guess it says something when you won't make any sacrifices."

She was grateful for his honesty. She made a decision on an impulse.

"I should tell you the whole story. I'm seeing Kyle Langahan."

His eyebrows shot up high. "No way. Really?"

"Yes, really. It happened very suddenly. I'm sorry I didn't tell you."

"Nah, Maeve, it's cool. No worries." He thought it over for a minute, then went back to his bowl of rice. "He seems like a pretty cool guy. I'm glad. Good for you."

Maeve watched him from across the table, admiring the familiar sight of him. For years, they'd relied on each other, had been there whenever needed. They'd been bonded by mutual respect, and mutual desire for individual freedom. It had been a carefree friendship, but a dear one, and they'd gotten to know each other well. But Maeve had realized there were many more parts of her, parts she was only first recognizing herself. She had realized the problem wasn't that she didn't do relationships; the problem was that she couldn't do one with him.

"You're a good friend," she said, tearing up, and not trying to stop it. "I've really enjoyed all my time with you."

He met her gaze and smiled, that handsome, dark, suave smile she'd always loved. "So are you," he told her. "Likewise."

"Please keep in touch. I want to know how you're doing."

"I will. You do the same."

They looked at each other with fondness and understanding. Then they ordered dessert, chatted about the world, and took in the sound of each other's hearty laughter. They left arm in arm and said good-bye, parting with a friendly hug and wishing each other the best.

308

CHAPTER TEN

EPILOGUE: SIX WEEKS LATER

"To the congressman!"

"To the congressman!"

Dozens of hands rose into the air, all clasping champagne flutes filled with celebratory champagne. Wes had won reelection, by a margin wider than expected. Sarah and Charles were hosting a party with family, friends, and closest supporters. Everyone was in good spirits, mingling cheerfully and enjoying the fantastic lunch at the Bickharts' spacious home.

Wes had already given an upbeat speech, peppered with casual witticisms that always charmed his retinue. He was grateful, of course, for their support, but also eager to continue building togetherness. It was times like these, he'd said, that we need to remember what we have in common. It was not the time to compromise values. It was a time to fight for the vulnerable, to tear down antiquated structures and rebuild one that supported us all.

"I sensed a little Langahan language in there," Maeve said to Wes. She was nursing a glass of white wine—it would probably be the only one she had.

"Oh? How so?"

"He likes to talk about tearing things down."

Wes laughed heartily. "Hey, come now. Langahan doesn't have the monopoly on tearing things down."

"Stop. You'll hurt his feelings."

This, as Kyle approached, his right hand holding an iced tea, his left resting on his daughter's shoulder.

"Hurt whose feelings?"

"Yours. I was just telling Wes I detected your influence in his language. He said you're not the only one who likes to tear things down."

"Hey, the more people tearing, the better," said Kyle.

Some light chatter ensued, the mood friendly and upbeat. The conversation turned, as it inevitably did, to Virginia ClearStream and Brown & Little.

"Grady did such great work," said Kyle, with a sip of iced tea; he seemed comfortable—relaxed, even—among the family, who had eagerly embraced him and Nicole into their lives. He smiled warmly now, a sight Maeve was delighted to see frequently these days. "I saw him earlier, and he told me a little more about the process."

"Grady knows his stuff," agreed Wes, with a sip of his own drink. "Don't let his reticence deceive you. He's a killer when he needs to be."

"I'll bet." Kyle nodded, clearly impressed. He had reason to be: there'd been a lot of good news lately. First, the lawsuit against Brown & Little had been settled, with the company agreeing to pay an extremely large sum to the plaintiffs in compensation for their health issues, relocation costs, and property damages. But in addition, Grady and his team had finally revealed that in fact, Virginia ClearStream had been fully aware of the safety violations, and had covered them up in exchange for bribes and other kickbacks—just as the Langahans had always insisted. It was in no small part due to Aditi, who finally had managed to secure a series of consequential meetings with George Collier, the grassroots organizer who had stood Maeve and Kyle up for dinner so many months before and who'd convinced several whistleblowers to come forward. A class-action lawsuit was building, and a number of executives faced criminal charges. And the new water bills would help prevent similar malfeasance in the future.

Wes was joined by Catherine; Nicole scurried off with Amy and Olivia. As Wes and Kyle drifted into a separate conversation, Catherine turned away from them, indicating Maeve should do the same.

"So, did you tell her?"

Maeve eyed Catherine crossly, shushing her with her finger to her lips.

"No, not yet! Keep your voice down."

"When are you going to tell her?"

"Whenever we find the right moment."

Catherine's face was the picture of excitement. Maeve had to laugh and shake her head. Her sister's lips had risen into grin of anticipation, and her wide green eyes were positively sparkling with glee.

"When will it be the right moment?"

"I don't know!" Maeve's own voice was louder than she'd expected. She lifted her chin a little, recovering her composure. "I don't know," she whispered. "I have to leave it to Kyle."

Maeve and Kyle were going to tell Nicole that they were seeing each other. Maeve had agreed with him that they should wait to see where things were going. Now that they were sure they were in it long-term, they were ready to reveal their secret. Maeve was excited but unbearably nervous. On the one hand, it meant she could relax in Kyle's presence. It meant they could do things all together without arousing Nicole's suspicion. But on the other hand, Nicole might recoil at the idea of someone replacing her mother. Maeve didn't want to intrude, and she didn't want to offend. Most of all, she didn't want to damage the relationship she had with Nicole. Nicole trusted her, and Maeve cherished her trust like a jewel. If Nicole thought Maeve was usurping Melissa's place, she might resent her, or hate her, and what then?

"You're scared," said Catherine. "I can see it in your face."

"Yes, I'm scared, all right? But not for the reason you think."

"How do you know what I think?"

"Because I just know. You think I'm afraid of commitment and that once we tell Nicole, the stakes are higher, and I'm more involved."

"I was going to say that you're afraid Nicole will resent you for taking her mother's place, but that's also a good reason."

Maeve sighed and closed her eyes; calmer, she reopened them and took a deep breath.

"I think Nicole will be happy," said Catherine. "She loves you. She already calls you 'Aunt Maeve.' How could anyone not be happy to have you in their lives?"

"That's my sister, the incorrigible optimist."

"That's my sister, the incorrigible grump."

Maeve looked at her, her eyebrows high. She laughed suddenly, the sound like bubbles filtering through the room.

"God, Catherine," said Maeve, patting her sister's shoulder and gingerly sipping her wine. "Don't ever change."

Wes and Catherine stepped away to speak with someone, and Maeve and Kyle were left standing by themselves.

"Hello, Langahan," Maeve said, her voice like velvet, nodding to him formally.

"Hello."

"Would you mind following me, please? There's a spreadsheet I'd like you to see."

"I'm occupied presently." He looked awkwardly about the room, and Maeve grinned. He was still so self-conscious when it came to anything sexy. The slightest innuendo or word play sent flames of heat rising into his cheeks.

"Fine, I'll stop teasing you." She looked around the room for Nicole. "I'm too nervous for teasing."

"Do you want to find her? Are you ready?"

"Ready as I'll ever be."

The two walked out of the room and into the hallway, where they nodded hello to colleagues and peeked into rooms for Nicole. They found her sitting in a spare room with Amy and Olivia. The three girls were playing some version of make believe: they were clearly involved in a story, but Maeve couldn't tell what invisible things they were seeing.

"Hi, girls," said Kyle. "Having fun?"

"Yes, Daddy." Nicole was not interested; she and the others were play acting in the corner.

"Honey, would you mind taking a break so Maeve and I can speak to you for a minute?"

Nicole looked at them curiously, then recomposed her face. "Okay."

She followed them out of the room and back down the hallway. There were people everywhere, nowhere for a quiet conversation. Kyle went to the door, and they walked out and around the side of the house toward the spacious backyard. All around them were flowering shrubs and fruit trees; in the distance, the Blue Ridge Mountains cascaded in gradually fading layers of blue. It was an unseasonably warm day in November, and the bare trees offered a clear vision of the rich Virginia landscape.

Nicole stood there waiting, her hands clasped in front of her waist. Kyle crouched down before her, looking up into his daughter's eyes.

"Honey," he said, "I have something to tell you. It's something good, but you may have a lot of different feelings about it. Whatever your feelings are, I want you to tell me. Promise?"

Nicole nodded solemnly, her face expressionless.

Kyle took a deep breath. "What I have to tell you is that Maeve and I"—he gestured up toward Maeve, smiling at her—"are seeing each other. Romantically." When Nicole said nothing, he added, "What do you think about that?"

Nicole stood frozen for a second, and Maeve's heart sank to her gut. After a moment, Nicole relaxed, shifting her weight, and shrugging.

"Fine," she said.

Kyle raised his eyebrows. "Fine? That's it?"

"Yes, it's fine."

Maeve stepped toward her and rested her hand on her shoulder. "I really want you to be okay with this."

"I am okay with it."

Kyle was watching her, his eyes narrow with thought. "Sorry, honey," he said. "I just thought you'd have stronger feelings, like you'd either be mad or excited."

"Oh, I am excited." Nicole's face brightened, and she nodded vehemently. "I just didn't know it was a secret."

Maeve's eyes opened wide. "What?"

Nicole looked up at her. "I just figured. You know? You're always with us, and I know my dad likes you. I mean, he didn't tell me he did. It's just so obvious!"

Maeve had to cover her face to stop from giggling. Kyle stood and straightened his clothes. He cleared his throat, clearly speechless.

"Well. I just..." he stammered. "I just thought you should..."

"You just thought I should know? I do."

Maeve put her arm around Nicole and squeezed her tight against her hip. "I'm glad you're really okay with it. And listen." She turned Nicole to face her, her hands now on both her shoulders. "You can come to me with any question or problem. No judgment. I'm always there for you." She swallowed. "But I would never try to take your mom's place."

"It's okay." Nicole's eyes met hers. "You couldn't. She'd never tell me to come to her with my problems."

Maeve's smile faded, and she watched wordlessly as Nicole sauntered away. She stared after her for a minute, amazed, and overwhelmed by the warmth in her chest.

Kyle's hand on her shoulder brought her out of her reverie.

"Wow," he said.

"I know."

"Did you hear that?"

"Yes, I did."

He pulled her close, and she melted into him, closing her eyes at the safety of being enclosed. She rested her head on his shoulder, and he rested his cheek on her head. They stood there for many moments, deep in thought, a brisk November breeze whipping around them in soft caresses.

"It means a lot to me," he said finally, "that my daughter has you on her team."

"It means a lot to me that I have you both on mine."

They shifted to face each other, and kissed on the lush green lawn. Maeve had kissed men before, but they'd never held her face so, had never squeezed her hips gently in patient anticipation. They'd never looked at her with warm, tender eyes, never touched her lips with slow, soft reverence. They'd never been honest, or apologized; they'd never made her trust them, and they'd never even tried. Being with Kyle was like doing it all for the very first time. It was frightening but liberating; she felt light, and deliciously free. This time, she wasn't running; she wasn't hiding from his gaze, nor hiding from her own.

They separated and sighed, then walked back toward the house, hand in hand.

"Listen," he said, kissing the top of her head. "Now that she knows, I have an idea."

"You think she should stay at your parents' so we can have a night to ourselves."

He looked at her. "Yes. How did you know that?"

"Because I've been thinking about it myself pretty much nonstop for six weeks."

He chuckled once, silently. "It would be better than sneaking it in on our lunch break."

315

"Indeed."

They were approaching the house; the sounds of laughter and conversation were reaching them from within. Soon, their dreamy intimacy would dissipate, and they'd be thrown back into the tedious world of small talk.

"Your place or mine?" she asked him, as they made their way around the front of the house.

"It doesn't matter."

"Well, why don't you come to me. It'll be like a little vacation for you."

"Do I get to stay in your secret bedroom?"

"Yes. But only if you stay until morning."

They exchanged a quick kiss and went back inside, looking forward to the future, and to morning.

THE END

CATHERINE'S STORY

In a poignant tale of intertwining lives, two women discover their destinies are intricately linked and that inner strength is found in the reconciling of differences.

Catherine Sheering is perfectly content with her quiet, predictable life. A successful chocolate maker, she enjoys living alone and keeping her own company—until she's swept off her feet by rising political star Wes Bickhart. The problem is, she suspects Wes may have a lingering affection for his seemingly perfect ex, Meredith Kelly, who remains an important part of his life. Now she's torn whether to simply enjoy the most satisfying love she's known or to avoid the risk of being hurt again.

After years of personal struggles of her own, Meredith Kelly thought her life was finally perfect, with a wonderful husband and a growing family. But when her dying father, a famously irascible journalist and political luminary, requests her help drafting his memoir, she must reckon with their difficult relationship and with their family's haunted past. It's a task she can't accomplish alone

—and the one person who can help her is her politically ambitious ex, Wes Bickhart.

Now both women are put to the test as they balance their seemingly idyllic lives with their mutual uncertainty about where Wes's heart really lies, leading them to surprising revelations about each other and themselves.

Easily read as a standalone novel or as an extension of Amanda Gale's *Meredith* series, *Catherine and the Wind* is a tale of human frailty and fear, of growth and redemption—and of the sacrifices we make for the people we love most.

ALSO BY AMANDA GALE

Meredith Out of the Darkness
Meredith Against the Wind
Meredith Into the Fire
Meredith With the Waves
Love in the Lavender
Strawberry and Sage
Sweet Lavvy
Catherine and the Wind
Gwyneth in the Garden
The Magic You Bring
Dahlia Almost Drowning

ACKNOWLEDGMENTS

Thank you Gina, Jessica, Erica, Jami, Judy, Rusty, Kimberli, and kind WFWA members for your help, advice, and encouragement.

www.ingramcontent.com/pod-product-compliance
Lightning Source LLC
Chambersburg PA
CBHW030639020726
47493CB00006B/1784